Praise for *The Bull*

"Osman concocts a satisfyingly complex
wrong turns. But unlike most crime novelists, he ensures his book's strength and momentum stem not from its plot or its thrills but rather its perfectly formed characters."

—*The Washington Post*

"Not to be missed."

—*Parade*

"*The Bullet That Missed* hits on every front. Its quandaries stymie, its solutions thrill, its banter is worth reciting, and its characters exemplify an admirable camaraderie. One can only hope that the Thursday Murder Club's next outing appears before long."

—*The Wall Street Journal*

"This book is as delightful as the others. A remarkable achievement, Osman up there effortlessly balancing on that very high bar."

—*Star Tribune*

"It's charming and, as always, will leave you guessing the murderer until the very end."

—*Town & Country*

Praise for *The Man Who Died Twice*

"The club makes a triumphant return. . . . *The Man Who Died Twice*, like its series predecessor, is an unalloyed delight, full of sharp writing, sudden surprises, heart, comedy, sorrow, and great banter."

—*The Wall Street Journal*

"Richard Osman's action-packed second outing with the Thursday Murder Club overflows with wit, friendship, and derring-do."

—*The Christian Science Monitor*

"It's taken a mere two books for Richard Osman to vault into the upper leagues of crime writers. . . . No wonder readers, myself included, have surrendered to [the Thursday Murder Club members'] abundant charms."

—*The New York Times Book Review*

"[Feels] like a reunion with old friends. Clever, witty, and touching, this thriller has it all."

—Lisa Gardner, #1 *New York Times* bestselling author of *Before She Disappeared*

"A thing of joy."

—Kate Atkinson, #1 *New York Times* bestselling author of *Big Sky*

"By turns moving, hilarious, and brilliantly suspenseful, the novel keeps us flipping pages from start to finish."

—Jeffery Deaver, #1 international bestselling author of *The Final Twist*

"Osman's novels are so much more than just brilliantly engineered mysteries. . . . These books are absolute gold."

—Joe Hill, #1 *New York Times* bestselling author of *The Fireman*

"Fun and ingenious . . . Osman blends humor and pathos while weaving his tangled web of intrigue and deception. This is the perfect book with which to unwind."

—*Star Tribune*

"Think of the Thursday Murder Club itself as a senior version of *The A-Team*. . . . So delicious, even adorable."

—*The Washington Post*

Praise for *The Thursday Murder Club*

"Witty, endearing, and greatly entertaining." —*The Wall Street Journal*

"An amusing debut that finds gold in getting older." —*People*

"Don't trust anyone, including the four septuagenarian sleuths in Osman's own laugh-out-loud whodunit." —*Parade*

"Mystery fans are going to be enthralled."
—Harlan Coben, #1 *New York Times* bestselling author of *Win*

PENGUIN BOOKS

THE BULLET THAT MISSED

Richard Osman is an author, producer, and television presenter. Each of his novels—*The Thursday Murder Club, The Man Who Died Twice,* and *The Bullet That Missed*—were number one, million-copy international bestsellers as well as *New York Times* bestsellers. He lives in London with his wife, Ingrid, and Liesl the cat.

Look for the Penguin Readers Guide in the back of this book

Also by Richard Osman

The Thursday Murder Club

The Man Who Died Twice

The Last Devil to Die

The Bullet That Missed

A Thursday Murder Club Mystery

RICHARD OSMAN

PENGUIN BOOKS

PENGUIN BOOKS
An imprint of Penguin Random House LLC
penguinrandomhouse.com

First published in Great Britain by Viking, an imprint of
Penguin Random House, Ltd., 2022
First published in the United States of America by Pamela Dorman Books/Viking,
an imprint of Penguin Random House LLC, 2022
Published in Penguin Books 2023

A Pamela Dorman/Penguin Book

ISBN 9780593299395 (hardcover)
ISBN 9780593299418 (paperback)
ISBN 9780593299401 (ebook)

Library of Congress Control Number: 2022940734

Printed in the United States of America
4th Printing

Set in Adobe Jenson Pro
Designed by Cassandra Garruzzo Mueller

To Ingrid.

I was waiting for you.

The Bullet That Missed

Bethany Waites understands there is no going back now. Time to be brave, and to see how this all plays out.

She weighs the bullet in her hand.

Life is about understanding opportunities. Understanding how rarely they come along, and then rising to meet them when they do.

"*Come and meet me. I just want to talk.*" That's what the email had said. She has been playing it over in her mind ever since. Should she?

One last thing to do before she decides: send Mike a message.

Mike knows the story she is working on. He doesn't know the details—a reporter has to keep her secrets—but he knows it's a risky one. He's there if she needs him, but there are some things you have to do alone.

Whatever happens tonight, she would be sad to leave Mike Waghorn behind. He is a good friend. A kind and funny man. That's why the viewers love him.

But Bethany dreams of more, and maybe this is her chance. A dangerous chance, but a chance all the same.

She writes her message, and presses send. He won't reply tonight; it's late. That's probably for the best. She can hear his voice now: "Who texts at ten p.m.? Millennials and sex pests, that's who."

Here we go, then. Time for Bethany to spin the wheel of fortune. Will she live, or will she die?

She pours herself a drink, and takes one final look at the bullet. Really, she has no choice at all.

To opportunities.

PART ONE

Around Every Corner, a Familiar Face

1.

"I don't need makeup," says Ron. He's in a straight-backed chair because Ibrahim told him you mustn't slouch on television.

"Do you not?" replies his makeup artist, Pauline Jenkins, taking brushes and palettes from her bag. She has set up a mirror on a table in the Jigsaw Room. It is framed by lightbulbs, and the glow bounces off her cerise earrings as they bob back and forth.

Ron feels the adrenaline pumping a little. This is the stuff. A bit of TV. Where are the others though? He told them they could come along "if they fancied, no big deal," and he will be gutted if they don't show.

"They can take me as they find me," says Ron. "I've earned this face, it tells a story."

"Horror story, if you don't mind me saying?" says Pauline, looking at a color palette, and then at Ron's face. She blows him a kiss.

"Not everyone has to be beautiful," says Ron. His friends know the interview starts at four. They'll be here soon surely?

"We're agreed there, darling," says Pauline. "I'm not a miracle worker. I remember you back in the day though. Handsome bugger, weren't you, if you like that sort of thing?"

Ron grunts.

"And I *do* like that sort of thing if I'm honest with you, right up my street. Always fighting for the working man, weren't you, throwing your weight around?" Pauline opens a compact. "You still believe in all that, do you? Up the workers?"

Ron's shoulders go back a touch, like a bull preparing to enter a ring. "Still believe in it? Still believe in equality? Still believe in the power of labor? What's your name?"

"Pauline," says Pauline.

"Still believe in the dignity of a day's work for a fair day's pay, Pauline? More than ever."

Pauline nods. "Good oh. Then shut your mush for five minutes and let me do the job I'm paid to do, which is to remind the viewers of *South East Tonight* what a looker you are."

Ron's mouth opens, but, unusually for him, no words come out. Pauline starts on his foundation without further ado. "Dignity, my arse. Haven't you got gorgeous eyes? Like Che Guevara if he worked on the docks."

In his mirror, Ron sees the door to the Jigsaw Room open. Joyce walks in. He knew she wouldn't let him down. Not least because she knows Mike Waghorn will be here. This whole thing was her idea, truth be told. She chose the file.

Ron notices that Joyce is wearing a new cardigan. She just can't help herself.

"You told us you weren't going to have makeup, Ron," says Joyce.

"They make you," says Ron. "This is Pauline."

"Hello, Pauline," says Joyce. "You've got your work cut out there."

"I've seen worse," says Pauline. "I used to work on *Casualty*."

The door opens once again. A camera operator walks in, followed by a sound man, followed by a flash of white hair, the quiet swoosh of an expensive suit and the perfect, masculine yet subtle scent of Mike Waghorn. Ron sees Joyce blush. He would roll his eyes if he wasn't having his concealer applied.

"Well, here we all are, then," says Mike, his smile as white as his hair. "The name's Mike Waghorn. The one, the only, accept no substitutes."

"Ron Ritchie," says Ron.

"The same, the very same," says Mike, grasping Ron's hand. "Haven't changed a bit, have you? This is like being on safari and seeing a lion up close, Mr. Ritchie. He's a lion of a man, isn't he, Pauline?"

"He's certainly something or other," agrees Pauline, powdering Ron's cheeks.

Ron sees Mike turn his head slowly toward Joyce, slipping off her new cardigan with his eyes. "And who, might I ask, are you?"

"I'm Joyce Meadowcroft." She practically curtsies.

"I should say you are," says Mike. "You and the magnificent Mr. Ritchie a couple, then, Joyce?"

"Oh, God, no, my goodness, the thought, no, heavens no. No," says Joyce. "We're friends. No offense, Ron."

"Friends indeed," says Mike. "Lucky Ron."

"Stop flirting, Mike," says Pauline. "No one's interested."

"Oh, Joyce'll be interested," says Ron.

"I am," says Joyce. To herself, but just loud enough to carry.

The door opens once again, and Ibrahim pokes his head around. Good lad! Only Elizabeth missing now. "Am I too late?"

"You're just in time," says Joyce.

The sound man is attaching a microphone to Ron's lapel. Ron is wearing a jacket over his West Ham shirt, at Joyce's insistence. It is unnecessary, in his opinion. Sacrilegious, if anything. Ibrahim takes a seat next to Joyce and looks at Mike Waghorn.

"You are very handsome, Mr. Waghorn. Classically handsome."

"Thank you," says Mike, nodding in agreement. "I play squash, I moisturize, and nature takes care of the rest."

"And about a grand a week in makeup," says Pauline, putting the finishing touches to Ron.

"I am handsome too, it is often remarked upon," says Ibrahim. "I think perhaps, had my life taken a different turn, I might have been a newsreader too."

"I'm not a newsreader," says Mike. "I'm a journalist who happens to read the news."

Ibrahim nods. "A fine mind. And a nose for a story."

"Well, that's why I'm here," says Mike. "As soon as I read the email, I sniffed a story. A new way of living, retirement communities, and the famous face of Ron Ritchie at the heart of it. I thought, 'Yup, viewers will love a bit of that.'"

It's been quiet for a few weeks, but Ron is delighted that the gang is back in action. The whole interview is a ruse. Designed by Joyce to lure Mike Waghorn to Coopers Chase. To see if he could help them with the case. Joyce sent an email to one of the producers. Even so, it still means that Ron is going to be on TV again, and he is very happy about that.

"Will you come to dinner afterward, Mr. Waghorn?" asks Joyce. "We've got a table for five thirty. After the rush."

"Please, call me Mike," says Mike. "And, no, I'm afraid. I try not to mix with people. You know, privacy, germs, whatnot. You understand, I'm certain."

"Oh," says Joyce. Ron sees her disappointment. If there is a bigger fan of Mike Waghorn anywhere in Kent or Sussex, he would like to meet them. In fact, now he really thinks about it, he wouldn't like to meet them.

"There is always a great deal of alcohol," says Ibrahim to Mike. "And I suspect many fans of yours will be there."

Mike has been given pause for thought.

"And we can tell you all about the Thursday Murder Club," says Joyce.

"The Thursday Murder Club?" says Mike. "Sounds made up."

"Everything is made up, when you really think about it," says Ibrahim. "The alcohol is subsidized by the way. They tried to stop the subsidy, but we held a meeting, a number of words were exchanged, and they thought better of it. And we'll have you out by seven thirty."

Mike looks at his watch, then looks at Pauline. "We could probably do a quick supper?"

Pauline looks at Ron. "Will you be there?"

Ron looks at Joyce, who nods firmly. "Sounds like I will, yeah."

"Then we'll stay," says Pauline.

"Good, good," says Ibrahim. "There's something we'd like to talk to you about, Mike."

"Which is?" asks Mike.

"All in good time," says Ibrahim. "I don't wish to pull focus from Ron."

Mike sits in an armchair opposite Ron and starts counting to ten. Ibrahim leans into Joyce.

"He is testing the microphone level."

"I had worked that out," says Joyce, and Ibrahim nods. "Thank you for getting him to stay for dinner—you never know, do you?"

"You never do know, Joyce, that is true. Perhaps the two of you will marry before the year is out. And, even if not, which is an outcome we must prepare for, I'm sure he will have plenty of information about Bethany Waites."

The door opens once more, and Elizabeth enters the room. The gang is all here. Ron pretends he is not touched. Last time he had a gang of friends like these, they were being hospitalized by police riot shields at the Wapping print-workers' strike. Happy days.

"Don't mind me," says Elizabeth. "You look different, Ron, what is it? You look . . . healthy."

Ron grunts, but sees Pauline smile. That's a cracking smile, to be fair to her. Is Pauline in his league? Late sixties, a bit young for him? What league is he in these days? It's been a long time since he'd checked. Either way, what a smile.

2.

It can be hard to run a multimillion-pound drugs gang from a prison cell. But it is not, as Connie Johnson is discovering, impossible.

Most of the prison staff are on side, and why wouldn't they be? She throws enough money around. There are still a couple of guards who won't play ball, however, and Connie has already had to swallow two illegal SIM cards this week.

The diamonds, the murders, the bag of cocaine. She had been very skillfully set up, and her trial date has been set for two months' time. She is eager to keep things ticking over until then.

Perhaps she will be found guilty, perhaps she won't, but Connie likes to err on the side of optimism in all things. Plan for success, her mum used to say, although soon afterward she died, having been hit by an uninsured van.

Above all it's good to keep busy. Routine is important in prison. Also, it is important to have things to look forward to, and Connie is looking forward to killing Bogdan. He's the reason she's in here and, eyes like mountain pools or not, he is going to have to go.

And the old guy too. The one who helped Bogdan set her up. She has asked around, and found his name is Ron Ritchie. He'll have to go as well. She'll leave them until after the trial—juries don't like witnesses being murdered—but then she will kill them both.

Looking down at her phone, Connie sees that one of the men who works in the prison admin block is on Tinder. He is balding and standing next to what appears to be a Volvo of all things, but she swipes right regardless, because you never know when people might come in handy. She sees immediately that they are a match. Quelle surprise!

Connie has done a bit of research into Ron Ritchie. He was famous apparently, back in the seventies and eighties. She looks at the picture of him on her phone, his face like an unsuccessful boxer, shouting into a megaphone. Clearly a man who enjoyed the limelight.

Lucky you, Ron Ritchie, thinks Connie. *You'll be famous again by the time I've finished with you.*

One thing is for sure: Connie will do anything she can to remain in prison for as short a time as possible. And, once she is out, the mayhem can really begin.

Sometimes in life you simply have to be patient. Through her barred window Connie looks out over the prison yard, and to the hills beyond. She switches on her Nespresso machine.

3.

Mike and Pauline have joined them for dinner.

Ibrahim loves it when the whole gang is together. Together, and with a mission in mind. Joyce had been adamant that they were to investigate the Bethany Waites case. Ibrahim was quick to agree. Firstly because it is an interesting case. An unsolved case. But mainly because Ibrahim has fallen in love with Joyce's new dog, Alan, and he is worried that if he upsets her, Joyce might restrict his access.

"You want a drop of red, Mike?" Ron asks, bottle raised.

"What is it?" asks Mike.

"How do you mean?"

"What wine is it?"

Ron shrugs. "It's a red, I don't know the make."

"OK, let's live dangerously, just this once," says Mike, and lets Ron pour.

They have been very keen to talk to Mike Waghorn about the murder of Bethany Waites. It is assumed that he will have information that was not in the official police files. Mike doesn't know that yet, of course. He is just enjoying free wine with four harmless pensioners.

Ibrahim will be patient before he starts asking about the murder, because he knows that Joyce is excited to meet Mike, and she has lots of other questions for him first. She has written them down in a notebook, which is in her handbag, in case she forgets any of them.

Now that Mike has a glass of unidentified red in front of him, Joyce clearly feels able to begin. "When you read the news, Mike, is it all written down, or are you allowed to put it in your own words?"

"That's an excellent question," says Mike. "Perceptive, gets right to the heart of things. It is all written down, but I don't always stick to the script."

"You've earned that right over the years," says Joyce, and Mike agrees.

"Gets me into trouble from time to time though," says Mike. "They made me go on an impartiality course in Thanet."

"Good for you," says Elizabeth.

Ibrahim sees Joyce take a sneaky peek at the notebook in her handbag.

"Do you ever wear any special clothes when you read the news?" asks Joyce. "Special socks or anything?"

"No," says Mike. Joyce nods, a little disappointed, then takes another look at her book.

"What happens if you need the loo during a show?"

"For heaven's sake, Joyce," says Elizabeth.

"I go before the show starts," says Mike.

Fun though this is, Ibrahim wonders if it isn't time to kick off this evening's proceedings himself. "So, Mike, we have a—"

Joyce places a hand on his arm. "Ibrahim, forgive me, just a couple more things. What is Amber like?"

"Who's Amber?" says Ron.

"Mike's co-host," says Joyce. "Honestly, Ron, you're embarrassing yourself."

"I do that," says Ron. He says this directly to Pauline, who, in Ibrahim's opinion, had very deliberately sat next to Ron at the start of dinner. Ibrahim usually sits next to Ron. No matter.

"She's only been there three years, but I am already starting to like her," says Joyce.

"She's terrific," says Mike. "Goes to the gym a lot, but terrific."

"She has lovely hair too," says Joyce.

"Joyce, you should judge news presenters on their journalism," says Mike.

"And not their appearance. Female presenters, particularly, have to put up with that a lot."

Joyce nods, knocks back half a glass of white, then nods again. "I do take your point, Mike. I just think that you can be very talented *and* have lovely hair. Perhaps I'm shallow, but both of those things are important to me. Claudia Winkleman is a good example. You also have lovely hair."

"I'll have the steak, please," says Mike to the waiter now taking their orders. "Rare to medium rare, err on the side of rare. Though if you err on the side of medium, I'll live."

"I had read you were a Buddhist, Mike?" Ibrahim spent the morning researching their guest.

"I am," says Mike. "Thirty-odd years."

"Ah," says Ibrahim. "I had been under the impression that Buddhists were vegetarian? I was almost sure."

"I'm Church of England too," says Mike. "So I pick and choose. That's the point of being a Buddhist."

"I stand corrected," says Ibrahim.

Mike has started on his second glass of red, and seems ready to hold court. This is perfect.

"Tell me about this Thursday Murder Club, then," he says.

"It's fairly hush hush," says Ibrahim. "But we meet up, once a week, the four of us, to look over old police files. See if we can solve anything they were unable to."

"Sounds like a fun hobby," says Mike. "Looking into old murders. Keeps you busy I bet? The old gray cells ticking over? Ron, should we get another bottle of this red?"

"It's mainly been new murders recently," says Elizabeth, laying the bait still further.

Mike laughs. He clearly doesn't think Elizabeth is being serious. Which is probably for the best. Don't want to frighten him off just yet.

"Sounds like you don't mind a bit of trouble here and there," says Mike.

"I've always been a magnet for trouble," says Ron.

Pauline tops up Ron's glass. "Well, watch yourself, Ron, because I've always *been* trouble."

Ibrahim sees Joyce give a tiny, secret smile at this. Ibrahim decides that, before they try to move the conversation, gently and slowly, on to Bethany Waites, he has a question of his own. He turns to Pauline.

"Are you married, Pauline?" he asks.

"Widow," says Pauline.

"Ooh, snap!" says Joyce. Ibrahim notes that this evening's combination of wine and celebrity is making her quite the giddy goat.

"How long have you been on your own?" asks Elizabeth.

"Six months," says Pauline.

"Six months? That's no time at all," says Joyce, placing her hand on Pauline's. "I was still putting an extra slice in the toaster at six months."

Was it time? Here goes, thinks Ibrahim. Time to make small, subtle shifts in the conversation so they can start talking about Bethany Waites. A delicate dance, with Ibrahim as master choreographer. He has his first move all planned. "So, Mike. I wonder if you—"

"I'll tell you this for nothing," says Mike, ignoring Ibrahim, wine glass circling the air. "If you want a murder to solve, I've got a name for you."

"Go on?" says Joyce.

"Bethany Waites," says Mike.

Mike is on board. The Thursday Murder Club always get their man. Ibrahim notes, and not for the first time, that people often seem very willing to walk into their traps.

Mike takes them through the story they already know from the police files. They nod along, pretending it's all new to them. The brilliant young reporter, Bethany Waites. The big story she was investigating, a massive VAT fraud, and, then, her unexplained death. Her car driving off Shakespeare

Cliff in the dead of night. But there is nothing new. Mike is currently showing them the final message Bethany sent him, the night before she died: *I don't say this often enough, but thank you.*

Touching, certainly. But also nothing they don't already know. Perhaps the biggest revelation they are going to get from this evening is that Mike Waghorn goes to the toilet before he goes on air. Ibrahim decides to chance his arm.

"What about messages in the few weeks before that? Anything out of the ordinary? Anything the police haven't seen?"

Mike scrolls back through his messages, reading some highlights. "Do I fancy a pint? Have I watched *Line of Duty*? There's one about the story she was working on here, but from a couple of weeks before. Interested?"

"One never knows what might help," says Elizabeth, pouring Mike another glass of red.

Mike reads from his phone.

"*Skipper* . . . that's what she used to call me."

"Among other things," says Pauline.

"*Some new info. Can't say what, but it's absolute dynamite. Getting closer to the heart of this thing.*"

Elizabeth nods. "And did she ever tell you what the new information was?"

"She did not," says Mike. "I'll tell you what, this red is half decent."

4.

PC Donna De Freitas feels like someone has just punched a hole through the clouds.

She is flooded with heat and warmth, alive with a pleasure both utterly familiar but completely new. She wants to weep with happiness, and to laugh with the uncomplicated joy of life. If she has ever felt happier, she cannot immediately bring it to mind. If the angels were to carry her away this very moment—and if her heart rate was anything to go by that was a possibility—she would let them scoop her up, while she thanked the heavens for a life well lived.

"How was it?" asks Bogdan, his hand stroking her hair.

"It was OK," says Donna. "For a first time."

Bogdan nods. "I think maybe I can be better."

Donna buries her head into Bogdan's chest.

"Are you crying?" asks Bogdan. Donna shakes her head without lifting it. Where's the catch here? Perhaps this is just a one-night thing? What if that's Bogdan's style? He's kind of a loner, isn't he? What if he's emotionally unavailable? What if there's another girl in this bed tomorrow night? White and blonde and twenty-two?

What was he thinking? That was the one question she knew not to ask a man. They were almost always thinking nothing at all, so were thrown by the question, and felt compelled to make something up. She'd still like to know though. What was going on behind those blue eyes? Eyes that could nail you to a wall. The pure blue of . . . wait a minute, is *he* crying?

Donna sits up, concerned. "Are you crying?"

Bogdan nods.

"Why are you crying? What's happened?"

Bogdan looks at her through his gentle tears. "I'm so happy you're here."

Donna kisses a tear from his cheek. "Has anyone ever seen you cry before?"

"A dentist once," says Bogdan. "And my mother. Can we go on another date?"

"Oh, I think so, don't you?" says Donna.

"I think so," agrees Bogdan.

Donna rests her head on his chest again, comfortably settling on a tattoo of a knife wrapped in barbed wire. "Maybe next time we do something other than Nando's and Laser Quest though?"

"Agreed," says Bogdan. "Next time perhaps I should choose instead?"

"I think that's for the best, yes," says Donna. "It's not my strong point. But you had fun?"

"Sure, I liked Laser Quest."

"You really did, didn't you?" says Donna. "That children's birthday party didn't know what had hit them."

"It's a good lesson for them," says Bogdan. "Fighting is mainly hiding. It's good to learn that early."

Donna looks over at Bogdan's bedside table. There is a body-builder's hand-grip, a can of Lilt and the plastic gold medal he won at Laser Quest. What has she found herself here? A fellow traveler?

"Do you ever feel different from other people, Bogdan? Like you're outside looking in?"

"Well, English is my second language," says Bogdan. "And I don't really understand cricket. Do you feel different?"

"Yes," says Donna. "People make me feel different, I suppose."

"But sometimes you like to feel different maybe? Sometimes it's good?"

"Sometimes, of course. I'd like to choose those times myself. Most days I just want to blend in, but in Fairhaven I don't get the chance."

"Everyone wants to feel special, but nobody wants to feel different," says Bogdan.

Just look at those shoulders. Two questions come to her at once: Are Polish weddings like English weddings? And would it be OK if I rolled over and went to sleep?

"Can I ask you a question, Donna?" Bogdan suddenly sounds very serious.

Uh-oh.

"Of course," says Donna. "Anything." Anything within reason.

"If you had to murder someone, how would you do it?"

"Hypothetically?" asks Donna.

"No, for real," says Bogdan. "We are not children. You're a police officer. How would you do it? To get away with it?"

Hmm. Is this Bogdan's downside? He's a serial murderer? That would be tough to overlook. Not impossible though, given those shoulders.

"What's happening here?" asks Donna. "Why are you asking me that?"

"It's homework for Elizabeth. She wanted to know my thoughts."

OK, that makes sense. What a relief. Bogdan is not a homicidal maniac; Elizabeth is. "Poison, I suppose," says Donna. "Something undetectable anyway."

"Yes, make it look natural," agrees Bogdan. "Make it look like not a murder."

"Maybe drive a car at them, late at night," says Donna. "Anything where you don't have to touch the body, that's where forensics will get you. Or a gun, nice and simple, one shot, *blam*, and get out quick, the whole thing away from security cameras. Plan your escape route, of course, that's essential too. No forensics, no witnesses, no body to bury, that's how I'd do it. Phone off, or leave your phone in a cab, so it's miles away when you're committing the murder. Bribe a nurse, maybe get vials of blood from strangers and leave them on the body. Or . . ."

Bogdan is looking at her. Has she overshared there? Maybe move the conversation on.

"What's Elizabeth up to?"

"She says someone got murdered."

"Of course she does," says Donna.

"But murdered in a car, pushed off a cliff. Is not how I'd murder someone."

"A car over a cliff? OK, I can see that," says Donna. "Why is Elizabeth investigating it?"

Bogdan shrugs. "Because Joyce wanted to meet someone off the TV, I think. I didn't really understand."

Donna nods—that sounds about right. "Were there any marks on the body? Like they'd been killed before the car went over the cliff?"

"No body, just some clothes and some blood. The body was thrown from the car."

"That's convenient for the killer." Donna was not used to this type of post-coital talk. Usually you had to hear about someone's motorbike, or the ex whom they'd just realized they still loved. Or you had to give a reassuring pep-talk. "Spectacular though. If the killer wanted to send a message to someone. Difficult to ignore."

"I think it's too complicated," says Bogdan, "For a murder. A car, a cliff, come on."

"And you're an expert in murder now?"

"I read a lot," says Bogdan.

"What's your favorite book ever?"

"*The Velveteen Rabbit,*" says Bogdan. "Or Andre Agassi's autobiography."

Maybe Bogdan could kill Carl, her ex? She's fantasized about killing Carl a few times. Could Bogdan push Carl's stupid Mazda over a cliff? But, even as the thought flashes through her mind, and she stretches like a cat finding a patch of sunshine, she realizes she no longer cares about Carl. Be the bigger person, Donna. Let Carl live.

"She could have asked me and Chris to help," says Donna. "We'd have been able to take a look at it. Do you remember the name?"

Bogdan shrugs. "Bethany something. But they like to do these things by themselves."

"Don't they just," agrees Donna and throws her arm across his endless chest. Rarely has she felt so thrillingly puny. "I like talking about murder with you, Bogdan."

"I like talking about murder with you too, Donna. Although I don't think this was murder. Too convenient."

Donna looks up, one more time, into those eyes. "Bogdan, do you *promise* that's not the last time we're ever going to have sex? Because I'd really like to go to sleep now, and then wake up with you and do it again."

"I promise," says Bogdan, his hand stroking her hair.

This is how you're supposed to fall asleep, thinks Donna. How has she not known about this before? Safe and happy and sated. And murders and Elizabeth, and tattoos, and being different and being the same, and cars and cliffs and clothes, and tomorrow and tomorrow and tomorrow.

5.

Joyce

I will admit that the murder of Bethany Waites was my idea.

We were all looking through the files for a new Thursday Murder Club case. There was a spinster in Rye in the early eighties, for example, who had died, leaving three unidentified skeletons and a suitcase containing fifty thousand pounds in her cellar. That was Elizabeth's favorite and, I agree, it would have been quite jolly, but, as soon as I saw the name "Bethany Waites" on another file, my mind was made up. I don't put my foot down often, but, when I do, it stays down. Elizabeth sulked, but the others knew not to argue. I'm not just here for tea and biscuits you know.

I remembered Bethany Waites, of course, and I had read a piece Mike Waghorn had written in the *Kent Messenger* about her murder, so I thought to myself, hello, Joyce, this looks suspicious, *and* you might get to meet Mike Waghorn.

Is that so wrong?

I have been watching Mike Waghorn on *South East Tonight* for as long as I can remember. If anyone gets murdered or opens a fête anywhere in the South East, Mike will be there, with that big smile on his face. Actually, he doesn't smile for the murders. Then he does a serious face, which he is also very good at. I actually prefer his serious face, so if there has been a murder, at least that's a silver lining. He looks a little bit like if Michael Bublé were more my age.

Mike has done *South East Tonight* for thirty-five years now, but every five years or so they get a new woman to host it with him. Which is where Bethany Waites came in.

Bethany Waites was blonde and Northern and she died in a car that drove over Shakespeare Cliff, near Dover. (It's just off the A20, I looked it up, because I suspect we'll be going there at some point.) This must have been almost ten years ago. You would have thought it was just a suicide, cliffs and cars and what have you, but there were all sorts of other things. Someone had been seen in the car with her just beforehand, there were ambiguous messages on her phone, the waters were muddied. So the police called it murder and, looking through their files, we were inclined to agree.

It was very big news around here at the time. Not an awful lot happens in Kent, so you can imagine. They had a special tribute show and I remember Mike crying, and Fiona Clemence having to put an arm around him on air. Fiona was the new co-host by then.

Fiona Clemence is so famous now, lots of people don't realize she started on *South East Tonight*. I asked Mike if he watches her quiz *Stop the Clock*, but he said he doesn't. Which must make him the only one in the country who doesn't. Pauline—she's the makeup artist, and we will get back to her—said he's just jealous, but Mike said he doesn't watch TV.

I will be honest with you. I'd hoped that this evening I would flirt with Mike, and he would tell me how much he liked my necklace, and I would blush and giggle, and Elizabeth would roll her eyes.

But nothing doing, I'm afraid.

"All wag, no horn," was how Ron put it. Mike gave me a peck on the cheek, and at one point he brushed my hand and there was electricity, but I think that was the combination of the deep carpet outside the restaurant and my new cardigan.

He interviewed Ron this afternoon: they're doing a piece about retirement living on *South East Today*. This was all Elizabeth's suggestion; she made me email one of the producers. If you want to lure someone, go to Elizabeth.

I have to admit Ron was actually rather good. He knows when to turn it on. He talked about loneliness and friendship and security, and I was very proud of him for being so open. You can see that Ibrahim rubs off on him. At one point he got distracted and started talking about West Ham, but Mike steered him back on course.

What we really wanted out of this whole plan, though, was information about Bethany Waites, and Mike was certainly happy to chat. He was three sheets to the wind, and he told us a lot of things we already knew from the files, but he was fired up.

The basic facts are these. Bethany had been investigating a huge VAT fraud. To do with importing and exporting mobile phones. The scheme had made millions.

A woman named Heather Garbutt had been behind it. She worked for a man named Jack Mason, a local crook, and it was widely believed that she was managing the operation on his behalf. Heather later went to jail for the fraud, but Jack Mason did not. Lucky Jack Mason.

One March evening, Bethany had sent Mike a text message, and Mike had expected to see her bright and breezy the next morning. But the next morning was never to come for Bethany.

That night she had been seen leaving her apartment building—we used to call it a block of flats, didn't we—at about ten p.m., and had then gone AWOL for several hours, no one knows where. She next reappeared on a CCTV camera near Shakespeare Cliff at around nearly three a.m. She had an unidentified passenger in her car.

The next time the car is seen is at the bottom of Shakespeare Cliff, wrecked, and containing her blood and her clothes but not her body. Which makes me suspicious, but is apparently common, with the tides around there. A year later, without the faintest sign of her, and with her bank accounts having not been touched, a Presumption of Death certificate had been issued. Again, par for the course, but still you must ask yourself, where's the body? I didn't say that out loud to Mike, because you can tell Bethany Waites means a great deal to him.

He gave us one new piece of information. A text message Bethany had sent him. She had found some new evidence, something important. Mike never found out what it was.

Heather Garbutt was obviously the key suspect, with all the evidence Bethany had been gathering about her, but they couldn't link her to Bethany's death in any way. Try as they might, they couldn't link Jack Mason either. Soon enough, Heather Garbutt was in prison for the fraud, and everyone moved on to something else.

But Mike never moved on. The key questions, as Mike sees them, are:

What was the new evidence Bethany messaged him about? It was nowhere in the court documents, but had she kept a record somewhere? Would it link Jack Mason to the crime maybe? He is still a free man today. A very rich one too.

Why did Bethany leave her apartment at ten p.m. that evening? Was she going to meet someone? To confront someone? And why did it take her more than four hours to reach Shakespeare Cliff? She must have stopped somewhere, but where? Did she meet someone?

And finally, of course, who was the passenger in her car?

There's enough for us to be getting on with there. I could tell even Elizabeth was taking an interest by the end.

After that we all had a few more drinks. Pauline and Ron shared a dessert, which might sound normal to you, but I've never seen Ron willingly share food, let alone a Banoffee Pie. So watch this space.

Before we knew it, it was nearly eight p.m.! Alan was beside himself when I got in. I say "beside himself": he was curled up on the sofa and raised an eyebrow at me that said, "What sort of time is this for my dinner, you dirty stop-out?" You know how dogs can be. I had brought him back some steak though, so that soon changed his tune. He wolfed it down without a backward glance. Alan is many things, but he is clearly not a Buddhist.

I am Googling Heather Garbutt and listening to the World Service. She is difficult to Google, because there's also an Australian hockey player called Heather Garbutt, and most of the results are about her. I actually ended up quite interested in the hockey player, and I follow her on Instagram now. She has three very beautiful children.

Heather Garbutt is still in prison (not the hockey player, but you know that). In fact, it turns out she is in Darwell Prison, which might work out very nicely for all concerned. Because, of course, we already know someone in Darwell Prison. I've messaged Ibrahim with an idea that he will like very much.

They are talking about cryptocurrency on the World Service now, so I'm going to look that up too. Bitcoin, that's the big one. It sounds very interesting, and it's all the rage according to this program, but quite risky. They just spoke to someone who made a million from it before his sixteenth birthday, and he was all in favor.

Gerry and I used to have some Premium Bonds, but that's as far as I've experimented with money. Maybe I should live a little? Do something different? Be someone different? Different to what, though? Who am I?

Who am I? I'm Joyce Meadowcroft, and that will do me to be getting on with.

Night-time is for questions without answers, and I have no time for questions without answers. Leave that to Ibrahim. I like questions you can answer.

Who killed Bethany Waites? Now that's a proper question.

6.

Morning has broken at Coopers Chase. From the window of Elizabeth's flat you can see the dog-walkers, and a few latecomers rushing to Over-Eighties Zumba. The air hums with friendly greetings, and the sounds of birdsong and Amazon delivery vans.

"Why you keep looking at your phone?" asks Bogdan. He is sitting across the chessboard from Stephen, but has been distracted by Elizabeth.

"I get messages, dear," says Elizabeth. "I have friends."

"You only get messages from Joyce," says Bogdan. "Or me. And we are both here."

Stephen makes a move. "There you go, champ."

"He's quite right," says Joyce, sipping from a mug. "Is this tea Yorkshire?"

Elizabeth gives a "How on earth would I know?" shrug, and goes back to the documents laid out in front of her. Evidence from the trial of Heather Garbutt. Readily available to the public if you're happy to wait three months or so. Or readily available in a couple of hours if you are Elizabeth. She must stop looking at her phone. The last message had read:

> You can't ignore me forever, Elizabeth. We have a lot to speak about.

She has started receiving threatening messages, from an anonymous number. The first had arrived yesterday, and it read:

Elizabeth, I know what you've done.

Well, you could narrow it down a bit, she had thought. More had come through since. Who was sending her these messages? And, more importantly, why? No point worrying about it now though. No doubt all would become clear eventually, and, in the meantime, she has the murder of Bethany Waites to solve.

"I really think it is Yorkshire." Joyce again. "I'm almost sure. You must know?"

Elizabeth continues to look through the documents. Financial records, dense and unyielding. Paper trails showing nonexistent mobile phones leaving the docks at Dover, and the same nonexistent phones coming back weeks later. Reams and reams of VAT claims. Bank statements totaling millions. Money disappearing to offshore accounts, and then nothing. Bethany Waites had uncovered the lot. You had to admire it.

"Never mind," says Joyce. "You're busy. I'll take a look in the cupboard."

Elizabeth nods. This paperwork was enough to get Heather Garbutt convicted of fraud. But did it also contain a clue to Bethany Waites's death? If it did, no one had yet found it. Elizabeth didn't fancy her own chances either, not really her area, all this. So what to do? She has a thought.

"Yes, it's Yorkshire," shouts Joyce from the kitchen. "I knew it."

Joyce had been insistent that she was coming round to visit. And it doesn't matter how high up one might have been in MI5 or MI6, it doesn't matter how many times you've been shot at by a sniper, or met the Queen; you won't stop Joyce once she has her mind set on something. Elizabeth had acted quickly.

Stephen's dementia is getting worse, Elizabeth knows that. But the more he slips from her grasp, the tighter she wants to hold him. If she is looking at him, surely he can't disappear?

Stephen is at his very best when Bogdan comes around to play chess, so Elizabeth has invited Bogdan over, and taken the risk with Joyce. Perhaps he will be in fine form. And perhaps that will be enough to keep the charade going for another few weeks. She has given Stephen a shave and washed his hair. He no longer finds this unusual. Elizabeth looks over to the chessboard.

Bogdan has his chin in his hands, contemplating his next move. There is something different about him.

"Are you using a different shower gel, Bogdan?" Elizabeth asks.

"Don't put the boy off," says Stephen. "I have him in a funk here."

"I used an unperfumed body scrub," says Bogdan. "Is new."

"Hmm," says Elizabeth. "That's not it."

"It's very feminine," says Joyce. "It's not unperfumed."

"I play chess," says Bogdan. "No distractions please."

"I feel like you're keeping a secret," says Elizabeth. "Stephen, is Bogdan keeping a secret?"

"Lips are sealed," says Stephen.

Elizabeth returns to the documents. Something here got Bethany Waites killed. By Heather Garbutt? Elizabeth doubts it very much. Heather Garbutt's boss, Jack Mason, is ostensibly a scrap-metal dealer, but in reality is one of the most well-connected criminals on the South Coast. Heather Garbutt seems like a soldier, not a general. So was Jack Mason the General? Is his name somewhere in these papers? Time for her plan B.

"How's Joanna, Joyce?" Elizabeth asks. Joanna is Joyce's daughter.

"She's doing a Skydive for Cancer," says Joyce.

"Be lovely to catch up with her," says Elizabeth.

Joyce sees straight through this. "Do you mean, it would be lovely for her to take a look through those documents, because you don't understand them?"

"Wouldn't do any harm, would it?" Joanna, and her colleagues, will get through this stuff in no time, Elizabeth is sure. Maybe turn up a name or two.

"I'll ask her," says Joyce. "I'm in her bad books because I said I didn't see the point of sushi. Why *do* you keep looking at your phone, by the way?"

"Don't be tiresome, Joyce," says Elizabeth. "You're not Miss Marple."

On cue, Elizabeth's phone buzzes. She doesn't look. Joyce nails her with the minutest raise of an eyebrow, then turns to Stephen, with a much gentler look.

"It's very nice to see you, Stephen," says Joyce.

"Always nice to meet one of Elizabeth's friends," says Stephen, looking up. "You pop round any time. New faces always welcome."

Joyce doesn't react, but Elizabeth knows what she has heard.

Bogdan makes a move, and Stephen gives a gentle round of applause.

"He might smell different," says Stephen. "But he doesn't play different."

"I don't smell different," says Bogdan.

"You do," says Joyce.

Elizabeth takes the opportunity to sneak a look at her phone.

I have a job for you

Elizabeth feels the blood pumping. Things have been too quiet recently. A retired optometrist crashed his moped into a tree, and there has been a row about milk bottles, but that was about it for excitement. The simple life is all well and good, but, in this moment, with a murder to investigate, and threatening texts arriving daily, Elizabeth realizes that she has missed trouble.

7.

DCI Chris Hudson is walking along a freezing cold beach, in a howling gale. He is nursing a lukewarm cup of something approximating tea. He has just bought it from a seafront café that refused to give him change, or let him use the staff toilet.

But nothing can ruin his mood. For once, things are going very well for Chris.

The Scenes of Crime Officer pokes her head out from inside the burned-out minibus currently squatting among the seaweed and the pebbles like a dreadful crab.

"Won't be a moment."

Chris gives a "no bother" wave, and means it.

Why is Chris so happy? The answer is simple, but also complicated.

Chris is in love with someone, and that same someone is in love with him.

No doubt it will all implode at some point, but it hasn't imploded yet. A crisp packet, performing acrobatics in the air, blows into his face. Love, you just can't beat it.

Perhaps it won't implode at all? Is that possible? Perhaps this is it now? Chris and Patrice. Patrice and Chris. Chris narrowly avoids stepping on one of the many needles strewn alongside the minibus. Heroin addicts love the beach. Perhaps he will grow old with Patrice? Watching box sets and going to farmers' markets? One hand, one heart. She has just made him watch *West Side Story,* and it actually wasn't bad once you got past the singing and dancing. Wouldn't that be a thing?

He looks over at PC Donna De Freitas, almost doubled up against the wind, face barely visible through the hood of her waterproof coat. She is his partner—officially still his "shadow," but that doesn't seem to be how their relationship works—and she is Patrice's daughter. What a lot he owes her already.

Donna also seems quite happy despite the weather. She turns her back to the wind and, pulling off a glove with her teeth, starts to reply to a message she has just been sent. Donna had a date last night and is being very coy about the whole thing. Chris is not *certain* it went well, but he caught her humming "A Whole New World" in the car over here, so he has his suspicions. Perhaps Patrice will be able to find out who the mystery man is.

The minibus, now just a twisted, melted frame, coal-black against the gray of the sea and sky, had belonged to a children's home. The corpse in the driver's seat is, as yet, unidentified. Chris has never really thought about how beautiful the sea is before. His foot crunches the broken neck of a beer bottle. The wind picks up still further, blowing icy needles into Chris's face. Glorious, when you stop to look at it. When you drink it all in.

Chris has also lost a stone and a half in weight. He recently bought himself a T-shirt in size L, instead of his usual XL, or occasional, shameful XXL. He eats salmon and broccoli now. He eats so much broccoli he can spell it without looking it up. When was the last time he had a Toblerone? He can't even remember.

Chris's phone buzzes. Donna is not the only one who can be sent mystery messages. Checking the name, he sees it is from Ibrahim. If Elizabeth messages, you know you should worry. When it's Ibrahim, it's fifty-fifty. He reads:

> Good afternoon, Chris, it is Ibrahim here. I hope I haven't messaged you at an inconvenient time? One never knows the schedules of others, let alone those working in law enforcement, where hours are irregular at best.

There are dots, indicating Ibrahim is working his way through a second message. Chris can wait. Six months ago none of this was his. There was no Patrice, there was no Donna, there was no Thursday Murder Club. In fact, he realizes, it all started with them. They carried a kind of magic, the four of them. Sure, they recently condemned two men to their death on Fairhaven Pier, and stole an unimaginable amount of money, but they carried a kind of magic all the same.

"Who are you texting?" he calls to Donna, over the sound of the wind. Might as well give it a go.

"Beyoncé," shouts Donna, and keeps typing.

Chris's phone buzzes. Ibrahim again.

> I was wondering, and forgive me if this is outside the ambit of our friendship, if you might be able to look into two old cases for me? I believe you might also find them interesting, and I hope you understand that I wouldn't ask, were it not that the situation in which we find ourselves requires it.

Dots indicate there is a part three.

Chris and Donna have recently been in to see the Chief Constable of Kent, a man named Andrew Everton. Good copper, sticks up for his troops, but merciless if anyone crosses the line. He writes novels in his spare time too, under a pen-name. The Chief Constable publishes the books himself, and you can get them only on Kindle. Another officer was telling Chris that's where the real money is these days, but Andrew Everton still drives an old Vauxhall Vectra, so it may not be true.

Andrew Everton told them they are both going to get a commendation at the Kent Police Awards. For their work catching Connie Johnson. Nice to get a bit of recognition. The walls of the Chief Constable's office were garlanded with portraits of proud police officers. Heroes all. Chris looks at this sort of thing through Donna's and Patrice's eyes these days, and had noticed the portraits were all of men, save for one of a woman, and one of a police dog. The police dog had a medal. Chris sees a used condom curled up in a seashell. Life is a miracle.

Another text from Ibrahim. Cutting to the chase, hopefully.

> The cases to which I referred in my previous message are the death of Bethany Waites. And the conviction of Heather Garbutt for fraud. Both from 2013. With particular emphasis on where Bethany Waites might have been between 10 p.m. and 2:47 a.m. on the night of her death. And who might have been in her car with her. All information gratefully received. Talk soon, my good friend. Love to Patrice, you really have found yourself a fine woman there. Often, in relationships, the key is to . . .

Chris stops reading. He remembers both cases, Bethany Waites and Heather Garbutt. Will he take a look? Who is he kidding, of course he will take a look. One day the Thursday Murder Club will get him sacked, or possibly killed, but it's worth the risk. He feels as if someone must have conjured them up just for him, to save him. The Thursday Murder Club brought him Donna, Donna brought him Patrice, Patrice brought him stir-fried tofu. And all of that, it turns out, brought him happiness.

Donna looks up from her phone. "Why are you smiling?"

Chris shrugs. "Why are *you* smiling?"

Donna shrugs. "You getting texts from my mum?"

"Can't open those in public," says Chris. "Vice Squad would pull me in."

Donna sticks out her tongue.

"Ibrahim wants us to look into a case."

"Don't tell me," says Donna. "Someone called Bethany drove her car off a cliff?"

"How on earth would you—"

Donna waves this away.

Chris looks out to sea, and Donna joins him. The gray clouds are turning an angry black, and the whipping wind lashes their faces with stinging salt spray. The smell of burned metal and plastic from the minibus mixes with the stench of the decaying corpse, and catches in their throats. Two seagulls fight, loudly and angrily, over a plastic shopping bag.

"So beautiful," says Chris.

"Stunning," agrees Donna.

8.

Elizabeth has been thinking about the CCTV cameras. How on earth did they not pick up Bethany's car as she drove through Fairhaven? Before leaving for her walk, she had rung Chris about it, and he had said, "Ah, I've been expecting you."

She asked if he might have a look into it, and he said he was rather busy with a corpse of his own, so Elizabeth had congratulated him on the commendation he had just received from the Chief Constable, and reminded him of her part in catching Connie Johnson for him.

So he has agreed to take a look.

Elizabeth and Stephen have started taking a walk at the same time each afternoon. Rain or shine, same route, same time.

They walk through the woods, along the western wall of the graveyard, where Elizabeth had gone digging not so very long ago, and out into the open fields beyond the new buildings, which are beginning to spring up on top of the hill. There they stop, take out a hip flask and talk to the cows.

Stephen has given all the cows their own names and personalities, and, every day, gives Elizabeth a running commentary of all the latest cow developments. Today, Stephen tells her that Daisy has been cheating on Brian with Edward, a younger, more handsome bull from a nearby field, and Daisy and Brian are now trying cow counseling. Elizabeth takes a nip of whisky and says that Daisy is an unimaginative name for a cow.

"No dispute there," agrees Stephen. "The blame lies squarely with her mother. Also called Daisy."

"Is that so," says Elizabeth. "And what was her father called?"

"No one knows, that's the thing," says Stephen. "Quite the scandal at the time. Daisy senior had been on holiday to Spain, rumors of a fling."

"Mmm hmm," says Elizabeth.

"In fact, if you listen closely, you can hear Daisy has just the slightest hint of a Spanish accent."

Daisy moos, as if on cue, and they both laugh.

It is time now though to head back through the woods, along the path that she has made herself, quiet, private, all their own. Keeping Stephen away from prying eyes. Away from inconvenient questions about the state of his mind.

Their hands stay clasped together as they walk, arms lightly swinging, hearts beating as one. This routine has quickly become Elizabeth's favorite time of the day. Her handsome, happy husband. She can pretend for a little while longer that all is well. That his hand will forever be in hers.

"Nice day for a walk," says Stephen, the sun lighting up his face. "We should do this more often."

God willing, thinks Elizabeth, I will take every walk with you that I can.

Bethany's body had never been found. That worries Elizabeth. She has read enough detective novels to know you must never trust a murder without a corpse. To be fair, she has also faked a number of deaths herself over the years.

Her attention elsewhere, Elizabeth sees the man only for a split-second. But she instantly realizes she has made a mistake.

It happens. Not often, but it happens.

This happy routine of hers, these familiar walks with Stephen, this familiar pleasure, was, of course, Elizabeth's big mistake. As love so often is.

Routine is the spy's greatest enemy. Never travel the same route two days in a row. Never leave work at the same time. Don't eat at the same restaurant every Friday evening. Routine gives your enemy an opportunity.

An opportunity to plan ahead, an opportunity to hide, an opportunity to pounce.

Her split-second is up. Her last thought is "Please, please don't hit Stephen." She doesn't even feel the blow she knows is coming.

9.

"And then, in the late seventies, I went out with a member of UB40, but I think we all did back then," says Pauline.

"Which one?" asks Ron, trying to eat his soup with a little decorum.

Pauline shrugs. "There were so many of them. I think I slept with one of Madness too, or he said he was at least."

Ron had rung his son, Jason, and asked where might be good for lunch, somewhere that was classy, but wouldn't make a fuss if he didn't know what knife to use. Somewhere that did food he would recognize, but would have proper napkins, and nice loos. Somewhere you didn't have to wear a tie, but you could if you wanted, just hypothetical, say, but to remember he was a pensioner, and not made of money, though, you know, he had a few bob put away, don't you worry about that.

Jason had listened politely, then said, "And what's her name?" Ron had said, "Whose name?" Jason had said, "Your date," and Ron had said, "What makes you think . . ." and Jason had said, "Le Pont Noir, Dad, she'll love it," and Ron had said, "Pauline," and Jason wished him the best of luck. Then they spoke about West Ham for a bit until Ron asked Jason if he could book the restaurant for him, because he could never work out websites, and was too shy to ask Ibrahim to do it for him.

"Your mate really going to Darwell Prison today?" Pauline asks.

"We have a habit of interfering," says Ron. "So, what's your take on this Bethany Waites thing? You were around at the time?"

Le Pont Noir is what they call a gastropub. Ron had to scan the whole menu twice before he saw there was a steak. Even then it said "bavette" of steak, but it came with chips, so he was hoping it was going to be safe.

"She was a terrier, that's for sure," says Pauline. "In a good way. Mike was very cut up when she died. They looked out for each other. Rare in this business."

"A looker too," says Ron. "If you like blondes, which I don't. Not my type, not that I have a type. I'm not fussy. Well, I'm fussy, but—"

Pauline puts a finger to Ron's lips to help him out of his cul-de-sac of a sentence. He nods gratefully.

"She'd just started dating a new fella too," says Pauline. "Some cameraman, as always. In telly, the women all date their cameramen, and the men all date their makeup artists."

"Oh, really," says Ron, eyebrow raised. "So you and Mike Waghorn? You ever—"

Pauline laughs. "You've no worries there, darling. Mike dates cameramen too."

"There go Joyce's chances," says Ron, as his "bavette" of steak arrives. He is mightily relieved to see it is just a normal steak that someone has already cut up for him. Bingo. "You reckon the story got her killed?"

Pauline is pretending to look enthusiastic about a dish of braised cauliflower that has just been put in front of her.

"Maybe," she says. "Let's talk about something else; I get enough of this from Mike."

Ron is trying to work out who Pauline looks like. A bit Liz Taylor maybe? The new head judge on *Strictly Come Dancing*? He has decided, on reflection, that she is definitely out of his league. And yet here she was. "How's your cauliflower?"

"Take a wild guess."

Ron smiles.

"You enjoy yourself last night, then?" says Pauline. Ron had stayed over at hers for the first time. If you can eat braised cauliflower suggestively, then that's what she's doing.

Ron feels his cheeks flush. "I, look, yeah, it's been a while for me, so maybe I'm not what you're used to. It's been a long time. It was nice, just staying up talking. I hope that was OK?"

"Lover, it's been a long time for me too," says Pauline. "It was perfect. You're a gent. And a handsome, funny gent at that. Let's just go at our own pace, shall we?"

Ron nods, and eats some more of his steak. They hadn't brought any ketchup, but other than that he couldn't fault Le Pont Noir at all. Thank you, Jase.

"You fancy a walk along the front after this?" says Pauline. "While the sun's still in the sky? Get an ice cream on the pier?"

Ron thinks about his knees. How much they hurt when he doesn't use that blasted stick Jason bought for him. How they make him feel like an old man. Every step will hurt, all the more so for hiding it from Pauline. He'll be laid up in bed all day tomorrow.

"I'd love to," says Ron. "I'd love to." Perhaps he doesn't need to hide anything from Pauline?

"And I know your knee gives you gip," says Pauline. "So let's get you a stick for goodness' sake. I don't need a tough guy slowing me down. I just want an ice cream and a kiss from Ron Ritchie on the pier."

Ron smiles again. He still won't be using a stick—he's got standards—but it's nice to hear.

Pauline gestures to her bag. "I've got a couple of spliffs in here too. They'll help."

10.

How long has Elizabeth been unconscious? Impossible to tell.

So what *does* she know?

She is lying on the cold, metal floor of a speeding vehicle. Her hands are cuffed behind her, and her feet are bound. A blindfold covers her eyes, and white noise is being played at deafening volume through a pair of headphones. A familiar torture technique.

But, on the plus side, she is not dead. Which at least gives her options.

All she can control right now is her breathing, and so she does just that. Slow, deep and steady. Nothing to be gained by panicking. She suspects she is going to need all her energy when she finally discovers where she is being taken.

Would they have hit Stephen too? Or not seen the need? Is he here with her?

Elizabeth wriggles backward across the floor of the vehicle—she has now deduced it must be a van—until she brushes up against another body. They are back to back. She knows it is Stephen, she can tell by the electricity.

With her hands behind her back, she feels for his hands. He is doing the same and their hands clasp, like those of sleepy, waking lovers. She squeezes Stephen's hand, then worries that that is perhaps emasculating. Should he be squeezing her hand? In the circumstances it is probably right that she is being the reassuring presence. Stephen has not been in this sort of position before.

She puts her finger on his wrist, in what could easily be a sign of affection, but really she is checking his pulse. She is seeing if *he* is panicking.

His pulse is rock-steady: sixty-five beats per minute. Of course it is. Stephen will also be controlling his breathing, trusting that his wife will get him out of this.

But will she? Well, it very much depends on what this is, Elizabeth supposes. It's the man sending her the texts certainly. Finally made good on his threats. But who is it? And what job does he have for her?

The van is beginning to slow down. As if it has left a major road and joined a minor one. Elizabeth takes note.

She will be missed in Coopers Chase, that's a good thing. Joyce will spot that her light is not on this evening. Or will she? Will she be busy looking into Heather Garbutt? Will Ibrahim be thinking about Connie Johnson? Will Ron be busy with . . . well, that goes without saying. Will they even notice her absence? Will they raise the alarm?

Elizabeth knows she is already too far from home anyway. There will be no cavalry to save her this time. She has got herself into this mess, and she will have to get herself out of it.

The van comes to a halt. Elizabeth waits and breathes. She feels a hand on her shoulder, roughly dragging her up.

But whose hand?

11.

"So you're not from the *Sunday Times?*" asks Connie Johnson, not unreasonably in Ibrahim's view. She is chewing gum. Again, fine by Ibrahim, good for dental health so long as it is sugar-free.

"No, I lied," says Ibrahim, crossing his legs, then tugging down the hem of his trouser leg. "I thought you might be more likely to speak to me if you thought I was a journalist."

They are sitting in a visiting room at Darwell Prison. Tables are spread out, but close enough that everyone can hear everyone else's heartbreak if they choose to. Ibrahim is listening to every conversation, while conducting his own with Connie. That is his habit.

"Then who are you?" asks Connie. She is in a prison jumpsuit, but is surprisingly well made-up for someone with no obvious access to high-end cosmetics.

"My name is Ibrahim Arif. I'm a psychiatrist."

"Well, that's fun," says Connie, and she sounds like she means it. "Who sent you? Prosecution lawyer? See if I'm batshit?"

"I already know you're not batshit, Connie. You are a very controlled, intelligent, motivated woman."

Connie nods. "Mmm, I'm very goal-oriented. I scored ninety-six on a Facebook quiz about it. That's a nice suit. Someone's doing all right."

"You set goals, Connie, and then you achieve those goals. Am I right?"

"I do," says Connie, then looks around her. "Though I am in prison, aren't I, Ibrahim Arif? So I'm not perfect."

"Who among us is?" asks Ibrahim. "It is healthy to admit that to ourselves. I wonder if you might like a task, Connie?"

"A task? You need coke? You don't look like you need coke. You want someone murdered? You look like you could afford it."

"Nothing illegal at all," says Ibrahim. He absolutely loves talking to criminals, he can't deny it. It's the same with famous people too. He loved talking to Mike Waghorn. "Quite the opposite."

"The opposite of illegal, OK. And what's in it for me?"

"For you, nothing at all," says Ibrahim. "I just suspect it's something you'd be rather good at. And therefore you'd rather enjoy."

"I mean, I'm quite busy," says Connie, smiling.

"I see that," says Ibrahim, smiling back. Connie's smile looks real, and so his is real in return.

"OK, what's the task?" says Connie. "I like your cheek, and I like your suit—let's talk business."

Ibrahim quietens a little, keeps his voice flat and under the radar. "There's an inmate here called Heather Garbutt. Do you know her?"

"Is she the Pevensey Strangler?"

"I don't think so, no," says Ibrahim.

"There's a Heather on D-Wing," says Connie. "Older, looks clever. Like a teacher who robbed a bank?"

"Let's assume that's her for now," says Ibrahim. "Do you think you could befriend her? Perhaps find something out for me?"

"Sounds like the sort of thing I could do," says Connie. Ibrahim can already see her mind is in motion. "What do you need to find out?"

"I need to find out if she murdered a television reporter called Bethany Waites in 2013. By pushing her car over a cliff."

"Cool," says Connie, a small grin creeping onto her face. "I'll just ask her. Nice cup of tea, isn't it mild for the time of year, and did you murder someone?"

"Well, I'll leave it up to you how you approach the question," says

Ibrahim. "Your area, not mine. And maybe she didn't do it—that would also be useful information."

"I bet she did, though," says Connie. "I've never pushed a car off a cliff, always wanted to."

Ibrahim raises his palms. "There's still time, I'm sure."

"And there's really nothing in it for me?" asks Connie. "You can't smuggle in a SIM card for me or something?"

"I don't think I could," says Ibrahim. "I could Google how to do it, though, and give it a go."

"Don't stress, I've got plenty. And you don't want to know how they get smuggled in."

Ibrahim thinks he will Google it anyway. He is really enjoying himself. He hasn't been out much since his mugging, but, bit by bit, he is regaining his confidence, and, bit by bit, he is feeling his old self return. There are scars, yes, but that at least means the bleeding has stopped. And it's nice to remember he's good at this sort of thing. At reading people. At understanding trouble, and redirecting it. He likes Connie, and she likes him. Although one has to be careful: she is a ruthless killer and, without wishing to be judgmental about it, that is fairly bad. He will have good news to report back to the gang later though. He starts thinking about SIM cards. They are very small, Ibrahim knows that, so he wonders how you . . . Ibrahim realizes that Connie has just said something, and that he has missed it. That is unlike him. Very unlike him. Time to sharpen up.

"I'm sorry," says Ibrahim. "I didn't catch that?"

"You were off in dreamland, Ibrahim," says Connie. "Let me ask you again. As a psychiatrist, what do you think motivates me?"

This is easy meat for Ibrahim. Sure, we are all different, all unique snowflakes leading unique lives, but we are all the same under the bonnet.

"Momentum, I would say. A desire for movement and change." Ibrahim steeples his fingers. "Some people need everything to stay the same—I am a little like that. If they changed the music on the *Shipping Forecast*, for example, I would hyperventilate. But some people need everything to change. You need everything to change. That chaos is where you are able to hide yourself."

"Hmm," says Connie. "How wise, Mr. Ibrahim Arif. But do you think honesty is important to me?"

Where's this going? Ibrahim has a sinking feeling. "I imagine so. In your line of work, honesty is, ironically, paramount."

"You imagine so, do you?" asks Connie. "Where did you get my name, mate? How did you hear about Connie Johnson? Who sent you?"

"A client," says Ibrahim. He is a bad liar, and tries to avoid lies whenever he can. But he's had to lie more and more often since he met Elizabeth, Joyce and Ron.

"Because I've heard your name before," says Connie. "Ibrahim Arif. Do you know where I heard that name?"

Ibrahim is all out of lies, as Connie leans over and whispers in his ear, "From your mate Ron Ritchie, the day I got arrested."

She settles back in her chair. Your move, Ibrahim.

"He told you to come here, did he?" asks Connie. "You're working for him?"

"No, I'm working for Elizabeth Best, of MI5. Or MI6. One of them."

Connie takes this in. "So MI5, or 6, want me to talk to Heather Garbutt?"

"Indirectly, yes," says Ibrahim.

"And will this help me in court? Can a gang of men in balaclavas bust me out of the dock?"

"No, I'm afraid not," says Ibrahim. Though it occurs to him that they probably could. Elizabeth would know. Best not to promise anything.

"Ibrahim," says Connie, "I don't like being lied to."

"No," says Ibrahim. "I apologize."

"And," continues Connie, "it's important that you know that the moment I'm out, I'm going to kill your friend Ron Ritchie for landing me in here."

"Noted."

Connie thinks for a moment. "And do you know Bogdan?"

"I do," admits Ibrahim.

"I'm going to kill him too. Will you tell them both for me?"

"I will pass on the message, yes."

"Is Bogdan seeing anyone, do you know?"

"I don't think so," says Ibrahim.

Connie nods. A prison warder approaches the table.

"Time's up, Johnson, that's your twenty."

Connie turns to him. "Five more minutes."

"You don't run this jail," says the warder. "We do."

"Five more minutes, and I'll get your son an iPhone," says Connie.

The warder thinks for a moment. "Ten minutes, and he wants an iPad."

"Thank you, Officer," says Connie, and turns back to Ibrahim. "I'm so bored here, let's do it. Give me everything you've got on Heather Garbutt. I'm still going to kill your friends, but until that happens let's all agree to get along and have a bit of fun."

Ibrahim nods. "You know you could just choose not to kill my friends, Connie?"

"How do you mean?" asks Connie, genuinely confused.

"All that happened here is that they outsmarted you. Is that such a bad thing? They took advantage of your greed. Is your self-esteem so fragile that you can't be outsmarted once in a while?"

Connie laughs. "But it's my job, Ibrahim, it's how I make my money. Surely you get that, you're a bright man."

"Thank you," says Ibrahim. "I once took an IQ test, and—"

"Say I didn't kill Ron and Bogdan," Connie cuts across. "Let's workshop that. Every chancer in Fairhaven would think they can take me on. Do you know my company slogan?"

"I wasn't even aware you had one," says Ibrahim.

"Immediate and brutal retaliation," says Connie.

"That makes sense," admits Ibrahim. "Are there no ethical drug dealers?"

"In Brighton there's a fair-trade cocaine dealer. He gets all his wraps stamped and everything. Cocaine from family-run farms, no pesticides."

"Well, that seems like a start," says Ibrahim.

"He still threw someone off a multi-story car park for stealing money from him."

"Small steps," says Ibrahim. "You know, perhaps I could bring Ron in to see you? You might not want to kill him quite so much if you really got to know him." Ibrahim thinks this through for a moment. Actually, Ron often has the opposite effect on people.

Connie considers this. "You're interesting. Would you like a job?"

"I have a job," says Ibrahim. "I'm a psychiatrist."

"A proper job though?" says Connie.

"No, thank you," says Ibrahim. Though it would be fun to work for a crime organization. All that planning, smoky backrooms, men wearing sunglasses indoors.

"Then would you like to be my psychiatrist?"

Ibrahim takes this in for a moment. That would actually be a lot of fun. And interesting. "What would you want from a psychiatrist, Connie? What do you think you need?"

Connie thinks. "Learn to exploit weaknesses in my enemies, I guess. How to manipulate juries, how to spot an undercover police officer?"

"Umm . . ."

"Why I always pick the wrong men?"

"That's more my sort of thing," says Ibrahim. "If someone asks for my help, I always start with one question. Are you happy?"

Connie thinks. "Well, I'm in prison."

"But that aside?"

"I mean. Maybe I could be happier? You know, five percent. I'm OK."

"I can help with that. Five percent, ten, fifty, whatever it might be. That's my job. I can't fix you, but I can make you run a little better."

"You can't fix me?"

"Humans can't be *fixed*," says Ibrahim. "We're not lawnmowers. I wish we were."

"Might be fun, mightn't it?" says Connie. "Unburden all my secrets. What do you charge? To buy suits like that?"

"Sixty pounds an hour. Or less if someone can't afford it."

"I'll pay you two hundred an hour," says Connie.

"No, it's just sixty."

"If you charge less for someone who can't afford it, then charge more for someone who can. You're a businessman. How often can we meet?"

"Once a week is best at first. And my schedule is pretty flexible."

"OK, I'll sort it here. They lap this sort of thing up, mental health. And I'll look into Heather Garbutt in the meantime. Girly chat, what's your star sign, did you push a car off a cliff."

"Thank you. I shall look forward to speaking with you," says Ibrahim. "And seeing if I can persuade you not to murder Ron."

"Great," says Connie. "Let's do Thursdays."

"Actually," says Ibrahim, "can we do Wednesdays? Thursdays are the one day I have something on."

12.

The last time Elizabeth had a bag and blindfold pulled from her head was in 1978. She was in the harshly lit administration block of a Hungarian abattoir, and was about to be questioned and tortured by a Russian Army general with a chest of bloodstained medals. As events transpired, there was to be no torture, as the General had left his tool bag in the car, and the car had driven off for the evening. So, in the end, she had got away with light bruising and an anecdote for dinner parties.

What had he wanted, the General? Elizabeth forgets. Something that no doubt seemed terribly important at the time. She knew people who had died for the blueprints to agricultural machinery. Very few things are so important you would risk your life for them, but all sorts of things are important enough to risk somebody else's life.

As her blindfold is removed this time, there is no glare of strip lights, no grinning General and no blood-smeared filing cabinets. She is in a library, in a soft leather chair. The room is lit by candles, the kind Joyce buys. The man who removed her blindfold and uncuffed her has silently left the room and is out of her sight.

Elizabeth looks over to Stephen. He arches an eyebrow at her, and says, "Well, this is a to-do."

"Isn't it?" she agrees. "Are you OK?"

"Right as rain, darling, you just keep your wits about you. I'm out of the old comfort zone here. Bash on the bonce, but no harm done. Probably knocked some sense into me."

"Your back all right?"

"Nothing a Panadol won't fix. Any idea what's afoot here? Anything I can do to help?"

Elizabeth shakes her head. "This might be one for me."

Stephen nods. "I'll look after morale, and follow your lead. I don't suppose we'd be in such comfortable chairs if they meant to kill us? You'd know better than me?"

"I suspect they want to speak to me about something or other."

"And decide whether to kill us based on what you have to say?"

"Possibly."

They are both silent for a minute.

"I love you, Elizabeth."

"Don't be so sentimental, Stephen."

"Well, either way, there's never a dull moment," says Stephen.

The door to the library opens, and a very tall, bearded man stoops through the doorway.

"Viking, is it?" Stephen whispers to Elizabeth.

The man takes his place in an armchair opposite Elizabeth and Stephen. His frame overflows the chair, like a teacher sitting on a classroom chair.

"So you are Elizabeth Best?" he asks.

"That rather depends on who you are," says Elizabeth. "Have we met?"

The man takes something from his pocket. "Do you mind if I vape?"

Elizabeth holds out her palms in invitation.

"Terribly bad for you," says Stephen. "I read a thing."

The man nods, takes a drag on his vape and turns to Stephen.

"And you must be Stephen? Sorry to drag you into this."

"Not a bit of it. Par for the course with this one. Afraid I didn't catch your name?"

The man ignores Stephen's question, and returns his attention to Elizabeth.

"You have been very busy for an old woman."

What is the accent? Swedish?

Elizabeth notices that Stephen is scanning the shelves of the library, eyes opening in wonder from time to time.

"Now, Elizabeth," says the Viking. "To business. I believe you stole some diamonds?"

"I see," says Elizabeth. At least she knows where she is now. No ancient history, simply their last little adventure. It felt like she had wrapped the whole thing up with a pretty little bow, but no good deed goes unpunished. "Am I to take it that I stole them from you, and not from Martin Lomax after all?"

"No, no," says the Viking. "You stole them from a man named Viktor Illyich."

"Viktor Illyich?" Elizabeth takes it all back. Ancient history at its very finest. "The most dangerous man in the Soviet Union," they used to call him. She has to hand it to herself, however. Whatever jolt of electricity passed through her body at the mention of the name "Viktor Illyich," no outside observer would have guessed she had ever heard it before.

"And you work for this Viktor Illyich?"

The Viking laughs. "Me? No. I work for no one. I am a lone wolf."

"We all work for someone, old chap," says Stephen, eyes still scanning the books. He's up to something, God bless him.

"Not me," says the Viking. "I'm the boss." He howls like a wolf, for an uncomfortably long time. Elizabeth waits, patiently, for his howl to end.

"So why am I here?" asks Elizabeth. "Not your diamonds, not your boss's diamonds, not your business."

"I don't care about diamonds. You think I care about twenty million? It's nothing."

The Viking leans forward in his chair, tilts his head and looks Elizabeth straight in the eyes.

"You are here because, for some time now, I have been looking into the possibility of killing Viktor Illyich."

"I see," says Elizabeth.

"And it isn't easy," says the Viking.

"I'm sure," says Elizabeth. "If murder were easy, none of us would survive Christmas."

"And so," says the Viking, "I want you to kill Viktor Illyich for me."

The Viking leans back, his cards on the table now. Elizabeth is thinking at speed. What has she found herself in the middle of here? Only this morning she had been thinking about traffic cameras and missing bodies. Now she is being threatened by a Viking. Or propositioned. Often the same thing in her line of work.

Whatever it is, at least it seems that she and Stephen will live to see another day. Let this new game begin, then. She sits back in her chair and clasps her hands together.

"I don't kill people, I'm afraid."

The Viking settles back into his chair, and smiles. "We both know that's not true, Elizabeth Best."

Elizabeth concedes the point. "Here's your problem though. I've only ever killed people who wanted to kill me."

The Viking reaches for a laptop from a side table, and gives a broad smile. "Then we are in luck. Because I am shortly to send an email to Viktor Illyich, with two photographs attached. One photograph of you at Fairhaven train station, opening a locker, and one of you at Fairhaven Pier on the day of the shootout. A situation that has caused Viktor Illyich a great deal of inconvenience."

"Banged to rights there, darling," says Stephen.

Elizabeth hadn't known that Viktor was involved with Martin Lomax and the business with the diamonds. But it made sense. Viktor was freelance these days.

"So you see," says the Viking, "as soon as he receives these photographs, Viktor Illyich will want to kill you. He will be consumed with revenge. It is very neat. All you need to do now is kill him first."

"Kill him yourself, old chap," says Stephen. "Look at the size of you."

"Much easier for me if somebody else does it," says the Viking. "And who better than a former spy, a little old lady, a woman who knows how to kill, and who has just pulled off one of the thefts of the century? Who better, Stephen?"

"It's cowardly," says Stephen. "Never taken the Swedes for cowards."

Elizabeth is mulling. Pretending to mull at least. Just arranging her cards in order before playing the first one. She doesn't have a great hand, though she does have an ace. She will have to proceed with care.

"Still not for me, I'm afraid," says Elizabeth to the Viking. "If I refuse, the worst you can do is kill me, which is a nuisance for you, and, honestly, I've had a fairly good run. And this would be a nice room to die in. Very cozy."

The Viking smiles. "I think your husband might not agree with that. Perhaps he might like you to stay alive."

Stephen shrugs. "We all go at some point, my Viking friend. I'd rather she wasn't killed by a cowardly Swede, but best to bow out doing something decent. I'm sure I'd miss her, but someone else would turn up soon enough. Beautiful spies everywhere you look. Falling out of trees."

Elizabeth smiles. But what if she really were to die? What then? What then for Stephen? Her heart cracks in two, but her face remains placid. Because she knows something the Viking doesn't know.

"I think if it's all the same to you," she says, "I'm going to take my husband home and forget this conversation ever happened. Put the bags back over our heads: I don't need to know where I am, and I don't have any interest in finding out who you are. I understand your position, and I understand why I'm the perfect woman to kill Viktor Illyich, but I'm not going to do it. Which leaves you with two options. Either you kill me—which would be very messy, an awful lot of admin, probably a lot of heat from MI6 when they realize I've vanished—or you simply let us go, no more said about it."

"Viktor Illyich will kill you though," says the Viking. "He will find out where you live. I found out easily enough."

"I will take my chances," says Elizabeth.

Viktor Illyich will not kill Elizabeth, she knows that. That's her ace. The Viking has been unlucky here. Elizabeth and Stephen will be home before dawn, and will be quite safe. Depending on where they are, of course. "So kill me or let me go. Those are your two options. Which do you choose?"

"I think I choose option three," says the Viking. "The option where I send Viktor Illyich the full photos."

"The full photos?"

"Yes, for sure. The photos with your friend Joyce Meadowcroft by your side. Both pictures, both names."

"Bit below the belt," says Stephen. Elizabeth still feels safe. Viktor won't go after Joyce either. Not if they're in the photo together. A friend of Elizabeth is a friend of Viktor.

"Viktor might not have the heart to kill Joyce, of course," says the Viking. "She is more of a civilian, I think? So here's my deal. Just as insurance, if Viktor Illyich isn't dead within two weeks, I will kill your friend Joyce."

13.

The second date was, if anything, even better than the first. They have just been to Brighton to watch a Polish film. Donna hadn't realized there were Polish films, though obviously there must be. In a country that size, someone is going to make a film once in a while.

It was an art-house cinema, of course it was, it was in Brighton, and that meant you couldn't get proper pick 'n' mix. No chocolate mice, no Kola Cubes, nothing. Just healthy snacks.

But they did let you bring wine into the cinema, so Donna supposed it was OK to put up with a handful of unsalted cashew nuts. Also, everyone stayed quiet during the film, which Donna was not at all used to.

They took the train from Fairhaven. Donna drank a Mojito in a can, and Bogdan drank a large energy drink into which he had mixed a sachet of protein powder.

They walked from the station to the cinema, her arm hooked through Bogdan's. At one point they walked past a house on Trafalgar Street that Bogdan told her was a crack den, and then past an old forge on London Road where a Lithuanian was buried. Bogdan would make a very good tour guide for a very specific type of tourist.

There were other black people in Brighton, and that was nice to see. Though still few enough for a subtle nod to be exchanged as they passed each other. Donna likes Brighton; she could see herself raiding a few crack dens here before her career was out.

They talked a little about Bethany Waites, and about Heather Garbutt.

Donna is putting together a map of all the CCTV cameras in Fairhaven for Chris. It is not an enjoyable job.

Now, not only do people in Poland make films, it turns out they make very good ones. Donna had worried it might be a searing portrayal of love and loss across the generations of a remote farming family, and she would have to keep turning to Bogdan and pretending to nod wisely. But not a bit of it. There was murder, there was fighting, there was a cop in a ripped shirt; it wasn't bad at all. Every few minutes Bogdan would lean into her and she readied herself for a kiss, but he was just pointing out occasional inconsistencies in the subtitles. She held his hand, her red wine slipped down a treat, the gal got the guy, and someone shot down a helicopter. Eight out of ten, would recommend.

They went back to his, there wasn't even a question. Where would they have parted? And why?

Bogdan is currently in the bathroom, and Donna is frantically rehydrating, and trying to recall if she has ever been happier.

They had talked a little more about Bethany Waites. Donna had looked into the files on Jack Mason, the businessman. A record as long as a Post Office queue. Charming but dangerous.

Talking of which, Bogdan walks back into the room, and gets into bed. She puts her arm around him, sleepy and safe.

They laugh. God, this feels right. It feels natural, and true, and unforced. It feels like all those things you read about relationships, but assume are lies.

Bogdan's mobile phone rings on the bedside table. They both look over at it. It is two a.m.

Well, here we go, thinks Donna, her reverie immediately broken. All those things *are* lies. There's another woman. Of course. Once again, Donna, nice try. There is *always* something. She is suddenly not so sleepy, and not so safe.

Bogdan looks at the number, then back at Donna. "I have to get this. I'm sorry."

Donna shrugs. She had been planning to stay until morning, but now she starts scanning for her clothes.

14.

Elizabeth and Stephen have been dropped by the side of a small road in a big wood. The moon is high and full, and pale light zigzags through winter's bare branches above them.

"You gave quite the start when he mentioned Viktor Illyich," says Stephen.

"I gave a start? I thought I covered it pretty well. Does anything get past you?"

"That's a kind thing to pretend. Old friend is he, Viktor?"

"Old enemy if anything. KGB Head of Station in Leningrad, eighties," says Elizabeth, her breath smoke in the clear air. "Then upward and upward."

One of the photos of Viktor in the folder the Viking had given her was of Viktor in his prime. Not prime exactly perhaps: the head was already balding, the thick, pebble-lensed glasses too big for his face. But young at least. The most recent photo brought the shock of age. Old, lined, strands of gray hair clinging to the cliff edges. The glasses still too big, but look behind them and there he was. Viktor. The mischief and intelligence in his eyes. The rival who became her friend. The enemy who became . . . her lover? Had they? Elizabeth doesn't recall, but she wouldn't put it past herself.

Viktor will look at her photograph in the same way, she is sure. Who is this old woman?

Elizabeth's phone is dead, and Stephen doesn't have his, so on they walk.

"Without speaking out of turn," says Stephen, "you have a look that says you don't much want to kill him?"

"No, I don't," says Elizabeth.

"And do you imagine he will try to kill you?"

"Goodness, no. He'll take one look at the photograph and roar with laughter."

They listen to the owls talk for a while, and hold each other close for warmth as they walk. How often do you walk down a new road with an old lover? Elizabeth looks at the moon, and at her husband, and thinks to herself that this is an unusual time to feel happy.

"But if you don't kill him," says Stephen, "then our Viking friend will kill Joyce?"

"That's where we find ourselves." This takes the edge off her mood somewhat.

"Hell of a choice. And, as yet, we have no idea who this Viking is?"

"Not yet we don't," agrees Elizabeth, as she spies a public phone box on the roadside ahead. "But, first things first, we need to get you home. I don't suppose you have twenty pence?"

Stephen fishes in his pocket and hands Elizabeth a coin.

"It's the middle of the night, dear, don't forget? Everyone will be asleep."

Elizabeth dials the number she knows by heart. She knows all her important numbers by heart. It must be two a.m., but the phone is answered before the first ring is completed.

"Hello, Bogdan," says Elizabeth.

"Hello, Elizabeth," says Bogdan. "What do you need?"

"A little help," says Elizabeth. "Right away if possible."

"OK, are you at home?"

"Bogdan, I hear a noise in the background. Is somebody there?"

"Is the TV."

"Well, it isn't the TV, but let's not argue about it now. I'm in a public phone box, I have no idea where but the number is 01785 547541. I wonder if you could possibly find out where that is, and then possibly also come and get me?"

She hears the sound of a laptop being opened.

"Where is Stephen? You need me to see him?"

"He's with me, dear." Elizabeth puts the receiver to Stephen's mouth.

"Hello, old chap," says Stephen. "Sorry to be a nuisance. A right pair of waifs and strays you have on your hands."

"Is no problem," says Bogdan. "Put me back to Elizabeth."

Elizabeth gets back on the call.

"OK, you're in Staffordshire," says Bogdan. "You heard of Staffordshire?"

"Of course I've heard of Staffordshire," says Elizabeth. "Any chance you could head up? It's very cold."

"Already dressing," says Bogdan.

"Thank you. Any clue how long it will take you?"

Bogdan goes quiet for a moment. "Google says three hours and forty-five minutes. So I will be there in two hours and thirty-eight minutes."

"I'm almost sure I can hear someone else there, Bogdan."

"It's the sat nav," says Bogdan. "You hold tight and I get there as soon as I can. Do you need me to bring you anything?"

Elizabeth thinks for a moment. Viktor Illyich, the Viking, Joyce. Is a plan forming? She believes it may well be.

"Yes, please, dear," she says. "Could you bring me a flask of tea, and a gun?"

15.

Mike Waghorn sits in a leather swivel chair, in a darkened edit suite. He holds a pen like the cigarette he would dearly love to smoke. But you can't smoke now that everyone has an HD television. It is very aging.

There is a row of television monitors in front of him, and, in front of the monitors, a control panel that wouldn't look out of place on an Airbus 380. Mike has recently flown in an Airbus 380 simulator on a corporate away-day he hosted for Delta Airlines at Gatwick. He crashed it into the Adriatic, trying to show off.

The face of Bethany Waites fills the screens in front of him. Mike is watching the tribute show he had hosted with Fiona Clemence. Fiona, with her game shows, her adverts, her magazine front covers. She has recently brought out her own diet book. But look at the two of them onscreen in 2013. Mike Waghorn, the famous one, Fiona Clemence, the producer over-promoted to presenter. Mike hadn't thought she would last.

Fiona was no fan of Bethany, that was for sure. And vice versa, to be fair. Huge rows, the two of them would have. Mike has thought about this a few times over the years. Could Fiona have killed Bethany? It is an absurd thought, but Bethany's death had given Fiona her big break, so who knew? Television was a cutthroat business at the best of times. He has looked further back in his texts after the other night. Bethany had been receiving anonymous notes at work. *Just leave. No one wants you here. We are all laughing at you.* Schoolyard stuff, really. But perhaps not? Were they from Fiona? And, if not, who were they from?

There are clips from Bethany's time on *South East Tonight*. It's mainly action shots, the type of stuff that looks good in montages. Bethany Waites on Kent's largest rollercoaster, Tom Jones flirting with Bethany Waites backstage at the Brighton Center, Bethany Waites at the top of a Dubai skyscraper, interviewing a Faversham woman who had made a fortune in plastic surgery, Bethany Waites being pushed into a swimming pool by a group of schoolkids from Deal.

But the real memories are never the ones that make the highlights reel. The real memories were of quiet afternoons watching Bethany work. The skill with which she found and told stories. The small jokes, the private looks, the squeeze of the hand every evening when they were "five seconds to air." Every day, "Anything from the canteen, Mike?" "No, thanks, Beth, my body's a temple." The Twix she would then bring him back.

Not rollercoasters, not skyscrapers, just the accumulation of small moments that turn acquaintance into friendship.

Mike finds it hard to cry, because he started having Botox treatments before they'd really got the hang of them, and his tear ducts are blocked. But he knows the tears are there, and he welcomes them. The tears only exist because Bethany existed.

Can he really trust this "Thursday Murder Club"? Mike has the peculiar sensation that he is being manipulated, but in such an enjoyable way that perhaps he will stay on the ride for now? See exactly what they're capable of.

He freezes the picture in front of him. Bethany's face. It's not a smile, or a laugh. He freezes it on a look of calm determination, eyes staring directly into his. He checks the code onscreen and sees this is a week before Bethany died.

When you look backward, everything is inevitable. Looking at her face, Mike knows that one week later Bethany would be dead. Mike leans forward and looks into those eyes. Did they know? He could swear now that they did. What on earth had she got herself into?

The edit door opens.

"Thought I might find you here," says Pauline, walking in with two cups of tea.

"Just wanted to remind myself," says Mike. "That Bethany was a real person, and not just a story."

Pauline nods. "I know you loved her."

"She could have done all sorts, couldn't she?" says Mike. "So full of ambition, full of ideas."

"Would have left us behind, wouldn't she?" says Pauline.

"You'd hope so," says Mike. "Do you remember those notes she was getting? *No one wants you here*. On her desk, on her windscreen, all of that?"

Pauline shakes her head. "Made you a cuppa."

"Thanks," says Mike. "What do you think happened though? I mean really happened?"

Pauline puts her hand on his. "You know you might never find out, Mike? You know you have to prepare yourself for that?"

Mike looks at Bethany's face on his screen once more. Looks into those eyes. He'll find out all right.

Pauline opens her bag. "Let's watch some more together, shall we?"

Mike nods.

Pauline pulls a Twix out of her bag and puts it next to his cup of tea.

16.

Remand prisoners at Darwell Prison are often kept in their cells for up to twenty-three hours a day. Connie Johnson reflects on how inhumane and unproductive that is, as she walks past all the locked cell doors on her evening stroll.

One of the warders doffs his cap to her as she makes her way along the steel walkway to Heather Garbutt's cell, the clang of her Prada loafers echoing through the cavernous building.

Connie knocks, then swings open the cell door without waiting for a response. This is exactly the Heather she thought it was. Dark hair turning gray, skin loose and pale, but nothing a bit of Botox wouldn't fix. Connie knows someone who can come in and take a look at her if need be.

Heather Garbutt, sitting on a plastic chair at a metal desk, gazes up at Connie with unhappy eyes. No shock or surprise. Connie knows the life of a prisoner is one of unexpected visitors and unwanted interruptions. The life of a normal prisoner, at least. Connie has got a doorbell.

"I don't have any money," says Heather. "I don't have cigarettes. I don't think I have anything you need."

Connie sits on the lower bunk of Heather's bed. "You want money? You want cigarettes? I can do that."

Heather is weighing her up, and Connie knows that is no easy job. On first meeting, people always find Connie affable. Fun even. But Heather has been in prison long enough to smell the danger on her too. So she is wary, and Connie doesn't blame her one bit. Connie would be terrified in Heather's shoes.

"I don't need anything, thank you. A bit of peace and quiet."

"I'll be gone soon enough. What were you writing?" asks Connie, tilting her head toward the desk.

"Nothing," says Heather.

"I'm Connie Johnson," says Connie. She gets up, walks behind Heather and starts to knead her shoulders. "Good friend, terrible enemy, but you're in luck, because you and I are going to be friends. You feel very tense, by the way."

"Please, I don't have anything." If Heather could make herself any smaller in her chair, she would disappear altogether.

Connie stops the massage, and walks back to the center of the cell. "Everyone has something, Heather. You're in for fraud, then? Ten years. Must have been a hell of a fraud."

"It was," says Heather.

"They make you pay back the money too?" asks Connie. "Knocked a couple of years off? Proceeds of Crime Act?"

"They asked me to," said Heather. "But there weren't any proceeds."

"Sure," says Connie, laughing. "But you'll be out soon?"

Heather nods.

"You must be happy about that?"

"I'm happy when they lock my door at night," says Heather.

Connie looks around Heather's cell. No family photos on the wall. A few prison library books on her desk. One is called *Small Pleasures,* and it has oranges on the cover. Connie thinks about the flat-screen TV in her own cell. And the mini-bar.

"What a ball of fun you are," Connie says. "I can cheer you up. What do you like? Chocolate? Men? Booze? I can get you anything."

"Connie, I want to be left alone," says Heather. "Can you get me that?"

"I can definitely get you that. I'll be out of your hair in a heartbeat. I just need you to answer a question."

"Where did I hide the money?"

"No, not where did you hide the money," says Connie. "Although where did you?"

"There is no money," says Heather. "That's why I'm still here."

Connie nods. "You stick to your story, girl, good for you. No, I need to ask you the other question, Heather."

Heather looks down at the floor. "No."

"Chin up, come on, we're a team. Look at me."

Heather looks up at Connie.

"Heather, did you kill Bethany Waites?"

"I can't talk to you about that."

"Does that mean you did or you didn't?"

"It means I can't talk to you about that. And shame on you for asking."

Connie looks at Heather Garbutt, eyes back down to the floor, shoulders slumped. Why can't she charm this woman? It absolutely infuriates Connie when people are resistant to her charms. She simply won't allow it. Connie starts crying, and that gets Heather looking up all right.

"Please don't cry in here," says Heather. "It's seen enough tears."

"I'm sorry," says Connie, trying to wipe the tears away. "It's just you remind me so much of my mum. And we lost her last year."

Heather looks at her, shakes her head the slightest amount and shrugs. "Don't lie about that sort of thing, Connie."

Connie stops crying immediately and sighs. "All right, we don't have to be friends, but I've been given a job, and I want to do it. Just tell me, and we're done. Bethany Waites was a journalist, she had worked out what you were doing, which was making millions sitting in a nice little office, doing bugger all. She was about to go public and suddenly someone pushes her car off a cliff. What does that look like to you?"

Heather gives the smallest of shrugs.

"Come on," says Connie. "You killed her—"

"No."

"Or you know who did?"

Connie notices that Heather does not say no to this question.

"You know who killed Bethany? You're covering for someone?"

"Please," says Heather quietly. "It's not safe."

"You're safe with me, princess," says Connie. "Why would you cover for someone? They got something on you? I could kill them for you, you know?"

Heather is silent for a long moment. She then gets up, walks to the door of her cell and opens it. She shouts down the corridor to a warder. "Mr. Edwards, there is someone in my cell. I'm being threatened."

Connie hears footsteps climbing a metal staircase, and Heather walks slowly back into the cell and sits down again.

"Sorry," Heather says. "I'm going to have to ask you to leave."

The footsteps from outside reach the doorway and a prison warder appears. "OK, let's get you back to . . . oh, Connie, it's you."

"Hello, Jonathon. Just visiting my friend Heather."

"Right you are," says Jonathon. "I'll shut the door and give you a bit of peace."

The door shuts behind him, and Connie turns back to Heather. "Listen, it was worth a try. Just tell me, Heather. It looks like you did it. But you don't seem like a killer. And there was no evidence. So what are we saying? Your boss did it? Jack Mason? I met him at a do once. Someone was trying to stab him in the car park."

Heather is having a long think.

"It's just you and me, Heather," says Connie, putting a hand on Heather's shoulder. "No one will ever know. Who are you covering for? Jack Mason? You scared of him?"

"You said you've been given a job?"

Connie nods.

"By whom?"

"No one you need to worry about."

"Don't tell me who I need to worry about," says Heather. Connie likes this. Heather is showing a bit of heart at last.

"You're right, fair point. Heather, listen, I'm a very difficult person."

Heather nods.

"And I will be back here every day for the rest of your sentence until you tell me. Who killed Bethany Waites?"

"You'll get the same answer every time."

"I can be patient. And next time I'll bring you something. Kit Kat? Coke Zero? A gun?"

Heather gives her first, small smile. This is more like it, thinks Connie. Finally.

"I like knitting," says Heather. "I have a godson who has just had a baby. I'd like to knit something, but—"

"But they don't trust you with needles? Don't blame them. Boy or girl?"

"Boy," says Heather. "Mason, of all things."

"I'll bring you a package straight away, blue wool, everything," says Connie. "And we'll see how you've got on tomorrow."

"Thank you," says Heather. "I find it hard to trust people. It takes time."

"Well, you must never trust me, but the one thing we've both got is time," says Connie. "I'll just keep coming back. I like to get a job done."

Connie stands to leave. She reaches out a hand, and Heather takes it and shakes it.

"I will quite look forward to seeing you again, Connie," says Heather. "I still won't tell you what you want to know though."

"We'll see about that, gorgeous," says Connie, and gives a little goodbye wink.

17.

Thursday. The Jigsaw Room.

"But your lights were off all night," says Joyce.

"Don't fuss," says Elizabeth. She will tell Joyce about the kidnapping once she has worked out her plan to deal with the Viking. In the meantime, she is glad of the distraction of the murder of Bethany Waites.

"I'm not fussing," says Joyce. "It's just unusual. Is Stephen all right?"

"We had a romantic evening in," says Elizabeth. "Candlelight in the bathroom, and an early night."

Joyce doesn't buy this, but Elizabeth thinks she has been fended off for now. She will have to tell her eventually. To business.

"So what do you have for us, Mr. Waghorn?"

Mike Waghorn and Pauline have joined them in the Jigsaw Room. Pauline is topping up Mike's glass.

"Just something I remembered," says Mike. "Someone was sending Bethany notes. Locker-room stuff, really, probably not important."

"Bullying."

"I can't stand a bully," says Ron.

"And did you find out who sent them?" asks Ibrahim.

"No. Bethany just laughed them off," says Mike. "She sent me a few messages about them, but we never got to the bottom of it."

"Do you still have her messages?" Elizabeth asks.

"Of course," says Mike. "I'll always keep her messages."

"I should think so too," says Joyce. "Gerry once had a letter in the *Radio Times,* and I've always kept it."

Mike is scrolling through his phone.

"It was about *Cagney & Lacey,*" says Joyce. "Which wasn't like him at all."

Mike has found Bethany's messages. *"Another note today, skipper. Slipped into my bag. 'If you don't leave, I'll make you leave.'* It was always that sort of thing: *Get out. Everybody hates you.* Playground stuff, but you never know. And it was something I didn't think to tell the police at the time."

"Could it have been Fiona Clemence?" asks Joyce. "I do hope not."

"Pauline, any idea?" asks Elizabeth.

"Don't even remember the notes," says Pauline.

Joyce puts her hand on Mike's arm. "More wine, Mike?"

"Yes, please," says Mike, and Joyce pours him another glass.

"You reading the news later, Mikey boy?" asks Ron.

"You'll have to do better than three glasses of wine to stop Mike presenting the news," says Pauline. "Do your trick, Mike."

Mike sits up, ramrod straight, and looks Ron in the eye. "Meanwhile, military maneuvers are continuing in Bosnia and Herzegovina, as the Serbian secessionist spokesperson initiated interventions with interested intermediaries."

Ron raises his glass. "The lad can take a drink."

"Thank you, Ronald," says Mike.

"I've trained him well," says Pauline.

"Well, aren't we all terrific," says Elizabeth. " But, if we could get on. Let's go through exactly what we know."

The Jigsaw Room has recently been repainted. Or one wall of it at least. They call it a "signature wall," and it is duck-egg blue. It was Joyce's idea: she had seen somebody do it on television, and had then raised it with the Amenities Committee. There had been objections, both in terms of cost and aesthetic, but Elizabeth could have told them to save their breath. If Joyce wants a signature wall, Joyce will have a signature wall.

The wall, which does actually look rather good, is currently covered in photographs and documents. There are pictures of Bethany Waites, and the wreck of a car at the foot of Shakespeare Cliff. There are grainy CCTV shots. The photos are surrounded by financial documents, and by timelines meticulously constructed, printed out and laminated by Ibrahim. They used to lay this sort of thing out on the jigsaw table itself, but Joyce has recently come across some sticky hooks you can peel on and off the wall without leaving any marks. Elizabeth much prefers it this way. It reminds her of a Serious Incident Room, the type of place where she has spent many happy hours.

"For reasons known only to herself," says Elizabeth, "or to her killer, Bethany decides to leave her flat. CCTV in the lobby of her building captures her at ten fifteen p.m., and, minutes later, we see her car pass by the front of the building."

"The car then seems to disappear," says Ibrahim. "It goes missing for several hours, until it is finally captured again at two forty-seven a.m., approximately a mile from Shakespeare Cliff."

"Meaning it has taken her more than four hours to complete a forty-five-minute car journey," says Elizabeth.

"Telling us," says Ibrahim, "that she must have stopped somewhere on the way. To meet someone, to do something, perhaps to die. And when the CCTV picks up the car again near the cliff, there appear to be two figures in it, not one."

"Very blurry though," says Pauline. "To be fair."

"The next morning," says Elizabeth, while registering Pauline's intervention, "Bethany's car is found at the bottom of the cliff. Her body is no longer in it, which is not altogether unsurprising. I once had to push a Jeep with a corpse sitting in the front seat into a quarry, and it popped out almost immediately."

"Why did you have to push a—" says Mike.

"No time, Mr. Waghorn, sorry," says Elizabeth. "The Conversational French class will scream blue murder if we're out of this room as much as a minute late. Traces of Bethany Waites's blood, and fragments of the clothing she was last seen wearing, were found in the wreckage of the car. A houndstooth jacket, and yellow trousers."

"Well, that's another thing," says Pauline. "Who wears a houndstooth jacket with yellow trousers?"

Elizabeth glances at Pauline. Two interventions now.

"Her body has never been found," says Ibrahim. "Usually it would wash up at some point, but not always. Her bank cards and bank accounts have never been used since, nor was there significant activity in her accounts before this incident. She wasn't squirreling money away for a disappearance."

"The secret might lie in Heather Garbutt's financial records," says Elizabeth. "We'll know more as soon as we've spoken to our consultant."

"When she says 'consultant,' she means my daughter," says Joyce.

"And that's pretty much where we are," finishes Elizabeth.

"You heard back from Connie Johnson?" Ron asks Ibrahim.

"Nothing useful yet," says Ibrahim. "She said something about knitting, but her Wi-Fi is quite patchy. She has complained to the Home Office about it."

There is a knock at the door. The Conversational French class that uses the Jigsaw Room after them is early. Elizabeth resolves to give them a piece of her mind.

18.

Chris and Donna are looking at a map of Fairhaven on the wall in their Incident Room.

There is a pin in the map, showing Bethany's apartment, and further pins showing the location of the CCTV cameras that had been checked on the night of her death. Her car hadn't triggered a single one until she got to Shakespeare Cliff. They are trying to plot her route out of Fairhaven, to see where she might have stopped. Once she was out of Fairhaven, a camera-free route was pretty easy. Just take the back roads. But in the town itself? Much harder.

Where on earth had she been for those missing hours? And who had she met?

"It's impossible," says Chris. "There are so many cameras in Fairhaven, and she could only take Rotherfield Road or Churchill Road. No other way out of town that takes you toward Shakespeare Cliff."

Strictly speaking, they are supposed to be investigating the death of the man in the burned-out minibus, but they are still waiting for a forensics report, so they thought they might spend the morning looking at the Bethany Waites case. Also, Elizabeth had asked them to. Elizabeth has access to many things, but not the exact position of every CCTV camera in Fairhaven.

Donna starts to plot a course from Bethany's apartment, avoiding the cameras. At every corner she turns, there is a camera. It's like a maze, with no way out. "And the cameras were all working?"

"For once," says Chris.

"Whatever happens," says Donna, tracing a finger along the map, "I can't get past Foster Road. She must have driven down it, but I can't take a left out of it, and I can't take a right out of it without hitting a camera. So how does she do it?"

Chris goes over to his computer and opens the Google Street View of Foster Road. "Let's see if there are any little cut-throughs we can't see on the map."

They scroll along Foster Road. It is largely residential, some big apartment blocks, some Victorian terraced houses, and a small parade of shops. No obvious cut-throughs.

"Stop there," says Donna. She takes control of the mouse now, and she revolves the image on the screen. It shows a large, modern apartment building called Juniper Court. On the left-hand side of the building is a ramp, leading down to the security grille of an underground car park.

"Worth seeing if there's an exit at the back of the building," says Donna. She navigates the arrows along Foster Road, up Rotherfield Road, past the CCTV camera, and then right into Darwell Road, which runs along the back of Juniper Court.

"You're very quick at this," says Chris.

"I spend a lot of time on Rightmove," says Donna. "Looking at houses I can't afford."

And there it is. The back of Juniper Court. Another ramp leading underground, this one with a no entry sign on it. The exit of the underground car park.

"If she'd driven through the car park, she could have taken the right turn onto Rotherfield Road and missed the cameras," says Chris. "It's the only way."

"Two possibilities, then," says Donna. "Either she's deliberately trying to avoid the cameras. Which is unlikely, given she wouldn't know where all of them were."

"Or . . ." starts Chris.

"Or . . ." continues Donna, "the person Bethany Waites went to meet that night lived in Juniper Court."

"And that could be our killer," says Chris.

"So Bethany leaves her building at ten fifteen, drives five minutes to Foster Road and into the underground car park at Juniper Court. Several hours later . . ."

"With somebody else now in the car with her . . ."

". . . she drives out of the exit onto Darwell Road, then right onto Rotherfield Road and heads toward Shakespeare Cliff."

"We're geniuses," says Chris. "Let's take a little trip down to Juniper Court, see who lives there."

"I ag—"

The door opens, and DI Terry Hallet walks in, a sheet of paper in his hand.

"Thought you'd be interested in this, Guv," says Terry Hallet. "Given who you were asking about the other day?"

Terry shows the piece of paper to Chris. Juniper Court will have to wait for now. He looks at Donna.

"Change of plan. We're going to see some old friends of ours."

19.

"Well, this is a pleasant surprise," says Joyce, ushering Chris and Donna into the Jigsaw Room. "Don't you look well?"

"Hello, all," says Chris.

"We have wine and biscuits," says Joyce. "There's red to go with the bourbon creams and white for the Jaffa cakes."

"No Jammie Dodgers, even though I asked," says Ron.

"Not now, Alan," says Donna. Alan has a particular fondness for her.

Chris pulls up a chair, and Donna does the same.

"What a look you have on your face, Detective Chief Inspector," says Ibrahim. "You seem quite troubled."

"We need to have a very serious conversation," says Chris. "Wait, you're Mike Waghorn!"

"Guilty as charged," says Mike Waghorn, offering his wrists for mock handcuffs.

"How do you know this lo—" starts Chris. "No, don't worry, of course you know them."

Ron reluctantly reaches for a Jaffa cake.

"You ever done any TV, Chris?" says Mike. "You've really got the bone structure for it."

"I . . . uh . . . no, I haven't," says Chris.

"Leave it with me," says Mike.

"Uh . . . sure," says Chris, as he takes off his jacket and hangs it over the back of his chair. "Really?"

Mike nods. "Great hair."

Chris snaps back to the matter at hand. "We need to have a serious conversation."

"A serious conversation about what, Chris?" says Elizabeth. "We have seven and a half minutes."

"You're investigating the death of Bethany Waites," says Donna.

"We're dipping our toe in, yes," says Elizabeth. "With your help."

Chris looks around at each of them in turn. "Been making inquiries into Heather Garbutt too?"

"Not really," says Ibrahim. "Minor inquiries. She's in jail, you know."

"Nothing else you want to tell me?" asks Chris.

"Nothing else to tell," says Ibrahim.

"For goodness' sake, Chris," says Elizabeth, "why do I feel we're being told off? I can practically hear Conversational French on the stairway, and I guarantee you won't want to keep them waiting."

Chris takes a moment. Composes himself.

"At six this morning," says Chris, "Heather Garbutt was found dead in her cell."

The gang share shocked looks. Pauline puts her hand on Mike's arm.

"There was a note," says Chris. "In one of the drawers of her desk."

"Suicide?" says Joyce. "Why would she—"

Donna looks down at her notebook.

"It reads," says Donna, "THEY ARE GOING TO KILL ME. ONLY CONNIE JOHNSON CAN HELP ME NOW."

PART TWO

Raise a Glass to New Friends

20.

I'm afraid that our systems show there's no fault in your area, so there's not a great deal I can do."

Viktor Illyich nods. "I understand, I understand, but still the television, it isn't working. So you see the position in which I find myself."

The young man on the other end of the line is beginning to sound exasperated, and has clearly had enough of this intellectual cut and thrust.

"I'm trying to tell you, Mr. Ill . . . Mr. Ill . . ."

"Illyich," says Viktor Illyich.

"Yes, as you say," says the voice. "I'm trying to tell you that, as far as our system can tell, it is working. And so I wouldn't be able to send an engineer to you today."

"Not today, then?" says Viktor. "No TV today?"

But *Bake Off* is on tonight. And it's the semi-final. Viktor scans the London skyline, laid out before him through his floor-to-ceiling windows. Viktor can see out, but no one can see in, which makes an old spy very happy.

"Not today, sir, no. If you log in to your Virgin Media app—"

"I don't have the app," says Viktor. "I don't work for Virgin Media, you see. I pay you to do the work."

"Understood, understood," says the voice. "You can do it online too. Log in to your account, find the 'Book an engineer' page and choose the next date that is convenient for you."

"OK, the next date convenient for me is today," says Viktor. He looks across his terrace. From his penthouse you can see the swimming pool suspended between two buildings. It caused quite a stir when they unveiled it. A swimming pool floating a hundred feet up in the air? Viktor doesn't use it much. Currently the only person in the pool is a Saudi princess. She is taking a picture of herself. No one really swims, it is too cold.

"As we've discussed, Sir," says the voice, "today is impossible."

"'Impossible' is a big word," says Viktor, lifting his legs onto his sofa and settling in. When Viktor worked for the KGB, they had a nickname for him. "The Bullet." If you wanted to question someone, the basic protocol was always to send in two operatives. "Good cop, bad cop," they called it in Great Britain. Usually they would get what they needed. Sometimes there was torture, though Viktor never approved. Torture got you nowhere. Sure, people would talk, but you had no way of knowing if it was the truth. Most people would talk to keep their teeth, their fingernails, to avoid the electrodes.

"Well, yes, I understand that . . ."

But sometimes people wouldn't talk, wouldn't crack, whatever you did to them. However you tried to break them. And on those occasions a call would go out to Moscow. Send for the Bullet. Viktor just had a way. He had a manner about him.

"I am an old man," says Viktor. "I live alone." He pours himself a brandy.

"I can quite appreciate that, Sir, but it doesn't—"

"And computers? I don't understand them so much." Viktor was the first man in Russia to hack into the IBM mainframe computers in the Pentagon.

"The system is simple: I can guide you through it if you have your computer there?"

Viktor's technique would always be the same. Enter the room, sit, chat. Build a rapport, maybe clear up a bit of blood, light a cigarette and find a consensus.

"You sound like my son, Aleksandar," says Viktor. Viktor never married, never had children, although the KGB encouraged it. They liked you to have a family, something they could leverage, something to keep you in Russia should you ever be tempted to stray. Many women were put in his path. Funny, brave, beautiful women. But Viktor's life was made of lies, and love doesn't blossom among lies. If it wasn't to be love, then Viktor wasn't interested. And now that he is out of the game, it is too late.

"Are you maybe twenty-one? Twenty-two? What is your name?"

"Umm, I'm Dale," says the voice. "I'm twenty-two. Would you like me to take you through the process?"

"You finished university, Dale? You didn't go, maybe?" asks Viktor. Viktor likes people, and he wants the best for them. These days that is seen as a weakness, but, over the years, it has been his greatest strength.

"I . . . I was at uni, but I dropped out," says Dale.

"Loneliness?" asks Viktor. He can hear it in the voice. "You found it difficult to make friends maybe?"

"Uh, I have to finish this call in under five minutes or there's a report," says Dale.

"There's always a report," says Viktor. "I have written many, and no one looks at them. So at uni, there were no friends? I too was very shy at twenty-two."

"Well, I suppose, yes," says Dale. "I didn't really know where to start. It got to me. Are you on the website?"

Sometimes you would walk into a room, and there would be a young man slumped in his chair, blood down his shirt, eyes swollen closed, and you just had to make a connection. Any interrogation is a conversation, and there have to be two people in a conversation. If you want something, you cannot take it; you have to let somebody give it to you.

"I was the same, this was many years ago though," says Viktor, as he looks out of the window. The Saudi princess is no longer in the pool. Now there is a young man eyeing the water. Viktor recognizes him: the man has a radio show, and once helped Viktor with his bags. Viktor likes him and tried to listen to his program once. It wasn't for him, but he couldn't fault the young man's enthusiasm. They gave a caller a thousand pounds for knowing the capital of France. And there were three options. "You think everyone around you knows some secret about how to live life. That there was a lesson you missed somewhere."

"Yeah," agrees Dale. "Are you on the website, I can take you through—"

"I still feel it, Dale. These people who know how to live. They can dance, they know what clothes to wear, how to cut their hair. I am not one of them, are you?"

"No," says Dale.

"It passes though," says Viktor. "It passes, and you become yourself. You were a boy, and now you have to be a man, and that's not easy."

"Right," says Dale. "My dad left, and, well, I always felt lonely after that. We used to do all sorts together."

"You swim alone, Dale, we all do. And you have to keep swimming until you reach the far shore. You can't turn around and swim back."

"I wish I could," says Dale.

"It's not an option. You don't want to work on the phones talking to old men like me, Dale—right?"

"Right," says Dale. "No offense."

Viktor giggles, high and tinkling. "None taken. What do you want to do?"

"I don't know," says Dale.

"Yes, you do," says Viktor.

"I want to work with animals, maybe," says Dale.

"Then you will," says Viktor. "You will work with animals. But you might have to wait. Might have to do this job for a while. Wait for the various pieces of you to come together and settle."

"You think?" says Dale. "I feel like I've already messed it up."

"You are young," says Viktor. "And I can hear that you are bright and kind. As the years go by, you will find that people need someone who is bright and kind more than they need someone who knows how to dance and has got the right haircut."

"So just—" says Dale.

"Just be patient and show yourself the same kindness you show others. It's difficult, and it takes time, but you can practice until you get good . . . Now, shall we go through this process and see when I can get an engineer?"

There is an encouraging pause on the other end of the line. "Look . . ." starts Dale, "I shouldn't really do this, but I can put an 'Urgent Need' flag on your request, and it'll jump to the front of the queue."

"Oh, I don't want to get you into trouble," says Viktor. This year on *Bake Off* there is a woman from Kyiv, called Vera, so he is even more invested than usual.

"We're only supposed to do it if someone is either clinically vulnerable or a celebrity. Are you either of those?"

"In my way, I am both," says Viktor.

"OK," says Dale, and Viktor hears the tapping of buttons. "You'll have someone out to you in the next ninety minutes."

"Thank you, Dale," says Viktor.

"No, thank you," says Dale. "Thank you for listening."

That's all it was in the end. People were always trying to tell you something, and all you really had to do was let them.

"My pleasure," says Viktor. "And good luck—it's all there ahead of you."

Viktor puts his phone down. He catches sight of himself in the mirror. That bald head, too big for his shoulders. Those pebbly glasses, too big for his face. A face he has grown to love. If you are disappointed with your face, eventually it shows.

An email alert pings on Viktor's computer and he turns toward the sound.

Viktor has an elaborate system of alerts. An alert for day-to-day emails, of course, the *Gardeners' Question Time* newsletter, Waitrose offers and so on. Then different sounds for different clients. For different levels of urgency. There were certain email addresses that were completely unique for, say, an important Colombian client or an impatient Kosovan. In all, Viktor had over a hundred and twenty email accounts, all changing, all the time. But the sound alert for each client would stay the same.

He also has an alert for an email address that he has given to nobody. It was a line of security, hidden deep on the dark web. It was an early warning system really. If anyone ever found this email address, he would know his security had been compromised. And if his security had been compromised, he knew he was in trouble.

The alert for the secret email is a gunshot. Viktor's little joke. A gunshot for the Bullet.

The alert that now rings around Viktor Illyich's apartment is a gunshot. Viktor pushes his glasses up the bridge of his nose.

He scans the skyline. Anything? Anyone? In the pool, the radio DJ is also now taking a selfie.

Viktor lights a cigarette. You would have to look long and hard to detect the slightest of trembles in his hand.

He opens the email. There are two photographs attached.

21.

Joyce

Heather Garbutt has been murdered.

The fraudster, not the hockey player.

They found her in her cell, where she had been killed in a very unpleasant way. Chris wouldn't go into the details, but it involved knitting needles.

She left a note in one of her drawers:

THEY ARE GOING TO KILL ME. ONLY CONNIE JOHNSON CAN HELP ME NOW.

It seems to tell us two things.

Heather has been murdered. Though by who, and for what? Is it a coincidence that this has happened so shortly after we started investigating?

Connie Johnson has some information. But what information?

Elizabeth suggested that Ibrahim might like to return to Darwell Prison and "be a bit more thorough this time." He took that about as well as you'd imagine.

There is another question here, of course. Did whoever murdered Bethany Waites also murder Heather Garbutt?

Ron said, "What if Connie Johnson killed her?" It was agreed that she would certainly have had the opportunity. But what would her motive have been?

Plenty to think about, then. Just the way we like it.

Chris was excited to meet Mike Waghorn, and, as he was leaving, he said, "You won't remember this, but I Breathalyzed you once. You were clean as a whistle," and Mike thanked him for his service.

We are doing a Zoom with Joanna tomorrow, to see if she's managed to uncover anything in Heather Garbutt's financial files, but I think we should also be looking at the notes Bethany had been sent? I know they seem fairly gentle, but that's how bullies start. One minute it's "nobody likes you," the next you are being pushed off a cliff. I'm being melodramatic, but you take my point? Things escalate.

So who sent the notes? A jealous lover? Someone from the newsroom? Fiona Clemence?

To be honest, wouldn't that be more fun than a VAT fraud? I will ask Elizabeth to let me look into it. I bet Pauline knows a few stories from the time, and questioning her would be a nice way for me to get to know her a bit better. I'm not saying she's here to stay, but Ron was wearing moisturizer today. He had a bit left over behind his ear. First Banoffee Pie, then moisturizer. That's all I'm saying about that.

Alan has just walked in, tongue out, and tail thumping the doorposts on his way. I know we sometimes credit our dogs with too much intelligence, but I honestly think he can tell there's been a murder.

22.

"Mum, you're muted," says Joanna.

"She's saying we're muted," says Joyce to Elizabeth.

"Yes, I heard," says Elizabeth. "*She's* not muted."

"Press the microphone button, Mum," says Joanna. Elizabeth notes it is all Joanna can do to not roll her eyes. Joanna has little patience for her mother. Elizabeth knows the feeling sometimes.

"I don't understand it at all," says Joyce, looking for whatever the microphone button might be. "It always works with Ibrahim."

"It sometimes works," corrects Ibrahim. "You are always sideways, for example."

"Let me look at it," says Ron.

Ron stares at the screen for four, perhaps five seconds, then sits back. "No, beats me."

"It is the little picture of the microphone, Joyce," says Ibrahim, leaning forward and moving the computer mouse.

"Ooh, I've never seen that before. Can you hear us?" asks Joyce.

"We can hear you now, Mum," says Joanna. "Hallelujah. Hello, everyone."

She gets hellos from everyone in return. Elizabeth recognizes the boardroom of Joanna's office, with its table made from the wing of an airplane, and its expensively terrible abstract art. She also recognizes Cornelius, Joanna's American colleague, who has a large pile of papers in front of him. The financial records from the trial.

"And hello, Cornelius," says Joyce. "Did Joanna tell me you're getting married?"

"No, my wife is leaving me," says Cornelius. "Close enough."

"Oh, I am sorry," says Joyce. "I knew it was something."

"Mum, you've got us for fifteen minutes," says Joanna. "Shall we start?"

"Of course," says Joyce. "Would you like to say hello to Alan?"

Joanna's mouth moves to form the word "no," then Elizabeth sees the faintest trace of a smile. "OK, but quickly though."

Joyce pats her dining-room table, and Alan puts his paws up, excited about whatever it is that might be happening now. Joanna and Cornelius wave. Alan licks Ron.

"Leave it out, Al," says Ron, though Elizabeth notices he doesn't push him away.

"I'll kick this off," says Cornelius, and places his palms on each side of the pile of papers. "Here are the headlines. This scam pulled in upward of ten million pounds in three years, very quickly, and all tax-free. The money goes into a single account, in the name of Heather Garbutt, then heads off into all sorts of directions. Jersey, the Caymans, the British Virgin Islands, Panama, all over."

"Still in Heather Garbutt's name?" asks Joyce.

"None of it in Heather Garbutt's name," says Cornelius. "None of it in anyone's name."

"Well, except . . ." says Joanna.

"Yes, except . . ." says Cornelius. "But we will get to that."

"It's basic money-laundering," says Joanna. "The money goes all over the world, into different accounts, all in places where you can keep your banking secret. Made-up companies, anonymous directors. You're not suddenly going to find the name of her killer here. We can only look for clues."

Cornelius riffles through a few of the papers. "Here're just a few examples for you, all from a single month in 2014. Eighty-five thousand paid to Ramsgate Cement & Aggregates, sixty thousand to Masterson Financial Holdings in Aruba, one hundred and fifteen thousand to Absolute Construction in Panama, seventy thousand to Darwin Securities in the Cayman Islands."

"And when you look into these companies?" says Elizabeth, knowing the answer already.

"Nothing," says Cornelius. "Just a registered office, and no accounts available to access. Unless you're the world's greatest expert on money-laundering, which I'm not."

"Don't do yourself down," says Joyce.

"And that's where the trail goes cold," says Cornelius.

Elizabeth takes charge. "So there's plenty we don't know, and you were right to start with that, but that's a big pile of papers, so I'm hoping there are some things we do know."

"Right as always, Elizabeth," says Joanna, which Elizabeth knows is designed purely to wind up her dear mother. "We know a couple of things. Heather Garbutt's bank records were made available to the court, and, as far as we can tell, she didn't see a penny of the ten million. There are no unusual outgoings, no big purchases. She stays in the same house, she drives the same car, her mortgage remains the same. If Heather Garbutt was the one laundering all this money, she hasn't spent any of it."

"And what else?" asks Elizabeth. She is distracted by her phone.

> I have sent the photographs to Viktor Illyich. The clock is ticking. Two weeks. You kill Viktor, or I kill Joyce. Tick tock. Tick tock.

One thing at a time please, thinks Elizabeth. I'm solving a murder here.

Cornelius steps up again. "All in all it's a pretty slick operation. The lawyers couldn't untangle it in court, and I couldn't untangle it. But the further back you go, the less sophisticated it becomes. That's usually the way. The longer a scam goes on, the better the scammers get at hiding the money. So the earlier in the scam you look, the more chance there is of spotting a mistake."

"What sort of mistake?" asks Ibrahim.

"The most common one is this," says Cornelius. "Obviously you have to invent names for all these imaginary companies. The rookie error is to choose a name that has some significance for you, however tangential. Now, the first few payments, and this is in the early days of the scam, were paid to a series of secret accounts in Jersey, namely Trident Capital, Trident Investments and Trident Infrastructure International."

"We did a little more digging," says Joanna. "And we found another company registered in Jersey, called Trident Construction."

"And that company," says Cornelius, "is completely legitimate. Information publicly available."

"Trident Construction had only one director," says Joanna. "Can you guess who?"

"Heather Garbutt!" says Joyce, rising from her chair.

"No, Mum," says Joanna, and Joyce deflates.

"Jack Mason," says Ibrahim.

"Jack Mason," confirms Joanna.

"So money goes out of Heather Garbutt's account, straight into an account run by her boss," says Ron.

"Probably run by her boss," says Joanna.

"And then disappears for good," says Cornelius. "Also worth noting too that when Heather Garbutt's house is sold, it's one of Jack Mason's companies that buys it."

"Jack Mason buys Heather Garbutt's house?" says Elizabeth.

"There are two further slip-ups," says Cornelius. "Very early on. A couple of payments that both go to named beneficiaries. Both seem to be fake identities, but, again, if they've been careless, those fake identities might give us a clue to somebody involved in the scam. One for forty thousand pounds is paid to a 'Carron Whitehead,' and one for five thousand is paid to a 'Robert Brown MSc.' The first two payments that ever left the account. But, as the scam gets bigger, everything just gets locked down tight, and there are no more named beneficiaries. Heather Garbutt or Jack Mason must have worked out they needed to start hiding the money better."

"Carron Whitehead and Robert Brown," muses Elizabeth. She sees that Ibrahim is already writing down the two names in his notebook.

"What a splendid job you've done, Cornelius," says Joyce.

"And me, Mum," says Joanna. "I helped too. I'm not fifteen."

"Well, I already know you're wonderful," says Joyce.

"Wouldn't kill you to tell me now and again," says Joanna.

"Couldn't have done it without her," says Cornelius.

"So perhaps we need to pay Jack Mason a visit," interrupts Elizabeth. "Ask him about Heather Garbutt and Bethany Waites. Maybe even ask him about Carron Whitehead and Robert Brown. See how he reacts. And I think our fifteen minutes are up, Joanna, thank you."

"Oh, thank *you*," says Joanna. "Mum knows she can rely on me whenever there's a murder."

"I do," agrees Joyce. "And I know you'll find another lovely woman soon, Cornelius."

"Oh, I'm not looking," says Cornelius. "But thank you."

"Nonsense," says Joyce.

"Nonsense," agrees Ibrahim, nodding. "You must look."

After quite some rigmarole they manage to sign off the call and retire to softer chairs for tea.

"So," says Elizabeth. "Jack Mason?"

"Leave him to me," says Ron. "We move in similar circles."

"Ooh," says Joyce, "get you."

"Ibrahim and I will look into Carron Whitehead and Robert Brown," says Elizabeth.

"And I'll look into the notes that Bethany was being sent," says Joyce. "Ron, I might talk to Pauline—would you mind?"

"Don't need my permission," says Ron. "It's not like she's my girlfriend."

"Oh, Ron," says Elizabeth.

23.

Parking fine yesterday," says Mike Waghorn, the moment Chief Constable Andrew Everton takes his seat in the studio.

"Hello, Mike," says Andrew Everton, as a woman adjusts his lapel mic.

"On the front in Fairhaven," continues Mike Waghorn. "I was opening a charity shop—a charity shop, bear that in mind. Out I come, and there's a ticket."

"I see," says Andrew Everton. The *South East Tonight* studio is much smaller than it seems on TV. There are three cameras, two are fixed in place and one has a camera operator, who is currently scrolling through her phone. "Were you parked illegally?"

"Barely," says Mike Waghorn. The floor manager tells them it is two minutes until their interview. "Hardly at all. And, as I say, a charity shop, which I don't have to do. Goodness of my . . . whatever."

Andrew Everton sees himself on the studio TV monitor. Looking good. Salt-and-pepper hair, closely cut, the faintest remains of a tan from a Cyprus mini-break, topped up in a Fairhaven tanning salon this afternoon. He's aware that this is pure vanity, but, equally, he's pushing sixty now and has decided he should probably get all the help he can.

"One minute to studio," says the floor manager.

Andrew Everton goes on *South East Tonight* once a month. A Chief Constable needs to be accountable. A live chat with Mike is always combative but always fair. There's no Paxman nonsense unless it's really necessary, which sometimes it is. Andrew Everton is the friendly face of policing, when it needs all the friendly faces it can get. He likes Mike. Mike acts the fool, but is far from it.

"Anything you can give me on Heather Garbutt?" Mike asks.

"Heather Garbutt?" Andrew Everton replies.

"The one who died in Darwell Prison?"

"Not really across it," says Andrew Everton. "How long were you parked for, Mike?"

"Three hours, absolute tops," says Mike.

"Three hours to open a shop?"

"I went for a drink afterward," says Mike. There is now a filmed report playing on the studio monitor. An older guy is being interviewed. He appears to be wearing a West Ham top under a suit jacket. "Just a couple of pints on the pier. I come back, ticket. Daylight robbery. I got a speeding fine for doing forty in a thirty the other day. Everybody does forty in a thirty."

On the monitor there is now a shot of the man with the West Ham top walking through some sort of village, very green, but with modern buildings. He has three friends with him, and they are laughing and joking together as they walk. Probably for the cameras, but they seem genuinely happy. Andrew wonders where it is. Looks nice.

"If I send the ticket your way, can you have a word with someone?" asks Mike, now looking through the list of questions he is about to ask.

"Jeopardize my career for a parking fine," says Andrew. "No."

Mike looks up and smiles. "Good lad. I was only having you on. I was banged to rights to be fair. I even wrote 'Mike Waghorn—*South East Tonight*' on a card in the windscreen. Works sometimes. You ready?"

Andrew nods, then glances over to the monitor again. Something catches his attention, and he looks closer. The four friends walking through the village. He recognizes one of them. That surely can't be . . . His eyes stay on the screen.

"What's this report, Mike?" he asks. "Where is this place?"

Mike glances over to the monitor. "A retirement village, Coopers Chase. That's Ron Ritchie, the union guy from years back. You recognize him?"

Andrew Everton shakes his head. No, that's not whom he recognizes.

"Will you have a look at the Heather Garbutt thing for me?" Mike asks. "Just as a favor?"

Andrew Everton nods; he certainly will. The friends disappear from the screen, and the report ends, with beautiful shots of the English countryside. The floor manager counts down from five to cue the live interview. Andrew sits up, straightens his tie and prepares himself. But his mind is elsewhere.

"What a wonderful place," says Mike to the camera. "I have to admit I stayed behind for a drink or two afterward! A timely reminder that age is nothing but a number. And, talking of numbers, the crime statistics for Kent have just been published and they show . . ."

Chief Constable Andrew Everton, waiting to answer, knows exactly what the statistics show. They show he is doing a very good job. No complacency, of course—things can always go wrong, he knows that very well—but he's proud of what he's achieving. He turns on his smile, but really he is thinking of the face he has just recognized. He really, really must pay a visit to this "Coopers Chase." And quickly.

24.

Jack Mason is strong and squat, but showing his age. Like a last defiant East End house standing alone in the rubble of a demolished street. Ron knows that feeling.

Gray hair shaved to the scalp, deep brown eyes never missing a moment of action—you'd never kill Jack with a bullet, you'd have to use a bulldozer.

Ron's route to meet him has been fairly straightforward, all things considered.

Ron simply spoke to his son, Jason, who spoke to one of his old boxing pals, Danny Duff, who messaged a man named Pump-Action Dave, who happened to drink with a man who declined to be named, who happened to do some work from time to time with Jack Mason.

A message had come back along that same line—pausing briefly at Danny Duff, who had been arrested on suspicion of cocaine importation and wasn't allowed his phone for a couple of hours—and Jack had suggested he and Ron meet for a game of snooker in Ramsgate.

Ibrahim offered to drive Ron, but at the last minute Pauline said she'd drive, as Ramsgate had a number of interesting antique shops, and a tattoo parlor, so she was keen to "make a morning of it." She suggested Ibrahim come along too, but Ibrahim had decided to stay at home. Is Ibrahim acting a bit strange around Pauline? Ron wonders.

Ron asks for Jack Mason at the reception of Stevie's Sporting Lounge and is shown through to a private room, where Jack has already set up the balls on the table.

"Ron Ritchie, is it?" says Jack, holding out a hand. "The lad himself?"

Ron shakes Jack's hand. "Thanks for seeing me, Jack—know you didn't have to."

"Intrigued, aren't I," says Jack Mason. "What's an old bugger like you want with an old bugger like me?"

"Your name came up," says Ron.

"Did it now?" Jack replies.

Jack takes his first shot. Ron is glad they are playing snooker. It can be quite hard for two men to have a conversation together, but snooker, or golf, or darts, always seemed to make it easier. Men didn't really meet for a coffee. Perhaps they did these days? Perhaps the coffee shops of Ramsgate were full of men chatting about their hopes and dreams, but Ron doubts it. Ron bends down over the table and takes his shot.

"Used to drink with your brother," says Ron, tutting as a red ball rattles in the jaws of a pocket. "Lenny. I was sorry to hear about him."

"We all go sometime," says Jack, potting the red Ron had missed. "I know he liked you, I wouldn't be here otherwise. So my name happened to come up? Any particular reason?"

"Heather Garbutt," says Ron. If Jack Mason is fazed hearing the name, he doesn't show it. He pots a black with ease and lines himself up for his next red.

"Heard she died," says Jack Mason.

"You heard right," says Ron. "Wouldn't know anything about it, would you?"

"Nope," says Jack Mason. "Ain't heard a peep."

"Where were you Thursday morning?"

Jack stops playing for a moment. "Where was I Thursday morning? I'm meeting you as a favor, Ron. You get that? We've both been around the block, eh, so I'm not going to disrespect you. But make your next question a good one, or we're going to fall out."

Ron smiles. This is home ground for him, two men arguing, grievances being aired. You can't beat a bit of conflict. He lets Jack take his next shot. A miss.

Ron leans a hand on the table. "Here's where I am, Jack. Heather Garbutt worked for you, and fiddled millions while she did. Some of that money went into an account that sounds an awful lot like it belonged to you."

"What account?" asks Jack.

"Trident Construction," says Ron.

Jack nods, looking interested. "You got evidence of that?"

"Yup," says Ron, and misses another red.

"And that evidence," continues Jack. "Anybody else got it?"

"Nope," says Ron. "But we made the connection to you easy enough, so if anyone really starts poking around Heather Garbutt's death, someone else will find it too."

"Who's 'we'?" asks Jack, as he pots yet another ball.

"It would honestly take too long to explain," says Ron. "You're thrashing me here."

"I think you're a bit nervous," says Jack, potting a blue, and chalking his cue.

"You read me wrong, then," says Ron. "And I haven't finished. Just before Heather Garbutt goes to trial, a young journalist dies. Bethany Waites, from the local news. Drives herself off a cliff."

"Hell of a way to go," says Jack Mason, making another pot.

"Never found her killer," says Ron. "But, a few weeks before she dies, Bethany messages her guv'nor because she's just cracked a big story. Found a smoking gun."

"And the story is Heather Garbutt?" asks Jack, game forgotten for the moment.

"More than Heather Garbutt. Something bigger, someone connected to her," says Ron. "And *you* were connected to her, Jack. Coincidence, innit?"

"No such thing as coincidence," says Jack.

"Well, that's what we think. So there are minds cleverer than mine who say Heather Garbutt is stealing money for you, Bethany Waites uncovers the connection—maybe in the same way we have—so you have Bethany Waites killed."

Jack nods. "Thank you for bringing this to my attention."

"Just, people might start asking, you know," says Ron.

"I'd imagine they might," agrees Jack.

"And I wondered," says Ron, "between you and me, what you make of that story?"

Now it's Jack's turn to smile. "Between you and me? I'd say this. Look, I was up to my eyes in the VAT thing, course I was. No proof, no nothing, till you mentioned this Trident thing, but that could be a coincidence. They won't get me on that. I'm locked tight, Ronnie—they'll never find the money. Even I've lost track of it."

Ron nods. He really wants to play his next shot, but Jack hasn't finished.

"And this Bethany Waites. I won't pretend I haven't heard the name, I have, lots of the evidence in Heather's case came from her. But this message you're saying she sent before she died? Where would I have heard about it from? Makes no sense."

"You never met Bethany Waites?"

"Never."

"Never even spoke to her?"

"Never, God's honest," says Jack.

"You're not offended I asked though?" says Ron, and misses yet another red.

"No, I get it, I get it," says Jack. "But you must have thought this was a bit too amateurish for me? Leaving a loose end, killing a journalist. Bit offended if you thought that'd be my style."

"We all make mistakes, Jack," says Ron. "Especially when the pressure's on. But you're right, I figured it wasn't you. She might not even be dead, Jackie. They never found the body."

Jack Mason lines up another shot. He doesn't look at Ron.

"Oh, she's dead."

"I'm sorry?" Ron thinks he must have misheard.

"I said she's dead." Jack pots another ball, then chalks his cue.

"You know that for a fact?"

"I know that for a fact," confirms Jack Mason, lining up his next shot.

"How can you know it for certain?" says Ron. "Unless you killed her?"

"Listen, Ron. I know she's dead," says Jack Mason. "And I didn't kill her. But that's all you're getting from me. You work it out if you want to."

How can Jack Mason be sure that Bethany Waites is really dead? Unless he killed her. Or at least unless he knows exactly who did?

Ron bends over the table and pots his first ball of the game. He nods casually as if it was never in doubt. Two men playing snooker—you can't beat it. Fewer and fewer people to play against these days though. There used to be a whole gang of them, London, Kent, wherever you were you could get a game. But between death, prison and living in exile on the Costa del Sol, the gang was all gone. Ron now relied on Jason taking pity from time to time and playing against his old man. Ron pots a black. This is more like it.

"You do know who killed her, then?" Ron asks.

Jack smiles. "That's enough chitchat, I think. I'm always up for a game though, Ron. If you're ever free."

Ron looks up at Jack again, and sees another old man whose friends have died around him. "Me too, Jack."

It'll be just Ron's luck if his potential new snooker partner turns out to be a murderer.

25.

Chief Constable Andrew Everton gazes out at the sea of faces all looking up at him. Well, a couple of them are asleep, and two elderly gentlemen at the back are having a private discussion, but, other than that, everybody is looking up at him. He loves this sort of thing, he really does. Giving readings. He is not asked often and, in fairness, he has arranged this one himself, but it is still a thrill. Also, he spots the face he is looking for almost immediately. Bit of luck there.

He wears his uniform, of course, because it gives a sense of theater, and it also gives him a bit of authority. He knows it will give his reading extra power. Not that it needs it, his writing is very powerful. This is a generation who respects you if you are a chief constable. Not like this new generation, but then you reap what you sow, and trust has to be a two-way street.

The woman who just introduced him was called Marjory. Marjory had been surprised when Andrew had written to her, offering to do this reading, but she had given a quick "yes" and promised to rally the troops, and so here they were. The last thing Marjory had said to him was that the previous speaker at the Coopers Chase Literary Society had been a woman who had written a book about fish, and she had gone down very well, so please don't let us down. Andrew Everton didn't intend to. He has chosen to read from his fourth book, *Remain Silent*. It is a follow-up to his previous works, *Given in Evidence, Harm Your Defense* and his first book, before he'd stumbled upon his elegant new system of titles, *The Bloody Death of Archibald Devonshire*.

He scans the room, biding his time. He knows his silence, and his uniform, and his deep, brown eyes, are all building anticipation. He starts to read.

"The corpse was mutilated beyond all recognition . . ."

He hears several "oohs" and sees a woman in the front row wearing a tweed jacket and pearls lean forward eagerly.

"Black-red blood pooled around the body, limbs were splayed at grotesque angles, like a swastika of death. Chief Constable Catherine Howard liked to keep a cool head while, all around, others were losing theirs—"

A hand shoots up. That doesn't normally happen at readings. Andrew Everton decides to take the question, even though it is interrupting the narrative. He motions to the questioner, a woman in her nineties.

"Sorry, dear, did you say Catherine Howard? Like the Queen? Henry VIII's wife?"

"Yes," says Andrew Everton. "Well, I suppose so."

"The same name?" asks a man farther back in the room. "Or the same person?"

"Just the same name," says Andrew Everton. "The book is set in 2019."

There are murmurs as this is discussed. An unofficial spokesperson seems to emerge. It is the woman with the tweed jacket in the front row.

"Two things," says the woman in the front row. "I'm Elizabeth, by the way. Firstly, it's confusing that she's called Catherine Howard."

Agreement from the room.

"Well, I—" begins Andrew Everton.

"No, it is. And secondly," continues Elizabeth, "I suspect a series of books in which the real Catherine Howard was a detective might well be a bestseller. Are your books bestsellers, Chief Constable?"

"In their field, yes," says Andrew Everton.

"Google would disagree with you there," says Elizabeth. "But do go on, we are enjoying it."

"Are you sure?" says Andrew Everton, and the audience make it clear that they actually are.

"We just interrupt a lot," says the very man that Andrew Everton is here to see. Ibrahim Arif. Andrew had recognized him immediately from the filmed report on *South East Tonight*. "It's in our nature. Please, return to the spreadeagled corpse."

"Thank you . . ."

"Although," says Ibrahim, a new thought having clearly occurred to him, "when you say she keeps her head, is that an allusion to the beheading of the real Catherine Howard?"

"No," says Andrew Everton. "I hadn't really . . . no."

"I thought it might have been a literary trick," says Ibrahim. "You hear about them."

"*She*—"

"Am I the only one who hasn't heard of Catherine Howard?" asks a man in a West Ham shirt.

"Yes, Ron," says Elizabeth. "Now, let the Chief Constable continue."

"*She takes*—"

"Will there be a signing afterward?" asks a small, white-haired woman sitting next to Elizabeth. "The fish woman did a signing, didn't she?"

The room agrees that the fish woman had indeed done a signing.

"I'm afraid my books are e-books, and so are impossible to sign, unless you want me to make a terrible mess of your Kindle," says Andrew Everton. A line he has perfected in the backrooms of several Kent pubs and bookshops over the last few years. Though it has yet to get a laugh, he now realizes. "But I will give everyone a QR code after the reading to buy any of my books at a substantial discount."

A number of hands shoot up at this. Ibrahim turns and faces the rest of the crowd. "A QR code is a 'Quick Response' code that can be read by a computer and link you to a specific URL. A type of matrix barcode would be the simplest way of putting it."

Most of the hands go down, but three or four remain. Ibrahim turns back to Andrew Everton. "The remaining questions will be about the specific nature of the discount."

"Fifty percent," says Andrew Everton, and the remaining hands go down.

"Do continue," says Elizabeth. "We're holding you up."

"Not at all," says Andrew Everton. He will find a way to speak to Ibrahim Arif after the reading. Just engage him in conversation. Establish a rapport, and ask what needs to be asked. He's here, that's the main thing. He looks back at his notes.

"Should I start again from the beginning?"

"No, dear," says Elizabeth. "Mutilated corpse, Catherine Howard keeping her head. I think we're up to speed."

Andrew Everton nods.

"She took in the scene around her. Howard could see experienced officers turn ghostly pale—"

From the side of the stage, Marjory, the woman who had introduced him, chooses to interrupt.

"Is it confusing that she's a woman, but her surname is a man's first name? I'd be thinking, 'Who's Howard?' "

There are nods in the audience at this.

"Is it too late to change it?" asks the white-haired woman with friendly concern.

"Well, yes, the book has been out for several years already," says Andrew Everton. "She's the hero of all my books, and no one seems to have minded yet."

A few raised eyebrows.

"Carry on," says Elizabeth.

Andrew turns back to the text. He will sell a few copies, he thinks. Then he will thank Ibrahim for his questions, and ask a few of his own. He takes a sip of the water provided on the lectern. It turns out to be a vodka and tonic. Probably for the best.

"No one present had ever witnessed a crime scene this awful, this macabre, this depraved. No one except Catherine Howard. Because Catherine Howard had seen this exact crime scene before. Just three nights ago, in fact. In a dream."

Hands shoot up again.

26.

Andrew Everton settles into a battered old armchair, underneath a painting of a boat. Looking around, he sees glass-fronted shelves, absolutely stacked with box files.

"That was most enjoyable," says Ibrahim, walking in with the mint tea. "Most enjoyable. You have a rare talent."

"You just write one word, then another, and you pray that no one finds you out," says Andrew Everton. He had once heard Lee Child say something similar, and had liked it. "You have a lot of files. Is that a work thing?"

Ibrahim settles onto a sofa. "A life's work, yes. Well, many lives. I'm a psychiatrist, Chief Constable."

"Call me Andrew," says Andrew Everton, well aware that Ibrahim is a psychiatrist. "I'm afraid I need something from you, and so I want to appear as unthreatening as possible."

Ibrahim chuckles. "A fine tactic. Was the reading a ruse? Simply to come and see me?"

"Partly. I saw you on television," says Andrew Everton. Saw him on television, dug into his files. "With your friends. I recognized you. So two birds with one stone really," he says, blowing on his tea. "I wanted an informal chat with you, and I also thought perhaps I might sell a few books."

"I'm certain you will," says Ibrahim. "Chief Constable Catherine Howard is very tough. Haunted, but tough."

"I describe her as 'teak-tough' in *Given in Evidence*."

"Quite so, Andrew," says Ibrahim. "'Teak-tough.' Enough of literature though. You say you recognized me? I am intrigued."

"A couple of days ago, you made a visit to Darwell Prison, I believe?" Andrew Everton sees all the details of Connie's visitors. Lovely close-up from the prison security cameras too.

"Ah," says Ibrahim.

"Ah," says Andrew Everton. "You gave your profession as 'journalist,' though I could find no trace of you in relation to that. You visited a prisoner named Connie Johnson. A particularly brutal drug baron, currently on remand for a number of very serious crimes. You stayed with her for around half an hour, chatting, and I quote an official report here, 'animatedly at times.' Correct?"

"Well, I would say drug baroness, although I must learn to degender job titles," says Ibrahim. "But, other than that, correct."

"I wonder if I might ask what you and Connie Johnson spoke about?"

Ibrahim considers this. "I wonder if I might ask, in return, what business that is of yours?"

"You might also be aware that another prisoner, Heather Garbutt, was found dead shortly afterward, Mr. Arif. And that Connie's name was mentioned in a note found in her cell. That makes it my business."

"Indeed. Crime, and excellent writing, are your business," says Ibrahim. "Cigar?"

Andrew Everton shakes his head; he is having none of it. "Connie Johnson is possibly, in fact probably, the most dangerous woman my force has ever had to deal with. With luck she will be convicted and sent to prison for a very long time. If you jeopardize that in any way, I could make life very difficult for you, so I would counsel against it. If you're in a position to help me, however, I would strongly recommend you do so."

"I understand your position," says Ibrahim. "That is admirably clear. I see why people like you. I see why you are Chief Constable. In America they sometimes vote for their chiefs of police, did you know that? It's one of many idiosyn—"

"So I'm going to ask you politely, one more time," interrupts Andrew Everton. "Why were you visiting Connie Johnson, and what did you speak about?"

Ibrahim drums his fingers on the arm of his sofa. "You place me in a quandary, Andrew. If I might still call you Andrew?"

Andrew Everton nods, and takes a sip of his tea.

"You see, when I have a client," says Ibrahim, "everything we speak about is covered by patient-confidentiality laws."

"She is your client?" asks Andrew Everton.

"Well, that's just it," says Ibrahim. "At the start of the meeting she wasn't. But by the end of the meeting she was. So where does that leave us? Can I tell you what I spoke about, or can I not? Is the confidentiality retrospective, as it were? A thorny one, Andrew, no?"

"A thorny one." Andrew nods. "Let me see if I can help with your dilemma."

"You are most kind," says Ibrahim.

"The gentleman you were sitting with in the reading . . ." says Andrew Everton.

"Ron," says Ibrahim.

"I also saw him on the television," says Andrew Everton, "so I'm aware you're close. You will know, as I do, that today a pungent air of cannabis hung about him."

"I will take your word for that," says Ibrahim. "Ron always smells of something."

"You'll also know that searches for cannabis in my force, and in most other forces, disproportionately fall on young black men. Something I have tried to address in the last few years, with some, if not enough, success. So believe me it would really help my statistics if I were to sanction a drugs search on an old, white man. I can have officers in Ron's flat within an hour."

"Goodness," says Ibrahim. "That's very forthright."

"Would Ron like a team of officers rooting through his underwear?"

"I don't think anyone would like that," says Ibrahim. "Least of all the officers. But, also, I don't think you'd do it. Ron would kick up a fuss, we'd all be there to take photos. I might even get our friend Mike Waghorn to take an interest. All too visible and messy, I think."

Andrew Everton refuses to be outmaneuvered. "Then your other friends. The ladies?"

"Joyce and Elizabeth?"

"You might be comfortable with a chief constable questioning you. Ron might take it in his stride. But two elderly women? How do you think the two of them would react if I decided to question them? Because if I have to, I will."

Ibrahim laughs. "I wish you the very best of luck with that, Andrew. I must tell Elizabeth what you said—she will hoot. Of all the nuts to crack around here, I assure you I am very much the easiest."

"I need you to help me here, Ibrahim," says Andrew Everton.

Ibrahim leans forward. "Chief Constable. Andrew. I recognize it seems like I'm being obstructive. Really I understand that, and I can be very difficult at times. Unyielding, I was once described as. So I won't be telling you what I have spoken to Connie Johnson about, and, assessing the situation as best I can, I don't think you are particularly in a position to compel me to do so. But I can assure you that there is nothing that would concern you, and nothing that you need to worry about. Whether Connie Johnson is guilty or not is for the courts to decide. Whether she had some involvement with the death of Heather Garbutt, I doubt very much. But I can plainly assert to you that my chat with her, at the very least, was innocent."

"When will you see her next?"

"No plans," says Ibrahim.

Andrew Everton nods. He is not quite sure what to do next.

One thing he is sure of, however, is that Ibrahim Arif has just lied to him.

27.

Joyce

Carron Whitehead and Robert Brown MSc.

I have been Googling, but there's not much out there. I got so desperate I even used Bing, but the results were the same, if a bit slower. Ibrahim says there's no use searching. He thinks the names will be in some kind of code. But, then, Ibrahim thinks that everything is in code.

I have Mike Waghorn's email address now, but I am trying not to abuse it. I sent him what I thought was a very funny clip of a squirrel tasting almonds for the first time, but he replied saying that this was his work email and it wasn't for clips from the internet and, besides, he had already seen it.

I hadn't been brave enough to email him after that, so I was glad of the opportunity to send him the names. Whitehead and Brown? Ring any bells?

He thanked me, but said he'd never heard either name before. So perhaps they really are in code. He has passed them on to Pauline.

My big news is that we just had a reading at the Literary Society. And a good one too. The Chief Constable of Kent, if you can believe that? I have downloaded his books onto my Kindle. Ninety-nine pence each, thank you very much.

Ibrahim is going to Darwell Prison on Wednesday, to talk to Connie Johnson. He asked me what magazine she might like to read, but I wasn't sure. I like *Woman & Home*, but I didn't think it would be Connie's thing, so I asked Joanna, and I told her that Connie was a thirty-something drug dealer who always wore lovely shoes, and she suggested *Grazia*.

Ron reported back from Jack Mason. Jack Mason says he knows for a fact that Bethany is dead. And he can only know that if he knows who killed her. Elizabeth has told Ron to go back and find out more, but it has focused all of our minds.

I might watch *A Place in the Sun*. Yesterday they were looking for a house in Crete. The wife fell in love with a little farmhouse, but there was no room for the husband to keep his hang-glider, and so they didn't put in an offer. You could see the wife was heartbroken, but she married him, and so she must shoulder some of the blame.

I am also thinking about how we might be able to talk to Fiona Clemence. I know she doesn't fit in with Jack Mason, but if she wrote those notes to Bethany years ago, she is still a suspect. And all suspects must be questioned.

But how? I sent her a message on Instagram, but I don't know if she got it.

Even as I write this down, I know what Elizabeth will say. That I only wanted to look into the Bethany Waites case as a way of meeting Mike Waghorn, and now I only want to accuse Fiona Clemence as a way of meeting her. That there's no way of knowing if she wrote those notes all those years ago. And, yes, that is true. But just because I'd like to meet Fiona Clemence doesn't mean she isn't a murderer. Lots of famous people are murderers. The Krays, for example.

Joanna is coming down for lunch on Sunday, so I will ask her how someone might go about meeting Fiona Clemence. I know you can apply to get tickets to watch *Stop the Clock* being filmed, but I suspect you are not allowed to shout out questions about murders from the audience.

Perhaps I'll pop to the shop? They have almond milk now. Last time Joanna came down she brought her own milk, because "No one drinks cow's milk anymore, Mum." I protested and said I think quite a few people do still drink cow's milk, dear, but Joanna's definition of "no one" and my definition of "no one" are probably different. I wanted to say, "Do you mean no one in London," but it wasn't worth the fuss.

Either way, I can't wait to see her face when she opens the fridge. Unless no one drinks almond milk anymore either, which I'm prepared to admit might also be a possibility. It is very hard to keep up.

She's useful when you have to choose the right magazine for a drug dealer though. I will give Joanna that.

I've arranged to meet Pauline tomorrow, and am very much looking forward to it. Pauline suggested afternoon tea at a hotel by the pier. I looked it up and they give you a glass of Prosecco. I will feel like Jackie Collins.

28.

Jack Mason is looking at helicopters online. It would be nice to buy one. He can certainly afford it, but, really, how much use would he get out of one?

In the old days, sure, back and forth to Amsterdam, up to Liverpool, sitting in traffic, stuck in the Channel Tunnel. Helicopter would have been lovely. Would really have hit the spot.

But now? Where does he really go now? Down to the scrapyard? That's fifteen minutes in the Bentley. Maybe twenty minutes if there're temporary traffic lights. He pops up to London now and then, visits the few pals he has left. The few pals who aren't in Spain, or dead.

The clock in the hall chimes six, so Jack pours himself a scotch.

Had he told Ron Ritchie too much? It was just nice to talk to someone his own age. Jack knows who killed Bethany Waites, but no one would hear the name from his lips. You had to maintain standards, and grassing was grassing, no matter who you're speaking to.

But Jack had wanted to say *something*. Because, when you really thought about it, the whole thing was an absolute liberty. There'd been no need for Bethany Waites to die.

Jack's scrapyard still ticks along nicely, a few bits and pieces come his way now and again, favors are asked, favors are granted. He's sold most of his casino, and the bit that remains still makes him nice money. But the phone doesn't ring the way it used to. People don't need him. That's OK. Who has the energy to run drugs anymore? Leave all that to the kids. Jack has his house, his view over the English Channel, his snooker table. He even has stables, should he ever want a horse. And he doesn't start drinking till six. No grassing, and no whisky till six. Rules to live by.

Jack has plenty of *room* for a helicopter, that's for sure. He could land it on the croquet lawn. Buy a little golf buggy to drive him up to the house. And, really, there were some beauties. Someone in Estonia was selling a Bell 430 in gold and purple. That would impress a few people.

Though would it? Jack knocks back the rest of his scotch. Who would even see it these days? Who comes to visit? Jack wonders if he could invite Ron over to the house for a game of snooker? Would Ron like that? They got on.

Jack has made an awful lot of money in his life, but he hasn't, he realizes, made very many friends. One thing he has come to understand, after a lifetime in crime, is that your henchmen are not real friends.

Does he really want to spend six hundred grand on a helicopter he'll use twice a year? To watch it rusting on the lawn? Hmm.

He is typing "golf buggy how much uk" into Google, when an email alert pops up on his screen.

He recognizes the address. The email is from Bethany Waites's killer. They used to be in contact quite often. Less so now, which has been something of a relief. Though, with everything that has happened in the last few days, he has been expecting a message.

The email reads:

> Long time no see. Just a friendly warning to keep your eyes open. Talk soon.

You're telling me, thinks Jack. Jack Mason hasn't left too many loose threads in his life, but this is definitely one of them.

Jack wonders if, perhaps, it might be time to tell the truth?

29.

Juniper Court, the building they'd identified from their work with the CCTV cameras, is only fifteen minutes or so from Fairhaven police station, so Chris and Donna walk there.

"Who's the mystery man, then?" Chris asks.

"Haven't heard back from forensics yet," says Donna. "Nothing on the body, no ID, photo circulated to the press. You know all this?"

"Not the man in the minibus, Jesus," says Chris. "The guy you're seeing?"

"Some priorities you have there," says Donna. "Wow."

They turn onto Foster Road. Juniper Court is a purpose-built 1980s block, which might begin to look retro-fashionable in twenty years. A hundred or so flats, lawns to the front and, crucially, a large car park underneath.

Juniper Court has not cropped up often in police records. A few stolen bikes, the odd noise complaint, a man selling fake Banksys by post, and some graffiti about the Mayor that they'd had to take seriously. They can't even find the details of the management company online. It is the very definition of quiet and nondescript. But it could hold the key to who murdered Bethany Waites.

It's nice and near the station, so home to plenty of commuters into London or Brighton. That means it's deserted as they approach.

"You nervous about your audition?" Donna asks Chris. He's doing his screen-test for *South East Tonight,* just around the corner from here, on Wednesday.

"No, I chase villains for a living," says Chris. "You think a TV camera's going to frighten me?"

"I do, yes," says Donna.

"You're right," says Chris. "I'm terrified. You think they'll let me pull out?"

"I won't let you pull out," says Donna. "You'll be amazing."

Through wide double doors, Chris and Donna see a desk in the entrance hall of Juniper Court, and a man in brown overalls sitting behind it, reading the *Daily Star*.

"In London, they'd call him a concierge," says Chris, as he buzzes to be let in. He flashes his warrant card, but there is no need, as the man lets them in without looking up.

"Morning," says Chris. The man still doesn't look up. "Is there a building manager we can talk to?"

The man finally looks up. "That's me. I don't love talking though."

Chris flashes his warrant card again. "Kent Police."

The man puts down his paper. "This about my neighbor? You going to arrest him?"

"I'm . . . no, I don't think so," says Chris. "What's he done?"

"Built a conservatory," says the man. "No planning permission. I'm Len. I keep ringing you lot about it, and this is the first time I've seen you."

"That's more for the council, Len," says Donna. "Not the police."

"That right?" says Len. "I suppose if I killed him though, you'd be round soon enough?"

"Well, yes, obviously," says Chris. "If you murdered him we'd come round. Murders, yes; conservatories, no. We're looking for the details of the management company for this place, and we wondered if you could help?"

"You scratch my back, I'll scratch yours," says Len. "You come round and have a word with my neighbor, and maybe I'll remember—"

"Arlington Properties," says Donna, reading the notice board and copying down a number.

Chris starts taking a look in some of the post pigeonholes, noting down names. Illegal, really, but Len behind the desk seems to have a fairly loose relationship with legality.

"You allowed to be doing that?" Len asks.

"With a warrant, yes," says Chris. He obviously doesn't have one. Chris sometimes thinks the Thursday Murder Club are a bad influence on him.

"Anyone cause you any particular trouble?" Donna asks.

"The guy in seventeen broke two toilet seats," says Len.

"Thank you for your help, Len," says Chris. "We'll let you get on."

As they leave, the man calls after them. "Well, don't blame me if I kill him. That'll be on you."

Back out in the cold air, Chris and Donna start noting down car registration numbers. There is a car Chris is sure he recognizes, a white Peugeot with flames on the number plate. He notes down the number.

Chris would love to find a clue that Elizabeth has missed. Should he really be that competitive with a woman in her late seventies?

But he understands that this is a fishing expedition. Even if someone lives in Juniper Court now, it's meaningless unless they lived there ten years ago, on the night Bethany died.

He keeps noting down the numbers regardless. Most of police work is jotting down numbers.

30.

"He liked motorbikes," says Pauline. "He liked tinkering. He'd take them apart, and forget to put them together again."

"Gerry was like that with jigsaws," says Joyce. "I'd forever be telling him, don't start a jigsaw and not finish it, Gerry. If you've done the opera house, then, for goodness' sake, do the bridge. I'd end up having to finish them off. I don't suppose you can do that with a motorbike."

"He'd ride off with his mates at the weekend," says Pauline. "A whole gang of them—the Outlaws of Death, they were called. Two of them were accountants."

"But he looked after you," says Joyce.

"Did he, Joyce? I don't know," says Pauline. "He loved me, as far as it went, and it would have been a lot of trouble to get rid of him. But—"

"But?"

"Look, we got along fine. I've seen worse," says Pauline. "I don't know if it was love's young dream though. You had to get married in those days, didn't you? Had to find someone."

"I'm afraid I was terribly boring," says Joyce. "I wanted to get married."

"God, that's not boring, Joyce," says Pauline. "To really mean it, that's the dream. How did you fall in love with Gerry, can you remember?"

"Oh, I didn't fall in love with him," says Joyce. "Nothing like that. I just walked into a room and there he was, and he looked at me, and I looked at him, and that's all there was to it. Like I had always been in love with him, no falling necessary. Like finding the perfect pair of shoes."

"Christ, Joyce," says Pauline. "You'll have me crying."

"I mean, he had his bad points," says Joyce.

"Did he ever cheat on you with a tattoo artist called Minty?"

"No, but he'd always leave his used teabags in the sink," says Joyce. "And then there were the jigsaws."

The two women laugh. Pauline raises her glass in a toast.

"To Gerry," says Pauline. "I wish I'd met him."

Joyce clinks Pauline's glass. "And to . . . I'm sorry, I didn't catch your husband's name?"

"He called himself Lucifer," says Pauline. "He was a roadie for Duran."

"What was his real name?"

"Clive," says Pauline.

"Well, I wish I'd met Clive too," says Joyce. "I wonder if he and Gerry would have got along?"

There is a pause, and both women laugh again. A waiter brings them a cake stand, loaded with tiny pastries and sandwiches. Joyce claps her hands.

"I love a cream tea," says Pauline. "Now, while I eat a tiny eclair, why don't you tell me why we're here?"

"I thought it would be nice to have a chat," says Joyce. "Get to know you, have a gossip."

Pauline holds her hand up. "Joyce, spare me."

"OK," says Joyce, taking her first bite out of a two-bite sandwich. "I wanted to talk to you about Bethany Waites."

"You shake me to my core in surprise, Joyce," says Pauline. "Do you think you will want your eclair? I could swap it for a beef and horseradish?"

They make the trade.

"I keep thinking back to the notes that Mike mentioned," says Joyce.

"OK," says Pauline. "Do you think you'll want your lemon tart by the way?"

"No, please," says Joyce. "It's just that you don't always find things in the most obvious place, do you? I lost my tape measure the other day, for example, and it's always in my kitchen drawer. Always. But I needed it, to settle an argument with Ibrahim about whose television was bigger, and I opened the drawer, and was it there? It was not. It was not in the obvious place. In the end it was on the bookshelf, heaven knows why. I didn't put it there, and it certainly wasn't Alan, was it?"

"Have you lost your train of thought, Joyce?"

"Not a bit of it," says Joyce. "I just mean that while everyone is off looking at Jack Mason, I wondered if I might look at *South East Tonight,* and see if anyone there might have killed her? For an entirely different reason. Does that make sense?"

"As much sense as any of you make," says Pauline. "Ask me anything."

"So someone was leaving threatening notes for Bethany. In her bag, on her desk."

"So I hear," says Pauline.

"Could it have been you?"

"No."

"Could it have been Fiona Clemence?"

"Could have been Fiona Clemence," says Pauline. "I doubt it, but not impossible."

"Jealousy?"

"I don't think jealousy is the right word," says Pauline. "They were both strong women. And in those days people liked to make strong women compete with each other. Like you couldn't have two strong women in the same room at the same time. The world would explode."

"Perhaps I should speak to Fiona Clemence," says Joyce. "Do you think?"

"I think you would like to speak to her, Joyce. That's what I think."

Joyce passes Pauline her lemon tart. "No harm in it. Now, the other day. What were you saying about Bethany's clothes?"

"I've no idea," says Pauline.

"Houndstooth jacket and yellow trousers," says Joyce. "You asked who would wear that?"

"Well, you know," says Pauline.

"I don't know," says Joyce. "Why mention it?"

"Can I tempt anyone to another Prosecco?" asks a waiter.

"Yes, please," say Joyce and Pauline. As he pours, the two women are politely silent, save for the odd "ooh" as the glasses fill.

"Odd thing to wear, is all," says Pauline, and takes a healthy glug. "Not her style."

"Pauline," says Joyce. "Do you know something you're not telling me?"

"I think you'd work that out, don't you?"

"I'm not sure I would with you, no," says Joyce. "You're not protecting someone?"

"By talking about Bethany's clothes? No," says Pauline. "I'm just interested in clothes. That's the thing I would look at."

"They're all concentrating more on offshore accounts than trousers," says Joyce.

"Well, that's why you're a gang," says Pauline. "You don't all have to concentrate on the same thing."

"And you mentioned that the CCTV was very blurry? That was an unusual thing to say."

"Joyce," says Pauline. "You were all sitting around with your theories and I just wanted to join in. Just wanted to have something to contribute. You're quite an intimidating bunch when you get together."

Joyce laughs. "I suppose. That's mainly Elizabeth though, not me."

"Sure," says Pauline. "Tell me about Ron."

"What do you want to know?"

"The bad stuff," says Pauline. "Anything I've missed while I've been staring into those beautiful eyes."

"Where to begin," says Joyce. "He can't dress, he refuses to eat healthily, you can't disagree with him, he's too loud sometimes, especially in public, some of his attitudes are outdated, and he once gave me an hour-long lecture when I said I'd voted Lib Dem at the local elections."

"But is—"

"Sometimes he teases me, although when he teases Elizabeth I like it, so perhaps that's not a fault. He's very slow at responding to messages, he gets grumpy easily, especially if he hasn't eaten. He passes wind often. He once sulked for an entire day because we didn't ask him to see the corpse of an assassin someone had shot at Coopers Chase. He has terrible taste in music and, if he ever comes round in the evening, he talks when the TV is on."

"There was an assassin at Coopers Chase?"

Joyce waves this away. "If you ever send him to the shop, he'll get the wrong thing. And I don't mean dark chocolate digestives instead of milk chocolate digestives. I mean you'll ask for a four-pack of loo roll and you'll get a pineapple."

"That's fairly comprehensive," says Pauline. "Any good points?"

"That's a longer list," says Joyce. "So I'll boil it down for you. He's loyal, he's kind, he's funny, and I am very, very proud that, for whatever reason, he has chosen to be my friend. He is, and this is just an opinion, a prince. I sometimes daydream, and this will sound silly, but I sometimes daydream about Ron sitting there on my sofa, and Gerry is in his armchair, and the two of them just laughing and arguing until all hours. I can play the whole thing out in my head. Gerry would have loved him, and that's the greatest compliment I have."

There are tears in Joyce's eyes, and Pauline takes her hand. "It sounds like you love him too, Joyce."

"Of course I do," says Joyce. "How could you not love Ron? I mean, he is not the man for me, Pauline, for the many reasons listed. But if you like pineapple, and you've already got enough loo roll, he's the man for you."

"You know, you could just be right," says Pauline.

Joyce is smiling through her tears now. "How lovely, how lovely. I shall look for a wedding hat."

"Let's not go that far," says Pauline, smiling. "Early days."

Pauline lets Joyce's hand go. But Joyce now places it over Pauline's. She looks her directly in the eye.

"You promise me you're telling me everything, Pauline?"

"It looks like you ladies might need another top-up," says the waiter.

"Yes, please," say Joyce and Pauline.

31.

"You've put them through the old computer?" Stephen asks. "Nothing doing?"

"Nothing doing," says Elizabeth. A friend still in the Service had run the names for her. "Carron Whitehead" throwing up no matches, "Robert Brown" throwing up far too many. They have promised to look through them all, but there are only so many favors you can ask, and Elizabeth has asked rather a lot recently. Perhaps she should pay a visit to the Chief Constable, and see if he knew anything they didn't? Could she get an appointment? There must be a way.

"Your pal will crack it," says Stephen. "The one with the crosswords."

Ibrahim. He and Stephen used to be good friends. Ibrahim still asks to come round, and Elizabeth still puts him off.

"I'm trying to play chess here," says Bogdan. "There is a lot of talking."

Bogdan has come down from the construction site at the top of the hill to keep Stephen company.

"You still smell rather nice," says Elizabeth. "And the same smell as before. Almost as if you are seeing someone regularly?" Elizabeth has room for more than one mystery at a time.

Bogdan makes a move and sits back. "What are you going to do about the guy you have to kill?"

"I asked a question first, Bogdan," says Elizabeth.

She will get nothing from Bogdan. Perhaps she should start following him. Is that a bit much? She contemplates for a moment, and decides that, yes, that probably is a bit much. But, really, Elizabeth hates not knowing secrets. Spies are like dogs. They cannot stand a closed door.

"Wonderful books the Viking chap had," says Stephen, pondering his move. "Really quite extraordinary."

Stephen is her secret, of course. Her closed door. For now.

"You going to use the gun I gave you?" Bogdan asks. "The woman I got it from said it had been buried for a while, so make sure it works."

"He's giving me advice about guns now," says Elizabeth. She will actually have to check though. She'll take it out into the woods this evening. Scare the owls and the foxes.

"Bogdan, old chap," says Stephen, frowning at the chessboard. "Looks like you've got me again. Must be losing my marbles."

"Only thing you are losing is the game," says Bogdan.

Carron Whitehead and Robert Brown. The very first transactions with the stolen money. There must be a clue there, but Elizabeth feels like she's hit a dead end.

Ironically she can think of one person who might be able to help.

Viktor Illyich. A whiz at this sort of thing. Delving into records, following money trails.

It's time to put up or shut up though. Eliminate Viktor, and, thus, eliminate the risk from the Viking. Elizabeth will go into the woods tonight and test the gun. And then she will have to message Joyce, and tell her they are going to London tomorrow. Though she won't tell her why.

It is time to kill Viktor Illyich. And Elizabeth will need Joyce there when she does it.

32.

The morning rush hour has passed, but the train is still busy. Elizabeth has just come clean about her kidnapping.

"But why a bag over your head *and* a blindfold?" asks Joyce, as the train races through the horizontal English rain. "That's a bit much."

"Belt and braces," says Elizabeth.

Joyce nods. "I suppose I've packed a raincoat *and* an umbrella today, so I can hardly talk. How was Staffordshire?"

"I didn't see a great deal of it, Joyce," says Elizabeth. "I was driven there at speed, then forced into a house with a gun at my head, and eventually dumped on a freezing roadside at two a.m."

Elizabeth's phone buzzes, a message from a withheld number.

> I see you are on the train to London, Elizabeth. I have people everywhere. Please don't let me down.

It is meant to sound threatening, but it is starting to come across as needy. Elizabeth takes a look along the carriage, though, judging every face in turn.

"I'm not sure I've ever been to Staffordshire," Joyce continues. "But I must have been through it at some point, mustn't I?"

The ideal scenario would be to not have to murder Viktor Illych. But the Viking would kill Joyce in two weeks, unless given a good reason not to. The choice was Viktor or Joyce, and that was no choice at all.

So here they were, on the 9:44 from Polegate to London Victoria. She is still choosing not to tell Joyce about the threat against her. Was that right? Could Joyce handle a death threat? Elizabeth had yet to see Joyce's limits, but surely she must have some?

"You'll have been through Staffordshire, Joyce, yes. It's quite broad."

Joyce has been telling Elizabeth her new theory. That Fiona Clemence had been involved in Bethany Waites's murder and wouldn't it, all things being considered, be worth talking to her? Nice to think about that for a while, rather than what she is about to do.

Elizabeth feels the weight of the gun in the handbag sitting on her lap. A gun, a pen, some lipstick and a crossword book. Just like the good old days.

"Is there a trolley on this train?" Joyce asks. "Or do we have to go to the buffet car?"

"There's a trolley," says Elizabeth.

"Oh, good," says Joyce, and looks over her shoulder, to see if, perhaps, the trolley is on its way. "And is this trip to London connected to your adventure?" Joyce continues. "Or are we shopping?"

"It is connected. I will take you shopping another day to make up for it."

Another message on Elizabeth's phone.

Nice day for it, by the way!

Does the Viking have nothing else to do? They both sit back and take in the gray, wet view out of the window. Oh, England, you really know how to be drab when you want to.

Joyce finally cracks. "So where are we off to, then?"

"To meet an old friend of mine," says Elizabeth. "Viktor."

"We used to have a milkman called Victor," says Joyce. "Any chance it's the same Victor?"

"Very possible. Was your milkman also the head of the Leningrad KGB in the eighties?"

"Different Victor," says Joyce. "Though they finish milk-rounds very early, don't they? So perhaps he was doing two jobs?"

They laugh, and the trolley arrives. Joyce asks the woman behind the trolley a series of questions. Was the tea free? Were there biscuits? Were *those* free? Were those bananas she could spot? Was there much of a trade in bananas on the train, or were the biscuits the big draw? How much hotter would the coffee be at one end of the train than at the other? There were then a few supplementary questions, which elicited that the woman pushing the trolley had recently returned to work after having a baby, and that her husband, who worked in construction at the airport, was not really pulling his weight at home, and that his mother was being impossible and defending him at every turn. At the end of the questions Joyce had decided that actually she was fine, and wouldn't have anything, thank you. Elizabeth took a water, and the trolley, and the woman, continued on their way, wishing them both a safe journey.

"So why are we going to see Viktor?"

Elizabeth makes sure the trolley is out of sight.

"I'm afraid I have to kill him."

"Don't joke, Elizabeth," says Joyce. "We're right in the middle of an investigation. And we've been through a lot recently."

Joyce is right. Elizabeth thinks all the way back to the murder of Tony Curran. To Ian Ventham, and to Penny in Willows, with John holding her hand. It had all seemed a bit of a jape, but it was simply the start of a long series of events that has culminated in her sitting on the 9:44 from Polegate, with her best friend, and a gun in her handbag. "Best friend?" That was a new thought. She nods her agreement at Joyce.

"I know. And I'm afraid we're going to have to go through a little more, before this is all done."

"But you can't kill someone, Elizabeth."

"We both know that's not true, Joyce. And on this occasion I have to."

"Why? What happens if you don't kill him?"

"Someone will kill me." (Someone will kill you, Joyce. And I won't allow that to happen.)

"You really are ridiculous sometimes," says Joyce. "Since when do you do what you're told? Who is telling you to kill Viktor?"

"I don't know."

"MI5?"

"It would probably be MI6, Joyce, with respect. But no. A tall Swedish man."

"They're all tall in Sweden," says Joyce. "It was on *The One Show*. So is he paying you?"

"No, just the threat of death." (Your death, my lovely, kind, hugely over-talkative friend.)

"OK, well, I'm assuming I don't have the full picture, but I suppose I'm here to help, that's what best friends are for."

"I rather think we *are* best friends, Joyce, aren't we? It hadn't really occurred to me."

"Of course we're best friends," says Joyce. "Who did you think my best friend was? Ron?"

Elizabeth smiles again. Has she had a best friend before? Penny? Perhaps, but, really, they just shared a common hobby and a mutual respect. She's had husbands and lovers. Field partners, cell mates, bodyguards. But a best friend?

"Wait, is Stoke in Staffordshire?" says Joyce.

"Yes," says Elizabeth.

"Then I have been to Staffordshire. We did a coach trip to Stoke, years back. Lovely ceramics. I bought a pot with Gerry's name on it. It was spelt with a 'J,' but it was the closest they had."

"Glad to get that cleared up," says Elizabeth.

"Where does Viktor live?"

"Somewhere you're going to like very much," says Elizabeth.

Joyce nods. "You're not really going to kill him, Elizabeth? I don't think you'd bring me if you were really going to kill him."

Elizabeth studies Joyce for a moment. "Who on earth do you think I would bring? Ron?"

She hoped that might make her friend laugh, but, instead, Joyce looks scared.

The train begins to slow, as it approaches London.

33.

They are going to kill me," reads Ibrahim. "*Only Connie Johnson can help me now.*"

"She was frightened, I can tell you that," says Connie Johnson, her feet up on the desk. They have been allowed a private meeting room, because of the importance of "good mental health."

"Frightened," repeats Ibrahim. "Frightened of you?"

Connie shakes her head. "I know when people are frightened of me. Frightened of someone though."

"Perhaps you like it when people are frightened of you?" Ibrahim is making notes on his pad. "What would you say to that?"

"Are we doing therapy?" says Connie. "Or are we investigating a murder?"

"I thought we could mix the two," says Ibrahim. "In therapy you must never waste a crisis."

"People being frightened is not my thing," says Connie. "Thank you for my *Grazia* by the way, it's perfect. I don't get a kick out of people being scared of me, I just do it because it's easy to monetize."

"So who was she frightened of," says Ibrahim, "do you think?"

Connie shrugs and sips at the cappuccino a warder has made for her. It even has chocolate sprinkles. "Felt like she had a secret she was scared to tell."

"A secret that she seems to believe you know," says Ibrahim. 'Only Connie Johnson can help me now.' What did she say to you? She gave you a clue, perhaps?"

"If she did, I didn't pick up on it," says Connie. "But I'll keep thinking."

"If you would," says Ibrahim. "Do you have secrets, Connie?"

"Nah," says Connie. "The combination to the safe in my lock-up, I suppose, but I don't think that counts, does it? What are your secrets?"

"That's for another day," says Ibrahim. "Let's start from the beginning. When you heard what had happened—"

"With the knitting needles?"

"With the knitting needles, yes," says Ibrahim. "What did you think?"

Connie takes a pause, and breaks off a piece of the Kit Kat another warder had brought in. On a tray. "Well, first off, I admired the ingenuity. Not easy to kill someone with knitting needles."

"Agreed," says Ibrahim.

"And, second, I thought I shouldn't have given her the knitting needles," says Connie. "But you can't be ruled by hindsight, can you?"

"That is a wise thing to say."

"Too late for her now," says Connie, draining the last of her cappuccino with a wince. "If I look into it a bit more, do you think you could bring me a new coffee-maker? I've got a Nespresso, but I'd like a De'Longhi."

"I shouldn't think so," says Ibrahim.

Connie nods. "Well, try your best. Here's the only thing I can remember: when I went into her cell, Heather was writing something."

Ibrahim stops writing and looks up at her. "What sort of thing?"

Connie shrugs. "She hid it away pretty quickly. Worth looking for though. They'll have bagged up all her stuff."

"And what she was writing?" says Ibrahim. "It wouldn't have been the note she left?"

Connie shakes her head. "It was lots of writing. She was scribbling away."

"So what do you think, Connie? Why kill Heather Garbutt, and why kill her now?"

"What I think is this," says Connie. "I think this doesn't feel like the therapy I'm paying for. This feels like I'm an unpaid member of your gang."

"Well, we are all unpaid, but your point is valid," says Ibrahim. "It is a legitimate observation. Let's talk a little about you. Would you like to start, or shall I?"

"You start," says Connie.

Ibrahim thinks for a moment. "I think you are unhappy."

"Wrong," says Connie.

"I think you make other people unhappy," says Ibrahim.

"I'll give you that," says Connie.

"So you know you make other people unhappy, and yet you are happy? It must be hard to make peace with that fact?"

"Other people are their own responsibility," says Connie.

"Connie. You are very bright, you are hard-working. You spot opportunities. I think it is fair to say you are more powerful than many other people."

Connie drums her fingers on the table. "Maybe."

"So therefore you are a bully," says Ibrahim. "If you are strong, you have a choice in life: to protect the weak, or to prey on the weak. You use the strengths you have been given to prey on the weak."

"So does everyone," says Connie.

"I don't," says Ibrahim. "Only sociopaths do."

"Well, then, I'm a sociopath," says Connie. "You should try it, it's very lucrative."

"You sensed Heather Garbutt was frightened, Connie. And you sensed she was unable to tell the truth. And I think you cared about that."

Connie pauses. "Not especially."

"You didn't care?"

"Not really, no."

" 'Not really, no.' Yet you think I should find out what Heather was writing? You think maybe there's more to her death than meets the eye?"

"Maybe," says Connie.

"I have good news and bad news for you, Connie," says Ibrahim, shutting his pad.

"Enlighten me," says Connie.

"The good news is that you care. So you are not a sociopath."

"And the bad news?"

"The bad news is that means, at some point, you are going to have to come to terms with everything you've done in your life."

Connie stares at Ibrahim for a long while. Ibrahim stares back.

"You're a fraud," says Connie, finally. "Nice suits, I'll give you that, but a fraud."

"Perhaps so." There is a series of beeps on Ibrahim's phone.

"And that's our hour up. More next week, or is that us done? It's always your choice. Perhaps I am too much of a fraud for you?"

Connie gathers up her magazine and places the rest of the Kit Kat in her Hermès clutch. She stands, and holds out her hand to Ibrahim.

"More next week," she says. "Please."

"As you wish," say Ibrahim.

"I'll keep digging for you," says Connie.

"And I shall do the same for you," says Ibrahim.

34.

What did you make of Pauline?" asks Elizabeth.

"I like her," says Joyce.

"Well, I like her too," says Elizabeth. "But what did you *make* of her?"

"I asked her about the comments from the other day," says Joyce. "About Bethany's clothes. But she batted them away. And she said she had no memory of the notes."

"It's almost as if she were trying to lead us to something," says Elizabeth. "Or away from something."

"She agreed we should talk to Fiona Clemence though," says Joyce. "She thought that was a tremendous idea."

Elizabeth raises a doubtful eyebrow to her friend.

The black cab pulls in, and Elizabeth and Joyce step out. Elizabeth takes a good look around. Who is watching? There are guards at the door of the American Embassy up ahead, and there's a group of young women going through the revolving doors of a publisher's building on her left. Looking up, she can see plenty of windows, plenty of places in which to hide and watch. A sniper's paradise. Joyce is also looking around, but with an entirely different focus.

"There's a swimming pool!" says Joyce.

"I know," confirms Elizabeth.

"In the sky," says Joyce, looking up and shielding her eyes from the bright winter sun.

"I told you you'd like it," says Elizabeth.

The swimming pool runs between the tops of two tall, residential buildings. Its glass floor makes it seem suspended in mid-air. Elizabeth is unimpressed. It's just engineering plus money. Perhaps some imagination too, but she bets they copied it from somewhere. Perhaps if someone had built it for the public to use, she would marvel at it. But you can only swim in the sky if you have money, and if you have money you can do pretty much anything, so forgive her for not getting excited.

"And this is where he lives?" asks Joyce. "Viktor?"

"That's the information I have."

"Do you think he'll let us have a go in the pool?"

"Do you have your costume, Joyce?"

"I didn't think to. Do you think we'll be coming back anytime?"

Elizabeth feels the weight of the gun in her handbag again. "Not for a while, no."

They walk in through the huge double doors of one of the residential buildings, and make their way across the marble lobby, to the burnished walnut-and-copper concierge desk. The whole place feels very expensive yet deeply inoffensive, like a business hotel a divorcé might choose to kill himself in.

The concierge is very beautiful, East African, perhaps? Elizabeth gives her friendliest smile. She's no Joyce, but she does her best.

"We're here to see Mr. Illyich."

The concierge looks at Elizabeth very pleasantly, but very certainly. "I'm afraid we have no Mr. Illyich in the building."

That would actually make sense, thinks Elizabeth. Viktor Illyich had a hundred names. Why use the real one here?

"You're very beautiful," says Joyce to the concierge.

"Thank you," says the concierge. "As are you. Is there anything else I can do to help you today?"

Elizabeth's phone buzzes. The Viking again. She looks at the message.

> I hear you are in his building. Killing him at home is a nice touch. I look forward to hearing from you shortly.

How to get upstairs?

"Have you ever used the pool?" Joyce asks the concierge.

"Many times," says the concierge. "Just to let you know, a member of our staff is on his way to escort you to the exit at your earliest convenience."

"I think I'm more impressed with it than Elizabeth," says Joyce.

"Elizabeth?" says the concierge. "Elizabeth Best?"

"Yes, dear," says Elizabeth. Things are looking up.

"Mr. Illyich told me if an Elizabeth Best were to visit, to show her up straight away. He said she might also be called"—the concierge looks down at a list—"Dorothy D'Angelo, Marion Schulz, Konstantina Plishkova or the Reverend Helen Smith. He also told me to watch and learn, because Elizabeth Best is the cleverest woman he has ever known."

Elizabeth sees Joyce roll her eyes.

"You didn't think, when we walked in, asking for Viktor Illyich, that *I* might be Elizabeth Best? That didn't cross your mind?"

"I'm terribly sorry, no. The way Mr. Illyich spoke about you, I thought Elizabeth Best must be a much younger woman."

"Well," says Elizabeth. "I used to be much younger, so you're excused."

"Mr. Illyich is in the penthouse. I will show you up myself." The concierge turns to Joyce. "And I will show you the swimming pool when you leave. There are spare costumes for guests."

Elizabeth sees the delight on her friend's face. There will be no swimming today. But they might need towels.

After the trip up in a lift the size of a suburban sitting room, Viktor Illyich answers the door himself, thanks the concierge, and lets Elizabeth and Joyce into his penthouse. He couldn't look more thrilled to see them.

"There she is! How did I get so lucky? How long has it been, Elizabeth?"

"Twenty years?" says Elizabeth.

"Twenty years, twenty years," nods Viktor, and kisses her on both cheeks. "I look so terribly old. Don't you think?"

"You always looked terribly old," says Elizabeth.

Viktor laughs. "I did! Always! Finally I *am* old. Finally I make sense. Now, I think you are Joyce Meadowcroft?"

Joyce reaches out a hand, but Viktor kisses her on each cheek.

"Lovely to meet you, Viktor," says Joyce. "Do you know they kiss three times in Belgium? I only found that out recently."

Viktor smiles, and takes her elbow.

"Please, come with me and sit. It is too cold to sit outside, but we can enjoy the view. I hope you like gray clouds and red buses?"

Viktor leads Joyce over to a sunken sofa that, hypothetically, looks out over a huge vista of London. The gray clouds obscure most of the view today. The only things near enough to be made out are the building sites of Battersea Power Station, as a whole new swath of London takes shape on the banks of the river. Elizabeth follows behind them.

"Joyce," says Viktor. "I think you would like a gin and tonic? That's what I think. Tell me if I'm right?"

"You're right!" says Joyce.

"Then that's what we will have. I am so happy to have you both here. Elizabeth, you will join us?"

"Sit down, Viktor," says Elizabeth.

"I will, I will," says Viktor. "Come on, I'm excited. Let me make the drinks, then we can sit and talk. Two old spies. We can make Joyce's hair curl with our tales!"

"Sit down, Viktor," says Elizabeth again, her gun now in her hand.

35.

I speak, then you speak," says the producer. He is called Carwyn Price, and DCI Chris Hudson has been left in no doubt of that, because Carwyn Price likes to refer to Carwyn Price in the third person. "I speak, you speak; I speak, you speak; I speak, you speak."

"Got it," says Chris.

"I speak, you speak, that's my only rule. That's the Carwyn Price rule," says Carwyn Price.

"Do I look at the camera?" asks Chris.

"No, look at me, that's the other rule," says Carwyn. "Unless you're making an appeal, 'Have you seen this man?,' that sort of thing. You can do that down the barrel."

"Down the barrel?"

"Straight into the lens," says Carwyn. "That's what we call it in news."

"Down the barrel means something very different in the police force," says Chris.

Carwyn is wearing a woolen beanie hat indoors. Donna will have an opinion on that. Donna is watching from a chair at the side of the small *South East Tonight* studio. When Chris had received the call, come and screen-test, the guy on the phone had said, "Let's see if Carwyn Price likes you." "Who's Carwyn Price?" Chris had asked, and the guy on the phone had said, "I am."

"OK, I'm going to shoot a few questions," says Carwyn. "You zing back with a few answers, and we'll find out if the camera loves you."

"Good luck," calls Donna, from the side of the studio.

"Quiet on set," says Carwyn. "We're not in a zoo."

Why had he agreed to this, Chris wonders, a little too late now, of course. His mouth is drier than he had imagined possible. It's like he has just woken from a fitful sleep on a long-haul flight.

"I'm joined by Detective Sergeant Chris—"

"Detective Chief Inspector," says Chris with difficulty.

"Don't ever interrupt," says Carwyn. "I speak, you speak."

"Sorry," says Chris. "I just thought, you know, for accuracy."

"On live TV?" says Carwyn. "That's what you thought, was it? If I put you on my show, this is what I get? You piping up every five seconds?"

"We're not on live TV though," says Chris. "I promise I wouldn't do it if we were."

Carwyn mutters "Jesus Christ" under his breath. This seems to be going badly. Chris realizes he needs the loo too. How can he need the loo when his mouth feels so dry? He looks over at Donna. She gives him a thumbs-up, but it lacks conviction.

"I'm joined by Detective *Chief Inspector* Chris Hudson, of Kent Police," says Carwyn, not even looking up now. "Detective Inspector, robberies are up, violent crime is up, surely the people of Kent deserve better than this?"

"That's a very fair question, Mike, I think—"

"Mike?" says Carwyn. Which feels like an interruption, but Chris thinks it best to let it go.

"Yes, I thought you were being Mike Waghorn," says Chris. "Sorry."

"I'm Carwyn Price, mate," says Carwyn. "So I'm being Carwyn Price."

"Sorry," says Chris again. "I just thought you were the producer, so—"

"So I don't exist?" says Carwyn. "Because you haven't seen me on TV?"

"No, I just . . ." Chris looks over at Donna again, but she is pretending to look at her phone. "Sorry, I haven't done this before."

"That's coming across," says Carwyn. "I'm doing this as a favor to Mike, you understand that? I'm missing jujitsu for this."

Chris nods. "Sorry. Of course."

To his surprise, Chris realizes at this point that, actually, he really *would* like to be on television. He doesn't like Carwyn, sure, with his hat, and the chips on his shoulders, but he likes being in this studio, likes the camera pointed at him. It's quite a surprise for a man who would have avoided a mirror a few months ago. He sees Carwyn puff out his cheeks. *Last chance, Chris, let's nail this.*

"I'm Carwyn Price, and I'm joined by Detective Chief Inspector Colin Hudson of Kent Police . . ."

Chris lets this go. How much he has learned already.

"Robberies are up, violent crime is up, surely the people of Kent deserve better than this?"

"They do, Carwyn," says Chris. "It's the right question to ask, and if I had a simple answer I would give it. I'll start by saying we live in a very safe part of the world—I don't want your viewers to worry themselves too much. But one robbery is a robbery too many, one instance of violent crime is . . ."

Chris catches Donna out of the corner of his eye. A real thumbs-up this time.

". . . one too many. So I give this promise: my fellow officers and I will not rest—"

The studio door swings open, and Mike Waghorn saunters in, tossing his bag onto a chair.

"Here he is! My great find!"

Carwyn seems to find a politeness around Mike Waghorn that he hadn't been able to muster around Chris.

"Mikey boy!" Carwyn says. "Yep, just putting him through his paces!"

"I'll bet, I'll just bet," says Mike. "Hello, Chris, what do you make of all this?"

"Love it," says Chris. "To be honest. Didn't think I would, but I do."

Mike sees Donna. "And your better half? What do you think, Donna?"

"He's actually very good," says Donna.

"No need to screen-test him, Carwyn, I'll vouch for him—you know my instincts," says Mike.

"Of course, Mike," says Carwyn. "He's definitely got the X-factor."

"We're talking about knife crime in a couple of days," says Mike. "Put him on. That all right with you, Chris?"

"Umm, yes," says Chris. In a couple of days? On TV? Knife crime? It's like all his Christmases have come at once. He can't wait to tell Patrice.

"Well done, Boss," says Donna, rising from her chair and giving Chris a hug.

Chris's mind is galloping ahead. Perhaps this will turn into a regular slot. Your friendly bobby, dispensing advice, perhaps a little bit of wisdom along the way. Chris looks at the monitor on the studio floor. He looks good. Do his eyes twinkle? He could swear they do. He sees Mike look at the monitor too. But he realizes that Mike is not looking at him.

"Donna," says Mike. "You really pop on camera. I mean *really* pop."

"Pop?" says Donna. Chris has a sinking feeling.

"Shine, zing, pop," says Mike. "Last time I saw anything like this it was a young Phillip Schofield. Wow."

"I . . . uh . . . thank you," says Donna.

"What do you know about knife crime? I want you on instead of Chris," says Mike.

Donna holds up her hands in protest, Chris will give her that. "Sorry, Mike. Choose Chris."

Mike puts his hands on Donna's shoulders. "I don't choose anyone, Donna. The camera chooses. And it's chosen you."

Mike turns to Carwyn. "Carwyn, take Donna into wardrobe, see what we've got."

Carwyn takes Donna out of the studio. She gives an apologetic look over her shoulder as she goes. Mike places a hand on Chris's shoulder.

"Sorry, Chris," he says. "That's showbusiness."

Chris nods, the warmth of potential fame leaving his body.

36.

"Elizabeth, don't even joke," says Viktor Illyich, the gun pointed at his head.

"I wish I were joking, Viktor," says Elizabeth, and watches Viktor sit. Joyce is open-mouthed.

"Elizabeth," says Joyce.

"Don't get involved, Joyce," says Elizabeth. "Not this time. I need you to trust me. Killing Viktor is the only option we have."

"There are many options, Elizabeth," says Viktor. "Sit and talk, we will work it out. I chose not to kill you after I received the photographs. I could have, you know?"

"What photographs?" says Joyce.

"I know you could, Viktor, and I'm sorry," says Elizabeth. "You should have done. But the man who wants you dead knows I'm here. He has people watching everywhere."

She takes her phone from her bag and holds it up. "I can show you messages to prove it. So I have to kill you. I'll make it quick, and we'll bury you properly."

"Elizabeth . . ." says Joyce.

"Sorry, Joyce," says Elizabeth, putting her phone down on the table beside her. "I truly am. Now you get to see what I'm really capable of if my hand is forced. Where shall we do this, Viktor? Where is quietest? I don't want to alert your lovely concierge."

"If it was me, then the bathroom. It's quiet. And you can clean it easily," suggests Viktor. "But you really don't have to do this. We are friends, no?"

"We are friends, Viktor, yes," says Elizabeth.

"The guy who sent you," says Viktor. "He's Swedish, right?"

"I can't tell you, Viktor," says Elizabeth. "After this, I don't want to hear from him or think about him again."

"We team up together? We kill him? That's a better plan. Come on."

"It's all too late," says Elizabeth. "I don't know who he is, and you don't seem to know who he is, and I just want this over with. I want peace at home with my husband. I'm so sorry. Let's head to the bathroom. You lead the way."

Viktor stands. Joyce stands too.

"He's going nowhere," says Joyce. "Not while I'm here."

Viktor places a hand on Joyce's shoulder. "Joyce Meadowcroft, you have my thanks. But this is business. Someone is going to shoot me one day, and at least Elizabeth is a friend. This Swedish guy wants me dead, and maybe this is the best way."

Joyce looks at Elizabeth, and Elizabeth nods. "It can't always be a game, Joyce. I'm sorry."

"I will never forgive you," says Joyce.

"You have to trust me, Joyce," says Elizabeth. "Best friends."

"Not anymore," says Joyce.

She turns away from Elizabeth. Elizabeth is surprised at how much this stings, but she understands.

Viktor walks toward the bathroom, Elizabeth following behind, gun raised.

"No sudden movements, Viktor, let's just get this over with."

"Last chance to stop this now. You know I loved you, Elizabeth?" says Viktor.

"Where does love ever get us?" says Elizabeth, following Viktor from the room. "Tied up in the back of a van. Shot in a penthouse. I'm done with love."

Viktor opens the door to the bathroom. His voice is now loud, imploring. "Please, let me turn around and we can—"

Elizabeth pulls the trigger.

37.

The truth is, you simply don't get enough vitamin D in prison, and, in Connie Johnson's view, that contravenes her human rights.

She doesn't like the story her mirror is telling her one bit. She's too pale. When she gets out of here she is going to the Maldives. Life can't just be about work, and perhaps it's time to spend a bit of that money she's made? Perhaps St. Lucia? Or France? Where do civilians go on holiday?

Connie has been abroad only twice in her life. Once on a school trip to Dieppe, where she had been sick on the ferry and a Geography teacher had tried to kiss her behind a hypermarket, and once locked in the boot of a BMW and driven to Amsterdam by two Liverpudlian brothers with whom she had had a difference of opinion. The Liverpudlian brothers and the Geography teacher had all soon regretted their actions.

Slap on the fake tan all you like, have your Botox and your fillers, but the three things the skin can't survive without are vitamin D, vegetables and plenty of water, preferably sparkling. They don't serve fresh vegetables in prison, but, through the contact of a contact, Connie has an Abel & Cole box delivered once a week, and another of her contacts, in the kitchens, can work wonders with a parsnip and an aubergine. She takes her vitamin D tablets, but there's no real substitute for sunshine when you're supposed to be locked up for twenty-three hours a day. She has a machine for sparkling water.

Connie is thinking prison would be very, very difficult without a bit of money and some VIP status. It's still not *great*, but, much like traveling first class on the train, she's going to be stuck there for a while and the toilets aren't ideal, but at least someone brings her a cup of tea every now and again.

Either way, she's going to have to get out of here sooner or later. Sunshine on her face, a gun in her waistband and a gym where you can do Reformer Pilates. She doesn't need much.

Through the security gates and on to D-Wing now, Connie thinks about Ibrahim, that wise old owl. On the whole, Connie has not had good experiences with authority figures telling her what she should and shouldn't do. But Ibrahim? With his nice suits and his kind eyes? For once in her life she doesn't feel like she is being told off.

Connie passes a cell that is being hosed down with a pressure-washer. She gives the spray a wide berth, as she is wearing suede, and there is only so much the prison laundry can do, however much cannabis you smuggle in for them.

Connie has never really spoken to anyone the way she is speaking with Ibrahim. What is it? Honesty, perhaps? Connie can be a number of very different people, when the mood takes her. She puts on different faces if she wants to scare you, if she wants to sleep with you, or if she wants a prison warder to bring her a Nando's. But doesn't everyone? Isn't everyone doing that all the time? Presenting a certain side of themselves to other people?

So what side is she presenting to Ibrahim, and why does it feel so different? Connie climbs the metal staircase to Heather Garbutt's landing. Someone is shouting in their cell further down the corridor, something incoherent about asylum seekers. If you took everyone with mental-health issues out of this place they'd have to shut it down. Most people in here were, one way or another, just taking another step in a life of chaos, pulled by the tides of a world that neither wanted them nor needed them. Very few people in here were like Connie. Just plain bad.

Connie reaches the door of Heather's cell. It is still empty because of the internal investigation into Heather's death. The man in the admin block, the one with the Volvo from Tinder, has assured her that it has been left open. Connie walks into the cell, cold and empty in Heather's absence.

"ONLY CONNIE JOHNSON CAN HELP ME NOW." Well, let's see what we can do, Heather. Let's see if we can find what you were writing.

There are very few places to hide anything in a cell. Connie starts knocking on the walls, trying to hear a hollow sound. But the walls are too thick. No way through.

Connie reaches her arm around the U-bend of Heather Garbutt's toilet. Nothing.

Connie can fool anyone and everyone. She is very, very good at it, and it has served her well for many years. When her dad left, Connie kept smiling, just so someone in the house was. When her mum died, Connie plowed on, building the business. No one was any the wiser about Connie's pain.

The bed frame is made from tubes of cheap metal. Hollow tubes.

Of course, even while she's thinking it through, Connie knows what Ibrahim is doing. The mirror he's providing. He's letting Connie speak to herself. To see herself. And he's helping her understand that if you're fooling everyone, you're really only fooling one person, and that's yourself. Ibrahim had said to her, "Our great strengths are also our great weaknesses," and Connie had rolled her eyes. But, for some reason, that thought is with her all the time now.

Connie upends the bunk beds and pulls a loose rubber stopper out from one of the metal legs. Nothing but an empty space. Keep looking.

What if she wasn't just plain bad? What if that's a lie she has told herself all these years? That would be too much to take. She could just stop seeing Ibrahim, but it feels like he has opened a door that can never be shut again.

She pulls the stopper from the second leg of the bed. Nothing.

Plenty of people have dealt with an awful lot worse than Connie Johnson, she knows that. What she does for a living is despicable: how she makes her money, how she treats people, how she shuts off her brain to the pain that she has caused. It has always felt inevitable to her, though. As if she were born this way, and as if different rules applied to her.

She pulls out the third stopper. Still nothing.

But what if none of that is true? Does she really want to be confronted with everything she has done?

Connie pulls the stopper from the final leg.

On balance, no, she doesn't want to find that out—it is probably best to just keep on lying to herself. Best to remain the Connie Johnson that the little girl invented when her dad left her all those years ago. She will let Ibrahim know she doesn't want any more sessions with him. Thank you, but no thank you.

Connie hooks a finger into the hollow bed leg and feels the paper immediately. Rolled up tight. There are five or six pages perhaps, all tied with a rubber band, and she slides them out. Connie slips off the rubber band and flattens the pages as best she can. They are covered in neat handwriting. Blue ink. She reads the first line:

Through the bars I hear the birds

In the bare cell, with the thick walls, Connie has surely found something that will interest Ibrahim. Ibrahim had set her a task, and she has achieved it. She quickly scans what Heather Garbutt has written, but it seems to be, of all things, a poem. She was hoping for a nice, simple confession, or the naming of a co-conspirator, something to help solve the murder of Bethany Waites, but no such luck yet. Connie knows it could still be helpful though, feels it in her bones.

And, even if she can't make sense of it right now, she knows someone who will. She should probably do one more session with Ibrahim. Show him the poem. Just until they've worked out what's going on here.

38.

Where to begin?

Sitting on my sofa, watching a program about trains, is a man called Viktor Illyich. He's a former KGB agent. He's Ukrainian.

I told him I wanted to write my diary and he laughed and said I had plenty to write about today. I have left him with a glass of sherry and a slice of cherry-and-dark-chocolate cake. I saw it on Instagram and thought it had Ron's name all over it. But, as it turns out, Viktor is getting the first slice, which goes to show how plans can change. The rest is in Tupperware for Ron though.

Hold on one second.

OK, I'm back. I just went through to the living room and asked, and Viktor says the cake is very good. I know he would say that anyway, but he's had the whole slice, so let's assume he's telling the truth. I don't normally like dark chocolate, as a rule, but it really works here. It has Kirsch in it too, so that helps. The program Viktor is watching is about a train that goes through the Rockies in Canada. You should see the views. Viktor said they just spotted a bear.

I went to London today with Elizabeth. She told me we were going to see an old friend of hers, and that she was going to kill him. Which I didn't quite believe, but Elizabeth had been bundled in a van a few nights ago with Stephen, so things were certainly afoot, one way or another. As

I say, I didn't know quite what to think, but I trust Elizabeth. Also, there was a trolley service on the train, rather than a buffet car.

When we arrived in London, we went to the flats where Viktor lives. There is a swimming pool, but I will tell you about that another time, because I think I should get on with telling you what happened.

Wait another moment.

I'm back again. Viktor has just been to the loo, and couldn't get the flush to work. There is a knack, and I told him. Gentle, gentle, gentle, then all at once. I told him you can pause the TV when you go to the loo, but he already knew. I pause the TV during *Countdown*, just to make it less stressful. If ever I watch it with Ibrahim, he doesn't let me. He says I am only cheating myself.

Viktor lives on the top floor of the flats, the penthouse, and he's a funny-looking little thing. Like a very happy tortoise. He was delighted to see Elizabeth, and he even gave me two kisses, so I thought there was no way Elizabeth was going to kill him, and I was just waiting to hear what was up. Viktor offered me a gin and tonic, but then Elizabeth pulled out her gun. I had words with her about it, but she wasn't for backing down, and Viktor seemed to take the whole thing in his stride.

Honestly, I was scared, and I was angry with Elizabeth. I even told her I would never forgive her, which she reminded me of on the journey home. "You should always trust me," was her take on the thing, but, as it happens, I think my anger was useful.

Off they both went, to the bathroom, Viktor yelled out something or other, and there was a gunshot, and I heard Viktor fall to the floor.

I was shaking, I admit it. In fact, if I'm admitting everything, I was crying. Which, again, as it turns out, was also useful.

Elizabeth rushed back into the room and issued instructions. It was something like, "No time for tears, Joyce, I had to do it, and Viktor knew it, but now I need your help." She said she was on cleaning duties in the bathroom, which I was glad of at least, but she needed me to make a couple of calls. I was to call Bogdan on her phone and say, "Elizabeth needs a taxi," and then I was to take the SIM card out of her phone and cut it into pieces, and then wipe the phone clean and put it into the waste-disposal unit in the kitchen. There must be no physical or electronic evidence that we had ever been in the flat. I thought to ask about the concierge, but I didn't, because I feared the answer.

Off she disappears again and I call Bogdan, and he says hello, and I say Elizabeth needs a taxi, and he asks if I'm crying, and I say I'm not, and he says good, there is nothing to cry about, and he will be with us in an hour. Then I ask how he is, but he has already rung off.

So I took out the SIM card, which was difficult, because I was shaking, and cut it into pieces, and then took the phone into the kitchen and threw it into the chute. I heard Elizabeth call out, "Have you done it, Joyce?" and I called back, very quietly, that I had, and that's when Elizabeth and Viktor walked back into the living room, casual as you like.

I looked like I'd seen a ghost, and who can blame me? Then Elizabeth talked me through it all.

The text messages from the Viking had been the key. He knew our every move. He said he had people watching us at every step. But Elizabeth saw through it. She says she can't be followed without noticing, she's too canny. There was no one on the train, for example. So she knew the Viking had pulled a much simpler trick. He had simply cloned her mobile phone while she was at his house (I say "simply," you know what I mean) and was able to hear, and occasionally see, everything that happened right up to the moment I destroyed the phone.

That's why she had to keep me in the dark, so my reactions were natural, and believable, to the Viking. In fact, that's why I was there in the first place, to make the whole thing sound completely real. I told Elizabeth I could have acted, but she laughed. I asked if Viktor was in on it, and he said that, as soon as she held the phone up and told him about the messages, he understood her plan. I asked Viktor if he was worried before then that she was really going to kill him, and he said that he was assuming she wouldn't, but with Elizabeth you could never tell for sure. Elizabeth scoffed and said "as if" she would kill him, and Viktor said "you would," and, while Elizabeth kept protesting, Viktor finally poured me the gin and tonic I'd been promised.

An hour or so later, the concierge came up with Bogdan, who was carrying a very large holdall. Viktor told the concierge that he was dead, and she nodded and asked how long he would be dead for, so he looked at Elizabeth, and she said that a couple of weeks or so should do it.

The concierge works for Viktor, it turns out, and, in the end, she even helped Bogdan carry the holdall to the car, with Viktor keeping as still as possible inside, in case the Viking had someone watching the building. Viktor took two very heavy-duty sleeping pills, because he has been in this sort of situation before, and it was the only way through being locked up in a confined space.

After twenty miles or so, when Elizabeth was certain we weren't being followed, we went to the very top of a multi-story car park in East Croydon, opened the boot, unzipped the bag and let Viktor out. I promise you this is true: he was fast asleep, and we had to slap him awake. I said I wouldn't mind one of his sleeping pills, but he said they're too strong for me. You have to get them from America.

So here we are. Viktor couldn't stay with Elizabeth, so he will be in my spare room for as long as he is dead. The plan is to find out who this Viking is, and then find out where he is. After that I suppose the plan is to kill him, I don't know. I don't think we can keep Viktor dead forever.

I have questions about the Viking, and about Viktor, but tomorrow is Thursday, so they can wait until the whole gang is here.

Where does this leave us with the Bethany Waites investigation? It feels like it might be a distraction, but Elizabeth says it's actually enormous luck, as Viktor can help us while he's here.

Alan usually pops in to see me while I'm writing, but he is conspicuous by his absence, now there's a new, interesting Ukrainian man in the flat. How fickle he is. I will go and shake a packet of biscuits in a bit, and then we'll see who's boss.

I can hear from the other room that the train program has finished and Viktor is on his feet. It sounds like he is doing his own washing-up, which bodes well.

I know I was a stooge today, and I know it was important, but I'm not entirely at ease. Something isn't sitting right. There was the shock, of course, that can knock you sideways, but also something else, which I've been trying to put my finger on all afternoon. I think it's this.

You see, when Elizabeth pulled that trigger, I really *did* believe it. I really did believe she was murdering Viktor. That my best friend was capable of murdering a man she has known for many years, just to save her skin.

In fact, I didn't just believe it, I *knew* it.

So what does that say about Elizabeth? And what does it say about me?

39.

The Thursday Murder Club likes to meet at eleven a.m. in the Jigsaw Room. That is how things should be. It moves around from time to time, Ibrahim understands that, of course he does. There have been murders to deal with, and let no one say he is not flexible.

But, really, calling a meeting of the Thursday Murder Club at eight a.m. *at Joyce's flat*? When they have an active murder investigation ongoing? Words will have to be had.

He calls for Ron on the way, and he tells Ron that this is very much the thin end of the wedge. Ron agrees, or at least doesn't seem to strongly disagree, and so Ibrahim feels emboldened.

A schedule is a schedule is a schedule. A laminated schedule even more so. Again, Ron raises no objection to this point. In fact, Ron is unusually quiet all round.

"Do you smell of cannabis, Ron?" asks Ibrahim.

"I might do," concedes Ron.

"I'm of half a mind to declare this meeting unofficial, you know? Unless I'm given a good reason."

"Well within your rights, old son," says Ron. "You give 'em hell."

"Thanks, Ron, I will," says Ibrahim. "Why do you smell of cannabis all the time now?"

"Pauline," says Ron.

"Oh, I see," says Ibrahim. "That covers it."

"It's a lot stronger than I'm used to," says Ron. "I keep falling asleep on her bathroom floor."

Ibrahim presses the buzzer to Joyce's building, and the friends are let in.

"Lift or stairs?" asks Ibrahim.

"Lift? Why not?" says Ron. Ibrahim has noticed that he is trying to hide a limp. Still not using his stick.

They exit the lift, knock on the first door on the right, and Joyce lets them in. She gives them both a hug in turn.

"Ooh, Ron, are you wearing perfume?" asks Joyce. "It reminds me of something Joanna used to wear."

Ron grunts, and takes off his coat. Alan has approached him with interest, and starts to lick his hand with professional thoroughness. Ibrahim spots Elizabeth seated in the living room.

"Now, forgive me, but I must speak—"

"Must you?" asks Elizabeth.

"I must. Good morning, Elizabeth. And a very early morning, if I might be allowed the observation."

"And to you," replies Elizabeth, motioning for him to continue.

"We are the Thursday Murder Club, that is not news to anybody. We meet at eleven a.m. each Thursday in the Jigsaw Room. Let me take those three data points one by one—"

"Cup of tea?" asks Joyce.

"Thank you, Joyce, yes," says Ibrahim. "Point one, we meet on Thursdays. On this point I am satisfied, it is indeed Thursday, we need discuss this no further—"

"Ron, you absolutely reek of very high-grade skunk," says Elizabeth.

"It stays in the hair," says Ron.

"Point two, we meet at eleven a.m., and here, you see, our paths diverge, as it is eight a.m. Is there a reason, is there an explanation? None has been forthcoming."

"How is Pauline?" calls Joyce from the kitchen as she fills the kettle.

Ron grunts a non-committal reply.

"And from there onto point three," continues Ibrahim. "We meet in the Jigsaw Room, and, without putting the point too bluntly, I see no jigsaws."

"Skunk is very good for arthritis," says Elizabeth.

"I don't have arthritis," says Ron.

"And I've never seen the classified files on the assassination of JFK," says Elizabeth. "Pull the other one, Ron, it's got bells on."

"So before we go any further," continues Ibrahim, "I want to know if there is a good reason—and my definition of 'good' will be strict—as to why we are meeting here and now. Because it plays havoc with my spreadsheet."

Alan lollops into the room from the hallway, tail wagging, and makes an immediate beeline for Ibrahim. He starts tugging at Ibrahim's sleeve.

"Here is another man who is confused," says Ibrahim, now ruffling Alan's head. "Another man who understands the importance of consistency. A man who knows it is walk time, not meeting time."

Alan lies on the floor and exposes his belly for Ibrahim to tickle. Joyce puts his cup of tea on a side table.

"Thank you, Joyce. And so my point is this. I was expecting to meet at eleven a.m. to talk through the latest developments in the Bethany Waites case. To discuss, perhaps, the note left by Heather Garbutt. To hear from Ron about Jack Mason. I even have some exciting news for you from my source at Darwell Prison. Joyce, is Alan's collar a little tight?"

"No," says Joyce. "Unless you know better than the Supervet."

"So, unless something fairly spectacular has happened in the last twenty-four hours, and I think I might have spotted that, I see no reason why we can't move the meeting back to its regular time, and its regular place."

"You would spot it?" says Elizabeth. "If something had happened?"

"I am observant, yes," says Ibrahim. "Now, I want to show you something . . ."

"How many pairs of shoes were there in the hall?"

"I am not observant of shoes," says Ibrahim. "I am not perfect, Elizabeth."

"Why are we meeting at eight a.m.?" asks Elizabeth. "And why are we meeting at Joyce's? You want a good reason?"

"Were there four pairs?" asks Ibrahim. "That's my first guess."

"A number of days ago," starts Elizabeth, "while you were fluttering your eyelashes at Connie Johnson, and Ron was, I don't know, being seduced perhaps . . ."

Ron raises his cup of tea in a toast to that. "I've played a bit of snooker as well though."

". . . I was kidnapped, alongside Stephen, and driven to, of all places, Staffordshire. Not now, Alan, I'm talking. After regaining consciousness I met a very large gentleman we are calling the Viking, real identity as yet unknown, but we are working on it. He had a proposition for me. I was to kill a man named Viktor Illyich, a former KGB colonel. And, if I failed to kill him, or I chose not to, I would be killed."

"OK," says Ibrahim. "But even so."

"I haven't finished, dear. Yesterday morning, Joyce and I traveled up to London to visit Viktor Illyich."

"Wait till you hear about the swimming pool," says Joyce, Alan curled uncomfortably on her lap now, his eyes darting around, thrilled by all this unexpected company.

"Quite so," says Elizabeth. "We entered the penthouse apartment of Mr. Illyich, whereupon I proceeded to pretend to shoot him dead in one of his many bathrooms."

"I didn't know it was pretend at this point," says Joyce.

"Bogdan then kindly made his way up to London, and we stuffed Viktor Illyich into a holdall and he drove us all back here."

"Good lad, Bogdan," says Ron.

"As far as we are aware, the Viking believes that Viktor is dead, so we are out of immediate danger, but that situation will not last for long, and we need to find, and neutralize, the Viking, before he realizes what we've done. So we are meeting at eight a.m., because we don't have a second to spare, and we are meeting at Joyce's flat, because she is hiding a former KGB colonel and criminal kingpin in her spare room. He also has a great deal of experience in money-laundering and interrogation, so I will set him straight to work on the deaths of Bethany Waites and Heather Garbutt. Is that an explanation you find acceptable, Ibrahim?"

Ibrahim nods. "I knew it would be something like that, yes. Given the circumstances, I waive my objections."

"That is good of you, thank you," says Elizabeth.

Ibrahim looks up, and in the doorway sees Viktor Illyich with a cup of tea and some toast. Viktor gives him a huge smile.

"Everybody is here! The whole gang, now. Alan, you are too big for Joyce's lap, I think!"

"Viktor, I am Ibrahim."

"I have been told you were handsome," says Viktor. "But I didn't expect you to be this handsome."

Ibrahim nods. "Yes, it takes people by surprise sometimes. What is it like to be dead? Is it freeing?"

"Yes. This is my first slice of toast as a dead man, and it is delicious," says Viktor.

"It's Waitrose multi-seeded," says Joyce. "It's in the freezer for special occasions, so don't get used to it."

"I should get shot more often," says Viktor. "Maybe in heaven Joyce makes the breakfast?"

"I don't think either of us will be going to heaven to find out, Viktor," says Elizabeth.

"Maybe in hell, Ron makes you breakfast?" says Ibrahim, and everyone laughs, except Ron.

"Hello, I'm Ron," says Ron.

"A man with the heart of a lion," says Viktor.

"If you say so," says Ron.

"Ron is harder to compliment than Ibrahim," Elizabeth tells Viktor.

When Elizabeth first met Viktor, which would have been sometime around 1982, and somewhere around Gdańsk, he already had a fearsome reputation. A reputation for intelligence, rather than for violence, which marked him out as someone to worry about. He had risen from the ranks of the Leningrad KGB at that point, and was running agents in Scandinavia. He would later rise and rise until he was at the very top table of the KGB. Which was no mean feat. He had eventually fallen out of love with the whole system, however, and gone freelance. Which explained why he owned a penthouse.

They had met in a bar by the port to exchange prisoners without rigmarole, and, several bottles of vodka later, their friendship had been established. Eventually they were as close friends as sworn enemies could possibly be. Elizabeth had never imagined she would end up faking Viktor's death in a London penthouse, but neither had Elizabeth imagined having a best friend who didn't listen to Radio 4. Sometimes you simply have to swim with the tide.

"I think I should like to ask, if I may have the floor," says Ibrahim, "why did Elizabeth have to kill you? Not now, Alan."

"The criminal underworld is all linked," says Viktor. "The Colombians, the Albanians, the New York mob. They all do different things, they all fight, but sometimes they need each other. Sometimes they need someone to bring them together. Someone they trust with their money when it moves through the system. And that's me. I make sure everyone plays nice, everyone makes money, and I make sure people don't kill each other."

"But they do kill each other, old son," says Ron.

"I know," says Viktor. "But not as much as they would. I do what I can. Now, in every country I have men like Martin Lomax who work for me."

Elizabeth thinks back to Martin Lomax. That beautiful house they went to visit.

"So, you see, you killed one of my guys," says Viktor.

"Sorry, Viktor," says Joyce.

"You probably had your reasons," says Viktor.

"We did," says Elizabeth.

"What happened to his diamonds?" asks Viktor.

"Long story," says Elizabeth.

"So who is the Viking?" asks Ron. "Why does he want to kill you?"

"The new generation of criminals are different. And they like to launder their money in a new way. No gold, no diamonds, no bureaux de change or car factories, which is how I launder money."

Alan sneezes.

"Bless you, Alan," says Viktor. "The new generation clean all their money through cryptocurrency."

"Ah, like Bitcoin," says Joyce, nodding.

"Yes, like Bitcoin," says Viktor.

"And like Dogecoin and Ethereum," adds Joyce, taking a sip of her tea. "And Binance Coin, which is rocketing up this morning."

Elizabeth looks at her friend. They will have a conversation about this later.

"And cryptocurrency is the Viking's business? That's the story here?"

Viktor nods. "But I tell people to steer clear of cryptocurrency. It's too risky. I'm just doing my job, nothing personal. So I cost him a lot of money, and he would make a great deal more if I died. Of course, he could just wait a few years until everyone trusts cryptocurrency—"

"Why wouldn't you trust cryptocurrency?" asks Joyce.

"But I guess he wants me out of the way now. I get it, he's young. He's impatient."

"I'm not reading anything that suggests that cryptocurrency is going to collapse," says Joyce. "Quite the opposite."

"So we have to get to the big lad before he works out you're still alive," says Ron.

"Yes, or he will kill me," says Viktor. "And, if I understand correctly, he will also kill Elizabeth."

Elizabeth nods. And he will kill Joyce. Joyce, who is currently trying to hide the fact that she is secretly feeding a piece of croissant to an adoring Alan.

"This is certainly one of the most unusual meetings of the Thursday Murder Club," says Ibrahim. "Am I to assume that I shouldn't be writing up the minutes of today's meeting?"

"I think that might be for the best," says Elizabeth.

"What is the Thursday Murder Club?" asks Viktor. "I like the sound of it."

"We meet up every Thursday," says Ibrahim. "Usually at eleven in the Jigsaw Room, but you are forgiven on this occasion. And we try to solve murders. Though today seems to be about committing murders, so the remit is elastic."

"What are you working on now?" asks Viktor.

"We were supposed to be talking about a news reporter called Bethany Waites. She was murdered in 2013."

"I wondered, Ron," says Elizabeth, "if it might be fun to take Viktor with you the next time you see Jack Mason? See if Jack might open up?"

"He won't open up," says Ron. "We've got everything we're going to get from him."

"Well, who knows," says Elizabeth. "And, Viktor, I also have a pile of paperwork for you to look through. Might as well set you to work while you're here."

"I am at your service," says Viktor.

"But first things first," says Elizabeth. "I need to send a photograph of your dead body to the Viking, to prove I've killed you."

"Excellent," says Viktor. "Let us dig a shallow grave and throw me in it."

"And for a final touch," says Elizabeth, turning to Ron, "I wonder if anybody knows a makeup artist who might be able to help us out? I don't suppose you're seeing Pauline today?"

"Umm . . . yeah," says Ron, but without conviction. "Probably going tenpin bowling. Should probably head off actually."

Elizabeth nods, and wonders where Ron is really going.

40.

Ron wishes he was tenpin bowling. Wishes he was anywhere but here.

Pauline has persuaded Ron that he might like to have a massage.

The air is scented with eucalyptus, heavy and warm, and it thrums and trills with the sounds of the rainforests. He is wrapped, fairly insecurely, in a thick white towel, as he treads, barefoot, across Moroccan floor tiles, beside an azure pool, and he is deeply anxious about how relaxed he is supposed to be feeling. To think he could be interviewing Jack Mason about the murder, rather than going through this ordeal.

Pauline had asked him if he liked massages, and Ron had told her he had never had one, and Pauline had laughed, and Ron had told her, no, he was serious, what would he want a massage for, and she said to treat yourself, and then Ron laughed and said if he was going to treat himself he'd have a pint, and Pauline said, I'm taking you to a spa, and Ron said not on your nelly, not in a million years, and then Pauline kissed him and said just try it once for me and he said no, and then she kissed him again, and now here they are.

Susie is the name of the woman. She came to meet Ron and Pauline at the front desk of Elm Grove Spa and Sanctuary, and seems to be their gentle guide through this awful process.

Apparently aromatic herbal scrubs and Turkish cleansing rituals were real things that real people paid real money for. Every time Ron has walked past this spa before, he had just assumed it was a brothel. Neither spas nor brothels were of any interest to Ron. If someone wants to touch you, they had better be your doctor or your wife, or, at a push, a stranger next to you in the pub when England score.

Pauline holds his hand and tells him he can relax, and that there is nothing to be worried about. Nothing to worry about? What if his towel slips? What if he's too heavy for the massage table? What if the masseur is a woman? What then? Or, even worse, what if the masseur is a man? What will they make of his naked body? Do you keep the towel on? Do you have to turn over? Ron has seen himself in the mirror, and wouldn't wish that on anyone. Will he have to make conversation? What do masseurs talk about? Can you talk about football, or is it all essential oils and wind chimes? As he feels the seaweed-and-burned-umber face mask melt into his skin, Ron prays for his torture to end. Are the gentle sounds of the rainforest ever going to stop?

Ron reassures Pauline that he is relaxed, and that worries are the furthest thing from his mind. He can't wait. Pauline laughs and tells him he will enjoy it when it gets going, and Ron tells her that he is sure he will. Susie pours them both a glass of "deoxidizing watermelon juice" and bids them sit on an avalanche of cushions that Ron very much doubts he will ever be able to get up from.

"So you're booked in for the forty-five-minute couples' massage, in the Java Suite. Ricardo and Anton will be your masseurs."

Blokes, OK. Maybe that's for the best. They'll get that this whole thing is weird, surely?

"We'll start with the full body, then a gentle facial, and then a couples' steam bath to finish."

She is talking so quietly and calmly, it makes Ron want to fling himself out of a window. Except there are no windows. The walls are hung with ornate Persian throws, and mirrors reflecting the soft, warm light of the scented candles. There is no escape. He is going to have to be touched, and make conversation. He is going to have to relax, God help him.

Ron was once locked in the back of a police van with Arthur Scargill for eight hours, and that was more relaxing than this.

He takes a sip of his watermelon juice. It's actually not bad.

Over protests that he is quite capable of getting up by himself, Pauline helps Ron up from the sofa. Susie leads them through to the Java Suite. Two massage tables sit side by side, but no sign of Ricardo and Anton yet.

Good news, the sounds of the rainforest have stopped. Bad news, they have been replaced by the sound of whale song.

"If you lie face down on the beds, Anton and Ricardo will be with you presently. Namaste to you both."

"Namaste," says Pauline.

"Thank you," grunts Ron, as he plants his face through the hole in the massage table and grimly hopes for the best.

"You all right there, lover?" asks Pauline, as Susie leaves them alone.

"Yeah," says Ron. "I liked the watermelon juice."

"Anything you need?"

"Nah, nothing," says Ron. "Except, are we supposed to talk to them? The massagers?"

"Can if you want," says Pauline. "I usually just fall asleep. Land of nod, dream of horses."

"OK," says Ron. One thing he knows he won't be doing is falling asleep. Absolute vigilance will be the key here.

"Or just let your thoughts wander," says Pauline.

Let his thoughts wander? Wander where? Ron's thoughts don't do wandering. Whenever Ron is forced into actually doing some thinking, it's for a good reason. For example, what were the Tories up to today? Where did West Ham need to strengthen during the January transfer window? Why had they stopped doing omelets at the restaurant? He loves omelets. Was there an egg shortage he hadn't heard about, or was somebody taking a liberty? Important stuff. And when his mind wasn't thinking about important things, it was doing nothing. Recharging, for the next issue that needed his attention. Wandering was never on the agenda.

He looks over at Pauline, her eyes already shut. "You ever heard of a Carron Whitehead? Or a Robert Brown?"

"Just relax, Ronnie," she says, eyes still closed.

He senses Anton and Ricardo glide into the room. He is thankful that the towel is around his waist. God knows what his backside looks like these days. A moon landscape. He hopes these lads are well paid. Do they have a union? He waits for a greeting, but it doesn't come, just the feel of two warm, oiled hands on his shoulders. OK, it seems the forty-five minutes are starting right now. The hands draw long, deep strokes down his back. Ron reminds himself that, at some point, the agony will end.

Ricardo, or Anton, gets to work on Ron's neck and shoulders. Ron cannot avoid the fact that this is actually happening. Outside there will be cars and shops and dogs barking and mums shouting at kids. But in here, just the terrible whale sounds. Maybe he should think about the Bethany Waites case? Perhaps that could use up some time? He hears Pauline sigh in deep satisfaction. That, at least, makes him happy.

A hand is now drawing its way down his spine. Ricardo or Anton seems to be going about his business, and not, Ron will admit, without skill. Fair play. Perhaps they've seen worse than Ron in their time? The whales continue to sing, and, actually, when you get used to it, it's not so bad. He read once that whales were lonely.

He'll have a little think about Jack Mason, maybe. He likes him. Jack was always up to something, buying things, selling things, setting light to things. Now here he is, years later, legitimate business, lovely big house, lorries going here, there and everywhere. Still up to something? Of course, of course. How does he *know* Bethany is dead?

Two hands start to pummel Ron's thigh now. He'll go and see Jack again, that's what he'll do, take the KGB fella, talk about old times, buying and selling, all of them youngsters. Big house he has, Lenny. No, that's the brother, fell through a warehouse roof and died. Years ago. When you think about it, have West Ham ever had a better captain than Mark Noble? When you *really* think about it? Billy Bonds, yeah, Bobby Moore, course, but Noble's in with a shout. He'll ask Jack, Jack'll know.

Ron's swimming with the whales now, keeping them company, we all get lonely, son, everything's gonna be all right, floating on the warm currents. Pulled by the tides like Bethany Waites. Poor Bethany. Who killed her, all those years ago? Jack Mason knows all right. Jack Mason. Ron knew his brother . . . what was his name?

"Ronnie." It's his mum waking him for school. Just a couple more minutes, Mum. I won't miss the bus, I promise.

Ron feels so warm, cocooned. Maybe Jack Mason killed Bethany Waites himself? Ron doesn't buy it though. Was it really the story that got Bethany Waites killed, or something else? Something occurs to Ron in that moment, something he's missed . . . Robert Brown? He knows that name.

"It's me, Ronnie." A hand is stroking his hair, and Ronnie opens his eyes. Has he died? He's fairly sure he's died. Had to come sooner or later. Good knock.

"You were sleeping," says Pauline. "I told them not to do your front, you looked so peaceful."

"Just resting my eyes," says Ron, his body singing a new tune. What's that feeling? There's something familiar in it, from the old days. Ron tries to pinpoint it.

"For forty-five minutes, I know, lover," says Pauline. "Snoring like a little piglet. Now, shall we go to the steam room?"

Ron turns his head, and sees Pauline's smile. He has to catch a breath. You only get sent so many of those smiles in a lifetime. Ron reaches out a hand, and Pauline takes it. Ron realizes what the feeling is. He is not in pain. Not a single bit of his battered old body is nagging at him.

"Thanks for persuading me to come," says Ron.

"Told you you'd like it," says Pauline. "Maybe we can do it again?"

"Never," says Ron, shaking his head. A man has his limits.

"Let's see if you're still saying that after the steam room," says Pauline.

Ron levers himself off the massage table. What had he been thinking about just before he woke up? He tries to get hold of it, but it's not there.

No matter. If it's important it'll come back to him.

41.

But how do you murder someone in a prison?" asks Mike Waghorn.

Andrew Everton has done what he promised and made a few inquiries about Heather Garbutt. They are on the pier in Fairhaven, cups of tea in hand. Mike nods "hello" to a few excited passers-by.

"Easier than you'd think," says Andrew Everton, trying to blow through the tiny hole in the lid of his cup. "Though I've got the Home Office asking me the same questions now."

"There was no CCTV? Someone going into her cell?" Mike is opening a skate park at eleven a.m., and Andrew Everton agreed to meet him beforehand. Mike is aware that not everybody has the Chief Constable at their beck and call. Perks of the job.

"CCTV everywhere," says Andrew Everton. "But the one we need has mysteriously gone 'missing.' Two hours of Heather Garbutt's landing just erased."

"Jesus," says Mike. "That sort of thing common?"

"Used to be more common," says Andrew Everton. "But it still happens. A few quid in someone's pocket to erase the data."

"But that suggests definitely murder," says Mike. "That and the note she wrote?"

"You'd think so," agrees Andrew Everton.

"It must be connected to Bethany," says Mike, waving to a woman on a mobility scooter. "Has to be, doesn't it? Heather Garbutt's about to get out of prison, she fears for her life, and then she's dead?"

"Honestly," says Andrew Everton, "in prison, you never know. It's its own world. But, put me on the spot and I'd say yes, it has to be connected. That's not my official line, that's as a friend."

"Appreciate it, Andrew," says Mike. "So catch whoever killed Heather Garbutt and maybe we catch whoever killed Bethany?"

"Maybe," says Andrew Everton. He watches a young man in a tracksuit idle his way along the pier, hands in deep pockets. Where's he off to this early in the morning? What's in those pockets of his? The end of the pier is a good place for a private meeting. Who's this lad meeting? Andrew misses being out on the streets sometimes, back in the thick of things, trusting his instincts. He likes being a politician, but he misses being a detective.

"So who could get access to her cell?" Mike asks.

"Warders," says Andrew Everton. "We're looking into them. Other prisoners, if they're trusted."

"Another prisoner could have murdered her?"

"Lot of murderers in prison," says Andrew Everton.

"But to disable the CCTV as well? Surely a prisoner couldn't do that?"

"Some prisoners are better connected than others," says Andrew Everton.

"So another prisoner could just walk into her cell, pick up the knitting needles, and—"

"Do you mind?" asks a man in decorators' overalls, holding out a phone. "I wouldn't normally, but my mum's such a fan."

Mike nods, then smiles for a selfie with the man.

"I'll keep at it, Mike," says Andrew Everton. "I promise."

The man in the overalls walks on toward the café. He stops to put a tin down by some ornate ironwork covered in peeling paint, begins scraping it away and rubbing it down. The boy in the tracksuit joins him, takes a brush from his deep pockets and starts painting. Andrew smiles to himself. Can't win 'em all. Talking of which.

"I might . . ." Andrew Everton hesitates. "I might need a favor too, Mike, only if you can."

"Name it," says Mike.

"I don't really know very much about television, but it's just, I don't suppose you know anyone at Netflix? I keep sending them my books, but they haven't got back to me."

42.

Throw a bit more earth over me," says Viktor to Bogdan. "Just for warmth."

Viktor, being a professional to his bones, has insisted on being buried naked. He knows that any self-respecting murderer would leave as few clues in the grave as possible. If they are to raise no suspicions with the Viking, then it is the right thing to do. He had waited until the last possible moment, of course, nicely wrapped up as he watched Bogdan dig the grave. Viktor has seen many people dig many graves over the years, but few with the speed and efficiency of Bogdan. When this is all over, he wonders if Bogdan might like a job.

"I could pour you a cup of tea," says Joyce, looking down on him over the lip of the grave, flask in hand. "But I'm not sure how you'd drink it down there."

"It is a kind offer, Joyce," says Viktor, as another clod of earth from Bogdan's spade lands on his chest. "Perhaps later."

"Hold still," says Pauline, kneeling beside him with a brush, and a palette of red-and-black goop. She has been carefully painting a bullet hole on his forehead for five minutes or so.

"Sorry to make you work on a naked man in a freezing hole," says Viktor.

Pauline shrugs. "I work in television, darling."

"You smell lovely though," says Viktor. "Eucalyptus."

Pauline had originally painted on the bullet wound in the comfort of Joyce's flat. The situation had been explained to her, by Ron, and she had taken it in her stride. She had asked if what they were doing was illegal, and Elizabeth had said "define illegal," and that had been good enough for Pauline. She had also caked his face in powder, making him paler and paler, thinner and thinner, until they all agreed they were staring into the eyes of a ghost. They had then bundled Viktor back into his familiar holdall, and Bogdan had carried him out to a quad bike and driven him up to the woods. The others had followed, at a discreet distance, in the event that the Viking was somehow watching.

"And we're done," says Pauline, with a final flourish. She gives Viktor a last once-over, looking from every angle. "You look terrible."

It was Joyce who had spotted the original mistake. Pauline had first painted an entry wound on Viktor's forehead. The recording heard by the Viking would leave him in no doubt that Elizabeth had shot Viktor from behind. Which is why Pauline was now kneeling beside him in a grave, turning an entry wound into an exit wound. If Pauline had been surprised at how accurately both Viktor and Elizabeth could describe the exit wound of a bullet, it didn't show in her face.

Ron and Bogdan help Pauline out of the hole. Mainly Bogdan, Viktor notices, but done in such a way as to make it look like Ron is doing most of the work. Viktor sees the faces peering down at him.

Bogdan is now throwing down more earth onto Viktor's body. The idea is to give him a "just-dug-up" look. Ibrahim has his phone out, and now trains it on Viktor at the bottom of the hole. "Landscape or portrait?"

"Landscape," says Viktor. "Is grittier."

"Portrait," says Elizabeth. "I'm taking the photo, and I prefer portrait."

"You are insufferable, Elizabeth," shouts Viktor from the bottom of the hole.

Ibrahim has another question. "Close-up of the face, or the whole body?"

"Both," says Elizabeth. "But not too close to the face, just in case."

"Just in case what?" says Pauline. "You zoom in all you like, Ibrahim, that's good work."

"Yeah, zoom in," says Ron, and squeezes Pauline's hand.

"Of course we will need to talk about filters," says Ibrahim. "Personally I think Clarendon would be perfect, because of the earthy browns."

"If it is not too much bother," says Viktor. "Perhaps we discuss this after?"

Ibrahim nods. "Hypothermia, I understand completely. I also want to speak to you about Heather Garbutt's poem, but that can also wait until you are clothed."

Viktor looks up at the faces peering down. Elizabeth, his great love, how happy he is to spend a little more time with her. People drift in and out of your life, and, when you are younger, you know you will see them again. But now every old friend is a miracle.

Ron and Pauline. They are holding hands now. Viktor remembers Ron's name from many years ago. He was on a list. It was a long list, but he was on it. Someone, at some point, would have spoken to him, "sounded him out," seen if he was sympathetic with the Soviet way. Meeting him now, Viktor wouldn't fancy their chances. Bogdan, leaning on his spade, waiting patiently to fill the hole back in. Ibrahim, trying to find the perfect angle. Joyce, his flat-mate, his new protector, currently trying to stop Alan from jumping into the hole.

Looking up, Viktor realizes just how lonely his penthouse is. How lonely his life has become. Young, beautiful people taking photos in a pool that everyone could see, but no one could visit. Where were his friends?

Perhaps he could just stay here? Perhaps this photo will be enough to satisfy the Viking, and Viktor can just change his name, leave his old world behind and move down to Coopers Chase? Nothing like lying in your grave with a bullet hole through your head to make you think about your life.

Did he really need multibillion-pound deals, when there was Joyce and Elizabeth and Alan, and a whole gang to be a part of? Perhaps they will solve this murder? Perhaps he can walk Alan through the woods? And Ron had mentioned snooker. Viktor had no one to play snooker with anymore. He used to play with an old Kazakh who had a jeweler's in Sydenham, but he had died, what, three years ago. He looks up at the faces above him once more. Maybe he just got lucky.

"For God's sake, Viktor," says Elizabeth. "Stop smiling and shut your eyes. You're dead."

I think I was dead, yes, I think I was. Viktor shuts his eyes and, with some difficulty, stops smiling.

43.

The others are warming up somewhere, with cups of tea and blankets and gossip. But Ibrahim has work to do.

He has Heather Garbutt's poem spread out in front of him. There is a secret in these pages, no doubt about that. A hidden message, artfully concealed. Who was Heather Garbutt afraid of? Who was going to kill her?

Deciphering Heather Garbutt's poem and discovering that secret will take some time, Ibrahim is sure of that. He had wanted to talk the whole thing through with somebody, but Elizabeth, Joyce and Ron are not biting. They see it as a red herring.

He even tried Viktor, after they had dug him up again. You don't get that senior in the KGB without knowing a few things about cryptography. But Viktor had taken a look, with dirt-stained fingers, then handed it back, saying, "No message here. Just a poem."

As so often, Ibrahim's is a lone voice in the wilderness. So be it, that is his cross to bear. The prophet is often unheralded in his own land. There will be apologies aplenty when he uncovers Heather's message. He will nod, magnanimously, head bowed a little perhaps, as the plaudits rain down on him. He imagines the scene: Elizabeth is congratulating him ("I was quite wrong, quite wrong"), Joyce is handing him a plate of biscuits, while Alan sits in quiet, proud respect. Even Viktor will have to admit that Ibrahim has bested him.

He is lost in this reverie for a moment, and then the thought strikes him. Ibrahim knows exactly whom he should talk to. Someone who never judges him, someone who is always full of ideas. Someone who will *help*.

He looks at his watch. It is four thirty, which means that Ron's grandson, Kendrick, will be out of school, but won't yet be having his tea. The golden hour for any eight-year-old boy.

Ibrahim FaceTimes Kendrick. He is remembering the happy time the two of them spent together, spooling through hours of CCTV, looking for a diamond thief and a murderer.

"Uncle Ibrahim!" says Kendrick, and bounces on his chair.

"Are you quite well?" asks Ibrahim.

"I am quite well, yes," confirms Kendrick.

Ibrahim outlines the task at hand. That there had been a murder a few years before Kendrick was born ("Not *another* one, Uncle Ibrahim") and more recently another murder in prison ("Millie Parker's mum is in prison, she was off school"). The lady in the prison, Heather Garbutt, not Millie Parker's mum, had left a poem, which Ibrahim believes to be in code (a low, impressed whistle at this) and if Kendrick and he could decipher the code, they might find out just who had murdered her, and the whereabouts of a great deal of money stolen in a VAT fraud (a brief sidebar here, as Ibrahim explains VAT, having to start Kendrick off with the basic principles of universal taxation). They are now hard at it. Ibrahim has a brandy and a cigar; Kendrick has an orange squash ("It's less sugar, but you don't even know when you drink it").

Ibrahim reads:

My heart needs to reel like the eagles at wing
It wants to be heard, like the blackbirds that sing
But my heart she is broke, cleft in two 'round the wheel
The eagle can't fly, still my heart needs to reel.

"Well, you see why this is interesting, Kendrick. Terrifically bad, technically, but interesting. Her heart wishes to reel like an eagle, she says"—Ibrahim has sent Kendrick a copy of the text, and is reading from his own copy—"but two lines later that heart is 'cleft in two 'round the wheel.'"

"There are golden eagles and bald eagles, and black eagles," says Kendrick. "They eat mice. Do you know any other kinds of eagle? I don't know any more."

"A goshawk is a type of eagle," says Ibrahim, and Kendrick writes this down.

"Now I know four eagles," says Kendrick.

"If you break a heart around a wheel," says Ibrahim, "and I'm just thinking out loud here, Kendrick, are we to take it that Heather Garbutt wants us to take an anagram of the word 'heart' and combine it with another word for 'wheel'?"

"Maybe," says Kendrick. "Maybe she might do."

"Or," says Ibrahim, "if it is 'cleft in two,' perhaps she wants us to place a word for 'wheel' within the two broken parts of 'heart.'"

"Perhaps." Kendrick nods. "She has messy handwriting, doesn't she? I have good handwriting, but only if I concentrate."

"We need another word for 'wheel,'" says Ibrahim. "As a noun we have 'disk,' 'hoop,' at a push, 'circle.' As a verb—"

"A verb is a doing word," says Kendrick.

"Quite so," agrees Ibrahim. "Which would give us 'rotate,' 'revolve' and, again, 'circle,' such are the joys of the English language."

"What's a hundred, times a hundred, times a hundred?" asks Kendrick.

"A million," says Ibrahim, with a puff on his cigar. "Let's say that an anagram of 'heart' is 'Ath er . . .' and we add a word for 'wheel,' I wonder would 'hoop' work here? We fold 'Ath er' around 'hoop' and we come up with the name 'Ath Hooper.' Not a name, Kendrick. And the word 'around' can often signify the letter *c* in a cryptic crossword, from the Latin *circa*."

"The gladiators spoke in Latin," says Kendrick. "And Julius Caesar."

"So we add the *c* to the front of our answer. I wonder if you might search the name 'Cath Hooper' for me, and report back on anyone from either the Kent and Sussex area, or anyone with links to organized crime."

Kendrick busies himself for a moment. "There're about a thousand."

"Hmm—give me the top two," says Ibrahim.

"OK," says Kendrick. "One is in Australia, and one is dead."

"Hmm," says Ibrahim again. "The dead one. Did she die recently? Was she murdered?"

Kendrick scrolls down his page. "She died in 1871. In Aberdeen. Where's Aberdeen?"

"Scotland," says Ibrahim.

"Maybe that's a clue?"

Ibrahim continues to read the poem, with the awful realization that perhaps it is just a poem. Then he sees it.

"Did she write anything else?" asks Kendrick. "Because this seems quite a hard one."

"She wrote a note, before she died," says Ibrahim, still looking over his new clue, testing it for strength.

"A note?"

"A note, yes," says Ibrahim. "Foretelling her death. But I don't think your grandad would want me to show you it."

"Pleeeeease," says Kendrick. "I won't tell Grandad."

"I don't suppose it will do any harm," says Ibrahim. It'll keep Kendrick occupied for a few moments while he cracks the code. He finds Chris's original email and sends over the image of Heather Garbutt's note. He then returns to the matter at hand, and begins to read out loud from the poem again.

I recall, as a child, in the brook where we played
When our secrets were kept, and our promises made
Where the sun never ceased, and the rain never fell
In the brook where we played, I remember it well.

"'Where our secrets were kept,' well, that's worth investigating. Repeat of 'brook,' that suggests 'Brooks,' of course. And 'Where the sun never ceased,' could that suggest the word 'sun' without the *n*? So 'Su.'" Were they looking for someone called Su Brooks?

"Kendrick, Google Su Broo—"

"You played a trick on me, Uncle Ibrahim," says Kendrick.

"A trick?" says Ibrahim. Su Brooks. Su Brooks. Was she one of Heather's fellow accountants perhaps? A pseudonym?

Kendrick looks up from the note. "Well, the handwriting is different, isn't it? On the poem and on the note. The poem is so messy, and the note is so neat. So the note and the poem were written by different people."

Ibrahim looks back and forth between the note and the poem. Yes. Well. It couldn't have been much more obvious. Ibrahim was the only person who had seen both the note and the poem. But Ibrahim had seen things that were not there, instead of seeing what was right in front of him.

There was no secret message, there was just a lonely poem written by a woman who had given up hope. And a note, warning of death, appealing to Connie Johnson. Written by someone else entirely.

"I'm glad you picked up on that, Kendrick," says Ibrahim. "I knew you would."

"It was just a test, I know," says Kendrick. "What did you want me to Google?"

Ibrahim hears Kendrick's mum, Ron's daughter, Suzi, calling him down for his tea. Su Brooks indeed. Ibrahim recognizes, not for the first time, that he is given to over-complicating things at times.

"No need to Google anything. And maybe we keep the handwriting between ourselves for now," suggests Ibrahim.

"Great, like a secret," agrees Kendrick. "Bye, Uncle Ibrahim, I love you."

Kendrick's screen goes blank. "I love you too," says Ibrahim. Kendrick was, once again, the right man for the job. If life ever seems too complicated, if you think no one can help, sometimes the right person to turn to is an eight-year-old.

Heather Garbutt had written the poem, of that there was little doubt:

Connie had seen her write it. Which meant that Heather Garbutt had not written the note. So who had? And why?

Ibrahim will report his news to the gang immediately.

Though he might skip over a few details as to how his conclusion was reached.

44.

"You happy?" asks Mike Waghorn. "You look great."

"Happy as I'll ever be," says Donna, eyeing herself in the studio monitor. She doesn't look bad. Pauline had insisted on coming in on her day off to do Donna's makeup.

"Two minutes on this report," says the floor manager. *South East Tonight* is showing a report on a gluten-free bakery currently taking Folkestone by storm.

"I'll say, knife crime is on the up," Mike says to her. "You'll say it isn't as simple as that, Mike; I'll say come off it, don't give us that flannel; you'll say something reassuring, and then we'll play a report of some people complaining in Fairhaven. Then I'll ask if you have a message for those people, and you'll say don't have nightmares, or whatever comes to mind. You really look great, don't be nervous."

"Thank you," says Donna. Is she nervous? She doesn't feel nervous. Should she be? She looks around the small studio. The floor manager with her clipboard, the camera operator on Tinder, Carwyn, the producer, skulking, and, like a loyal hound, Chris, sitting and watching. This time he is giving her the thumbs-up. She returns it. If he is unhappy at being usurped, he is not showing it.

The floor manager has started a ten-second countdown. The camera operator reluctantly puts down her phone, mid-flirt.

"You got anywhere with the Heather Garbutt thing?" asks Mike, in a whisper this time.

"Trying," says Donna. "Not really our case, but we've got a lead we're working on." Donna has spent all morning looking through the vehicle registrations from Juniper Court.

"It's just—" says Mike.

"I know," says Donna. "I know what Bethany Waites meant to you."

"She was the real deal," says Mike. "Have you looked into—"

The floor manager cues the studio.

"Plenty of knives in a bakery, that's for sure," says Mike to camera. "And plenty of knives on the streets of Kent too. But this is less a case of 'our daily bread' and more a case of 'our daily dead.' To talk us through our area's latest worrying knife-crime statistics, I'm joined by PC Donna De Freitas from Fairhaven Police. PC De Freitas, knife crime is on the up?"

"Well, it isn't quite as simple as that," says Donna. "It's—"

"Oh, come off it," says Mike. "Either knife crime is going up or it isn't. That seems pretty simple to me, and it'll seem pretty simple to *South East Tonight* viewers."

"I wonder if you should give *South East Tonight* viewers a little more credit," says Donna, and Mike gives her a little thumbs-up out of shot. "We have targeted knife crime in the last six months, thrown an awful lot of resources at it. That means more investigating, and more reporting, and more convictions. So obviously the numbers are up. But knife crime is vanishingly rare on the streets of Fairhaven, or Maidstone or . . . Folkestone. And, by the way, next time I'm in Folkestone I'll be visiting that bakery, didn't it look delicious?"

"I'll join you, PC De Freitas, I'll join you," says Mike. "Makes you wish we had smell-o-vision."

"And call me Donna, by the way," says Donna, then looks straight into camera. "And that goes for everyone at home too. I work for you."

"First time on *South East Tonight*, Donna," says Mike, "but, I suspect, not the last. Let's see what the people of Fairhaven itself have to say about knife crime."

The report begins. Mike wags his index finger in admiration. "You're good. You're good."

"Thanks, Mike," says Donna. "It's quite fun, isn't it?"

Chris approaches, crouching over, as if he might otherwise be caught on camera.

"Wow," says Chris.

"You think?"

"I do think. The bakery thing, the look into camera. When did you plan all that?"

"I didn't plan it," says Donna. "I just felt it."

"Thirty seconds on this report," says the floor manager. "Clear the floor, please."

"You're a natural," says Chris. "Your mum just took a screenshot and sent it to me."

"People are much more impressed when you're on TV than when you're catching criminals," says Donna.

"You're good at both," says Chris.

"And we're back on in ten . . ." says the floor manager. Carwyn Price, the producer, approaches Donna.

"Brilliant, just brilliant," says Carwyn. "You and me, little drink afterward?"

"Plans, I'm afraid," says Donna. And then berates herself for how apologetic she tried to sound.

Donna gets a message on her phone. It is from Bogdan, watching her at home. She sneaks a peek as the studio count reaches five. His text is three emojis.

A star, a heart, a thumbs-up.

A heart, eh? The camera is just in time to catch Donna's beam.

45.

The photo looks good—very real. Viktor Illyich dead and buried. Well, Viktor Illyich buried, that much was for sure. The Viking is now using it as the lock screen on his phone.

Could it have been faked? Of course it could. Everything could. Scratching his beard, the Viking remembers he was once introduced to Brad Pitt at a party in Silicon Valley. Brad had refused a selfie, saying, "It's a private party, just relax," or some such Hollywood nonsense. So, when he got home, the Viking photoshopped a picture of Brad and himself, Brad laughing uproariously at a joke he was telling. It's in his kitchen now, and if anyone were ever to visit him, they wouldn't know the difference. Meeting people, not meeting people, it's all the same these days. Reality is for civilians.

As the Viking spies the building up ahead, he realizes that he has to stop being annoyed with Brad Pitt for a moment and concentrate on the matter at hand. He also feels shy, being out and about on the street. People look at him. He was born too big. He can't wait to get home again.

The killing itself? It certainly sounded real to him, as he sat listening, far away, in his library in Staffordshire. But why had Elizabeth Best thrown her phone away afterward? It could just have been admirable caution. Or Elizabeth and Viktor could be playing him. Two old spies thinking they can take a newcomer for a ride. Sometimes the Viking lacks confidence in himself. He curses his impostor syndrome.

The Viking looks up and sees the swimming pool, suspended in the sky high above him. If you fired a rocket launcher at it, the whole structure would collapse, and everyone would plunge to their deaths. Though no one is currently in it, so it would be a waste of a rocket. He thinks about firing a rocket launcher at Brad Pitt. "It's a private party, Brad. Just relax." Then, *kablammo,* maybe treat your fans with a bit of respect next time.

But, however tempting it is to kill people, it is also bad. And difficult.

Getting into the building is easy. The Viking has a client, a luxury car thief, on the twelfth floor. The client sends the Viking money, the Viking turns it into Bitcoin, or whichever crypto is riding high that week, then sends it back to the client perfectly washed. It was more complicated than that, of course it was. Otherwise everyone would do what the Viking was doing. But his genius was an algorithm that layered the transactions through the dark web, making his scheme virtually untraceable. In truth it has proved *completely* untraceable thus far. The Viking says only "virtually untraceable" because he is a Swede, and Swedes never like to show off.

His client base has grown and grown, and, with it, his personal wealth. The Viking gets a cut of every deal, and the bigger and more complicated the deal, the bigger the cut he takes. Ten years ago the Viking was working for an AI pornography start-up in Palo Alto. Today he is worth somewhere north of three billion dollars.

The Viking bypasses the twelfth floor and takes the lift up to the penthouse level, to the former home of Viktor Illyich. Anywhere you asked, Viktor was trusted, revered almost, a straight shooter in a spinning world. When he spoke, criminals listened, and when he gave advice, criminals took it.

Which is why the Viking needed him dead. Viktor always recommended laundering money the old-fashioned way. Through real estate, through casinos, through "smurfs" and "mules" and shell companies. Through gems or gold, or through good bureaux de change, which was very retro. It was all pretty safe, sure, but so time-consuming, and it cost lots of money. Rather than investing in cryptocurrency, which actually *made* you money.

Viktor is costing the Viking an awful lot of money. Sure, he's worth three billion, and that was probably enough to be getting on with, but Jeff Bezos is worth two hundred billion, and the Viking doesn't like being a hundred and ninety-seven billion poorer than anyone. Viktor knows that the Viking exists, and knows his business, but has no idea of his identity.

Viktor's immense front door was bought from, and installed by, an Israeli technology company. The lock is unbreakable, blockchain technology, graphene and Kevlar, all with a choice of veneer. Viktor has gone for Alaskan teak. The company has done very nicely indeed, servicing the security needs of international mafiosi. As the Viking knows well, as it's his company.

He lets himself in.

He's there for reassurance. Elizabeth Best had been highly motivated to kill Viktor Illyich. Threatening to kill her friend had been the masterstroke. But it is always worth checking these things. And Viktor's apartment is close to the heliport at Battersea, so it's an easy trip for the Viking. After this perhaps he will go for sushi, which is hard to come by in Staffordshire. There is a good place called Miso in Stoke, but the Viking is banned from there after he accidentally discharged a firearm in the bathroom. He is not good with guns. Shouldn't have one really.

The Viking looks around the penthouse. It is nice, sure. Perhaps lacking a feminine touch. The view is very pleasant. There's the London Eye, there's Big Ben, there's the Bank of England. You could launch a rocket attack on any of them from Viktor's balcony. Wouldn't that cause a stir? The Viking realizes he is thinking a lot about rocket attacks at the moment. Mainly because he has just bought a rocket launcher. It was an impulse buy, because, when you have as much money as he does, there are very few novelties left, and also because you can buy rocket launchers directly with Bitcoin. So far all he has done is blow up a barn.

The Viking works out the geography of the shooting, from the live audio he heard. He realizes that Elizabeth must have walked Viktor through a large open archway to his right, then down the carpeted corridor and into the shower room. He traces these steps.

No one has heard from Viktor since the shooting, which bodes well. The rumor mill is suggesting he is dead. It is causing some panic in certain circles, which is lovely to see. The Viking walks into the shower room.

It has been tidied up, of course it has, Elizabeth Best is a professional. At some point someone with a bit of authority will notice that Viktor is missing, and at that point the penthouse will be searched for clues. The Viking assumes that Elizabeth will not have left any. There will be no crimson blood spattered up the wall, no brain stuck in a plughole.

But there should be a bullet hole somewhere, maybe even the bullet.

The Viking holds out an imaginary gun, and points it at Viktor's imaginary head. He pulls the trigger, and estimates the path the bullet would have taken. It should really have passed straight through the shower screen, but it clearly hasn't. It should have lodged itself somewhere deep inside the Turkish marble wall tiles, but, again, it clearly hasn't.

The Viking knows that the bullet passed through Viktor Illyich; he has seen evidence of the exit wound. So where is it? Is Elizabeth Best taller than Viktor? Was she shooting downward? The Viking looks lower, scanning the walls. Nothing.

Was the gun angled upward? Was that how spies killed you? The Viking raises his gaze, but still there is no bullet hole. As his eyes scan the mirror on the far wall, he spots it. The hole in the ceiling. The Viking looks up, almost directly above the spot where he is standing. The spot where Elizabeth Best would have stood. A bullet hole. The bullet fired directly into the ceiling.

The Viking stares at the hole. He recognizes that it means a number of things.

It means, firstly, that Viktor Illyich is not dead. The bullet he heard was fired into the ceiling, not into Viktor Illyich. Which further means that

Elizabeth Best takes him for a fool. She has misunderstood his abilities. The Viking does not like that one bit. He sighs.

Because the most important thing it means is that he will now have to kill Viktor Illyich himself. And, of course, to punish Elizabeth, it means he will also have to kill Joyce Meadowcroft.

Which is vexing. Most vexing.

46.

Joyce

Joanna came down for lunch today with her man, the football chairman, and I, of course, have an ex-KGB colonel in my spare room. So I had some explaining to do.

I'm only glad she wasn't here the other day when Viktor was covered in mud. I know I have a power shower, but even that struggled.

I explained that Viktor was an old friend of Elizabeth's, and that he was staying, temporarily, while he was having work done on his flat. Joanna asked Viktor where his flat was, and Viktor replied that it was in Embassy Gardens, and Joanna said, is that the one with the swimming pool, and Viktor agreed that it was, and the football chairman (he is called Scott) said those places were worth millions, and Viktor agreed again, and Joanna said, so you're having a million-pound apartment done up but you're staying with my mum, and Viktor said he couldn't imagine a finer place to stay in all of England, and Joanna said, level with me, is something dodgy going on here, and we admitted that, yes, something dodgy was going on, and I showed Joanna the photo of Viktor in his grave and said we would tell her all about it at lunch. Joanna turned to Scott and said, well you can't say I didn't warn you, she didn't use to be like this. Scott asked Viktor which football team he supported and Viktor said Chelsea, so Scott said he knew people at Chelsea and could get Viktor a special hospitality box and to come and watch a game sometime, and Viktor said not to worry, he already has one.

I sent Joanna to the fridge on a pretext, and she clocked the almond milk straight away. She said I should really buy the low-sugar almond milk, but you could tell she thought it was a step in the right direction.

Alan likes Scott, by the way, which I'm taking as a good sign. Although, thus far, Alan has liked everyone.

They have just left. Scott has a Porsche; he showed it to Viktor, and Viktor nodded in that way men do. Joanna took me aside and asked me if there was anything going on between me and Viktor, and I told her there wasn't, and she gave me a look halfway between relief and disappointment. He is very lovely, Viktor, very kind, but he's not my type. Gerry was my type, Bernard was my type. Perhaps another one will be along one day. He'd better get a move on though, I'm nearly seventy-eight.

Ibrahim had us all round to his last night. He showed us Heather Garbutt's poem, the one that Connie Johnson found, and he showed us the note. The note that was not written by Heather Garbutt. So who wrote it?

I have persuaded Elizabeth to come on a little trip with me. To Elstree, where Fiona Clemence films *Stop the Clock*. You can get there on the train. Joanna knows someone who knows someone who knows someone, and I'm hoping we might get the chance to say hello. And, you know us, a chance is all we need.

By the way, I am reading *Given in Evidence*. One of the books by the Chief Constable. I only picked it up because there's a Hilary Mantel looming on my bedside table, and I didn't feel up to it yet.

It is not at all bad, he really draws you in.

Someone tries to murder the boss, Big Mick, in some gangland family in Glasgow, but the bodyguard dives in the way of the bullet. So the book is all about the gangland boss trying to work out who tried to shoot him.

It sparks this big gang war, and you can tell Andrew Everton is a policeman, because it all sounds real.

The fun thing in the end, after all this bloodshed and plenty of swearing, is we find out that the bodyguard was the intended victim after all: his girlfriend caught him cheating. So no one was trying to kill Big Mick, and all the carnage was for nothing.

I've read a lot worse, that's all I'll say. I can still see the Hilary Mantel out of the corner of my eye. I know I'll enjoy it, but I'm going to need a run-up.

Do you know another thing I thought when I was reading Andrew Everton's novel? I thought maybe I should write a book.

47.

The text comes through as Elizabeth is getting into bed. It is the Viking.

> You have made a big mistake.

Has she? Elizabeth thinks about the photo.

> The bullet. The bullet that missed.

The Viking has been into Viktor's apartment. How is that possible? He has seen the bullet hole. She has been sloppy. But, really, how on earth could he have got in?

> This is my final message. I am coming for you all.

So now they will have to find the Viking. Find him before he finds them. Stephen looks over toward her.

"Trouble?"

"Joyce can't get her thermostat to work," says Elizabeth.

"You have to reset it," says Stephen. "Losing battle otherwise, mind of its own."

What did Elizabeth know? Precious little. She has seen the Viking, of course. That is an advantage. But that he has let himself be seen suggests he is very safe and secure. He's somewhere in Staffordshire, for reasons best known to him. And in a very big house. The house has a library. That's about the extent of her knowledge. She remembers Stephen's eyes, widening as he scanned the library.

"What did you make of the Viking's library?"

"Come again?" says Stephen.

"The Viking's library? You seemed taken with it. Any reason?"

"Not getting your drift at all, dear," says Stephen. "Vikings? Libraries? You been on the gin?"

"You were looking at his books," says Elizabeth.

"You've either got the wrong stick, or the wrong end of the right one," says Stephen.

Elizabeth sits up and looks at him. "Stephen, the other night. The van, the man with the beard? You do remember?"

Stephen chuckles. "Even for you this is a strange one. What are we up to tomorrow? Thought I might pop over and see my mum. You know how she gets."

Elizabeth tries to control her breathing once more, but she is unable to. She feels like she is going to sob. Stephen puts his arm around her.

"What's got into you all of a sudden?" says Stephen. "I'm here, silly one, I'm here. If something's broken you know I'll fix it."

Elizabeth swings her feet out of bed and hurries to the bathroom. She locks the door and slumps back against it. The tears come now. Not easily, because tears never come easily to Elizabeth. Even now Elizabeth remembers crying when her dad would hit her. Because he loved her, because he loved her so. How he would keep hitting, and keep hitting until she stopped. Until one day she stopped crying forever.

She remembers too sitting by her dad's bedside, many years later, she on leave from Beirut, he dying of cancer in a Hampshire hospice. She held his bony, vicious hand, and thought of everything this man might have had in life. Everything she might have had. But still she didn't cry, frightened of what he might do if she did.

Will she be holding Stephen's hand in a hospice someday soon? Of course she will. But she will laugh with him, and she will love him, and she will give thanks for him, and for the woman he has made her. And she will cry the lifetime of tears she has denied herself.

48.

Bogdan is in love. There are no two ways about it. He is certain.

Or is he?

It *feels* like it.

But should you ever trust feelings?

They are off to see Jack Mason. With Viktor in tow this time. Bogdan is driving Ron's Daihatsu.

Bogdan wishes somebody would just tell him how to handle this. He had been in love at school, he remembers that, but there has been nothing that simple since. He needs to play chess with Stephen soon. Stephen will know.

He certainly likes Donna very, very, very much. But how many "verys" turn "like" into "love"? Four? Five? Bogdan wishes there were a definitive answer. There are six bullets in a gun, you can fit twelve bricks on a hod, there are thirteen grams of protein in an egg. But love? Try Googling it. There aren't any answers, Bogdan has tried.

Ron is in the passenger seat. He turns his head to the backseat to talk to Viktor.

"You know her from way back," says Ron. "Elizabeth?"

Viktor Illyich is stretching himself, and clicking his joints. They have just let him out of the boot of the car, and unzipped him from his holdall. They did this on a rutted track in the woods about a mile from Coopers Chase, as soon as Bogdan was sure they weren't being followed. Elizabeth had given him strict instructions.

"Way back," says Viktor. "A different lifetime."

"Tell us a secret, then," says Ron. "Something she wouldn't want us to know."

Viktor contemplates this for a moment.

"OK," he says. "Elizabeth is the greatest lover I ever had."

"Jesus Christ," says Ron. "I meant something about shooting Russian spies or something."

"She was so tender," says Viktor. "But also a caged animal."

Ron turns the radio on: talkSPORT.

Viktor is lost in memories. "She did things to me that no woman—"

Ron nods down toward the radio. "Liverpool are buying Sanchez? Waste of money."

Bogdan is tempted to join in the conversation. To talk about love. To ask a question maybe? But without giving anything away. Would he look foolish? The big Polish brute, what could he know about love? He decides to say something. He won't know what it is until it is out of his mouth.

"How much are they paying for Sanchez, Ron?" Oh, Bogdan.

"Thirty mill," says Ron. "In installments, but still."

Bogdan nods. He's really only here to drive, and to carry Viktor to and from the car.

While Ron is telling a joke about a parrot that used to live in a brothel, Bogdan thinks a little more about the case. Viktor had taken him through a few things before being zipped into his holdall. He now has a cushion in there, and also a copy of the *Economist* and a small torch.

Viktor had explained the basics of money-laundering, the complex network of anonymous shell companies and offshore accounts that could turn dirty money into clean money via a trail almost impossible to follow. Almost impossible.

Bogdan has missed the punchline of the parrot joke, and Ron has moved on to one about a nun on a train.

The real secret was to dig back in time, to follow the money back and back and back to try to find the original sin. The first transactions were the vulnerable ones. Viktor said it was like pulling up a carpet. You just needed to get your fingernail under a tiny fragment in the corner, and sometimes you could lift the whole thing up in one go. That's what had happened with Trident: an early transaction, a mistake. But that had led nowhere. So maybe they had to track back even further.

They reach the house at around two. It is an Elizabethan manor perched high on a Kent clifftop, the English Channel stretching off into the distance beyond. They park in a copse around a mile away, and zip Viktor back into his bag. How they will explain this Ukrainian in a holdall to Jack Mason is not Bogdan's concern. He just has to carry it.

Bogdan drives the Daihatsu up the long drive, and parks as close to the stone entrance steps as he can. The holdall sneezes, and Bogdan says, "Bless you."

If Jack Mason is surprised to see a large Polish man unzip a small Ukrainian man from a holdall, he hides it well.

"I will come back for you this evening," Bogdan tells Ron and Viktor.

"Thanks, old son," says Ron. "I'm not going back to Coopers Chase though. Staying at Pauline's place, but it's in Fairhaven if that's easy for you?"

"Is no problem at all," says Bogdan.

"You're a good lad," says Ron. "It's Juniper Court, just off Rotherfield Road."

49.

Joyce is combining business and pleasure. There was an advert on TV years ago, for sweets maybe, and the song went "These are two of my favorite things in one." And here she was, about to watch a television show being recorded, and, she hopes, interviewing a murder suspect.

Last time she and Elizabeth were on a train, Elizabeth had had a gun in her bag. Perhaps she has one today? She is certainly looking distracted.

"You seem distracted," says Joyce, as Elizabeth peers up and down the carriage.

"I seem what?" says Elizabeth.

"Distracted," says Joyce.

"Nonsense," says Elizabeth.

"My mistake," says Joyce.

They had changed trains at London Bridge, and then again at Blackfriars. Blackfriars Station is on a bridge, and Joyce was thrilled about it. Although there was only a Costa Coffee. Apparently there was also a WHSmith, but it was down the escalator, and Joyce didn't want to risk missing the next train. She would catch it on the way back. They spoke about Ibrahim's discovery. That the note found in Heather Garbutt's drawer was written by someone else. The killer presumably, but why would the killer mention Connie Johnson? Unless the killer *was* Connie Johnson, and even then it would make no sense.

They are now on a commuter service up to Elstree & Borehamwood, which is where Fiona Clemence films *Stop the Clock*. Joyce explains the rules to Elizabeth for the umpteenth time.

"Really, for an educated woman, you can be very slow, Elizabeth," she says. "Four players each have a hundred seconds on their clock at the start of the game. The longer they take to answer questions, the more time they lose, and once they get down to zero seconds they're out of the game."

"No, that much I understand," says Elizabeth. "It's all the other nonsense."

"Nonsense? Hardly," says Joyce. "They each have four lifelines. They can steal ten seconds from an opponent, they can freeze their own clock, they can speed up an opponent's clock, or they can swap a question. Steal, Freeze, Speed or Swap, simple as that. Though if your opponent steals from you or speeds you up, you receive an additional lifeline, Revenge, which you can play even when you're out of the game. All the winner's remaining seconds are converted to money, and to win the money they have to answer twelve questions, working their way around the clock from one to twelve before their time runs out. It couldn't be simpler."

"And they put this on television?" Elizabeth watches closely as a man walks past them.

"Every day," says Joyce. "You can watch it instead of the news, that's why it's so popular."

The train stops at Hendon, home of the famous police training college. Joyce texts Chris to say, *Guess where we are? Hendon!*, but Chris texts back and says, *I didn't train at Hendon*, so Joyce texts the same thing to Donna, but no reply yet.

"Tell me about Fiona Clemence," says Elizabeth.

"She was a junior producer when Bethany was the presenter of *South East Tonight*," says Joyce. "When Bethany died, she became the presenter. Ever so ambitious, but they only use 'ambitious' as a criticism about women, don't they?"

"I have been called ambitious many times," says Elizabeth.

"She hosted the show for about two years—you could really see she was starting to bed in—and then she went to work for Sky News. I always liked to keep up with her, you know, just in case she mentioned the South East. Then she started doing *Breakfast News* on the BBC, and now she presents everything. I even saw her doing Crufts the other day."

"I'm sure she's famous, Joyce, but I'm really only interested in what she can tell us about Bethany Waites."

"You have honestly never heard of her? I find that very hard to believe."

"Have you heard of Beryl Deepdene?"

"No," says Joyce.

"Then you see that different people have different interests," says Elizabeth.

"Who is Beryl Deepdene?"

"It was the cover name for a particularly brave British operative in Moscow in the nineteen seventies," says Elizabeth. "Well known in my circles."

"I doubt that Beryl Deepdene has won a TV Choice Award," says Joyce.

"And I doubt that Fiona Clemence has won a George Cross," says Elizabeth. "It's horses for courses, isn't it? Ah, look, we're here."

It is a ten-minute walk from Elstree & Borehamwood Station to Elstree Studios. Joyce likes nothing more than a high street she has never walked down before, and points out a number of things to Elizabeth. "Starbucks, Costa *and* Caffè Nero, as you'd hope," "Does that Holland & Barrett look bigger than usual?," "My goodness, they still have a Wimpy, Elizabeth."

A queue snakes from the security gates of the studio, but Joyce and Elizabeth are able to walk straight to the front. Joanna has a friend whose sister is a production manager, whatever that might be, on the show, and they have special guest tickets. They are ushered straight into a bar and offered tea or coffee. Joyce is wide-eyed.

"Isn't this something? Have you ever been on television, Elizabeth?"

"I was once called to give evidence to the Defense Select Committee," says Elizabeth. "But, legally, they had to blur my face. And I was once in a hostage video."

They are called through to the studio and given seats in the front row. It is freezing cold, but they are asked to remove their gloves ("Otherwise we won't be able to hear you when you clap"). There is no food allowed in the studio, but Joyce opens her bag wide enough to show Elizabeth that she has sneaked in some Fruit Pastilles. While they wait, Joyce gets her phone out of her bag. She spots a security guard.

"Are we allowed to take photos?"

"No," says the security guard.

"Righto," says Joyce.

"You're not going to stand for that, Joyce, surely?" says Elizabeth.

"I'm certainly not," says Joyce, taking a photo. "This is going straight on Instagram."

"Makes me wonder why you asked," says Elizabeth. "In a way."

"It's just polite, isn't it," says Joyce, taking another photograph. "Did you know Fiona Clemence has three million followers on Instagram? Can you imagine?"

"Barely," says Elizabeth.

As Joyce puts her phone away, she finally gets a reply from Donna. *I didn't train at Hendon, Joyce.* Where was everyone training these days, Joyce wonders.

She hopes Ron and Viktor are having a nice day too; she waved them off, with Bogdan driving, this morning. Jack Mason has a snooker table, and apparently that means they'll be gone for the day. Joyce can see the appeal of snooker. The waistcoats and so on. She thinks she would marry Stephen Hendry were the opportunity to arise.

The music being played into the studio fades now, and the crowd applauds as Fiona Clemence walks onto the set.

"Flawless skin," says Joyce to Elizabeth. "Flawless, isn't it?"

"How long is all this going to take?" asks Elizabeth. "I'm really only here to ask questions."

"Not long," says Joyce. "Three hours or so."

The famous theme tune starts up.

50.

They are fighting out a hard-earned draw. Bogdan with his bishop and his pawns, Stephen with his rook. They have played each other enough to know exactly where it is heading, but each is having fun regardless. Stephen is looking thin. He forgets to eat when no one is in the flat with him, and Elizabeth has been busy lately. He wolfed down the sandwiches Bogdan made for him. There is a shepherd's pie on the kitchen worktop, and Bogdan will put that on in an hour or so.

"Can I ask you something, as a pal?" says Stephen, eyes not leaving the chessboard.

"Whatever you need," says Bogdan.

"It's a ridiculous one," says Stephen. "Just to warn you."

"I am used to this already," says Bogdan. "You're a ridiculous man."

Stephen is nodding, and looking between his pieces and Bogdan's, looking for avenues that aren't there. He speaks without looking up. "Am I all right, do you suppose?"

Bogdan waits a beat. They have had this conversation before. Variations of it at least. "No one is all right. You're OK."

"If you say so," says Stephen, eyes still avoiding contact. "But something is muddled somewhere. Something isn't straight. You know the feeling?"

"Sure, I know the feeling," says Bogdan.

"Here's a for instance," says Stephen, and then waits a moment. "I don't know where Elizabeth is today."

"She's gone to a TV show," says Bogdan. "With Joyce."

"Ah, I met Joyce," says Stephen. "The other day. Where does she know Elizabeth from?"

"She's a neighbor," says Bogdan. "She's very nice."

"That came across," agrees Stephen. "But even so. Queer that I didn't know where Elizabeth was? Unusual?"

Bogdan shrugs. "Maybe she didn't tell you? She likes her secrets."

"Bogdan." Stephen finally looks up. "I'm not a fool. Well, no more than any of us. I miss things from time to time, people don't quite make the sense they did."

Bogdan nods.

"My father, God rest him, lost himself toward the end. In those days they said he went doolally—probably that's not what we say these days."

"I don't think we do," agrees Bogdan.

" 'Where's your mother?' he would ask me sometimes." Stephen moves a piece on the board. A holding move, nothing risked, nothing gained. "Only, my mother had died, many years previously."

Bogdan is looking down at the board now. Let Stephen talk. Only answer a question if one is asked.

"So, you see," says Stephen, "why it might worry me that I don't know where Elizabeth is today?"

OK, that sounds like a question. Bogdan looks up. "Some things we remember, Stephen, and some things we forget."

"Hmm," says Stephen.

"The first time I ever thought I was in love," says Bogdan. He has been thinking about this recently. "You know, when it makes you sick . . ."

"Don't I just," says Stephen.

"It was a girl from school, we were nine, in Mr. Nowak's class. She sat in front of me and to the left, and she would arrange her pencils so neatly. When she wrote, the tip of her tongue poked between her lips. She lived on the next street from mine, and sometimes we would walk home together, when I could make it happen, and she had silver buckles on her shoes, so she didn't like to go in puddles. I liked to go in puddles, but when I walked with her I would pretend I didn't. I was sick, Stephen, sick. Her father was in the air force, and they sent him overseas, so she left school, didn't even say goodbye, because she didn't know we were in love—why would she? But I still remember how I felt, still remember how she smelled, her laugh, all these tiny details. I remember them all."

Stephen smiles. "You old romantic, Bogdan. What was her name?"

Bogdan raises his eyes from the board, and raises his hands in a slow shrug. "We all forget things, Stephen."

Stephen smiles, and nods. "Very clever. But you would tell me? You would tell me if something was up? I can't ask Elizabeth. I don't want to worry her."

Again, Stephen has asked Bogdan this question a number of times. And Bogdan always answers in the same way.

"Would I tell you? Honestly, I don't know. What would you do, if it was someone you loved?"

"I suppose if I felt it would help, then I would tell them," says Stephen. "And if I felt it wouldn't help, then I wouldn't tell them."

Bogdan nods. "I like that. I think that is right."

"But you think I'm all right? A bit of fuss over nothing?"

"That's exactly what I think, Stephen," says Bogdan, and moves one of his pawns further up the board.

Stephen stares at the board. "But it leads me to another question. A worse question."

"We have all day," says Bogdan.

"Is Elizabeth OK?"

"Sure," says Bogdan. "I mean, Elizabeth is never OK, you know. But she is well."

"She was in a tizz," says Stephen. "The other night. She was talking about a library and a Viking, making no real sense, and when I questioned her about it, she took herself off. Dose of the waterworks, which she tried to cover up. Very unlike her. What's that, do you think?"

"Doesn't ring a bell at all?" asks Bogdan.

"Good question actually," says Stephen, making his next move. "The question of the day, I'd say. 'The Viking'—your guess is very much as good as mine, but the library. I didn't think about it at the time, but I have been in a library recently. I'm sure I hadn't told Elizabeth about it though."

"What library?" asks Bogdan.

"Friend of mine," says Stephen. "Bill Chivers, you know him?"

"Bill Chivers? No," says Bogdan.

"Where do I know you from, Bogdan?" asks Stephen. "Where did we meet?"

"I came to fix something in the flat," says Bogdan. "I saw the chessboard, and we started playing."

"That's it," says Stephen. "That's it. No reason why you'd know Bill Chivers, then. He's a book dealer. Bent as a nine-bob note, between you and me."

Bent as a nine-bob note. Bogdan always likes to discover a nice new idiom.

"Only he invited me up to his place, forget where, got Staffordshire in my head, but that can't be right. But big old pile, doing well for himself, and there I am in his library, and I'm looking around, Bogdan, being nosy, you know me . . ."

"You never know what you might see," says Bogdan.

"Always been that way," agrees Stephen. "And, anyway, I finally come to my point, there are books on the shelf that shouldn't be there."

"Shouldn't how?"

"Expensive," says Stephen. "Famously expensive. Not first editions but one-offs. Should be in museums, but some are in private collections. Worth tens of millions if you want to add them all together, but there they are in Bill Chivers's library. So what do we make of that?"

"In a library, in a big house in Staffordshire? You saw these books?"

"I feel like I did, yes," says Stephen.

"You remember the names of the books?"

"Of course," says Stephen. "He had the Timurid Quran, for goodness' sake, and a volume of the *Yongle Encyclopedia*. Not my area, but he had a Shakespeare First Folio. So, yes, I remember the names. I haven't gone loco."

"I know," says Bogdan.

"'Doolally,' they used to call it."

Bogdan nods. Elizabeth needs to find out the identity of the Viking. Could this help? Could they track him through these books? He will tell Elizabeth as soon as she is back, and Elizabeth will have a plan.

"I don't know when it would have been," says Stephen. "But recently, I think. Though I feel as if I don't go out so much anymore?"

"You're always out and about," says Bogdan. "Walking with Elizabeth. All sorts."

"This will seem another very silly question to you," says Stephen. "And forgive me. But do I have a car?"

Bogdan shakes his head. "Lost your license."

"Blast it," says Stephen. "Do you have a car?"

"I have access to cars, yes," says Bogdan.

"When is Elizabeth back?"

"This evening," says Bogdan.

"Righto," says Stephen. "Could you run me down to Brighton?"

"To Brighton?"

"Old pal of mine runs an antique shop. Dodgy as they come—"

"Bent as a nine-bob note?" says Bogdan.

"Never a truer word spoken," says Stephen. "I want to ask him about these books. See how Bill Chivers came to have them. Bit of detective work, if you fancy it?"

OK, perhaps Bogdan won't have to wait for Elizabeth to come up with a plan.

"And, speaking of detectives and fancying," says Stephen, "why don't we invite your pal Donna along too? Been dying to meet her. Elizabeth really hasn't clocked that you two are dating?"

"She knows something is up, but she hasn't worked out what," says Bogdan.

"Oh, Elizabeth," says Stephen. "You can see why I worry about her?"

Bogdan and Stephen shake hands on a draw. Now to get Stephen changed and shaved, and then a trip to Brighton. Should he ask Elizabeth's permission?

No, he has Stephen's permission. He will do as Stephen wishes.

51.

I'm a dreadful nuisance, I can't apologize enough," says Elizabeth, stretched out on a sofa in an Elstree Studios dressing-room.

"Don't be silly," says a paramedic, removing a blood-pressure sleeve from Elizabeth's arm. "Blood pressure all normal, but people faint for all sorts of reasons. It happens all the time."

"Silly sums it up," says Elizabeth. "A silly old woman spoiling everyone's fun. I think it's because they don't let you have any food. I'm elderly, you see." Elizabeth tries to sit up, but the paramedic is having none of it.

"Not a bit of it," says the paramedic, turning to Joyce. "She's not spoiling anyone's fun, is she?"

"I mean, I was enjoying it," says Joyce. "But these things happen."

"Must have been a bit of a shock for you too?" says the paramedic. "Your friend keeling over twenty minutes into the recording?"

"Yes and no," says Joyce, then looks straight at Elizabeth. "Yes and no."

"I'll leave you in peace for a bit," says the paramedic. "I'll come back and check on you in a while. I'm sure someone from production will come and see how you are between shows too."

"You've been so kind," says Elizabeth, and tries to raise her hand to thank her. "I should have had something to eat; it's my own fault."

Elizabeth watches the paramedic leave and, as soon as she hears the door shut, removes the cold towel from her forehead and sits up.

"What a nice woman," says Elizabeth. "A credit."

"You really couldn't have waited?" says Joyce. "Twenty minutes? I barely saw the first round."

"You could have stayed," says Elizabeth.

"Fine friend I would have looked then," says Joyce. "They don't know you're a terrible fake, do they? I couldn't say, oh, she's a spy, she does this sort of thing all the time. Honestly, slumping to the floor and groaning. You might have warned me."

"Oh, Joyce," says Elizabeth, helping herself to a banana from the dressing-room fruit bowl. "How were we ever going to be able to ask questions from the audience?"

"We can't ask questions from here either," says Joyce. "I've missed the whole thing."

"You'll thank me when Fiona Clemence walks through that door to check on me," says Elizabeth.

"Why would she do that?"

"Joyce, a frail old woman just collapsed on the set of her show," says Elizabeth. "A frail old woman who collapsed because she wasn't allowed anything to eat. A frail old woman who would be mollified by Fiona Clemence simply popping her head around the door between shows and asking after her health."

"And then what?"

"And then we play it by ear, Joyce," says Elizabeth. "As we always do."

"I will bet half my Bitcoin account that Fiona Clemence won't—"

There is a knock at the door. Elizabeth springs back onto the sofa and lies down, just in time for a man in a headset to poke his head around the door.

"Now, you ladies must be Elizabeth and Joan?"

"Joyce," says Joyce.

"We are the laughing stock, I know," says Elizabeth.

"Not a bit of it. A little someone wanted to say hello," says the man. "If you're up to it?"

"She is," says Joyce.

"Right you are," says the man, and disappears again. Now the door opens, and Fiona Clemence pops her head around it. That auburn hair, so famous from the shampoo adverts, the full smile, so famous from the toothpaste adverts, and the cheekbones honed by genetics and Harley Street.

"Knock, knock, guess who," says Fiona Clemence. "You must be Elizabeth and Joan?"

"Yes," says Joyce. Elizabeth sees she is mesmerized.

"Just wanted to check there was no lasting damage?" Fiona gives a warm laugh. She is leaning around the door, not troubling the threshold. Clearly not planning to stay. "Before I head back out."

"If we could detain you for just one moment?" says Elizabeth.

"Have to get back," says Fiona, smiling. "Bosses cracking the whip. Just wanted to check in."

"Perhaps we could get a photo?" Joyce suggests. Good, Joyce, good. Elizabeth sees indecision in Fiona's eyes, and then resignation.

"Of course," says Fiona. "Quick one. Forgive the rush."

Fiona commits to the room, albeit reluctantly, and perches by Elizabeth on the sofa, as Joyce rummages in her cardigan pocket for her phone. Fiona's photograph smile is already fixed in place.

"Now," says Elizabeth. "Time is short, and I need to convey a lot of information to you."

"I'm sorry?" says Fiona, smile still in place. For now.

"I didn't faint, I'm not ill, and I don't want a photograph," says Elizabeth quickly. "I also pose you no risk, wish you no harm and, indeed, before today, I had no idea who you were."

"I . . ." says Fiona, smile now drifting off. "Really need to be getting off."

"I won't keep you," says Elizabeth. "Myself and my friend Joyce, by the way, not Joan . . ."

"You can call me Joan," says Joyce.

". . . are here to investigate the murder of Bethany Waites, who, I know, you knew—"

"OK, I don't know what this is . . ." says Fiona.

"Fiona, Fiona," says Elizabeth. "I won't be a second. We're very happy to wait around and speak to you later."

"I'm going to talk to security," says Fiona. "Come on, you know this isn't right."

"Oh, gosh, right, wrong," says Elizabeth. "Who cares? Two harmless old women, a couple of questions about a murder I'm sure you had nothing to do with."

"No one's saying I had anything to do with it," says Fiona. "And this is . . . weird."

"A colleague is murdered, and you step into her job," says Elizabeth. "Threatening notes had been written. You would be a clear suspect, Joyce has left me in no doubt about that."

"Well, no, I didn't exactly say—" says Joyce.

"And another woman, Heather Garbutt, has also just been murdered," says Elizabeth. "Now we've spoken to Mike Waghorn, your erstwhile colleague, and we would love to speak to you. I had to fake a fainting fit to get the opportunity, so what do you say?"

"I say no," says Fiona. "Obviously."

There is a knock at the door. "Fiona? Back on floor, please."

"I have to get changed," says Fiona, getting up.

Elizabeth stands with her. "Fiona, I shouldn't be telling you this, but I mention it in case you find it interesting. My friend Joyce here would not be able to tell you herself, for obvious reasons, but she was, for many years, a very highly decorated member of the British security services."

Fiona looks at Joyce.

"I know, you wouldn't believe it to look at her," says Elizabeth.

"I actually would believe it," says Fiona.

"So we are many things," says Elizabeth. "A nuisance, yes. Something you could live without, certainly. A pain in the backside, spot on, you've got us. But we are also serious, we are also no threat, and we are, believe it or not, once you get to know us, rather a lot of fun."

There is a knock on the door again. "Fiona?"

"So what I'd love," says Elizabeth, "is for you to go out and finish your shows, for Joyce to sit in the audience and watch, and then afterward the three of us can have a drink and a chat, and see if you can help us solve the murder of Bethany Waites."

Fiona looks between the two of them.

"There's a Wimpy on Borehamwood high street," says Joyce.

"Admit it," says Elizabeth. "We do seem fun? And we *are* investigating two murders."

Fiona looks at Joyce. "You were really in MI5?"

"I can't say," says Joyce. "I wish that I could."

"Take a look in her bag if you don't believe her," says Elizabeth.

Joyce, understandably, looks puzzled as Fiona peeks into her bag. There, in pride of place, is Elizabeth's gun.

"Whoa," says Fiona.

"I know," says Elizabeth. "The worst thing I've got in my bag is a packet of Fruit Pastilles."

Elizabeth sees Joyce take a quick look into her own bag, and, seeing the gun Elizabeth recently slipped into it, shakes her head and gives her friend a despairing look.

"And you've spoken to Mike Waghorn?" says Fiona.

"We do little else these days," says Elizabeth.

Fiona's mind is made up. "OK, done. A quick drink after the show. I was very fond of Mike Waghorn."

"And Bethany?" asks Elizabeth. "You were fond of her?"

Fiona is about to respond, but thinks better of it. "Well, we can discuss that after the show, can't we?"

"You have been very patient with us, Fiona, thank you," says Elizabeth. "I promise you will enjoy talking to us."

"I don't doubt it," says Fiona.

"Unless you murdered Bethany Waites," says Elizabeth. "In which case we will be your worst nightmare."

"I should think if I murdered Bethany Waites and have been smart enough to get away with it all these years," says Fiona, her brilliant smile filling the dressing-room once more, "then I might just be *your* worst nightmare."

Elizabeth nods. "Well, I must say I'm looking forward to this immensely. See you anon. Break a leg."

52.

"That's impossible," says Kuldesh Sharma, pushing eighty, handsomely bald, and wearing a lilac suit and a white silk shirt unbuttoned to a point beyond the confidence of any ordinary man.

"Improbable, certainly," says Stephen. "But not impossible. I saw them with my own eyes. Book after book, all just sitting there."

Donna is browsing at the back of the dark shop. "This is beautiful," she says, holding up a bronze figurine.

"Anahita," says Kuldesh, looking over. "The Persian goddess of love and battle."

"Love *and* battle, good for you, Anahita," says Donna. "I love her."

"Unless you love her two thousand pounds, I might have to ask you to put her down," says Kuldesh.

Donna places Anahita down very carefully, her eyebrows rising in counterweight as she does so.

"Is full of stuff, your shop," says Bogdan. "Is very beautiful. Very beautiful."

"One acquires things," says Kuldesh. "Over the years."

"And if I put everything you've acquired through a police computer," says Donna, "is there anything that would raise an alarm?"

"Save yourself the time," says Kuldesh. "The only dodgy old things in this shop are Stephen and me." Donna smiles. "Now, shall we get to the business at hand?"

Stephen shows Kuldesh the list he wrote in the car. "And these were just the ones I could identify. Books everywhere."

Kuldesh runs a finger down the list, puffing his cheeks as he goes. "*The Deeds of Sir Gillion de Trazegnies?*"

"A few million?" guesses Stephen.

"At least," says Kuldesh, still reading the list. "This list is completely insane. You would need billions to buy all of these. *The Monypenny Breviary*? How does Billy Chivers have all of these?"

Bogdan pulls up a wooden chair to sit with Kuldesh and Stephen.

"I wouldn't sit on that," says Kuldesh. "It's worth fourteen grand, and you are tremendously large. There's a milking stool somewhere."

Bogdan locates and pulls up the milking stool. "Maybe don't worry about Billy Chivers. Maybe someone else bought them."

"Chivers is just looking after them," agrees Stephen.

Kuldesh folds the list up and puts it in the pocket of his suit jacket. "I will ask around. But this is pretty big, even for me." He looks over to Donna. "I am but a humble shopkeeper, I don't really know any criminals."

"And I'm the goddess of love and battle," says Donna, now looking at a pewter inkwell in the shape of a chihuahua.

"But you might know someone who knows someone?" Stephen asks Kuldesh.

"I might," says Kuldesh. "I would like to help."

Donna wanders over. "And would you ever be tempted to help the police, Mr. Sharma?"

Kuldesh shrugs a little. "Let me tell you a story, Donna. A story that I suspect will not surprise you. I've been in this shop for nearly fifty years, opened up in the nineteen seventies, *Kemptown Curios, proprietor Mr. K. Sharma,* written so beautifully over the window. Like a British shop, you know? Like the shops I'd seen in films; I did it myself. The first night, bricks through the window. I fixed, I repainted, I reopened. The moment I reopen, bricks through the window. Every night until they got bored, until they moved on to someone new."

"I'm sorry," says Donna.

"Not at all," says Kuldesh. "A long time ago. But perhaps you can guess how helpful the Brighton police were to me in the nineteen seventies?"

"Not particularly?" guesses Donna.

"Not particularly," agrees Kuldesh. "If you'd told me the bricks were theirs, it wouldn't have shocked me. And so I have steered clear of them ever since and, largely, they have steered clear of me. Best for everyone, I think."

Donna nods. She can only imagine.

"Stephen," says Bogdan. "I need to speak to Kuldesh by myself for a moment. Is OK?"

"You know best," says Stephen. "I'll fetch the car."

"Maybe . . ." Bogdan says. "Maybe Donna could go with you? Keep you company."

Donna gives Bogdan a wink, and takes Stephen by the arm.

"Thank you, Kuldesh, old chap," says Stephen. "Knew you'd be the man for the job. Give my love to Prisha. Dinner soon?"

"Dinner soon," says Kuldesh, rising and embracing Stephen. "I will tell Prisha I saw you, and I will see her face light up, I know."

"You're a lucky sod with that one," says Stephen.

Donna leads Stephen from the shop. Bogdan and Kuldesh wait until the final reverberations of the shop bell have silenced.

"Prisha is dead, I think?" asks Bogdan.

"Fifteen years ago," says Kuldesh. "But I will tell her I saw Stephen, and she will smile."

Bogdan nods.

"And I was a lucky sod, he's right there. How ill is he? Getting worse? I cannot tell you how kind Stephen has been to me over the years. Lucrative too, but the kindness is the real treasure."

"He remembers what he remembers," says Bogdan. "And for now he doesn't really know what he forgets."

"That's a mercy," says Kuldesh. "For now."

"You can help with Stephen's list?" asks Bogdan.

"If one person owns all of these books," says Kuldesh, "then I might be able to find out who. Difficult. I'm guessing it's not Bill Chivers, though?"

"No, is not Bill Chivers," says Bogdan. "Is someone who wants to kill Stephen's wife."

"Elizabeth?"

Bogdan nods. "Elizabeth."

"Then I will find out," says Kuldesh. "That is my promise. She's still firing on all cylinders I hope?"

"Most of them," says Bogdan. "I'm sorry I brought a police officer into your shop. But is only Donna."

"A friend of Stephen is my friend," says Kuldesh. "Even if they're in a uniform. Give me a couple of days to see what I can find."

Kuldesh shakes Bogdan's hand and starts to usher him to the door. But Bogdan seems reluctant to leave.

"Is there something else?" asks Kuldesh.

Bogdan is shifting his weight from foot to foot. Then he nods his head toward the back of the shop.

"The statue that Donna liked?" asks Bogdan. "How much for cash?"

53.

Joyce

I met Fiona Clemence today, that's my big news. Also, I had a gun in my handbag, which, on any other day, would probably be the big news. Thirdly, Blackfriars Station has the tiniest branch of WHSmith you've ever seen in your life.

What a day we've had of it, though. We left at about ten, and we weren't back till gone seven. Viktor is still not back from seeing Jack Mason. All his bits of paper are scattered all over the floor. The financial records. This morning I asked him if he'd had any luck, and he said there was no luck involved, and I said, well, I was just making conversation, and he said, yes, I was quite right, and then he put the kettle on. We rub along just fine.

Normally Alan would have a field day with all those bits of paper. Chewing them, tearing them. But he was stepping around them politely. Viktor has explained their importance to Alan, and asked him to be very careful with them. Viktor does have a persuasive tone. For example, he had me watching the Formula 1 the other day, even though there was a *Poirot* on ITV3. He makes everything feel like it was your idea in the first place. Alan and I just sit there nodding half the time.

Before I come into the flat now, I have to do a special knock so Viktor knows it's me. It's just four quick knocks, and it sort of matches the rhythm of the moonpig.com advert. Viktor says that if he hears the door open without the knock, I will find him behind the sofa with a handgun. "I don't want to shoot you by accident," he said, "but I will."

Elizabeth and I have been to watch *Stop the Clock* being filmed. They filmed three episodes, and I saw the second and third one. The first one was interrupted by Elizabeth pretending to faint. All in a good cause, as it turns out. The couple in the second show won two thousand seven hundred pounds, and they are getting married, so it is going toward their wedding. He must have been fifteen years older than her. I know you shouldn't judge but really. I wanted to shout to her, "Get out while you can!"

Through a combination of pretending to faint and showing her a gun, Elizabeth persuaded Fiona to speak to us afterward. We sat in her dressing-room, and somebody who can't have been long out of school brought us all a herbal tea. I had chamomile and raspberry, because it was the first one I was offered and my brain switches off when someone reads me a long list.

Now, I didn't dislike Fiona Clemence, let me say that. She is not as warm as you might think when you watch her on TV. I think some of that is just for the cameras, but she wasn't rude, even though she had every right to be after the fainting and the gun.

She had only half an hour, because she was heading off to interview Bono, so Elizabeth and I took it in turns to ask questions. I left all the Bethany Waites questions to Elizabeth, because I probably won't get another chance to meet Fiona Clemence, and I wanted to make the most of it.

So the whole thing went something like this.

ELIZABETH: Tell me about your relationship with Bethany Waites.

FIONA: We disliked each other.

ME: What's the most money anyone has ever won on *Stop the Clock*?

FIONA: I don't know. About twenty grand, I think.

ELIZABETH: Why did you dislike each other?

FIONA: She disliked me because she thought I was an airhead. And I disliked her because she thought I was an airhead.

ME: A few weeks ago on the show you were wearing red shoes, I don't know if you remember them? But I wondered where they were from?

FIONA: I don't know, sorry.

ELIZABETH: Were you aware you might be next in line to present the show were Bethany ever to leave?

FIONA: I'd done a screen-test. I knew they liked me. But, and forgive me here, Joyce, co-hosting *South East Tonight* was not a particular ambition of mine.

ELIZABETH: Didn't do you any harm though?

FIONA: OK, I murdered her so I could read the local news.

ME: Are people talking to you through an earpiece on the show?

FIONA: Yes.

ME: What are they saying?

FIONA: All sorts. Reminding me of the scores, telling me to cheer up, letting me know someone in the audience has fainted.

ELIZABETH: Where were you on the night of Bethany's death?

FIONA: I was doing coke in a hotel with a cameraman.

ME: We bought ten thousand pounds' worth of cocaine recently. Who's the nicest person you've ever interviewed?

FIONA: Tom Hanks.

ELIZABETH: What do you know about notes that Bethany received before her death? At work?

FIONA: What sort of notes?

ELIZABETH: "Get out," "Everybody hates you." That sort of thing.

FIONA [laughing]: She got those too? I thought it was just me.

ELIZABETH: You got the same notes? Any idea from whom?

FIONA: No idea, but no one pushed me off a cliff, did they?

ME: What was it about Tom Hanks?

ELIZABETH [tiring of me, I think]: Is there anyone else you can think of who might have had reason to kill Bethany?

FIONA: The fashion police?

ME: You know on Instagram, where you do your live videos, and everyone can watch and comment? How do you do that? I can't find the button for it.

FIONA: It's called "Stories," you can look it up.

ELIZABETH: Is there anyone else we should talk to who was there at the time?

FIONA: Carwyn, the producer. Even if he didn't kill her, they should lock him up. And Mike's makeup artist. Pamela, something like that. Always a weird atmosphere there.

ELIZABETH: Pauline?

FIONA: If you say so.

ME: Would you ever do *Strictly*?

FIONA: Only if I was hosting it.

So, you see, she wasn't rude exactly, given the circumstances, but she wasn't exactly a thrill a minute. I just looked up how to do those live videos on Instagram, but I couldn't really make head nor tail of it. I will stick to photographs, I think. Ron made me post a picture of Alan today with two balls in his mouth. Joanna liked it, which is a first.

We made our way back to the station via the Wimpy, and I had a snooze on the train. I told Elizabeth she could snooze, and I would keep an eye out for our stop, but she wanted to stay awake.

I wonder when Viktor will be back? I hope he is having luck with Jack

Mason. Elizabeth seems to have great faith in him. I asked her if they had ever slept together, and she said that she honestly couldn't remember, but they probably did. I told her I carry around a picture of everyone I've ever slept with in my purse. Then I opened it, and showed her that the only picture in my purse was one of Gerry, and she said, "Yes, I got it the first time, Joyce."

I wonder if Viktor will remember if he slept with Elizabeth. I think one probably would.

54.

The three men are sitting on Jack Mason's veranda in the moonlight, with a strip heater and a tumbler of whisky each, keeping them warm. Lights blink out at sea. Ron feels the whisky warm his chest, and his eyelids begin to droop. Give him this over a massage any day of the week.

What a lovely day they've had. BBQ on the heated terrace, snooker, cards. Couldn't wish for more. Viktor gently prodding here and there, Jack avoiding his questions.

The snooker is over for the evening. The first, everyone hopes, of a regular game. Three old men, three new friends. The gangster, the KGB colonel and the trades union official.

"It must be a burden, Jack," says Viktor.

"What's that?" Jack asks.

"Your scheme," says Viktor. "It should have been so clean. Then Bethany dies. And now Heather dies. That must weigh on you. Your responsibility?"

Jack nods, and raises his glass.

"I don't kill people, Viktor," says Jack. "Some people do, but I've never got a thrill from it. I like breaking the law, I like making money, I like getting one over on people."

"A man after my own heart," says Viktor. "Perhaps it haunts you," says Viktor. "Just a touch."

"A touch," agrees Jack.

"I understand," says Viktor. "And you must be angry, I think I would be, with the killer?"

"It was stupid," says Jack. "It was unnecessary."

"Just the thought," says Viktor, "of Bethany going over that cliff. It must wake you at times?"

"Nah," says Jack. "You got it wrong."

"I sometimes do get it wrong," agrees Viktor. "I am eager to know why I am wrong now though? That vision would trouble me."

"Lads," says Jack, with a small smile, "can I tell you something? Unburden myself a bit?"

This sounds like it might get uncomfortably close to discussing feelings, Ron thinks, but he sees that's how Viktor works. And they're investigating a crime, so he's going to have to put up with it.

"This is not for the police," says Jack. "It's for the three of us. What you choose to do with it, that's your business."

"No one here is speaking to the police," says Ron. "Go on, Jack."

"There *was* no one in the car when it went over the cliff," says Jack Mason, and takes another sip of his whisky. "Bethany Waites was dead hours before that."

Ron is awake now, that's for sure. He looks at Viktor, knowing the KGB officer might have better questions than he does.

"Well, this is an interesting development," says Viktor. "You know this for a fact, Jack?"

"I know it for a fact," says Jack Mason. "I know who killed her, I know why, and I know where she's buried. I know where the grave is."

"It sounds an awful lot like you killed her, Jack? Wouldn't you agree?"

"I would agree," says Jack. "But that's just the point, isn't it? More whisky, gents?"

Viktor and Ron both agree that's exactly what the doctor ordered. Jack Mason pours the drinks, and settles back again.

"You're missing someone," says Jack. "Someone else involved in my little scheme."

"Man? Woman?" asks Viktor, very casually.

"One of those, yeah," says Jack Mason. If you want someone to resist questioning from a KGB officer, a Cockney isn't a bad choice, Ron thinks.

"So this person," begins Ron. "Probably a fella, let's face it. They've killed Bethany Waites?"

"Here's what it is," says Jack Mason. "The scheme was coming apart. Bethany Waites was all over it—you've got to know when to quit? Right?"

"Crucial," says Viktor.

"I figure I'm covered. Whatever she's got, she hasn't got it on me, so I can just shut it down and move on."

"But this partner of yours?"

"My partner was more worried," says Jack Mason. "Left me in no doubt about that. I hadn't made any big mistakes, but my partner had. He—I'm going to say 'he' but don't read anything into it, I've been in this game a long time—he was worried about me talking, about Heather talking."

"You'd never talk," says Ron.

"Never have, never will," agrees Jack.

"You're talking now, Jack," says Viktor, very gently. Jack waves this away.

"So," says Ron. "This partner of yours kills Bethany Waites?"

"Before she caused more trouble," says Jack. "Killed her, drove to Shakespeare Cliff, pushed the car off. My partner wasn't the type at all, but he panicked. Happens to the best of us."

"But why wasn't the body in the car?" asks Viktor. "I wonder if you have an explanation for that?"

"Here's the thing," says Jack Mason. "Here's the big problem, the thing no one's seeing. My partner comes to me, tells me he's murdered Bethany Waites, tells me to switch on the news and see if it's true. Which I do, and it is. I'm not happy."

"Who would be?" says Ron.

"Who would be, like you say," agrees Jack. "I'm angry, of course I am, fly off the handle a bit. No one needed to die, we could have walked away, and he gives me a little smile and says no one's walking away, and I think he's going to kill me too. Which is a bit rich, but these things happen."

Ron and Viktor both nod.

"Then he says, 'You wanna see the body,' and I'm 'Wasn't the body in the car?,' and he's 'No, the body's buried somewhere safe.'"

"Jesus," says Ron. The whisky is giving him a bit of a headache. The lights blinking out at sea now look cold and lonely.

"And here's what he's done," says Jack. "He's killed Bethany, and he's buried her, and he's told me exactly where. And, here's the clever bit, I'll give him that, he's buried Bethany with a phone covered in Heather Garbutt's fingerprints that has a call history from one of my personal phones. And he's shot her with a gun that's buried somewhere else, also covered in Heather's fingerprints."

Viktor sits forward. "So Bethany is dead, she can meddle no longer. And your partner has framed Heather for the murder, and linked you as an accessory?"

"You're getting it," says Jack Mason. "He says to Heather, this fraud is going to trial. I need you to plead guilty, to admit everything, but not a word on who you were working for."

"Or I send the police in the direction of Bethany's grave?"

"Where all the evidence says Heather did it. So, do you want ten years in prison, or do you want life? It's blackmail, buried six feet underground."

"And that's been hanging over her the whole time she's been in prison?" asks Ron.

"She never said a word, and she never made a penny," says Jack Mason. "She just sat and did her time, knowing that one false move and she'd be a murderer."

"All that waiting," says Ron. "Then someone kills her too. That's, whatcha call it, bad luck."

The men nod, like the three wise monkeys.

"And what did he want from you?" asks Viktor.

"He wanted his money," says Jack Mason. "It was ten mill or so, and he couldn't access it."

"And you could?"

"Turns out no," says Jack Mason. "The rules changed back in 2015, everything had to be declared, hoops to jump through. And then other obstacles kept popping up, never really seen anything like it. Do you know much about money-laundering?"

"Yes," says Viktor.

"We washed it so thoroughly it was scattered to the winds. Heather was very good at her job. But when we needed it to start coming back the other way, as clean money, some of the things we needed to do to get it back were no longer legal. And some of the money had just vanished. We'd hid it so well even we couldn't find it."

"So it's still out there?" asks Viktor.

"Presumably," says Jack Mason.

"Any chance you're going to tell us who your partner was?" asks Ron.

"'Course not," says Jack Mason. "I shouldn't have told you as much as I have, but, if you can work it out, good luck to you."

"We'll work it out," says Ron. He can hear the car approaching in the distance.

"She shouldn't have died," says Jack Mason. "It's on me. And Heather shouldn't have died either, that's on me too."

"I'd like to disagree, Jack," says Ron. "But I can't."

Jack nods, and looks around him, at his house, his gardens, that view. "There was no need for any of it."

The headlights of Ron's Daihatsu sweep across the lawn. Bogdan is here. Jack rises to wish his friends farewell. But Viktor has a final question.

"Why did you not just dig the body up yourself? Problem solved."

"I tried to find it," says Jack Mason. "Over the years. Believe me, I tried. I knew where it was, and I've dug and dug, but—"

"Will you tell us where she's buried?" Viktor asks.

"I've told you enough to be getting on with," says Jack. "You buggers can work it out."

"Your candor has been admirable," says Viktor.

Jack puts an arm around Viktor's shoulders. "I can't help thinking these revelations have taken the edge off your snooker victory this evening. And Ron's shocking performance."

"Will we still be invited back?" asks Viktor.

"I can't think of anything more fun," says Jack Mason. "A couple of mates, a glass of whisky, a game of snooker. Everything else is ego and greed. It's taken me a long time to work that out."

"You still owe Viktor a tenner for winning though," says Ron.

"Among my many debts," says Jack Mason with a bow. "Among my many debts."

55.

Elizabeth is wide awake and thinking.

Viktor had rolled back late this evening, full of news and whisky. Ron was elsewhere, which is becoming an increasingly regular occurrence. A quick council of war had convened at Ibrahim's. Joyce and Alan had joined them, both excited to be out late.

The case had blown wide open.

So Bethany Waites hadn't been in the car at all. She had been buried somewhere else by her killer, as an insurance policy. Buried with evidence linking both Heather Garbutt and Jack Mason to her murder.

It was a neat trick. No one was looking for the body; it was assumed that it had been swept out to sea many years ago. But if Jack or Heather ever felt inclined to help the police with their inquiries, the killer would just have to remind them that their future was in his hands. Or her hands. Keep quiet about my involvement, or face the consequences. But there would be a flaw somewhere. A fatal mistake.

As Elizabeth had walked home, she had felt a plan forming. Her eyes had also been alert for the Viking. It would be rather bad timing to be killed now, just when things were getting interesting.

They would get nothing further out of Jack Mason, Elizabeth was sure of that. Viktor's work with Jack was done. So there were two options left open.

Take another look at the financial documents, knowing there was a partner involved. They had the name "Carron Whitehead," of course, but nothing else to connect her to the murder. Then there was the name Robert

Brown MSc. But were there others? Viktor would be back on the case tomorrow morning. He has yet to make much progress.

The second option, just as difficult, but at least something Elizabeth could help with, was to find the grave that Jack Mason has spoken about. The general consensus is that it could be anywhere. But Elizabeth rarely lives her life by the general consensus.

A question that had been troubling her for a while has risen to the surface again. Why had Jack Mason bought Heather Garbutt's house? The proceeds had gone straight to the government in lieu of the laundered money, so he hadn't been buying Heather's silence. He hadn't lived in it, hadn't rented it out, hadn't renovated it and hadn't sold it at a profit.

So it seemed that Jack Mason must have bought the house simply to stop anyone else from living there. From living there and, let's say, relaying the patio or deciding on a whim to dig a pond or two? Elizabeth wonders if it wouldn't be fruitful to have a little dig in Heather Garbutt's garden? Bogdan will have a spade to hand somewhere.

But how do you just dig up someone's garden without permission? Jack Mason certainly won't be inviting them onto the property if the body is there.

As Elizabeth lies in bed, Stephen's hand interlaced with hers, she thinks of someone who might be able to help.

And now she really thinks about it, the same person might be able to help with her other problem too. Stopping the Viking. Stephen wakes and takes her in his arms. He says he is off to see his friend Kuldesh tomorrow, will probably take the car if she isn't using it? Elizabeth agrees that sounds lovely and strokes his hair until he falls asleep again.

56.

They must have gossiped on the way back?" Donna says. Her head is in Bogdan's lap. He wants to watch the International Biathlon on Eurosport, because someone he went to school with is in it. Biathlon is skiing followed by rifle shooting. She is getting into it.

"They swore me not to tell," says Bogdan. He then gestures at the television. "Jerzy is having a nightmare here."

"But you can tell *me,*" says Donna.

"No police," says Bogdan.

"I'm not police," says Donna. "I'm your girlfriend."

"You never said you were my girlfriend before," says Bogdan.

Donna turns her head to look up at him. "Well, get ready to hear it a lot."

"So I am your boyfriend?"

"I honestly don't know why people think you're some sort of genius," says Donna. "Yes, you're my boyfriend."

Bogdan gives a smile of delight. "We are Donna and Bogdan."

"We are," says Donna, reaching up to touch his face. "Or Bogdan and Donna, I don't mind."

"Donna and Bogdan sounds better," says Bogdan.

Donna props herself up and kisses him. "Donna and Bogdan it is, then. So, tell me what Ron and Viktor found out."

"No," says Bogdan. He is then distracted by the television again. "This Lithuanian guy is a cheat."

"Just tell me something," says Donna. "Throw me a bone."

"OK," says Bogdan. "Ron didn't go home tonight. He is staying at Pauline's."

"Oooh," says Donna. "That's good. You're forgiven."

Bogdan is shaking his head at the screen. "If Jerzy doesn't finish in the top four, he doesn't qualify for the European Shootout in Malmö."

"Poor Jerzy," says Donna. "Pull your finger out, mate. Where does she live?"

"Huh?" Bogdan is distracted.

"Pauline," says Donna sleepily. "She live round here?"

Bogdan nods. "Off Rotherfield Road, that big block. Juniper Court."

"Juniper Court?"

"Yes. You heard of it?"

Donna certainly has heard of it. Pauline lives in the building Bethany Waites visited on the night of her murder.

57.

The office is warm oak, and deep-red carpet. Elizabeth's eye is drawn to the large painting of a dog wearing a Police Bravery Medal. Also, a framed sign saying CRIME DOESN'T PAY. She has learned over the years that this is nonsense. Look at Viktor's penthouse for example.

It can be difficult to get an appointment with a chief constable. They are busy people, their diaries are carefully controlled. Try ringing 999 and asking to speak to a chief constable. See where that gets you.

Elizabeth had rung Andrew Everton's office that morning, saying she was a literary agent who had read and loved all the Mackenzie McStewart novels, and would he have a moment to spare for her?

The call came back within a minute, saying that a window had magically opened up in his diary that very afternoon. Whatever it was that Andrew Everton had planned on doing then, catching a serial killer perhaps, could be put on the back burner.

Elizabeth had seen the disappointment in his eyes when she walked in. He recognized her from the reading. There was a brief moment of regrouping hope, as he considered that, yes, this was the old woman from the reading the other day, but she might also actually be an agent, some grande dame of the literary world. But as soon as she had said, "I haven't actually read your books, though I know Joyce is enjoying one," she saw the wind depart his sails. By this point she had sat down, however, and she knew that common politeness would allow her a couple of questions.

"Bethany Waites," says Elizabeth. "You remember the case?"

"I remember the case," says Andrew Everton. "I don't remember asking you to come in and talk to me about it?"

Elizabeth waves this away. "We're all taxpayers, aren't we? Anything you can tell me? Any suspects at the time?"

"Mmm," says Andrew Everton. "Are you familiar with police procedure?"

"Very," says Elizabeth.

Andrew Everton starts to tap a pen on his desk. "And does this conversation feel like it tallies with police procedure? Given what you know?"

"Here's what I think," says Elizabeth. "I think you're the Chief Constable of Kent. I think you could probably tell me all sorts of things if you chose to. I also think you failed to close the Bethany Waites case—"

"Not me personally," says Andrew Everton. "To be fair. I was a smaller cog in those days."

"Quite so," agrees Elizabeth. "But a high-profile case, still unsolved. I'm offering you some help, and it feels only fair that you offer me help in return."

"What help are you offering me?"

"We'll get to that in good time," says Elizabeth. "You'll know that Heather Garbutt is dead. Was she your prime suspect?"

"She was a suspect," says Andrew Everton. "Again, what help can you give me? What do you know that I might not?"

"And Jack Mason?" asks Elizabeth. "Another suspect?"

"We spoke to him," says Andrew Everton. "He had an alibi, but he's not the type of man to do the deed himself, so it was fairly meaningless. I don't quite understand why we are having this conversation?"

"Anyone else?" asks Elizabeth. "Anyone we're missing?"

"Who is we?"

"My friends and I," says Elizabeth. "People you would like. I believe you've met Ibrahim, for instance."

"Ah, yes," says Andrew Everton. "Ibrahim Arif. A friend of Connie Johnson's?"

"A professional acquaintance of hers," says Elizabeth. "We have fingers in pies, Chief Constable. I am sure you would find us useful."

Andrew Everton is weighing her up. Elizabeth has seen it countless times before. People trying to get the measure of her. It's a fruitless endeavor.

"OK," says Andrew Everton. "I'll bite. Does Connie Johnson have anything to say about Heather Garbutt's death? Is that information that you have?"

"She thinks Heather Garbutt was frightened of someone," says Elizabeth.

"Well, with respect we could gather that much from the note; that's not new information," says Andrew Everton. "I'll need better than that. Did she say who?"

"I'm afraid that is information I don't have. But you'll be delighted to hear I can help you with the note," says Elizabeth. "It wasn't real."

"Wasn't real?" Elizabeth sees Andrew Everton think this through, working the angles. Experience tells her he is no fool. He might actually be useful to them.

"She didn't write it?" Andrew Everton still looks confused. "Then who did?"

"We're working on that," says Elizabeth. "But until then I have a different question for you. Where do you think the money is? If we can't find Bethany Waites's body, can we at least find the money?"

"You're aware we did try," says Andrew Everton. "We're not bumpkins. We had forensic accountants go through every page of every file. They covered their tracks."

Elizabeth laughs. "Honestly, we've found out more about the money in two weeks than you did in your whole investigation."

"I doubt that," says Andrew Everton.

"Doubt away, dear," says Elizabeth. "It won't change the facts. You didn't find the forty thousand pounds paid to Carron Whitehead. You didn't find the five thousand pounds paid to Robert Brown MSc. You didn't find the connection to Jack Mason's construction companies. You didn't really find anything."

Andrew Everton tries to form a reply. "I'm . . . I'm going to need those names. The details. Where you found them."

"There's the answer to your question about how we can help you, and"—Elizabeth takes out a file from her bag and puts it on his desk—"we can start with this."

Andrew Everton looks at the file in front of him. "It's all in here?"

"It is," says Elizabeth. "And it's all yours. But I will need a couple of favors in return."

"Yes, you have that air about you," says Andrew Everton. "If I can help, I will."

"Jack Mason bought Heather Garbutt's house," says Elizabeth. "Over the odds too. Why do you think that might be?"

Andrew Everton has no answer. "Honestly? I wasn't aware of that."

"Perhaps you should have been?"

"Perhaps I should," says Andrew Everton. "Agreed."

"Now that you know," says Elizabeth, "what do your detective instincts tell you?"

"That perhaps he was hiding something there? Or knew that Heather was hiding something there?"

"That's what my instincts tell me too," says Elizabeth. "It feels like it wouldn't do us any harm to go digging to see? If you could arrange that?"

Andrew Everton thinks for a moment. Elizabeth suspects there are all sorts of forms he would need to fill in to make this happen. Protocols.

"I think I could," says Andrew Everton. "I think that sounds a very good idea. See what we can see."

"See what we can see," agrees Elizabeth. "I knew we'd get along."

"What was the other favor?" asks Andrew Everton.

"There's a money-launderer trying to kill me," says Elizabeth. "Trying to kill Joyce too, but that's between us. I wonder if you might spare a couple of officers to guard us for a while?"

"A money-launderer?" says Andrew Everton.

"Best in the world, they say. Let's hope he's not such a good assassin."

"Let me look into it," says Andrew Everton. "That might be quite hard to explain away."

"I'm sure you'll try your best," says Elizabeth. "And you might just catch the biggest money-launderer in the world in the process. That feels like something that would be good for your career."

Andrew Everton smiles. "This has been an unexpected pleasure."

"Well, strap in," says Elizabeth. "Next time I see you I expect you to have a spade in your hand."

Elizabeth stands to leave. This has all been most satisfactory. If anyone can get permission to dig up a back garden, it's a chief constable. Andrew Everton rises with her.

"Before you go," says Andrew Everton, "I have a question for you."

"People usually do," says Elizabeth. She senses Andrew Everton is nervous. "Fire away."

"I need an honest answer," says Andrew Everton.

"If an honest answer is available, you shall have it," says Elizabeth.

"Your friend Joyce . . ." says Andrew Everton.

"What about her?" says Elizabeth.

"Did she *really* say she was enjoying my book?"

58.

Donna has very quickly come to understand that one of the key functions of a television makeup room is to be a central hub for all and any gossip.

Though, on this occasion, she is going to have to tread carefully.

Donna is back on *South East Tonight* to discuss online fraud. Dodgy emails or texts pretending to be from banks. Fake dating profiles. Basically, any of the number of ways someone can part you from your cash without ever having to actually meet you. She has been doing homework all afternoon.

"A little bird tells me you live in Juniper Court," says Donna.

Pauline pauses for a moment. Donna has to keep this as light as possible. They had run all the car registration numbers. The white Peugeot with flames on the number plate belongs to Pauline.

Pauline continues teasing Donna's hair into shape. "That little bird wouldn't be Bogdan, would it?"

"Maybe," says Donna. "We've been trying to keep it quiet."

"Can't hide anything from a makeup artist," says Pauline. "You landed on your feet there, what a fella. I'd climb him like a tree."

Donna smiles and keeps it chatty. "You been there long?"

"Juniper Court? Donkey's years," says Pauline. "You can walk to the studio, it's perfect."

So there it is, the information she was here to get. Pauline has lived at Juniper Court for years. Which means she will have been living there the night Bethany died. Which, in turn, potentially makes her the chief suspect in the murder of Bethany Waites. Things are moving uncomfortably fast for Donna.

Pauline taps Donna's forehead. "Relax, you're frowning. The makeup chair isn't for thinking."

"Sorry," says Donna. She takes the briefest of glances at Pauline in the mirror. Pauline gives her a reassuring smile.

What reason would Pauline have for murdering Bethany Waites? What was buried in the past? What about the notes? Had Pauline written them? Chris and Donna are keeping this new line of inquiry secret from the Thursday Murder Club. For a number of obvious reasons. But if Bethany had been visiting Pauline that night, they wouldn't be able to keep it secret for much longer. It was too much of a coincidence, Bethany visiting the building where Pauline lived. There had to be a connection.

"That's why I moved to Juniper Court in the first place," says Pauline, over the sound of her hairdryer now. "Loads of the crew live there. Cameras, sound, all sorts. The show even keeps a couple of flats there, you know, freelancers come down for a few months, that's where they get put up. Mike had a place there years back. It's like a hall of residence half the time."

Donna nods. Well, that complicates things. If it's true. All sorts of people Bethany might have known. All sorts of people she might have been visiting. Donna needs more information.

"Bethany ever visit?" Donna asks. Trying to be casual, but over the sound of the hairdryer.

"How do you mean?"

"Would Bethany have ever visited Juniper Court?"

"I'd have thought so," says Pauline. "People were in and out. Fiona Clemence had a thing with one of the camera ops who lived there. It was open house."

"Did she ever visit you there?" Donna asks.

"Me? No," says Pauline. She switches off her hairdryer. "Don't think she even knew I lived there."

"You'd think she'd have bumped into you," says Donna. "At some point. If she was there a lot?"

"I'm a bit more private than some of them," says Pauline, shrugging.

Donna had plenty to report back to Chris. The good news: Pauline had lived in Juniper Court when Bethany Waites disappeared. The bad news: so had everyone else. Convenient for Pauline. Too convenient?

"That's you done, darling," says Pauline. "Don't you look a picture?"

Donna looks at herself in the mirror. Just perfect. Pauline is very, very good.

59.

He thought he might have to kill the dog, but, in the end, there was no need. From the moment he broke in, the dog seemed very happy to see him. Had even licked his hand while he loaded the gun. He had been fast asleep until the key turned in the lock for the first time. The Viking would love a dog, but they take a lot of looking after. Walking and so on. And sometimes things go wrong with them. What if something went wrong and he didn't notice? The Viking would never forgive himself. He has heard that cats are easier. Maybe he will get a cat.

The first person through the door is Joyce; he recognizes her from the photograph. Joyce has a shopping bag in her hand. She is swaying slightly, and is whistling a happy tune. She stops whistling when she sees the gun, which makes the Viking feel guilty, but powerful. Mainly guilty, but he couldn't deny the powerful bit. He supposes that is why weak people like guns so much. Not that he is weak.

The dog bounds to greet her, and Joyce ruffles his coat without taking her eyes off the man with the beard and the gun who has just appeared in her living room.

"Bless you," says Joyce. "You must be the Viking?"

The Viking is confused. "The Viking?"

"You kidnapped Elizabeth," says Joyce. "And Stephen, which was very cowardly. Put your gun down; I'm seventy-seven, what do you think I'm going to do?"

The Viking puts the gun down by his side, but keeps hold of it. It is around seven p.m., and dark outside. He has closed the curtains already. Joyce is less scared than he thought she might be. She even feeds the dog. "Alan," he is called. She offers the Viking a cup of tea, but, wary of being poisoned, he declines. She sits opposite him while Alan eats, his metal bowl scraping noisily on the kitchen tiles.

"So you're here to kill Viktor?" she asks. "He's not in."

"I am here to kill Viktor, yes," says the Viking. "But also to kill you."

"Oh," says Joyce.

"They didn't tell you?"

"They didn't," confirms Joyce. "This seems like an awful lot of fuss. I hope it's over something very important?"

"It's business," says the Viking. "I told Elizabeth to kill Viktor. She didn't kill him. I told her I would kill you if she didn't."

"Well, she kept that quiet," says Joyce. "Have you ever killed anyone before?"

"Yes," says the Viking. His voice doesn't even waver. He is very impressed with himself.

"And yet you had to get Elizabeth to kill Viktor for you," says Joyce. "Have you really ever killed anyone?"

"No," admits the Viking. How could she tell? "I have never needed to. But now I need to. And I will."

"So you're going to start with me? That's in at the deep end, I'd say. A pensioner."

The Viking shrugs. "Maybe I'll just kill Viktor, then."

"I'd sooner you didn't kill either of us," says Joyce. "I've grown fond of him. Watches too many programs about trains, but who doesn't have faults? What's your disagreement with him? Are you sure you don't want a cup of tea? We'll be here some while if we're waiting for Viktor, and I promise I'm not going to poison you. The last thing I need on my hands is an unconscious Swede."

The Viking thinks he wouldn't actually mind a cup of tea. His whole plan doesn't seem at all right now he's here, with a gun in his hand, and a tiny old woman asking him polite questions. "OK, yes, please, just with milk. I have a dispute with Viktor."

Joyce walks through the open archway into the kitchen, and talks to him over her shoulder. "What sort of dispute?"

"I launder money," says the Viking. "Through cryptocurrency. Viktor tells his clients to steer clear of me. Says it's too risky. It is costing me a great deal of money. If I kill him, my problem is over."

"Oh, you poor love, that must be difficult," says Joyce. "Alan, I have literally just fed you."

"When are you expecting him?"

"You tell me," says Joyce, teaspoon clinking in a mug. "He's at an opera, if you can believe that. Might as well settle in. Can I ask you a question?"

"You won't persuade me not to kill him," says the Viking. "It is my destiny."

"No, no," says Joyce, walking back into the room with two mugs of tea, one with a picture of a motorbike on it, one with a floral scene. "Which mug do you fancy?"

"Motorbike, please," says the Viking. Joyce sits down with a satisfied sigh. "What's your question?"

"Cryptocurrency," says Joyce. "It's not really all that risky, is it?"

"Very risky," says the Viking. "Which is OK for money-laundering."

"Even Ethereum?" asks Joyce. "Is that risky?"

The Viking takes a sip of his tea. "You know Ethereum?"

"I have fifteen thousand pounds invested in it," says Joyce. "Everyone on Instagram seems very confident."

"Can you show me your account?" says the Viking. Honestly, amateurs will be the death of him. Cryptocurrency is complicated. One day it will be very important, but today it is the Wild West. Tiny old women should not be investing in Ethereum. Joyce opens up a page on her laptop and hands it to him.

"I only use the laptop for trading and for writing my diary," she says. "You'll be in it tonight if you don't kill me."

"I'm not going to kill you," says the Viking, but he knows he still might have to. He checks Joyce's Ethereum account, currently worth just under two thousand pounds. "Do you mind if I move things around a little? I will need your password."

"It's Poppy82, capital *p*," says Joyce. "And be my guest. If you promise not to kill Viktor, then there are biscuits too."

"Sorry, mind made up," says the Viking, as he drinks more of his tea, and launches Joyce's laptop into one of the more disreputable corners of the dark web. Playing on the computer relaxes him a little, as this is where he is at home. His heart rate slows, and he realizes how nervous he has been. The dog starts to lick his hand, and he feels his eyes start to puff up a little. He was allergic to dogs when he was younger, so avoids them now. He gently pushes Alan away, and rubs his eyes with the unlicked hand.

The Viking moves Joyce's money into two separate accounts. There were still bargains to be had if you knew where to look. There was still gold glinting in the streams, but not where everyone else was panning. The Viking feels this is the least he can do after breaking into Joyce's flat. If he doesn't kill her, she will make a tidy profit. Joyce is saying something now, but it isn't making sense. He is thirsty again. He looks up at Joyce, but his head is heavy. He starts a sentence.

"Could I get a . . ." Get a what? What's the word? "Uh . . ."

Alan is licking his face now. Why is he on the floor?

60.

Ron is aware that we live in a bright new world of sexual politics. A rainbow of gender and sexuality, and freedoms unimagined by his generation. Ron is all for it. If you let people be themselves, you let them flourish. But even in these happier times if you offer a man a choice between a motorcycle mug and a flower mug, he's going to choose the motorcycle mug. Lucky thing too: if Viktor's tablets could floor the Viking, God knows what they would have done to Joyce.

"You could have killed him, Joyce," says Elizabeth.

"With sleeping pills and worming tablets? I doubt it," says Joyce.

The Viking is beginning to stir. Bogdan has tied him to one of Joyce's dining-room chairs. After he had fallen asleep, Joyce had called the cavalry, and here they all were.

Bogdan for muscle, Viktor, back from the opera ("Exquisite. Almost transcendent") to face the man who wants to kill him, and Elizabeth, who has just had to explain why she hadn't told Joyce that the Viking was planning to kill her too. Ron and Ibrahim are there, presumably, thinks Ron, because Joyce and Elizabeth would never hear the end of it if they hadn't been invited.

Pauline is there because, well, because she is there an awful lot these days. Whether in Coopers Chase or Juniper Court, she and Ron like to be together. She's come straight from work. Bogdan has disappeared somewhere for now, who knows where with that guy?

Viktor is holding the Viking's gun. Ron had asked to hold it briefly. He had pointed it at the wall, closed one eye, said, "Pow," and handed it back.

The Viking looks a bit of a mess. Huge beard. Semi-conscious. Ron had tried to grow a beard many years ago, but he was not successful. Some men just can't grow beards, and you shouldn't read anything into that. Doesn't make them any less of a man.

Joyce has made them all a cup of tea, after thoroughly washing out the motorbike mug.

"Hey, sleeping beauty," says Viktor, as the Viking wakes. "Hey."

The Viking opens his eyes, just a touch. Then closes them again, unable to immediately accept what he sees.

"It's OK," says Viktor. "You can open them. You want some water?"

The Viking opens his eyes once again, and tries to focus on Joyce's carpet. With effort, he raises his head and looks toward Joyce. "You drugged me."

"I did," admits Joyce.

"You said you wouldn't," says the Viking.

"Forgive me," says Joyce. "You were going to kill Viktor. And you're very imposing."

"That is a fine beard," says Ibrahim. "How do you go about growing a beard such as that? Do you use oils?"

"Maybe a question for another time, Ibrahim," says Viktor.

"Anyone can grow a beard," says Ron.

Viktor gets down on his haunches. Ron remembers a time when he could get down on his haunches. Viktor has been lucky with his knees. "What's your name, Viking?"

"No one shall ever know my name," says the Viking.

"Well, we'll see about that," says Viktor.

"No one shall ever speak my name," says the Viking, and lets out a roar.

"Well, someone's woken up," says Joyce. Alan wanders in from the bedroom to investigate the noise.

Ron gives Pauline a reassuring wink. She is sitting forward, enjoying the theater.

"Best date ever, Ron," she says.

"Let's talk about why you want to kill me so much," says Viktor. "OK?"

"You will regret this," says the Viking. "Every one of you will regret this."

"I cost you money, I understand that," says Viktor. "I refuse to recommend you. But you understand why? Cryptocurrency is risky."

"No, it isn't," says Joyce. "Someone's been reading the mainstream media." She ruffles Alan's hair. "Haven't they, Alan? Yes, they *have*."

"You're living in the past," says the Viking.

"There is truth in that," says Viktor. "I live where I am comfortable. I live where my skills are. You will be the same in thirty, forty years. Talking about cryptocurrency while the youngsters laugh at you. But you know what is good for you here? I live in the past because I'm old. I am old, my Viking friend, and you know what that means? It means you don't have to kill me, you just have to be patient. The cells in my body, they atrophy as we speak. Everyone you see before you will be dead before you know it."

"Keep it light, Viktor," says Pauline.

"So I'm a fool. So I'm in your way, I cost you some money." Viktor shrugs. "You're doing OK, I heard about your house. Just go about your business—you do it well, I know. You know why no one has killed me yet?"

"Why?"

"Because I never kill anyone," says Viktor. "Honestly, once you start, that's it, you have to keep killing."

"That's like lip salve," says Pauline. "Once you start using it, your lips dry out, and so you have to keep using it."

Viktor gestures toward Pauline to show his point is proven. "So here is my suggestion. You get on with your life, launder money, enjoy your house, don't kill people. I'll get on with my life, do my job, then die of natural causes in five to seven years if you're lucky."

"And if I disagree? If I still think you cost me too much money?"

"Then kill me," says Viktor. "I'll put the word out today, to my many friends and associates, that you wish to kill me. And when my body is found, they will come to their own conclusions, and they will track you down and murder you."

A key turns in Joyce's door. Viktor throws himself on the ground, pointing his gun toward it. As it opens, Bogdan walks in, and Viktor reholsters the gun. Walking behind Bogdan is Stephen, looking very dapper in a suit. The Viking is focusing on Viktor, however.

"Your friends won't find me," says the Viking. "No one knows me. Look at you, a KGB colonel, and you have found out nothing about me. And you"—he turns to Elizabeth—"an MI6 officer, you have found out nothing about me. I am a ghost. You can't kill a ghost."

As the Viking makes his speech, Ron sees Stephen take a seat on one of Joyce's dining chairs. He pulls a notepad out of his pocket. Ron sees that Stephen's hands are shaking. But not from fear.

"Ghost are you, chief?" says Stephen, tapping his notebook. He has the immediate attention of the room. "Nice to see you again by the way. This is the Viking you were talking about, then, Elizabeth."

"Yes, dear," says Elizabeth. "The very one."

"Henrik Mikael Hansen, born in Norrköping on May 4, 1989," Stephen reads from his notebook. "Mum a pastry chef, dad a librarian. What do you say to that?"

"You are wrong," says Henrik Mikael Hansen of Norrköping. "You couldn't be more wrong. I'm Swedish, but apart from that. No one is a pastry chef."

"You love books, Henrik," says Stephen. "I love them too. You have quite the collection. A lot of them unique. And with unique books you can usually find a record of their sale. Nowadays you buy them all through a holding company, but when you first started collecting, you used your own name, and that's how we discovered your identity. It was a first edition of *Wind in the Willows* that gave you away."

"No," says Henrik. "This is impossible."

"Far from it, Henrik. It is an admirable way to get caught, at least. Once we had the name, everything else fell into our laps. Your sister is currently skiing, for example," says Stephen. "That's from Facebook."

"Stephen," says Elizabeth. "Stephen."

"Just doing my bit," says Stephen. "Mainly Kuldesh. We owe them dinner."

"You've really been to see Kuldesh?"

"I told you I had," says Stephen.

"Yes, I—" says Elizabeth.

"We drove down," says Bogdan. "Was a secret."

Elizabeth fixes Bogdan with a stare. "Full of little secrets at the moment, aren't you, Bogdan?"

Everyone else has turned to look at Henrik Hansen.

Ron is glad he was invited to witness this whole scene. Previously it's the sort of thing Elizabeth and Joyce would have taken care of themselves, only to fill him in the next morning. He is aware he hasn't yet been helpful, but he is grateful to be in the room.

"I am not Henrik Hansen," says Henrik Hansen.

"I think you probably are," says Elizabeth. "My husband doesn't get an awful lot wrong."

"Henrik, we can be friends," says Viktor. "Or, if not friends, then acquaintances who choose not to kill each other. If you leave me in peace, I will make sure my many clients leave you in peace too."

"No, I am not Henrik," says Henrik again, his anger rising. "You are all wrong, and you are all dead. Every single one of you."

"Henrik," says Joyce, kindly, "you couldn't even kill me."

"Then I won't kill all of you. I will kill one of you," says Henrik. "Yes. As a lesson for the others. The second you let me go, the hunt begins."

Henrik's eyes scan the room, looking for prey. They settle on Ron.

"You," says Henrik. "I will kill you."

Ron rolls his eyes. "It's always me."

"You will never see me coming," says Henrik.

Pauline stands, slowly and calmly. She walks over to Henrik and places a hand on either side of his face. The room falls silent.

"Henrik, listen to me carefully, my darling. I've met a thousand men like you, and I know you need things spelled out for you. So here goes. If you even dream of touching a hair on Ron's head, I will kill you. That man is under my protection, and if any harm comes to him I will put bullets in your knees, and then in your elbows, and then, when I've tired of hearing you screaming, which will take a long, long time, I will put a bullet in your head to finish you off. In fact, if Ron wakes up with so much as a *cough,* I will find you, and I will cut out your heart and eat it. And I will send the video evidence to your mum, the pastry chef. Do we have the beginnings of an understanding?"

Henrik is losing heart quickly. He points at Ibrahim now. "Then I will kill him."

Pauline squeezes his face even tighter. "That's Ron's best friend. Which makes him my best friend too."

Ron has not seen Ibrahim blush before.

"No one dies here today," continues Pauline. "Viktor has been very reasonable, so stop pretending to be a psychopath."

"I am a psychopath," protests Henrik.

"Darling," says Pauline, letting go of Henrik's face, "a psychopath would have shot Alan."

Alan gives a happy *woof*. He likes hearing his name.

Henrik looks beaten. "I thought this would be easier."

"I'm going to get you a water," says Joyce. "It will be quite safe, I promise you."

"Thank you, Joyce," says Henrik. "I should have chosen the flower mug. Even as I chose the motorbike mug, I thought, 'Oh, come on, that's so cliché.'"

"We're all programmed," says Joyce. "Joanna made me watch a YouTube video about it."

"I'm going to untie you now," says Viktor. "I can trust you, yes? Even if I can't, I have a gun, and I'm assuming Elizabeth has a gun too. Perhaps even Pauline has one."

Viktor loosens the baling wire around Henrik's wrists, and he wriggles his hands free. Joyce comes back in with the water and Henrik takes it from her.

"Thank you, Joyce," he says.

"I can take a sip of it if you'd like?" says Joyce.

The room falls into a momentary, contented silence. It is broken by Pauline again.

"Can I make an observation?"

Ron looks at Pauline, who, once again, has the attention of the room. My God, he's got a hell of a woman on his hands here.

"I love an observation," says Ibrahim. "It is grist to my mill. Especially coming from a good friend such as you, Pauline."

"OK, here's how I see things," says Pauline. "And I've only known you a short while. But this is just my take, and who am I to say? But each and every one of you in the room, each and every one of you, in your own different way, is absolutely barking mad."

Joyce looks at Elizabeth. Elizabeth looks at Ibrahim. Ibrahim looks at Ron. Ron looks at Joyce. Viktor and Alan look at each other.

Stephen surveys the room. "She has a point."

"I've known you for just over two weeks, and I've already been in a grave with a KGB colonel, I've seen a tiny old woman drug a Viking, and I've shared a bed with the most handsome man in Kent. For three or four years in the eighties I did a lot of magic mushrooms. I once did LSD in Bratislava with Iron Maiden. But nothing—nothing I've ever done—compares to a couple of days in your company. What else have you got in store?"

"Well," says Elizabeth. "Tomorrow we're digging up a garden with the Chief Constable of Kent, looking for a body and a gun."

"Bethany's body?" says Pauline. She is suddenly serious.

"Bethany's body," confirms Elizabeth. "Now, Henrik, I wonder if you might stick around here for a day or so? There's a spare room at Ibrahim's, if Ibrahim wouldn't mind?"

"It would be my pleasure," says Ibrahim. "Henrik has had a long and traumatic day."

"I just want to go home," says Henrik.

"All in good time, Henrik," says Elizabeth. "There's a task I think you might be able to help us with first."

61.

Joyce

Inspector Gerry Meadowcroft lit a cigarette, and inhaled deeply. A cloud of smoke drifted across his fierce blue eyes. Eyes that had seen too much killing, too much blood, too many widows. He felt the weight of a gun in his pocket. Would he have to use it?

Gerry could kill. He had killed before, and he would kill again if he was called upon. But not through choice, never through choice. Each time he killed, Gerry Meadowcroft lost a piece of his soul. How many pieces did he have left? Gerry was in no mood to find out.

He thought back to his training at Ashford Police College. Not everyone trained at Hendon, that was a misconception.

What do you think? I've been inspired to give writing a go. There is a short-story competition in the *Evening Argus*, first prize a hundred pounds and a Zoom call with a literary agent. I don't really want to do any more Zoom calls than I absolutely have to, but I could give the hundred pounds to Alan's rescue center, and it might be fun, mightn't it?

My detective is named after Gerry, though my Gerry had brown eyes, because you have to change some things. Also, my Gerry had hay fever, and I've changed that too. I can't just have my Gerry pottering about solving a murder. So this Gerry has blue eyes and a gun, while my Gerry had brown eyes and an organ-donor card. But my Gerry often said, "Well, then, Bob's your uncle," and I'm going to make that the detective's catchphrase too.

At the moment, the story is called "Cannibal Bloodbath," but I might change that, because it gives away too much of the plot.

62.

So they think they know where Bethany might be buried. Buried. That just makes no sense at all. Oh, Bethany, what on earth did you get involved in?

Mike Waghorn pours himself a glass of cider. He doesn't really drink cider in public, it doesn't look right. In public, he drinks champagne, good wine, the sort of stuff people would expect Mike Waghorn to drink. A beer if he's fitting in with the lads at a corporate do.

But when Mike was a teenager, he would only drink cider, and as he gets older he finds himself returning to it. He has tried expensive cider, you can get that now. Waitrose does one, but, really, the cheaper the better with cider. The one he is currently drinking is from a two-liter plastic bottle. He has poured it into a heavy cut-glass decanter, just for appearances, but he might stop doing that soon as well. Who is he trying to fool? There is no one here, so he can only be fooling himself.

He washes down his arthritis pills, then his beta-blockers, and his gout medication. You're not really supposed to drink alcohol with any of them, but no one is going to stop him.

He is watching *Stop the Clock* on a very big television. Fiona Clemence looks wonderful. He thought he should probably give it a go, after Joyce mentioned it. Admit some professional jealousy, swallow a bit of pride, he has plenty to spare, and watch it once. See if Fiona Clemence is any good. He hoped not.

Annoyingly, he watched an episode and is now hooked. Fiona is OK, friendly enough, good at reading out loud, but what a quiz. Mike imagines what he might have done with it. Every time a contestant says something, Mike thinks about how he would respond. Once or twice Fiona Clemence says the same thing as he would have done, and that irks him a little, but, overall, he thinks he'd be slightly better.

But isn't that just the thing, Mike? You can think all you like, but you never did it. Never took the risks. He filmed a pilot once, the late eighties or so. It went well, everybody agreed, ITV loved it, commissioned a series, but wanted one little change. Could they get a different host? Someone younger, someone—and these words remained etched in his mind for a long time—"more *authentic*, more *real*."

Mike never put his perfectly groomed head above the parapet again, never left the burrow, however much he could smell the air outside. "More authentic, more real"—for years he had railed against this insult. Mike *was* real, Mike *was* authentic, and if some twenty-somethings from London with fashionable hair and trainers couldn't see that, the problem was not with Mike, it was with them.

So there he sat, behind his desk, year in, year out, telling the people of Kent and Sussex about fires in care homes, building-society robberies in Faversham, or a Hastings man claiming to have the world's largest bouncy castle. And he was real enough and authentic enough for the people of Kent and Sussex, thank you very much. Walk through the streets of Maidstone or East Grinstead and see who thinks Mike is real. Everyone.

There were a couple more approaches from national TV, never anything concrete or exciting, but approaches nonetheless. But Mike refused even to consider them. He was happy where he was, thank you.

Except, Mike thinks back, looking at his cider in the ridiculous decanter, he wasn't happy at all. Did he know he wasn't happy? No, he had enough booze, and enough local adulation to keep him sedated, to keep his train on the tracks. He'd started to become a little more irritable, sure, a little bit more demanding of those he worked with, probably less fun to be around.

But that, to his mind, was just professionalism, in a world where the people around him started getting younger and younger. As the teams he was used to working with started drifting off to bigger things, to London, or, in one particularly galling case, to Los Angeles.

But Mike was not happy. And the reason that Mike was not happy was that Mike was not authentic, and Mike was not real.

And who taught him that lesson?

Bethany Waites.

How old was he when Bethany arrived? She was a researcher first, so maybe 2008? Wikipedia will tell you that Mike Waghorn was fifty-six in 2008, but he was sixty-one. Bethany would have been early twenties, he supposes, down from Leeds, with a Media Studies degree of all things. She would make him tea, he would tell her what a waste of time a Media Studies degree was, she would bring him stories her more experienced colleagues had missed, he would buy her a pint after work, she would challenge him, goad him, encourage him, and he would make sure she got safely into a taxi at the end of the night.

A year or so in, Mike told Bethany she should be appearing on air. Bethany, typically, did not disagree with this assessment. So she started filming reports. Then, every now and again, she'd pop into the studio to discuss those reports. Then, when Mike's co-host was on an ill-advised holiday, Bethany would step in, and, before you knew it, Mike and Bethany were the team at *South East Tonight*.

One evening they had been having a pint near the studio, as they often did, and there was a copy of *Kent Matters* on the bar. It was a local magazine, just photos from events, adverts for spas and expensive houses, that sort of thing. There had been a picture of Mike in the magazine. He was looking very suave, wearing a tux, at some business event or other. The Kent Accountancy Awards maybe. He remembered that one because he had fatally mispronounced the name of the awards very early on, and had the crowd firmly on his side from thereon.

He had taken Pauline as his "plus one," as he often did in those days. She liked a drink, and he liked having someone else to talk to other than an accountant from Sevenoaks who hadn't heard of him but demanded a selfie nonetheless.

Bethany had pointed the picture out, his arm around Pauline's waist, and Mike had smiled, and told her about the "Kent Accountancy" slip-up. Bethany then began the long process of making Mike a better, happier man.

"You should have been there with your boyfriend," she had said. Very matter of fact, bag of peanuts torn open and spatchcocked on the table in front of her. Mike can see it and hear it now.

They had another pint, and another, and another. Mike had never really spoken about being gay before. Not openly, in a pub, with a colleague. He was old enough to have kept his sexuality hidden, a rolled-up secret in a deep pocket. It had never seen the light of day before.

And why? Well, a hundred reasons. A thousand reasons. But those reasons were all tied together with a knot of shame. And it was that knot that Bethany began to unpick. Bethany refused to let Mike feel shame. She was from a different generation. A generation Mike envies. He sees them sometimes, out on the streets. He is certain they have their vulnerabilities and their insecurities, and they certainly still have many fights, but the joy with which they choose to present themselves—it makes Mike so proud and so jealous all at once.

The process wasn't quick, and the process wasn't easy, but Bethany was by his side throughout. Mike came out to friends. He came out to colleagues. He remembers telling Pauline for the first time. He was very serious, very solemn as he told her his secret. Pauline gave him a huge hug and just said, "At last, my love. At last."

Mike sometimes wonders why Pauline hadn't been the one to confront him, but, again, different generations.

Mike has never officially come out to the public, although they could find out if they really wanted. And he still goes to events with Pauline from time to time, but also with Steve, or Greg, or any of the other men he has managed to grasp but not hold.

And, bit by bit, he recognized that he was changing. He still looked amazing, sure, still wore the suits and the hairspray and flirted with the women, but he had started to become himself. To be authentic, and to be real. And, what do you know, happiness followed.

He became a better man, a better friend, a better colleague, a better presenter. If ITV had filmed their pilot now, Mike would get the job, without doubt.

The irony being that Mike wouldn't want it anymore. *South East Tonight* was no longer where Mike Waghorn hid, it was where he flourished. The building-society robberies, the bouncy castles and the twenty-five-year-old cats. He reported because he cared. Cared about himself, and about his community. Mike had Bethany to thank for that.

Was he still an idiot at times? Sure. Could he still be difficult? Yes, particularly when hungry. But he could look himself in the mirror without turning away.

Mike takes another swig of cider. He is waiting for the boxing to come on, and is currently having to sit through endless adverts for gambling companies. One of them is presented by Ron's son, Jason Ritchie. A fine fighter, he was.

Mike got the text from Pauline an hour or so ago. They start digging for the body tomorrow. Digging for Bethany's body. His wonderful, talented, headstrong friend. She could have done anything, she could have been anything. The world would have known her name.

Bethany saved Mike's life, and Mike was never able to repay that debt in her lifetime. But he could repay it now. With the help of the Thursday Murder Club. Find her killer, bring her peace. Heather Garbutt? Jack Mason? Someone they have yet to consider? Mike feels he is about to find out.

And that is the least he could do for Bethany Waites.

63.

Heather Garbutt's home is on an ugly road with a pretty name. To the front there is a driveway lined with hedges, now overgrown, that bends away from the road, hiding the house from the traffic. You could drive past this spot every day and never see the slow decline of a once-handsome house. To the back there is a garden, and then woodland, separating it from a municipal golf course.

The house itself is a bungalow. It had been pleasant enough at one point: they looked up the estate agent's pictures of the last time it had sold on Rightmove. Four beds, big sitting room overlooking the garden, a kitchen that the estate agents said was "in need of modernization," but which Joyce rather liked. Perhaps not the house of someone rich, but the house of someone who worked with someone rich. Comfortable, in every sense. It had been listed at three hundred and seventy-five thousand pounds, though a quick house-price search revealed that Jack Mason had paid four hundred and twenty-five thousand for it. He was clearly a motivated buyer, as Joyce supposes she would be if there was evidence buried in the garden that could send her to prison.

The whole place is running wild now. Jack Mason might have bought it, but it seems he doesn't visit it. Ron had rung Jack last night, to see if he could give them the keys, but Jack wasn't answering. Is he already regretting telling Ron and Viktor about the body? He hadn't named his co-conspirator, but, other than that, he had come dangerously close to grassing. Ron knows that won't have come naturally. And, if they do find something, what will that mean for Jack?

Two constables force open the door, pushing it unwillingly back against a pile of mail. Who is still delivering mail? Joyce wonders. Who takes a look at this house, clearly abandoned, returning to nature, and delivers a pizza leaflet? Joyce sees a National Trust magazine on top of the pile. She suspects she might have rather liked Heather Garbutt.

Elizabeth has gone around the side of the building with Chief Constable Andrew Everton, but Joyce goes through the front door because she wants to be nosy. And the lovely thing about investigating a murder is that you can be nosy and call it work. Joyce is disappointed that there is not much to see, however. All traces of Heather Garbutt are gone. The only clue she was ever here are the paler squares of wallpaper where pictures had once hung. At least there is no need to be careful, to tiptoe around and not touch. Joyce has free rein. The house had been searched many years ago, and any evidence there might have been here is long gone.

But no one had searched the garden. Why would you? With a body washed out to sea, what was there to dig for? Joyce walks into the sitting room, lovely patio doors framing the view of a large yellow digger, police tape flapping, and Chief Constable Andrew Everton, in a peaked cap and a hi-vis jacket, taking command of the scene. One of the constables slides open the doors, and Joyce walks out onto the patio decking. Joyce watches her step: decking gets too slippery, you are so much better off with stone. She has to admit, though, that this decking looks in better shape than the rest of the overgrown garden and fading house.

The digger has been here since eight this morning. The garden, and even bits of the woodland beyond, are pocked with holes. Two men in hard hats are just beginning to dismantle the decking. Tiny colored flags mark where holes have been dug and where they are yet to be dug. Joyce spots Elizabeth. She is, surprise, surprise, monopolizing the Chief Constable.

"What a lot of holes," says Joyce. "And I was right about that kitchen, even now it's very livable. Lots of storage."

"The holes are not all ours," says Andrew Everton. "Someone, let's assume

Jack Mason, has been doing their own digging over the years. Especially as you get into the woods."

Joyce looks into the woodland behind the garden. There are uniformed officers digging with shovels.

"That's a lot of police officers," she says.

"I'm the Chief Constable," says Andrew Everton. "People tend to jump when I ask for something. I'm told the only skeleton we've found so far was a guinea pig's."

"We were digging in Vladivostok once," says Elizabeth. "I forget why, a warlord had buried something or other. Anyway, we uncovered a prehistoric moose. Intact, antlers and all. We were all set to fill the hole back in, but the head of the Russian Service at the time was on the board of the Natural History Museum, and in the end we released a Russian spy from Belmarsh Prison in return for the moose. It's on display if you go there now."

"Right," says Andrew Everton.

"You stop listening after a while," says Joyce. "She's always digging something up, or upsetting Russia. Do you believe Jack Mason's story? About the partner?"

Andrew Everton considers the question. "It's an unusual thing to make up. And, if he's lying, he's lying for a reason, and I wouldn't mind finding out what that reason is."

"Any news back on Heather Garbutt's death?" asks Elizabeth. "Any forensics?"

Andrew Everton shrugs. "Here's the thing about dusting a prison cell for fingerprints. There are hundreds of them, and most of them belong to people with criminal records."

Elizabeth snorts.

"Honestly, ignore her," says Joyce.

A woman enters the garden from the side of the house. She wears white coveralls, and plastic sleeves over her shoes. Forensics. Just what Joyce has been looking for. She will let her settle and then go to speak to her. It never hurts to ask, does it?

There is activity in the woodland, and a constable in muddied uniform runs out toward them from the trees.

"Sir," says the constable. "We've found something."

Andrew Everton nods. "Good work." He turns to Elizabeth and Joyce. "You two stay here."

This time they both snort.

64.

"I don't know if there has ever been so much testosterone in this room," says Ibrahim, as he carries in a tray of sweet mint tea for everyone.

Viktor and Henrik are at the dining table, hunched over the financial documents from Heather Garbutt's trial. Ron is sitting on the sofa, watching something on his phone, and Alan is looking out of the window, wondering when Joyce might be back. Occasionally he spots someone who might look a bit like her, and gets excited.

"Five boys," says Ibrahim, pouring the tea. "Henrik, how is your murderous rage? Subsided?"

"It is forgotten," says Henrik. "It was tactically naive."

"You fellas found anything?" asks Ron.

"Nothing," says Viktor.

"Thought Henrik was the best money-launderer in the world?"

"I am," says Henrik. "That is provable."

"Well, Bethany Waites found something in there that you're missing," says Ron.

"And it got her killed," says Ibrahim.

"So at the moment you're just a guy with a beard."

"Ron, Henrik is a guest," says Ibrahim.

"A guest?" says Ron, still not looking up from his phone. "Yesterday he wanted to kill Joyce, and now he's a guest."

"And he wanted to kill me too," says Viktor.

"Guys, it was an error," says Henrik. "I wanted to be tough. I cannot keep apologizing."

"No need to apologize if you find out who killed Bethany Waites," says Ron.

"We will find out," says Henrik.

"Did Bethany Waites say anything to anyone?" asks Viktor. "About what she'd found?"

"Nah," says Ron.

"Nothing about 'Carron Whitehead' or 'Robert Brown MSc'?"

"Nothing about anyone," says Ron. "Far as we know. Henrik, you rich enough to buy a football club?"

"I already own one," says Henrik.

Ibrahim sits at the dining table. "Well, she did say something. To someone."

"What did she say?" asks Viktor.

"She sent a message to Mike Waghorn," says Ibrahim. "A couple of weeks before she disappeared."

"Do you have the message? It might be important," asks Viktor.

"I don't think there was anything in it," says Ibrahim. "But we could ask Pauline to ask Mike?"

"They're both coming over for lunch in a bit," says Ron.

"You are taken with Pauline, Ron," says Viktor.

"Well, you're taken with Elizabeth," says Ron.

"I know," says Viktor. "But I have no chance. You have every chance. What luck."

Ron shrugs, a little embarrassed. "We're friends."

"Love is very precious," says Viktor, and takes a sip of his mint tea.

"I wonder if I could ask you to put a lace doily under your teacup," says Ibrahim. "To prevent the wood from marking."

"Could I use your bathroom?" asks Henrik. "I forgot to moisturize this morning, and I can feel myself drying out."

Ron looks at Ibrahim. "So much testosterone in one room, mate. So much testosterone."

Alan barks at a chaffinch.

65.

They found the gun wrapped in a pale blue cloth, buried about thirty feet or so into the woodland. Elizabeth had taken a look before it had been driven away for examination. When she'd heard the word "gun," she had expected a revolver, some sort of handgun at least. But this was an assault weapon, semi-automatic. Andrew Everton looked as surprised as she did—it was a hell of a gun. There was no ammunition, but there was a metal box, which looked to contain around a hundred thousand pounds or so in cash.

So perhaps they had found the murder weapon, and, finally, some of the proceeds of the scam. Time and forensics would tell. The Forensic Officer on scene should presumably be heading back fairly soon, but is currently being monopolized by Joyce. They are sitting together on Joyce's raincoat, which has been spread over a mossy bench. What they are talking about, heaven only knows. Elizabeth is walking out of the woods with Andrew Everton.

"Seems like you owe us one," says Elizabeth.

"I'll owe you one when we find Bethany's body," says Andrew Everton. "We'll start concentrating the search in the same spot."

"Feels like it should be enough to arrest Jack Mason," says Elizabeth. "Ask him a few questions?"

"Leave that with me," says Andrew Everton. "You can't do everything."

That was a moot point, but Elizabeth doesn't feel the need to argue. "Do keep us informed though."

Andrew Everton bows to her, a little sarcastically for Elizabeth's liking. "Ma'am."

Elizabeth veers off in the direction of Joyce and the Forensic Officer. She hears Joyce's conversation as she approaches.

"But say that three bodies are left in a cellar for many years," Joyce is saying. "At what stage would the smell disappear?"

Is Joyce asking her about the case in Rye?

"Do they have wounds?" asks the Forensic Officer.

"They have been dismembered by a chainsaw," says Joyce.

That doesn't *sound* like the case in Rye.

"Well, they would bleed out very quickly," says the Forensic Officer. "So putrefaction would also occur fairly quickly. The smell would be awful for the first, let's say two months, then gradually things would return to normal."

"Bit of Febreze every now and again," says Joyce.

Elizabeth reaches the bench and addresses the Forensic Officer. "Is my friend bothering you? She does that sometimes."

"Not at all," says the FO. "I'm helping her with her story."

"With her story?" Elizabeth takes a look at Joyce, who won't meet her gaze.

"I thought I might give it a try," says Joyce to the flowerbed. "You know I like to write."

"Three bodies in a cellar," says Elizabeth. "That sounds familiar."

"You're allowed to base things on real cases," says Joyce. "Andrew Everton does it all the time."

"Where do the chainsaws come in?"

"You have to add bits of your own too," says Joyce.

"And you added chainsaws?"

Joyce nods, and gives a little smile. Elizabeth wonders, not for the first time, just how well she knows her friend.

"Shall we head home and see how the boys are getting on?" says Elizabeth. "And tell them we've found a gun?"

66.

Pauline and Mike have arrived for lunch.

Alan literally can't believe his luck. Even more people! If only Joyce were here, the whole scene would be perfect. Surely she won't be much longer. Pauline is tickling his belly as Mike Waghorn takes a seat.

"This is Henrik," says Ibrahim. "He is a cryptocurrency entrepreneur, and Swede."

Mike holds his hands together and says, "Namaste, Henrik."

"Henrik is also very good with money-laundering," says Ibrahim. "And this is Viktor, a former KGB colonel."

"Pauline has told me a lot about you, Viktor," says Mike.

"Has she now?" says Ron, and Pauline blows him a kiss.

"It's good to meet you, Mike Waghorn," says Viktor. "I will confess that two weeks ago I hadn't known who you were, but I am now very familiar with your work. Though often I don't catch everything you're saying, because Joyce likes to keep up a running commentary through the local news."

"Any news on the search?" asks Mike.

"Still waiting," says Ron. Pauline told him that Mike had taken news of the garden search very badly. It was such an extraordinary story. The body buried as blackmail. The killer some unknown accomplice. Mike wants the murder to be solved, but it will be very final for him.

"You arrive at an opportune moment, however," says Ibrahim. "Do you have the text of your message from Bethany to hand? About the new information? Viktor and Henrik would like to hear it in full. Perhaps it might unlock something."

Mike takes out his phone and scrolls until he finds the message. He addresses Viktor and Henrik. *Skipper. Some new info. Can't say what, but it's absolute dynamite. Getting closer to the heart of this thing.*

Viktor nods. "She would call you 'Skipper' normally? No clue there?"

"Completely normal," says Mike.

"And she would say 'info' instead of 'information'?" asks Henrik. "It was normal for her to be informal?"

"It was usually emojis and swear words, to be honest," says Mike.

"Now, when she says—"

Alan starts jumping at the window and barking hysterically, as if he simply cannot begin to comprehend what he has just seen.

Viktor rolls off his chair, and crouches behind a sofa with his gun drawn. Mike raises one eyebrow. Henrik takes a moment, and then taps Viktor on the shoulder.

"Viktor," he says. "You have to stop doing this. I'm the one who was trying to kill you. And I'm here."

Viktor thinks for a moment, then accepts the truth of this observation, and puts the gun down the back of his trousers.

"I'm glad I didn't try to kill you," says Henrik, looking at the gun.

"You should be glad," says Viktor, taking his seat once again. "I would be throwing your body off a North Sea ferry round about now."

Ibrahim has buzzed his door open, and Elizabeth and Joyce walk into the room. Alan leaps at Joyce, and she gives him a cuddle.

"Anything?" asks Mike.

"No body," says Elizabeth. "Not yet. But Jack Mason said there would be a gun, and there was. A big one."

"Was it the murder weapon?" asks Ibrahim.

"Yes, Ibrahim, it was," says Elizabeth. "The police handed me the gun, and I completed a full forensics check on it in the taxi on the way back."

Ibrahim turns to Mike. "She is being sarcastic." Mike thanks him.

"We will know soon enough," says Elizabeth.

"And they found money too," says Joyce. "They think around a hundred thousand. Just buried in a tin."

"Andrew Everton thinks they have enough to bring Jack Mason in," says Elizabeth. "Money and a gun in his back garden. Might be enough to get him to talk. Tell us who buried them there."

"Good luck with that," says Ron.

Henrik has been ignoring this conversation, tapping away at his computer. "Umm . . . OK, I have something."

The room turns to him as one, and he blushes.

"Well, *maybe* I have something."

"I knew you'd come in handy," says Elizabeth. "Spit it out, and we'll decide if it's something or not."

"Mike," says Henrik. "In her message Bethany says that her news is 'absolute dynamite.' Did she like to play little tricks?"

"It amused her to fool me from time to time, let's say that," agrees Mike.

"Because what she found wasn't 'absolute dynamite,'" says Henrik. "It was 'Absolute Dynamite.'"

"Absolute Dynamite?" says Mike.

"Very early in the money trail a hundred and fifteen thousand pounds is paid into an 'Absolute Construction' in Panama," says Henrik. "That money is still there, as far as I am able to tell, which is actually quite far, because I am very good at this sort of thing."

"Not so good at killing pensioners," says Joyce, and gets a "Hear, hear" from Viktor.

"When 'Absolute Construction' is set up, it seems that a web of subsidiary companies is set up beneath it, but no money was ever paid into them, so we have ignored them up to now. There is an 'Absolute Demolition,' an 'Absolute Cement,' an 'Absolute Scaffolding' and, in Cyprus, a company called—"

"Absolute Dynamite," says Ron.

Elizabeth looks around her. She puts a hand on Mike's shoulder. "And when you look into 'Absolute Dynamite'?"

"You find two named directors," says Henrik. "One is our old friend Carron Whitehead, so that doesn't really lead us anywhere. But finally we have a new name. The other director is a Michael Gullis."

"Michael Gullis?" says Elizabeth. "Pauline, Mike? Anything?"

They look at each other, then back at Elizabeth, and shake their heads.

"There was a Michael *Gilkes* who played for Reading," says Ron. "Midfielder."

"Thank you, Ron," says Elizabeth. Pauline taps Ron's hand.

The room falls quiet once again, save for the *tip-tapping* of Henrik's keyboard and Alan's happy panting as he moves from person to person to receive his due attention.

"Elizabeth," says Joyce. "I don't suppose you could join me outside for a moment?"

Elizabeth gestures that she certainly could, and they wander out to Ibrahim's hallway.

"Ask me," says Joyce.

"Ask you what?" says Elizabeth.

"Ask me if I know the name Michael Gullis," says Joyce.

67.

The team digging up the garden at Heather Garbutt's old house had dug up the gun this afternoon. They were still digging now, under the searchlights as evening turned to night. Andrew Everton thought they had enough evidence at least to talk to Jack Mason. Chris and Donna had got the call.

"You were so good again, I mean it," says Chris, reviewing Donna's latest appearance on *South East Tonight*. She had discussed online fraud and flirted with a vicar who was in the studio, raising money for a ramp. Chris thinks about overtaking someone on a blind bend, then remembers it's the dead of night, and he's a police officer.

"You just have to be yourself," says Donna. "Ignore the cameras."

"I've never been good at being myself," says Chris. "I wouldn't know where to start."

"Mum says you cried last night when you were watching *Sex and the City*."

"I did," agrees Chris.

"Well, don't start there," says Donna.

Chris especially loves his Ford Focus now there are no empty crisp packets in the footwell. He even had it shampooed the other day. Was that being himself?

"How is Jack Mason going to take it, do you reckon?" asks Chris. "An assault rifle and a hundred grand is tough to talk your way out of."

"He's a pro," says Donna. "He'll be charming. It'll be tougher for him if they find Bethany's body."

"He'll walk away," says Chris. "Don't you think? Doesn't matter if he owns the property; there'll be no forensic evidence after all this time."

"I saw this Polish film where they dug up a body after thirty years or something, and a tattoo had imprinted itself on a leg bone," says Donna.

"You've been to see a Polish film?" Chris asks.

"It's left here," says Donna. They had given up on the satnav some time ago. Jack Mason's house was on a private road, leading off a private estate, leading off a small track, leading off a country road. Deliberately hard to find, especially in this pitch darkness. As they take wrong turn after wrong turn, Chris thinks it would be easier to approach by boat and climb the cliff face.

Also, Jack Mason would be able to see anyone approaching from a mile away. Has he seen the lights of the yellow Ford Focus yet? Is he waiting for them? Does he know what's in store?

They finally reach a pair of iron gates. The gates remain firmly shut as they approach, so Chris leans out of his window and tries the intercom. He buzzes intermittently for thirty seconds or so, but there is no response. So perhaps Jack has seen them coming after all.

Old Chris would have got back in the car and driven the perimeter of the property wall, looking for a way in, tutting all the while. But new Chris, slim, athletic Chris, starts to climb the gates instead. This brings Donna out of the car. He feels the pleasing burn of his muscles as he climbs, the gratifying response of muscles doing what they're told. He must look great, he thinks, just as he snags and rips his trousers on an iron spike. Donna climbs up after him, at twice the speed, unhooks him, and they both clamber over the top of the gates and down onto Jack Mason's driveway. New security lights flick on with almost every step.

Chris's trousers are ripped beyond repair, and Donna gets full sight of a pair of Homer Simpson boxer shorts.

"Honestly," says Donna, as the seat of Chris's trousers flaps in the wind. "This is a perfect example of you being yourself. Did my mum choose those boxer shorts?"

"No, I forgot to take my washing out of the machine last night," says Chris. "These are my emergency boxers. Let's just arrest Jack Mason, shall we?"

As Chris walks up the driveway, Donna stoops to tie a shoelace. He keeps walking, until he hears a click.

"Donna, did you just take a photograph of my arse on your phone?"

"Me? No," says Donna, putting her phone back into her pocket.

The house itself soon appears, a silhouette in the halogen security lights. It is huge. Chris has never seen a private house this big. The only time you ever saw a house like this it had a gift shop and a tea room.

The wind is whistling around Chris's backside now. Perhaps Jack will have a sewing kit? Can you ask for a sewing kit when you've just arrested someone?

As they climb the stone front steps to Jack Mason's front door, Chris makes sure he is a step behind Donna. As he reaches to press the baronial bell, he notices the door is ajar, light streaming through a small gap out into the night. He and Donna share a look.

Donna pushes open the door, revealing the vast entrance hallway. There are sofas and side-tables, portraits of men in wigs, a locked cabinet full of shotguns, a suit of armor on a plinth.

And, on the hallway carpet, the body of Jack Mason.

Running, Donna reaches him first. He is on his back, a gunshot wound to the head. In his hand is a small gun. He is freezing cold, and very dead.

Donna starts to secure the scene as Chris calls it in. They will have a long wait with the body.

Chris takes a closer look. That really is a *very* small gun. Chris tucks this thought away.

"You OK?" he says to Donna.

"Of course I'm OK," says Donna. "You?"

Chris looks down at the body. "Yeah, yeah, I'm OK too."

They are both OK, but they put an arm around each other regardless.

Chris is thinking. The Thursday Murder Club starts looking into the Bethany Waites case and, before you know it, the two main suspects in her killing are dead. Hell of a coincidence. He glances at Donna. It looks like she's thinking the same thing.

"I'm just thinking," says Donna, "that we should really do something about your trousers before the circus arrives."

68.

Fiona Clemence thought she had heard the last of Elizabeth Best. With her questions about Bethany Waites. With her accusations. How wrong she was.

It was no secret that Fiona and Bethany hadn't got on. What of it? It doesn't mean you are going to drive someone off a cliff, does it?

So what if Fiona hadn't cried on the tribute show? There had been two letters in the *Evening Argus* about it, which was the *South East Tonight* equivalent of a Twitter storm. But it meant nothing. Everyone cried at everything these days. You got rewarded for it. Fiona had pretended to cry at the BAFTAs, for example, and it had gone down very well. The *Mail* Online headline had been "TV Fiona turns on waterworks as she flaunts gym-honed body in figure-hugging dress."

Does anyone ever actually cry for real, or is it always for attention? Her mum cried when her dad died, and within a week she was on a yacht with a dentist from her golf club. So spare us the histrionics.

You could point the finger all you liked at Fiona, but you wouldn't get what you wanted.

Fiona Clemence is still trying to work out how Elizabeth got her number. Presumably her friend Joyce had tracked it down through her government contacts. Either way, the message had turned up last night.

I wonder if you might be able to help us, dear?

A few messages later, and Fiona knew the score.

Does she trust Elizabeth and Joyce? No. Do they *really* know who killed Bethany Waites? Fiona doubts that very much. But will she help them? For reasons she can't quite access at the moment, yes, she probably will.

Fiona is filming an advert for yogurt this morning. Or for breakfast cereal. She forgets which. She knows she has to lick her famous lips and say, "It's delicious," but she hasn't looked into it beyond that. She sits on a plastic chair in a cavernous studio as lights are adjusted, and groups of men in glasses congregate, scratching their beards, while much younger people hand them coffees.

Fiona is scrolling through her Instagram. Three point five million followers now. She has promised her Instagram adviser, Luke, that she will post a story today. He is very strict with her, but, seeing as he can get her twenty-five thousand pounds a time to post about a free holiday to the Maldives, she lets him be. But it's all very regimented and boring. She is a brand now, and everyone wants to tell her what to do. And, worse, what *not* to do. Maybe she should push back against that a little? Next to her, a man dressed as a banana is eating a banana. She looks at the time. Just gone eleven a.m. It's make-your-mind-up time, Fiona.

Elizabeth isn't asking for much, in the grand scheme of things, but, even so, Fiona has a number of objections. At first she had told Elizabeth to speak to her agent ("Oh, I don't think we'll be doing that, dear, do you?"). Elizabeth did her very best to persuade her. What's the worst that could happen, Elizabeth had said. Well, plenty, is the truth. That's why Fiona remains of two minds.

A woman dressed as a yogurt pot walks past, so it probably is an advert for yogurt. Fiona doesn't eat yogurt, ever since Gwyneth Paltrow once said something or other about it on TikTok.

Was Fiona walking into some sort of trap? Should she just say no and have done with it? Why is she even entertaining the idea?

Elizabeth and Joyce had fired all sorts of questions at her when they first met, and, truth be told, Fiona had quite enjoyed it. Quite enjoyed being accused of murder by a woman who had pretended to faint, and another woman with a revolver in her handbag.

So, if they want her help, sure. Perhaps. Maybe. It will make a splash at the very least. Everything is about new content. Something new. Fiona wonders what the *Mail* Online headline will be this time.

One of the men with glasses and a beard approaches her.

"Hi, Fiona, I'm Rory, we've just done the tiniest rewrite, and I wanted to check you'd be OK with us putting a dab of yogurt on your nose? We think it could really work. You know, for humor?"

Fiona gives Rory her full-beam smile. "I won't be putting yogurt on my nose, Rory."

Rory nods. "Yep, yep, great. Let's do it without the yogurt on the nose. Love it."

He disappears. The man dressed as a banana asks her for a selfie, and Fiona lets him know, very gently, that he is being unprofessional.

She goes back to her phone, and types out the information that Elizabeth has asked for. For the final time she asks herself why. For fun, perhaps? For something new and interesting to do? To see how it all plays out, certainly.

And, maybe—*maybe*—for Bethany?

Fiona shakes her head. She is not the sentimental type. She is doing it for followers. That must be the explanation.

She presses send. The deed is done.

69.

Chris is having trouble hearing what Andrew Everton is saying. The room is very busy, and there is excited chatter all around. People are drinking on a weekday evening, and the air is heavy with that heady thrill. As they make their way to the table, Andrew Everton speaks directly into his ear.

"Suicide?"

"Looked like it," says Chris.

"I don't trust anything connected with this case," says Andrew Everton. "A friend of yours came to visit me."

"Oh, yes?" says Chris, back into Andrew Everton's ear.

"A woman named Elizabeth," says Andrew Everton.

No surprises there.

"Sorry about her," says Chris, as they reach their table.

"Not at all," says Andrew Everton. Chris searches for his name card. He is next to Patrice, thank goodness. Sometimes they split couples up at these things. "She has a job for me."

"That sounds like Elizabeth," says Chris.

"I can trust her?" he asks.

"God, no," says Chris, but his laugh says otherwise, and Andrew Everton nods.

Chris pulls Patrice's chair out for her and she sits.

"I could get used to this," says Patrice to Andrew Everton. "Who does Chris have to arrest to get invited back next year?"

Andrew Everton laughs.

Chris and Donna will both be receiving a "Highly Commended in the Line of Duty" medal. They are gold-plated. Terry Hallet has one and has shown Chris pictures.

Andrew Everton addresses Chris and Patrice. "Do you want to see the medal?"

"Go on, then," says Patrice. "Teachers don't see medals very often."

Andrew Everton reaches into a pocket and pulls out a small velvet pouch. He opens a drawstring and pulls out the gold medal inside.

"Worth a few bob on eBay, that," says Patrice. She squeezes Chris's hand.

Across from them are two empty chairs. Donna is bringing Bogdan. She had to come clean in the end. Polish cinema indeed. Patrice has yet to meet him, but she has just seen photos, and, as far as Chris is concerned, is a little too enthusiastic.

Bogdan is making Donna very happy though, and that is Chris's only concern.

Patrice kisses him. "You excited?"

"Never won anything before," says Chris.

"My heart?" says Patrice.

"I can't put your heart in my downstairs loo to show off to visitors, can I?" says Chris. "You excited about meeting Bogdan?"

"Oh my God," says Patrice. "So excited."

Again, a little over-enthusiastic. Chris suspects that Bogdan would be a tough stepson-in-law to match. A lot of weddings needed before that happened though. Well, two weddings. Stop thinking about weddings, Chris. Say something to impress Andrew Everton.

"I haven't had a Toblerone for three months now."

"Is that so," says Andrew Everton. Jesus, Chris.

The compère, a comedian Chris has seen on TV, Josh something, kicks things off with a monologue. He's very funny, ripping into everyone, and dealing with the drunken heckles that come his way. Chris sees Donna making her way through the side door of the Grand Ballroom. She is alone. Uh-oh. Both he and Patrice watch as she makes her way over, and sits, her face like a cliff in a dark storm. An empty chair beside her.

"No Bogdan?" asks Chris.

"Elizabeth needed him," says Donna.

Well, quite a theme was developing.

Was something going on they didn't know about?

PART THREE

Catch Up on All the News . . .

70.

Joyce

I am in Staffordshire. We all are, pretty much. Everyone who needs to be, at least.

Elizabeth and Stephen are here: they are down the hallway, though they haven't emerged yet this morning. Ron and Pauline are in the East Wing. This house has wings. Ibrahim drove Elizabeth and Stephen, and he is staying at the gatehouse at the end of the drive.

Henrik is here, naturally, it is his house. It's like Downton Abbey, but with a pinball machine, and a hot tub.

Mike Waghorn is also here. I suggested he join us for a brandy in the library last night, but he wanted an early night as we have given him a job to do today. He is taking it seriously.

In the end it was just me and Ibrahim, sitting up, drinking and chatting. He is feeling very perky because he has cracked the identity of "Carron Whitehead." He worked it out in the car on the way up here. When he told me, I double-checked and triple-checked, but he was quite right.

He really can be very clever. I'm still taking credit for "Michael Gullis" though. That's what really cracked the case.

I told Joanna I had worked it out and she said, "Well done," and sounded like she meant it. There was even a thumbs-up emoji.

As for "Robert Brown MSc," we are still none the wiser, but it doesn't matter so much now. I'm sure we will work it out sooner or later.

Stephen had been given a guided tour of the library when he arrived. He looked like a boy, eyes wide, smile even wider. The years dropped away from him.

Viktor is having breakfast in his room, and making notes for later. Interesting to see how he plans these things out. Andrew Everton is on his way up too. It was the Kent Police Awards last night and he couldn't miss it. They were giving Chris and Donna a commendation. I saw it on Donna's Instagram. I think Bogdan should probably have been with her, but he had to drive Elizabeth and Stephen up here. I wonder if Donna minded? No one else seems to have spotted they are dating, but Pauline and I had a quiet gossip about it earlier. Donna certainly wasn't smiling in the photographs.

One person who isn't here is Fiona Clemence, but that's not to say she isn't involved.

Alan has stayed at home.

I make that sound as if it was his choice, as if he had a few things he wanted to catch up on. If we are all up here in Staffordshire, who is looking after him, you ask?

There is a new resident in the village. He is called Mervyn, and he is Welsh. I have always had a soft spot for the Welsh. He used to be the headmaster of a school. You can tell that too. Strict but fair. Gray hair, dark mustache, you know the look. Don't mind if I do. I have shown him to Pauline at a distance and got a thumbs-up. I thought Pauline might have got a little upset about the way I questioned her at our afternoon tea, but not a bit of it. I suppose she just wanted the truth to come out as much as the rest of us.

Now, Mervyn has a Cairn Terrier called Rosie, and we bumped into each other a couple of days ago on a walk. Alan sniffed around Rosie and, I daresay if Alan were asked, he'd tell you I sniffed around Mervyn too. Long story short, we got chatting, and the same afternoon I dropped around a cherry Bakewell for him, just to say welcome to the village.

Mervyn is going to feed and walk Alan while I'm gone. I told him I would be very grateful, and he gave me a little smile.

And, before you ask, yes, Mervyn is heterosexual. He's had two wives and five kids, and there was a *Top Gear* DVD on one of his shelves.

We should only be here for twenty-four hours or so, unless something goes very wrong. Which reminds me, I must make sure that Ibrahim moves his car round to the back of the house. Bogdan didn't need telling—his is hidden away.

We're planning to kick off at about midday. I think everyone knows what they're doing. I don't really have a role as such, I just get to watch.

Which I think I've earned, given I worked out who murdered Bethany Waites.

Very soon the whole world will know.

I gave Mervyn my phone number, "You know, in case you want to send me a picture of Alan," but so far he hasn't used it. I keep checking, but nothing.

71.

It was an indignity to be dumped at the gates in a blindfold, but, if that's the price of entry, so be it. Paranoia is to be expected.

The approach to the house is magnificent. Long, gravel driveway, topiary hedges, fountains, statues of lions. But today there are no staff tending to it. No gardeners or chauffeurs poking their noses in, able to tell what they've seen. It's exactly as was promised. Looking up at windows ahead, no movement there either. You have to allow for the possibility that this is a trap, but, thus far, it doesn't look like one.

The house itself is too big. Way too big if this man, the Viking, lives here alone. Given the secrecy involved in this whole operation, and given the monosyllabic nature of their email exchanges, that's a fair bet. It will be just the two of them, and it will have to be played exactly right. Get what you've come for and go. Not easy, not easy at all, but the rewards will be worth it.

A push on the bell, and the sound of it reverberates deep inside this lonely house. How much would the Viking have paid for this place? Twenty million? At least.

Footsteps approach, and the huge oak front door opens. There he is, the man himself. What is he? Six six? Huge beard, Foo Fighters T-shirt clinging to a huge torso.

An offered hand, a shake.

"You must be the Viking?"

"And you," says the Viking, "must be Andrew Everton. Let me take you to my library."

Andrew Everton follows the huge figure through a marble entrance hall, and into a carpeted corridor. Every wall is covered in art, most of it too modern for the Chief Constable's tastes, but the odd sailing ship or Norman church here and there make up for it. The Viking leads him into a library, a cocoon of dark wood and red leather and soft lighting. Andrew Everton thinks about the sign on his office wall, CRIME DOESN'T PAY. We'll see about that.

The Viking gestures to the walls, lined from floor to ceiling with books. "Are you a reader, Chief Constable?"

"Love writing books more than reading them, if I'm honest," says Andrew Everton, and sits in an armchair indicated by his host. "We can probably skip all this chat if you'd rather? It's a lovely house, it was a pleasant journey, I don't need the loo, and I'm OK for water."

The Viking nods. "OK." He sits on, and nearly fills, a two-seater leather sofa, and switches on a lamp beside him. "What do you need from me, Mr. Andrew Everton?"

72.

Joyce

The lamp is the key to the whole thing.

Once you switch it on, you switch on the cameras and microphones. We're all in the staff kitchen at the back of the house, quiet as church mice, and now we can see the live images from inside the library. We can't see Henrik, because he didn't want to be on camera. Because of his criminal empire, not because he is shy. Although he is also quite shy, I think.

By the way, I checked my crypto account the other day, and it's now worth fifty-six thousand pounds. So thank you, Henrik.

Andrew Everton looks very sure of himself. Has no idea of what he is walking into. Elizabeth gave him a tip-off—"absolutely between us, Andrew"—about the Viking. The money-launderer who had been trying to kill us. "I can get you a meeting, don't ask me how, and don't ask me where, just thank me. Perhaps you could pay him a visit?"

And paying him a visit is exactly what Andrew Everton is doing now. Not to gather evidence, not to arrest him, but simply because he is a man in great need of a money-launderer.

Because Andrew Everton was the brains behind the VAT fraud. Andrew Everton killed Bethany Waites and blackmailed Jack Mason and Heather Garbutt into silence.

In his book *Given in Evidence*, I think I told you about it, the main character is a gangland boss called Big Mick. And Big Mick's full name?

Michael Gullis.

A silly error very early on in the scam. We all make mistakes.

And in case you're wondering if it might be a coincidence, the name of the other early payee also crops up in one of Andrew Everton's books.

I told you Ibrahim cracked "Carron Whitehead." It was simple really.

It's an anagram of "Catherine Howard." The teak-tough detective. Clever Ibrahim.

So our guess was that Andrew Everton, so far unable to unlock any of the proceeds of the fraud, might like to have a private chat with the Viking.

And that "private chat" is what we're watching right now.

73.

I'm a police officer," says Andrew Everton. "You understand that, of course?"

"I understand," says the Viking. "So long as you are not filming me or recording me, we are cool."

"Likewise," says Andrew Everton. "Though if you are taping me, not a single word of it would be admissible in court anyway, so you'd be wasting your time."

"No one is taping anyone," says the Viking. "That's not how I work. You say you need my help?"

Andrew Everton leans forward. "I have ten million pounds in various accounts around the world. I currently have no way of retrieving it without questions. I am hoping you might be able to help me."

"Ten million? Yes, easy," says the Viking. "What's in it for me?"

"Half a million," says Andrew Everton.

The Viking laughs.

"And a chief constable on your payroll. You look after me, I'll look after you."

The Viking nods. "I need to know where the money is from. Some money I won't touch."

"A VAT fraud, from about ten years ago. Mobile phones in and out of Dover. Easy money."

"Your idea?" asks the Viking.

"Guilty," says Andrew Everton. "I was writing a book. I write, for my sins, and I came up with this scheme, just a plot really. But the more I thought about it, I realized, you know what, I'm not going to put it in the book, I'm going to do it for real."

"Clever."

"Well, sometimes I use real crimes for my plots. This time I used one of my plots for a real crime."

"How did you do it?" asks the Viking.

"I wasn't a chief constable back then, but I knew a few people. Talked to a man called Jack Mason. Ran all sorts of dodgy enterprises, but he was always too smart to get caught. And that's exactly what I needed. I told him the plan, and we went into business together."

"And you made ten million?"

"Thereabouts," says Andrew Everton.

"Why did you stop?"

"A journalist was looking into it. She was getting a little too close for comfort. Managed to send one of our team to jail, so we backed off."

"And did the journalist back off?"

"Well, no," says Andrew Everton. "She died."

74.

Joyce

Elizabeth and Viktor look very happy with how this is all going.

You have to hand it to Henrik. "Your idea?" "How did you do it?" "You made ten million?" "Why did you stop?" All the questions that they drummed into him. The perfect confession.

Elizabeth knew Andrew Everton would be completely honest. He needs the Viking to trust him and help him, he has the ego to want credit for his own scheme, and, as he said himself, nothing on the tape could be used in a court of law.

But, of course, it doesn't have to be. That's the beauty of Elizabeth's plan. Andrew Everton will be found guilty long before he sees the inside of a court.

Mike is pacing up and down the kitchen, practicing his lines for later.

75.

Fiona Clemence has so many messages from concerned friends.

Fi u been hacked

Insta hacked!

Have u seen ur Insta?

Fi, WTF?????

Fiona gets a few influential friends to spread the word.

Guys, @FionaClemClem has been hacked. Don't watch!

summin weirdz going down on @FionaClemClem. Some crazy hack.

Before you knew it there were over two hundred and fifty thousand people watching her Instagram Live, with the number rising by the second. And what they were all watching was not Fiona Clemence shopping for makeup, or giving hot yoga tips.

Instead, they were all watching the Chief Constable of Kent Police admitting to a multimillion-pound fraud on a livestreamed video.

You couldn't see who he was talking to, but he was in some sort of library, and he was talking about mobile phones, and doing deals with criminals. The viewership continues to rise and rise as word is getting out. Insta, Twitter,

TikTok, even people's dads are WhatsApping now. They're all watching, they're all commenting, they're all calling for the head of this Andrew Everton guy.

Even the hair-straightening technician she is with this morning shows Fiona his phone, and says, "You seen this?"

Apropos of nothing, Fiona also sees her number of Instagram followers race above four million as the saga unfolds on her "hacked" account. At the moment, the Chief Constable is looking around the room, and you can hear someone tapping on a keyboard. The comments section is going crazy.

That's all Elizabeth had asked for. The login and password for Fiona's Instagram. "Only for an hour or so, dear," she had said. "I'm sure you won't even notice."

76.

Andrew Everton sits patiently while the Viking types something into his laptop. So far, so good. He likes the Viking; the Viking seems to like him. More importantly, he trusts the Viking, and he feels safe in this cozy room, in the middle of nowhere. Andrew Everton gets the feeling he is going to leave here considerably richer than when he entered it.

The Viking closes his laptop. "You kill anyone?"

"No," says Andrew Everton. "It was clean."

"You sure?"

"Listen, I made money, I broke the law, I did bad things, but I didn't kill anyone." What if the Viking decides this is too risky for him?

"It says the journalist was called Bethany Waites," says the Viking. "Bethany Waites, she used to work at *South East Tonight*, she was the journalist who reported your story?"

"That's the one, yes," says Andrew Everton.

"And she died," says the Viking. "Someone killed her?"

"Yup," says Andrew Everton. "Not me though. You've got no worries with me."

"I think I do have worries maybe," says the Viking. "The woman who went to jail, she was called Heather Garbutt?"

"That's right," says Andrew Everton.

"And she died too?"

"Again, yes, she did," says Andrew Everton. "And, again, nothing to do with me. She killed herself. Tragic, but—"

"And your accomplice, Jack Mason?"

"Let me stop you there," says Andrew Everton. "Yes, he died too."

"A lot of people dying around you," says the Viking. "That worries me."

"Of course, absolutely, it should do," says Andrew Everton.

"So I need you to be honest," says the Viking. "There's just you and me here, and I need to trust you. Did you kill them?"

"No," says Andrew Everton.

"Perhaps you killed one or two of them," says the Viking.

"I didn't kill any of them," says Andrew Everton.

"It's a big coincidence," says the Viking.

"Yes," agrees Andrew Everton. "It's a big coincidence. But you can trust me."

77.

Joyce

Ibrahim has everything open in front of him. Thousands of people are watching Fiona's hacked livestream. "Bethany Waites" is trending at number one on Twitter. People are sharing clips of her, posting newspaper articles from the time she disappeared. Her face is everywhere.

As is the face of Andrew Everton. The comments section is really going to town on "You can trust me." Kent Police have had to disable their Twitter account. It's even on Sky News. They're not allowed to show pictures, but they're talking people through it.

So he's admitted to the fraud, admitted to being Jack Mason's partner, but he hasn't admitted to the killings yet. I can't say I expected him to. Even when there're just two of you in a room no one wants to admit they're a murderer, do they?

But that's what we really want. For Andrew Everton to admit to what he has done. To tell the world the truth. To get justice for Bethany.

Elizabeth and Viktor are conferring in a corner. Whatever Elizabeth is saying, Viktor is nodding. I think it is time to send in the Bullet!

78.

Behind the Viking is a closed door, which now opens. A man walks into the library. He is short and bald, and wears glasses too big for his face. What is going on here?

"No," says Andrew Everton to the Viking. "No. It's just you and me."

"This is my associate," says the Viking. "His name is Yuri."

"A pleasure to meet you, Chief Constable," says Viktor. "You have been a busy man."

"I didn't agree to this," says Andrew Everton.

"Give me one minute," says Viktor. "If you don't like what I have to say, then I leave, and you may also leave too. You are quite safe."

"One minute," says Andrew Everton, his eyes looking for an exit.

"My friend here, they call him the Viking, he is the genius in the room. Though you may be a genius too, Andrew. Might I call you Andrew?"

"Certainly, Yuri," says Andrew Everton.

"It is clear you are very clever, Andrew. A chief constable, congratulations. An acclaimed author, also, under the pen-name Mackenzie McStewart. I have recently read, and much enjoyed, *To Remain Silent*, a tour de force, in my opinion. Like John Grisham. Further to this list of accomplishments, we now discover you are a master criminal? Cop, crime writer, master criminal. I imagine the skills overlap somewhat?"

Andrew Everton nods. There is something about this man he likes. And he is right about *To Remain Silent*. It is very Grisham-esque.

"Well, you are almost a master criminal, shall we say? You pulled off the robbery, very simple, very elegant, but have yet to see the proceeds. Which is where we come in. Can we track down your money? Yes, at least my friend can. Would we like to be in business with you? Again, yes, you are a powerful man, and you would be able to help us, I think, in a number of areas. Should you be willing?"

"I would be willing," says Andrew Everton. "You get me that ten million and you can have whatever you want."

"We are of like minds, I see," says Viktor. "I imagined we would be. We both like money, certainly we do, but we are both moral men. We bend the rules at times, that is undeniable, but rules aren't for everyone, are they?"

"Agreed, agreed," says Andrew Everton. He is going to get his money, he can just feel it. All those years slogging away, and it's finally going to come good. A house in Spain, a room to write in, overlooking the sea. He'll pretend he's signed a lucrative publishing deal, very hush-hush, and he'll quit his job for good. This man, with his oversized glasses, is the final piece of the jigsaw.

"But I need to trust you too," says Viktor. "I feel that I will. I feel that we are similar men. That we believe similar things about this tough world we live in."

"Goes without saying," says Andrew Everton. He saw a place online, on the Costa Dorada. It had *two* swimming pools, for goodness' sake.

"So I need you to tell me the truth," says Viktor. "About the journalist. And about your two friends. Three deaths, all connected to your fraud. I want to trust you, so I need you to come clean with me. You killed them, yes? It's OK."

Andrew Everton mulls over his reaction. What does this man want to hear? That he killed them? That he didn't kill them? What is the "moral" answer here? He makes up his mind.

"I didn't kill them," says Andrew Everton. "I am not a killer."

Viktor nods. "So they each just died?"

Andrew Everton nods. "Yes, they each . . . just died."

"I am disappointed, Chief Constable," says Viktor. "I had hoped for the truth."

This puts Andrew Everton in a bind. Can this man possibly know the truth? He weighs up the different lies he might tell. He's so close. Don't blow it now. Stick to your guns; he will respect that.

"I didn't kill them."

Viktor pulls a pained face. "Andrew, that is hard for me to hear. Given the information I have."

"What information?" says Andrew. This has to be a bluff. It's just a test. Keep denying, keep denying, and you'll be in Spain before you know it.

"That you murdered Bethany Waites. You buried her body in the garden of a house in Sussex, and used it to blackmail your co-conspirators, Jack Mason and Heather Garbutt, into keeping quiet about your fraud. That you had Heather Garbutt murdered in Darwell Prison, and, further, that you murdered Jack Mason two evenings ago." The Jack Mason bit is guesswork, but Andrew Everton doesn't need to know that.

Andrew Everton is stunned, paralyzed. Where could he possibly have got the information about Bethany's body and the blackmail? It was impossible. Jack Mason would never have named him, not in a million years. And Heather Garbutt was too scared of what he could do. So how did he *know*?

"Just the truth, Andrew," says Viktor. "And then we are sure what we're dealing with. Then we can move forward with trust."

Andrew Everton has to make a big decision. Confess? How can he stick to his version of the story when this Yuri seems to know the whole truth? Trust Yuri, and trust the Viking? Say the words? It's just three men in a room, miles from nowhere. He's very aware that the next sentence out of his mouth could make him ten million pounds.

"OK," says Andrew Everton. "And you guarantee this information never leaves this room?"

"No one is watching," says Viktor. "And no one is listening."

Andrew Everton clasps his hands together, as if in a prayer of forgiveness. "I murdered Bethany Waites."

79.

Connie Johnson is watching the action unfold on her flat-screen TV. The Wi-Fi is behaving itself for once, and she is watching a feed of the action on YouTube.

That was that, then, all wrapped up. Andrew Everton in the frame. The Chief Constable. She'd met him a couple of times, seemed nice enough. But a killer? Who'd have thought? And how handy for Connie.

One person he definitely hadn't killed was Heather Garbutt.

Connie had found Heather's body when she'd gone back to visit her for another chat. Knitting needles and all. There had been a suicide note by the body, a few last goodbyes, etc. Heather Garbutt was terrified of something, and, watching Andrew Everton on screen, Connie now at least knows what.

Connie had thought quickly. Ibrahim and his gang were on the trail of Bethany Waites's killer, and, in her estimation, would probably find the killer. She was right about that, wasn't she? Connie figured it wouldn't do any harm to get involved. To help out. The court might look a bit more kindly on her if she'd helped track down a murderer.

So she'd torn up Heather's note—*Farewell, can't take it any more,* something or other like that, she'd only skimmed it—and written her own. Made Heather sound like a murder victim, and cast herself as someone with information. A savior.

Now that Connie knows that Andrew Everton killed Bethany Waites, she can put part two of the plan into action. She just has to invent a bit of evidence to show he killed Heather Garbutt too. The guy in the admin block, the one with the Volvo who had wiped the tapes of her going into Heather's cell that night? She bets he might just remember Andrew Everton visiting the prison that evening. And Connie will, no doubt, remember something Heather had said to her. Something innocuous about the police. "This goes right to the top," some nonsense. She'll have fun inventing the memory.

Everton will be convicted, and Connie will get a few years knocked off her sentence for cooperating with the authorities. Beautiful. And the sooner she's out, the sooner she'll deal with Ron Ritchie.

She had to hand it to Ibrahim, he really came good.

Though she remembers him telling her that she cared about Heather Garbutt. And the fact that she cared was proof she wasn't a sociopath.

And, all the while, she had Heather Garbutt's torn-up suicide note in her pocket.

Therapy really is a fascinating process. She can't wait for more.

80.

Joyce

You can imagine the hullaballoo here when he said it.

"Viktor strikes again," Elizabeth said. "The Bullet never misses."

There are now more than three million people watching Fiona's Instagram Live. They have all just heard the same thing, and they are not being shy in giving their opinion. They all want to see what happens next.

I'm typing as I watch. It's all very relaxed now, the three of them just chatting about bank accounts. Viktor is pouring them each a scotch.

Ron has just been telling a story about a policeman in Yorkshire who hit him with a truncheon. I asked if a lot of people hit him in those days, and he agreed that they did.

Even for us, this was a hell of a team effort. Cracking the names on the financial documents, getting Jack Mason to open up, making friends with Fiona Clemence. "Friends" might be pushing it, although, looking at the numbers on her Instagram account now, perhaps we will be. Henrik doing his bit, lovely Viktor getting the confession. And Pauline and Mike still to come. Pauline is having to reapply Mike Waghorn's makeup, because he's been crying. I've just told him that three million people are watching, and he says he's ready.

Earlier, I asked Bogdan how Donna was, and he said how do you mean, and I said how do you think I mean, and he gave me the cutest little smile and a thumbs-up.

Talking of which, a text came through from Mervyn. I was excited to see his name on my phone, and all a-flutter as I opened the message.

Alan OK.

Well, we can work on him. We've all just wished Mike luck. Time to get back to the action.

81.

Donna and Chris are watching on Donna's computer. Everyone in their office is watching. Everyone in Fairhaven police station is watching. Everyone in Fairhaven is watching. Everyone, full stop, is watching.

It is safe to say that Andrew Everton is today's newest "Most hated man in Britain." Though Donna notes that *To Remain Silent* is currently number one on Amazon's "Movers and Shakers" book chart.

What a masterstroke from whoever hacked Fiona Clemence's Instagram. Speculation is rife as to who it might be. As if Chris and Donna couldn't work out exactly who it was.

The latest development for the crowd huddled around Donna's computer, all desperate not to be called away to some sort of crime or other, is that the old guy from *South East Tonight*, Mike Waghorn, has just walked into the Viking's library.

"There's your mate, Donna!" says DS Terry Hallet.

"He was my mate first," says Chris. "I Breathalyzed him!"

On the screen, Mike takes a chair, opposite an incredulous-looking Andrew Everton. Mike looks straight into whatever hidden camera is filming the scene.

"Hi, I'm Mike Waghorn, reporting for *South East Tonight*—"

"Mike, what are you—" says Andrew Everton, but Mike hushes him.

"I wanted to say a few words to the millions of people currently watching this livestream. The millions who have just heard the confessions of Chief Constable Andrew Ev—"

Andrew Everton leaps out of his chair and almost out of shot. He is caught and brought down by a muscled arm. You wouldn't know whose arm it was unless you recognized the tattoos. Donna recognizes them instantly. So that's where he was last night. "Trust me," he had said. Perhaps she should start making a habit of trusting him? She wonders if the whole gang is up there? Of course they are.

Mike Waghorn, ever the professional, waits for Andrew Everton's muffled cries to disappear into the distance, before continuing.

"This is a five-minute wonder, I understand that. To see a man confess to terrible crimes. To see a *chief constable* confess to fraud, to corruption, to blackmail and to murder. It certainly seems to have caused the stir we hoped for. At some point there will be a trial, no doubt complicated by the very scenes you are witnessing, but a trial at the very least. Andrew Everton will go to prison, of that we can be fairly sure, even with the lenient, mollycoddling justice system we seem to have in this country at the moment. But let's not get started on that. We will cut this feed fairly soon, and return Fiona's Instagram to its rightful owner. Thank you from the bottom of my heart, Fiona, for your help today. I can't think of a finer tribute you could have paid to Bethany. You will all go back to work soon, you'll have your dinner, you'll watch a bit of TV, whatever you have planned for today. You will talk about what you have seen, I am sure of that. And you will talk about it tomorrow too, although a little less. And maybe you'll have the odd word about it the day after, but then it will be gone. That's how news works. There will be other excitements to replace it. One of the Kardashians will have a baby, perhaps. So I am aware I have your attention only for a short while. Some of you will be drifting away already, as our main business is done here: Andrew Everton is being handcuffed in the hallway to my left, and the Staffordshire constabulary are on their way. But if I could ask of you just a minute or so more? It will be quick, I promise. I want to tell you about a friend of mine, Bethany Waites, who was murdered almost ten years ago. If she hadn't been murdered, you would know the name already, I'm sure.

She was a grafter, Bethany, a worker, no one ever handed her a thing. She could argue all night long, beat you in an arm wrestle, and she could drink you under the table. Northern, you see. If I'm allowed to say that. Bethany Waites was a fine journalist, but above all else she was a fine friend, and I loved her. I don't even mean I loved her, I mean I love her. So when your attention moves on, when your interest is piqued by the next shiny story, I'd just ask that you remember her name from time to time. Bethany Waites. Because she deserves to be remembered long after Andrew Everton has been forgotten. Well, that's all the news we have for you this lunchtime. So from me, Mike Waghorn, thank you all for watching, take care of yourselves, and take care of each other."

82.

All of Kent is shivering in the cold air, and Christmas isn't far away.

"I've told you before," says Donna. "You're forgiven."

"But it was important," says Bogdan. "It was an award. What if you never win another award?"

"Thank you for the vote of confidence," says Donna. "Here's the basic rule: if I'm up for an award, I want you to be there—unless you're catching a murderer by livestreaming a confession from the Instagram account of a famous television presenter. Then you're excused."

Carwyn Price has just been charged with threatening behavior. Donna saw him slip a note into her bag. It read: *We all hate you. You're a joke.* A man who doesn't respond well to being turned down. Bethany, Fiona, Donna, probably countless more over the years. He'll only get a slap on the wrist, but he won't be back at *South East Tonight* anytime soon.

They haven't solved the mystery of Juniper Court though. So perhaps she and Chris had got that wrong all along?

Bogdan parks carefully. The Coopers Chase Parking Committee have lost none of their power. If anything, it has only increased after a recent failed coup. Elizabeth is going to a cliff today, and Bogdan has promised to visit Stephen. He knows Stephen will be happy to see Donna too.

Before he gets out of the car, Bogdan turns to Donna.

"I have an award for you."

"You have an award for me?"

"Sure," says Bogdan. "I feel bad."

Bogdan reaches into a holdall in the back of the car and presents Donna with the statue of Anahita, goddess of love and battle.

"Donna, I highly commend you."

"Bogdan!" says Donna.

"I wanted to get it engraved, but apparently you're not supposed to."

Donna can't believe what she's holding. "Bogdan, it was two thousand quid! We could have had two weeks in Greece for that."

Bogdan smiles. "Kuldesh sold it to me for one pound. And he said to tell you to keep dodging the bricks."

Donna looks at her statue, her award. And then back at Bogdan.

"Why did he sell it to you for one pound?"

"Well," says Bogdan, opening his car door. "He asked me if I was in love with you. And I said yes."

83.

Ron had suggested it, for his own reasons, admittedly, and now here they all were. Freezing cold, that was for sure, but he was right. They stand high on the top of Shakespeare Cliff, the English Channel stretching away forever. Angry waves batter the foot of the cliff, hundreds of feet below, the noise rising to greet them like a muffled argument from a downstairs flat.

It's not where Bethany had died, they know that now, but it's the best place they have to drink to her memory.

Andrew Everton is keeping quiet about the whole thing. No surprises there. So they still don't know what really happened that night. Where had Bethany gone? Where had Andrew Everton killed her? Who were the two figures in Bethany's car as it approached this very cliff? No one had cracked the mystery of "Robert Brown MSc" either. Ibrahim had driven himself half mad with anagrams.

Other questions had been answered, though. One of the guards at the prison says that Andrew Everton visited Heather Garbutt on the night of her death. He denies it, but of course he would.

And Jack Mason. Ron has thought back to their last evening together. The guilt Jack had spoken about.

They each have a single rose to throw into the sea below. Elizabeth and Joyce, Ibrahim, Mike and Pauline. Even Viktor has come down to pay his respects. They had asked Henrik, but he had said, "I don't understand, I didn't know her, why would I throw a rose into the sea?" He had a point. Not everyone wants to be in a gang, do they?

One by one they throw their roses. Joyce's is blown back into her face by the wind, so she has to have another go. The sky is cloudless, so if Bethany is in a position to look down, she'd see them all today. Ron doesn't hold with that sort of thing in his head, but there is plenty of room for it in his heart.

Mike Waghorn says a few words, a number of which have to be repeated because the wind is picking up. He then suggests a little walk along the clifftop. Ron had known that he would.

"I'll sit this one out," Ron says. "You know what my knee's like."

A few raised eyebrows—they all know Ron doesn't talk about his knees. But it shuts them up, and they are soon on their way. Pauline sits with him, as he knew she would.

"You all right, lover?" she asks.

"I'm not so bad," says Ron. "Just thinking about my bathroom."

"You never fail to surprise me, Ronnie. You thinking about getting an air freshener?"

Ron smiles, but a little sadly. "Nah, just not used to having a woman around, am I? All the gear, you know, the creams, all the makeup and what have you."

"I'm taking up too much room, am I? You got no space for your Lynx Africa?"

"I love it, if I'm honest," says Ron. "Feels intimate, doesn't it? I've always been honest with you, you know, Pauline?"

"I know, darling," says Pauline, looking concerned. "What's all this about?"

"Have you always been honest with me?"

" 'Course," says Pauline. "I have the odd fag when you're not looking, but apart from that."

"Robert Brown MSc," says Ron.

"What about him?"

"I know I'm not the clever one," says Ron. "But it's about time I cracked something."

"Ron?"

"It's the makeup," says Ron. "It's been sitting there in the bathroom all this time. All lined up under the mirror where I shave. Staring me in the face."

Ron looks at Pauline. He doesn't want to say it, but he has to.

"Your mascara," says Ron. "Bobbi Brown, your favorite. Bobbi Brown Mascara. 'Robert Brown MSc.'"

84.

Donna and Bogdan kiss outside the car, they kiss in the hallway, they kiss by Elizabeth and Stephen's front door. Bogdan is unused to public displays of affection. What if somebody sees? Also, he has a bag full of food that needs to go in the fridge.

But he is in love, and he accepts that will bring its own challenges. Bogdan knocks, then opens the door, calling Stephen's name.

Stephen is sitting on the sofa in his pajamas, which is not in the least unusual.

"Here's the happy couple," he says. "Look at you both."

"The very happy couple," says Donna. "Hello, Stephen."

Donna is still holding her statue. Stephen levers himself up, and walks over to take a look.

"Our old friend Anahita," says Stephen, his eyes lighting up. "Goddess of love and battle. Most appropriate."

Donna smiles, and pops into the kitchen to put the kettle on.

Bogdan loves to see Stephen's eyes sparkle. Loves to see that intelligence. Bogdan had seen the list that Stephen made of Henrik's books. So detailed, so beautiful. He will give Stephen a shave later, and then a post-shave balm. Then a moisturizer. Stephen has never had a skin-care regimen before—"Soap and water, old boy"—but it is never too late to start. Maybe he should start giving him vitamins too? Would Elizabeth object? Just C and D to start with. He doesn't get out enough.

"Speaking of battle," says Bogdan, taking his seat by the chessboard. "We play?"

Stephen waves this away.

"We don't play today?" says Bogdan. Maybe they will watch a film instead? Or just tell stories. Bogdan will cook a paella.

"Not me, old chap," says Stephen. "Elizabeth's the chess player round here."

"Elizabeth?"

"I tried chess a few times," says Stephen. "Never got the hang of it. You play?"

"Yes, I play," says Bogdan.

"Any good?" says Stephen.

"Depends," says Bogdan, determined to stop the tears forming. "In chess you're only really ever as good as the person you play against."

Stephen nods and looks down at the board. Bogdan wonders what he is seeing.

"Better man than I," says Stephen. "Devil's own job, that game."

Donna walks back in with two mugs of tea. Stephen beams.

"That's the stuff, all right," says Stephen. "Cup of tea. That's the stuff."

85.

Ron can see the others returning. But they're in the distance, and their walk back is uphill. They will be a while yet. Joyce has her arm linked with Mike Waghorn's.

"The whole truth?" says Pauline.

"I think I'm due that," says Ron.

"I think you are too, Ronnie," says Pauline. "But I don't want the others to know. I don't want Mike to know."

Ron gives a small shrug. Is this where it all ends? On a clifftop high above a wild sea?

"It was about half ten," Pauline begins, barely able to look Ron in the eye. "I was getting ready for bed, believe it or not, early start the next day. There's a ring on the door. I ignore it, nothing good comes at night unless you've ordered it. It rings again, and again, and eventually I'm 'bugger this' and I look on the entry camera and there she is."

"Bethany Waites?"

"Bethany Waites. I buzz her up and wait for her to knock. In you come, I say, what's all this about? I could see something was up, else I'd have just sent her packing. She's wearing a houndstooth jacket and yellow trousers, looked like she'd just picked them up from a jumble sale. No makeup. She sits, and she says, Pauline, I need a favor, and I say, at ten thirty at night, and she tells me to sit down and listen to a story. I say, should I ring Mike, and she says, you can't ring Mike, I don't want him to worry."

"What was the story?"

"Bethany says, you gotta believe this, Pauline, someone's trying to kill me. I've got this story they don't want coming out, I've just had this message, threatening me, and you know me, Ronnie, I've heard it all in my time, but I don't know what to believe. But something in her eyes tells me I'm hearing the truth. Close to the truth at least, so I'm like, what can I do? What's the favor? If I can help, I'll help."

"And what was the favor?" asks Ron. He can just hear Joyce's laugh now, the top notes carrying on the wind.

"She's going to meet someone, she says. And she needs to look different. She knows I can't work miracles, but can I make her up, lend her a wig? Change her appearance just enough to fool someone. She had a picture she showed me, and it didn't look impossible."

"So you said yes?"

"First off, I tried to talk her out of it. If you're in trouble, go to the police. Not really my style, as you know, but they have their uses sometimes. She says she can't go to the police, she just needs this one favor, and the whole thing will be over soon enough. She says trust me, I know what I'm doing, and I'll pay you too."

"Five grand?" says Ron.

"I say I don't want money, come on, if you're in trouble, let's get started. So I make her up, like the picture. I get one of my wigs, fit it, give it a bit of a trim, and, ninety minutes later, it ain't bad. Really not bad. She's happy. She's looking at her watch the whole time, and now she says, Pauline, that's us, wish me luck, and I say where are you going, and she says, if you don't hear from me by tomorrow morning, call the police, anonymous though, and I said I don't want you going out there, I'm calling Mike, and she says, I have to. She gives me a hug, which she never does, and she gives me a bit of paper with numbers on it and says, 'That's the money for you,' and she takes off."

Ron drums his fingers. "That's the story?"

"That's the story," says Pauline. "You believe me, Ronnie?"

"I believe you, Paul," Ron says. "I believe you're telling me the truth. But you're missing something out, darling. You're missing out why you've never told anyone all this before. You knew where she was those missing hours. You knew she was heading off to meet someone. And you never told a soul? That doesn't make any sense. You'd have been straight on to Mike, and straight on to the police. Come on."

Ron sees Pauline glance toward the advancing walkers.

"There was one more thing," says Pauline. "When we were fitting the wig. I have my wigs and a few costumes on dummies, see, you know, mannequins, and before she leaves, Bethany says, can I borrow one? And I say, borrow a mannequin, you mad? But the whole thing's been mad, so in the end I say go ahead."

"A mannequin?"

"The next morning, they find her car at the bottom of the cliff, release the CCTV, all that, so I'm ready to ring Mike, but before I do, I have a little think. I think about the makeup, the photo she showed me, I think about the wig, I think about the mannequin, and the CCTV of the two figures in the car. I think about the clothes she's wearing, Ronnie. I think I even said to her, 'I wouldn't be seen dead in those.'"

"So, you think—"

"I don't think, I know. And, Ron, Mike was destroyed when Bethany died. He loved her, she loved him. And I took the view, for better or for worse, it would be a hundred times worse for him if he knew she'd faked the whole thing, run off to goodness knows where, with goodness knows what money, and not told him a dicky bird. Why on earth did she do it? I've never worked that out."

Pauline looks out to sea.

"There was no comeback. No one was accused of the murder, no harm done to anyone, and I kept quiet. Then you lot showed up, and there're people dying left, right and center, so I tried to drop a few hints. I knew I couldn't tell the truth after all this time, but I thought you lot might figure it out, and Mike might have to face the truth. Thought it was about time."

"Stone me," says Ron.

"I just tried to do what was best," says Pauline.

"And the money?"

"Never touched it," says Pauline. "Threw the piece of paper away, never thought about it again. Robert Brown MSc was Bethany's joke, not mine."

"A pretty good one too," says Ron.

"Yeah, you'd have liked her," says Pauline. "Can you forgive me, Ron?"

"Nothing to forgive," says Ron.

"Massage tomorrow? Little treat?"

"Don't push it," says Ron.

The others are nearly with them.

Ron looks over at Pauline. "Where do you think she is now?"

Pauline smiles, and stands to welcome the walkers back. "I think she's in heaven looking down on us."

Joyce takes Pauline's seat next to Ron.

"That was bracing," says Joyce. "I can't believe you missed the whole thing."

Ron puts his arm around his friend, and sees Pauline do the same with Mike.

86.

For years she has had Google Alerts on her phone. If anyone anywhere mentioned the name "Bethany Waites," she would know about it. She would take a quick look, assess any risks, and then continue on with her new life. Around the anniversary of her death, there would usually be a few mentions, but every year there had been fewer and fewer, until they eventually dried up altogether. To all intents and purposes, Bethany Waites had ceased to exist.

Until three days ago, when Bethany Waites suddenly became one of the most famous people in the world for a whole afternoon. Bethany Waites had seen all the fuss, of course she had, how could you miss it, even in Dubai.

She had stayed indoors, canceled her appointments. There was no real need though, she knew that. Bethany has been Alice Cooper for many years now. People laughed at her name, but it serves a purpose.

Back when she was investigating the VAT fraud, Bethany had been learning everything she could about money-laundering. Taking professors and criminals out for lunch. Bothering all the experts. A German police investigator had told her that the best alias for a fraudster was that of a famous person. "It makes you impossible to Google," he had said. And he was quite right. Google "Alice Cooper" now, and you will have to scroll through an awful lot of pages before you get to her "Media Training and PR Solutions" company on the eighth floor of an office building in the Dubai Marina.

She learned an awful lot more than that little trick too. Learned so much, in fact, that not only could she follow the trail of the VAT money, but also access it herself.

And then Andrew Everton sent her the bullet. The bullet with the name scratched, crudely, into its side.

That's when she knew she was in danger. Knew Andrew Everton had discovered she was on his tail. Knew that he meant her harm. He must have been bugging her phone. Seen the "absolute dynamite" message to Mike.

So she had a choice. Keep digging, keep investigating, be brave. Or find a way out?

Was she ever going to be able to beat Andrew Everton? A high-ranking police officer. Someone with the resources to access her messages, someone with a heart cold enough to send her a bullet.

Really she had no choice at all.

So she did the next best thing. Over the next few weeks, using what she'd learned, she started to channel Andrew Everton's money into new accounts. She didn't take any out, that's the real danger time, but she diverted it. She hid it.

After her death, poor Andrew Everton and Jack Mason had spent so long trying to retrieve their money, but the web they had devised was so opaque, and so *clever,* that they had no way of seeing that the money had already gone.

She had her plan in place. Her murder, her disappearance, the new passport with the new hair and makeup, taking her own blood with home-testing kits to smear in the car. She had picked up all sorts of tricks. But she didn't believe she would really go through with it. Until the night she had received the email from Andrew Everton. *"Come and meet me. I just want to talk."*

Bethany knew it was time to say goodbye. To her life, to her story, to Mike. And hello to Dubai, to a new life, and to ten million.

Bethany had waited a year or so before she started collecting her money. She'd siphoned off a hundred thousand from an obscure account in Panama, just to see her through, and to pay for the surgery. She'd reported, many years before, about a woman from Faversham who had made her fortune in plastic surgery, and the woman was only too glad to help, for a hefty cut. You could get pretty much anything you wanted in Dubai if you had ten million pounds in your pocket. And what Bethany Waites bought was anonymity.

She got away with it, sure. But got away with *what?*

She had regrets, certainly. Before she disappeared, she had received a couple of knockbacks from the BBC. Her confidence had been dented. Bethany had begun to think she would never make it, would never get out. That made the ten million, the new life, even more tempting. But maybe she should have stuck it out? Look at what happened with Fiona Clemence. But Bethany didn't have Fiona's confidence. Didn't have Fiona's looks either, although she resembles her a little bit more since the surgery. She could have toughed it out, but an opportunity came her way and she chose to take it. Mike had told her to keep fighting, told her she would make it, but she was too young to know that was true.

And Mike is the worst of all. The regret that still wakes her in the night. It would kill Mike to know she had left him voluntarily. She knows that, and she knew Pauline would know that too. She could have stuck around, been brave. She could have brought Andrew Everton to justice, could have risen through the ranks, enjoyed her career, popped in to visit Mike for a drink whenever she was in the area. That's what she could have done.

But her mind keeps coming back to the bullet. The bullet, with the name scratched into the side, sent by Andrew Everton. Designed to scare her, no doubt, but a bullet that ultimately cost him ten million pounds.

After that Bethany really had no choice. She has the bullet in front of her now. She weighs it in her hand, just as she had done that night many years ago. Beware the bullet with your name on it.

And the name is what had finally made her mind up. Because the name scratched into the bullet was not "Bethany Waites." She could have handled that.

The name was "Mike Waghorn."

87.

Mike Waghorn scrolls back through his emails. Every year, on the anniversary of Bethany's death, viewers send him their condolences. Not many, and fewer and fewer as the years ticked by, but enough to make a difference.

This year, there had been just four. Three from regular correspondents, and one from an account he had never identified. With a no-reply email address. It got lost among the throng for the first few years, but it is very visible now. The message would always comprise just a single red rose. Mike had never really thought anything of it.

They had never found Bethany's body. All sorts of people had told him why, tides and so on, and Mike had accepted what he was told. There were plenty of similar cases if you looked into it, and Mike had looked into it.

Then they were told that Bethany had been buried in Heather Garbutt's garden. But, despite the digging, the body has not been found there either. Andrew Everton continues to protest his innocence.

So what if? Mike has begun to think. What if?

Mike looks at the email with the red rose. He searches back. Same email every year. All from the same no-reply email address.

What could the red rose signify? Love, for one. Lancashire? That was a stretch. But Bethany liked to stretch things. Liked to tease him. "Absolute dynamite" indeed. As if he were ever going to be the one to work that out.

Of course, the emails are not from Bethany, of course they're not. They are just roses from a well-wisher. But it's a nice fantasy. The idea that

Bethany wasn't dead, but living it up somewhere, perhaps on the proceeds of the VAT fraud? No one else seemed to have the money, and even Henrik has said that at some point the money seemed to just vanish. Had it vanished with her?

Would Bethany really have left him without saying goodbye?

For ten million, why not? It was foolish, and it was greedy, but who hasn't been foolish and greedy in their life? Mike had been foolish his whole life, until Bethany had shown him the truth. He wishes Bethany could have hung around long enough for him to return the favor.

Maybe the emails are from Bethany. Mike can choose to believe it if he wishes. And, if they are, he hopes she saw the broadcast the other day. The tribute he paid her. He hopes she knows, wherever she is, up above, down below, or somewhere in between, that he loves her.

Mike pours himself a cider straight from the plastic bottle now. Why not? He raises his glass.

"To absent friends."

88.

Joyce

A few days have passed since all the excitement. I should probably fill you in on everything that's happened since.

I finished my short story. It is no longer called "Cannibal Bloodbath." Instead it is called "Life Is but a Dream—A Gerry Meadowcroft Mystery." I sent it off to the *Evening Argus*, and they immediately responded to say that my submission had been received. I replied to say thank you, and to wish them a nice weekend, but that email didn't get through. I haven't heard anything back since.

I have started a new story in which Inspector Gerry Meadowcroft goes to Morocco. I have never been to Morocco, but I watched a Rick Stein documentary in which he went to Marrakesh, so I am basing a lot of the descriptions on that.

Andrew Everton is in prison. Belmarsh, high security. For his own protection as much as anything, I think. He's been charged with the fraud, but they are still investigating the killings of Bethany, and Heather. It's interesting that, in any normal case, the livestream video we did would have prejudiced the trial, but the reaction to it was so huge I think even the authorities worked out that justice was going to have to be seen to be done. Andrew is still protesting his innocence, but, whatever happens, he'll be going to jail for a long time.

The irony is his books are now huge bestsellers. Top of the Kindle charts, and some publishing company is rushing out real, physical copies too. Netflix have bought the TV rights. It's true what they say about publicity. He's not seeing a penny of the money, though. It's all being held by the court until he pays back the ten million he stole.

I don't think they'll ever charge him with the murders. Where's the evidence? They dug every inch of the garden and the woodland behind Heather's house, and found no body. What they have found is many more guns, piles of cash, fake passports, stolen goods, everything you could think of. It seems that every time Jack Mason dug a hole over the years, looking for the body, he hid something in it before filling it back up again. The first gun we found, the assault rifle, had never been fired, and the hundred thousand was from a Post Office robbery in Tunbridge Wells.

I went shopping in Tunbridge Wells recently; Carlito took us all up there in the minibus. I had read in a book somewhere that Tunbridge Wells had a Waitrose, but it didn't. It had a lovely big Waterstones, though, and I bought a book by Stephen King called *On Writing*, and a new Marian Keyes.

The biggest news is probably Mike Waghorn. The world and his wife watched his tribute to Bethany, and he says the phone hasn't stopped ringing since. He's signed up to do a series on ITV called *Britain's Most Notorious Serial Killers*. He co-hosted *The One Show*—my favorite—for a week, and they've asked him back. And next week I'm going up to Elstree again to watch him on *Stop the Clock—Celebrities*! Elizabeth has a prior engagement apparently, so Pauline is going to come with me.

Fiona Clemence is taking us all out to dinner afterward, as well she might, given she now has eight million Instagram followers and is about to film an American version of *Stop the Clock*.

Pauline and Ron have just got back from a long weekend in Stratford-upon-Avon. I asked Ron what Shakespeare they had seen, but he looked at me blankly, so I think they spent the whole weekend in the pub. Ibrahim looks a bit lost without Ron. I know he is very happy for him, but perhaps I need to keep an eye on him? We often walk Alan together, and he natters away quite happily, but even so.

And, talking of walking dogs, I do often bump into Mervyn and Rosie. Mervyn is so handsome I have to stop my tail from wagging when I'm around him. He doesn't say much, but sometimes that can be a relief, can't it? With some men you spend most of your time just nodding in agreement.

I take Mervyn a casserole every now and again, always enough for two, just to see if he takes the hint, but he just says, "Thank you, that'll last me two days." But the way he says it, in that deep, commanding voice—well, it's worth it just for that. He hasn't yet shown any real sign of interest, though the other day he did bring round his copy of *The Times* and said, "There's an article in there about Margaret Atwood. About how she writes her books. Thought you might be interested." That must be the longest sentence he has ever said to me, so you never know. I read the article, so we will have something to talk about next time I see him.

Christmas is just around the corner, and I'm hoping Joanna and Scott might come down. I haven't really asked what everyone is doing. I wonder if Ron will be with Pauline? Perhaps they'd like to come round here? And Ibrahim, without question. I wonder what Viktor is doing for Christmas? I will ask him tomorrow, as we have all been invited for lunch at his. This time I will be bringing my swimming costume, I don't care how cold it is.

My crypto account, which was somewhere over sixty-five thousand pounds at one point, is now worth eight hundred. I emailed Henrik, and he replied saying, "Joyce, you must believe." Believe what, I don't know. But, whatever you might say about cryptocurrency, it's more fun than Premium Bonds.

Such a lot has happened this year, and my favorite thing of all has just bounded into the room looking for trouble. Alan thinks it is time for bed, and, as so often, he is quite right.

89.

Greed, that was the thing. The fatal flaw. Why wasn't he happy with what he had?

Actually, it was greed and being too clever. The two fatal flaws.

Sitting here in Belmarsh, when he should be on a Spanish terrace with a cold beer and a hot typewriter.

"A cold beer and a hot typewriter." Andrew Everton writes that down in his notebook. The new book, *Guilty or Not Guilty,* is going to be his best yet, just as soon as they let him use a computer. Perhaps after he's been convicted they'll let him use one? How many books will he have to sell to pay back ten million pounds under the Proceeds of Crime Act? A lot, that's his guess.

The VAT scheme, so simple, so victimless. How had it gone so wrong? The plot for a book, turned into a real-life crime. He should have left it as a book. Trusted his writing. "Grisham-esque," someone had called it, he forgets who.

He should never have sent the bullet to Bethany either. He had hoped it might scare her off. Never should have emailed asking to meet her. He should have stayed in the shadows. Life was not a book.

So many bodies and he had only murdered one of them. He'd told Jack and Heather he had murdered Bethany, sure. That was a masterstroke: blackmail them with a corpse that was never there. The coastguards had told him that if the body hadn't washed up within a week, it was probably not going to be washed up at all, and that's what gave him the idea. Such a clever idea. Too clever in the end; it was so unfair. You shouldn't be penalized for being too clever.

And he'd told the guy with the pebbly glasses that he'd killed Bethany too. Because that's what he thought the guy wanted to hear. That's how he thought he was going to get his money.

Greed. And being too clever. Look where it gets you.

Who had killed Bethany Waites? Andrew Everton has no idea. It wasn't him, and he knows it wasn't Jack Mason, or his little blackmail scheme wouldn't have worked. And where did all that money end up? He has no idea about that either. Who was the guy in the glasses? Was Elizabeth Best everything she seemed? His whole life had begun to unravel after he'd first met her. So many questions, and so few answers.

As he looks at the four walls of his cell, segregated from fellow prisoners, locked up for twenty-four hours a day for his own safety, and doing his business in a metal bucket bolted to a wall, it occurs to Andrew Everton that, for someone so clever, there seem to be an awful lot of things he doesn't know.

There is some good news, and you should always focus on the good news. There was no material evidence to link him to Bethany's or Heather's deaths. His solicitor would make short work of the "eyewitness" at Darwell Prison. Maybe he would beat the murder charges? The public was baying for his blood, but the public was always baying for something. They would move on soon enough, Mike Waghorn had been right about that.

Perhaps he would only be convicted of the fraud. And what would he serve? Maybe he'd do five years of a ten-year sentence? Write a series of best-selling books where a prisoner solves crimes from inside his cell? Call it "Hard Cell" or "The Wing Man."

Yes, focus on the good things.

Ironic that in the one murder he actually *had* committed, it looked like he wasn't even going to be a suspect. The moment Jack Mason started talking, Andrew'd had to kill him. No choice. Make it look like a simple suicide. Jack knew it the second he opened the door.

"Death Comes Knocking." Andrew Everton writes that down in his notebook too, under "Good Titles."

If he can beat these murder raps, five years will just fly by.

90.

Chris is celebrating solving the case in the way that all hard-bitten cops have done throughout the ages. He is drinking blueberry kombucha and dipping celery sticks into organic hummus, as he watches the darts.

He is thinking that murdering people must have been so much easier before the era of DNA evidence. You almost had to feel sorry for homicidal maniacs these days.

If you kill somebody, particularly at close range with a gun, then, and there's no nice way of putting it, their DNA will spatter all over you. All over your hands and your clothes. And that DNA is then transferred to anything you might touch.

At the Kent Police Awards, Patrice had wondered who Chris could arrest next to get another commendation? To get another night of black tie and free prosecco next year. Another cute, shiny badge in another cute, velvet pouch.

Well, after the message he has just received, Chris knows he will definitely be invited back next year. And it is all thanks to Patrice.

The start of the whole thing was this. The gun was just so small. It had been niggling at Chris. For a man with access to so many guns, legal and illegal, why would Jack Mason have shot himself with a gun small enough to be slipped into someone's pocket?

The answer, as so often, was very simple. It was because the gun *had* been slipped into someone's pocket.

When Andrew Everton had stolen it from the dig in Heather Garbutt's garden, he had chosen the smallest gun possible. Simply because he was going to have to walk out, past any number of police officers, without a soul spotting it. He couldn't have hidden an AK-47, even though they had actually found two of them.

Chris had asked for more tests on the gun, and those tests proved the gun had been buried alongside four others uncovered on the dig. Same fibers from the cloth they were wrapped in, same acids from the soil. The ammunition too. So Andrew Everton had seen the gun, stolen it, and had then used Jack Mason's own gun to shoot him.

It was good evidence, that's for sure. But it was not perfect. No one saw Andrew Everton pocket the gun. Anyone at the dig might have stolen it. Jack Mason himself might have dug it up weeks previously. Planning his suicide, Jack might have thought, "I know what I'll do, I'll dig up a tiny gun I buried ten years ago." In court a decent lawyer would soon throw doubt on the gun, and Andrew Everton will have a decent lawyer.

But it was good enough evidence for Chris to know that Andrew Everton had killed Jack Mason. He just needed to prove it.

He and Donna had talked it through. They didn't want Everton taking the stand and wriggling out of a murder charge on a technicality. Chris needed to find some evidence that placed Everton directly at the scene of Jack Mason's murder, and at the moment it was happening. Some DNA.

But where to find it?

It was Patrice who had the idea in the end. She made the suggestion about exactly where the DNA might be found. Chris was dubious. More than anything it would just be too ironic. But, after a few more prompts, he had contacted the forensics lab, and today the results had come back. She was right. He has just texted her at a Parents' Evening to let her know.

Everton would have cleaned himself thoroughly, of course. The blood and the gore, and the DNA of Jack Mason they contained, should have been long gone. But Andrew Everton had been sloppy. Or, knowing the man a little now, Chris thought it more likely he had been cocky. Perhaps he hadn't destroyed his clothes until the day after the murder? The day he was all laughs and smiles, sitting next to Chris and Patrice at the awards ceremony? Perhaps he recontaminated himself while he was disposing of them?

Whatever the reason, it is going to be very hard for Andrew Everton to explain where traces of Jack Mason's DNA have just been found.

On the cute, shiny badge and the cute, velvet pouch Andrew Everton had handed to Chris at the Kent Police Awards.

Chris pops another celebratory celery stick into his mouth.

Get out of that one.

91.

There is something Bogdan isn't telling her, Elizabeth can see that. It's not about Donna—three cheers for the two of them and all that—but it's definitely something. She has left him with Stephen again today, regardless. They will discuss it when she gets home.

"It has been an adventure," says Viktor. "I am grateful for that. I have been shot, buried and brought back to life. And I've played a lot of snooker."

"Welcome to the Thursday Murder Club," says Elizabeth.

They are sitting on Viktor's terrace, laptop open and gin and tonic poured. London spreads out before them in a vast panorama of greens and blues and grays. The buses like red blood cells. It all looks so genteel from up here, but they both well know the secrets that lie beneath the roofs of London. The money, the murder, the evil that people do. It was simply their stock in trade. Where you saw a cozy family chimney, they saw a corpse being burned. Such is the way of things after nearly sixty years in the business.

It is cold, but the cold helps them both think. Andrew Everton is behind bars, awaiting trial. Jack Mason and Heather Garbutt are in the ground. Henrik is back in Staffordshire, but has started sending Viktor cat videos from the internet. That feels a lot like a ceasefire to Elizabeth. She is pleased. Now that she has found Viktor again, she would rather not lose him.

But Viktor and she were agreed it was a job half done. Viktor had made Andrew Everton confess; Viktor made everyone confess sooner or later. But it didn't feel right. To either of them. They had discussed it at length. Had they uncovered the full story? Had they got the wrong man?

"How is Stephen?" asks Viktor.

"Another time," says Elizabeth.

Henrik has kept up the search, but everywhere he looked, the money had simply disappeared. They had cleared up "Carron Whitehead" and "Michael Gullis." They had never got close to "Robert Brown MSc." Perhaps there was some genius who could crack that one in time, but Elizabeth and Viktor have both stopped trying.

Henrik has uncovered one lead though. It was another early payment, this time for a hundred thousand pounds.

Viktor and Elizabeth scan the file in front of them. Henrik has tracked the payment as far as the British Virgin Islands, where it was further broken down into four separate payments. One of the payments found its way to the Cayman Islands, but that path has gone cold. One headed to Panama, and one to Liechtenstein, and into the endless corridors of banking secrecy. But the fourth payment was the interesting one. To the International Bank of Dubai. It seems out of place.

"Why pay money to Dubai?" says Elizabeth. "Surely there are plenty of places much safer, much darker."

"Access perhaps?" says Viktor. "Was this a little bit of spending money for someone?"

Elizabeth thinks she might take some time investigating the Dubai connection. She knows people there. Ten million pounds has gone missing somewhere, but sometimes a hundred thousand is all you need to catch someone. And Elizabeth would love to catch whoever killed Bethany Waites.

But perhaps she is a fool? Perhaps she is missing something obvious—it certainly feels that way. In her bones she knows it's not quite right. Are her powers waning? She is getting old. She uses a foot spa these days. She's even going to get Joyce one for Christmas. Is it time to quit all this nonsense? All this running around after shadows?

Viktor shivers in the cold. Elizabeth adjusts his blanket.

"Thank you," says Viktor. "Your country is so cold."

"So is yours," says Elizabeth, and Viktor concedes the point.

Time to quit all this nonsense? Elizabeth laughs to herself. What is there in life other than nonsense?

"Perhaps," says Elizabeth, "a little winter sunshine would do us some good?"

"Perhaps," agrees Viktor. "Any suggestions?"

"I hear Dubai is very temperate this time of year."

"I hear that too," says Viktor. "And they say the shopping is very good. There are even art galleries."

"Well, we could have a poke around the art galleries, couldn't we?"

"Spot of shopping," says Viktor. "Soak up the sun?"

"Wouldn't do any harm, would it?" says Elizabeth. She may be old, but she knows she will find something there. The missing piece.

"You know," says Viktor, "I remember being at the bottom of that hole, having all that earth shoveled over me. I remember looking up at everybody, and wondering if this might be the life for me. Coopers Chase. The tea, and the cake, and the birds and the dogs, and the friends. If it might be where I belong. You will understand that."

"Only too well," says Elizabeth.

"I was lonely," says Viktor. "You fixed that for me. You and your friends. My friends. They are quite something, aren't they?"

"They are quite something," agrees Elizabeth.

"Did I tell you I'm going to get a snooker table?"

"Ron spoke of little else in the car up here," says Elizabeth. "I had to feign sleep."

"It's the people, in the end, isn't it?" says Viktor. "It's always the people. You can move halfway around the world to find your perfect life, move to Australia if you like, but it always comes down to the people you meet."

Elizabeth looks over to the swimming pool, suspended in the sky. There is Joyce swimming laps, her head above water so as not to get her hair wet.

The boys, Ron and Ibrahim, are by the side of the pool, wearing overcoats on daybeds. Ibrahim is struggling to read the *Financial Times* in the wind. Ron is trying to work out how the lid goes back on his coffee cup.

It is far too cold to swim, but Joyce would not be dissuaded. Elizabeth had told her not to be so silly, and that the pool would still be here in the summer.

"Ah, but we may not be," Joyce had replied, and she was right. It was best to grab everything while you could. Who knows when your final swim might come, your final walk, your final kiss? Elizabeth has an idea what secret Bogdan is keeping from her. So be it.

Joyce sees Elizabeth looking, and gives her a wave. Elizabeth waves back. You keep swimming, Joyce. You keep swimming, my beautiful friend. You keep your head above the water for as long as you can.

ACKNOWLEDGMENTS

These acknowledgements are literally the last thing I have to write, and as soon as I finish I am allowed to go on holiday.

I could probably have gone on holiday at other points during the writing, but, honestly, publishers have a way of looking at you that says, "Do you *really* need to be going to CenterParcs this close to your deadline?"

I write this with, as so often, Liesl Von Cat stretched out on my desk. Her paw idly flicks out at me every now and again when my typing gets too loud for her delicate ears.

Whether Liesl is sleeping on my keyboard, blocking my screen or meowing loudly for food, even though she has literally just been fed, I know that she is constantly trying to help.

Indeed, I am indebted to so many people who have helped, cajoled, supported or, in her case, miaowed at me during the process of writing *The Bullet That Missed*.

First of all, readers. Nothing happens in this business without readers, and that's you. Unless you are just reading these acknowledgements in a shop while you're waiting for someone to buy wrapping paper. In which case, maybe buy a book? It doesn't have to be this one. Buy a Mark Billingham or a Shari Lapena.

But if you *have* read the book, then I thank you from the bottom of my heart. I have had a blast spending more time with the gang, and I hope you have too. My only job is to try to entertain you, and I really, really want you to have a good time. Even if that "good time" involves crying in public, or missing your stop on the bus.

Thank you also to all the incredible booksellers around the world. I think I have met almost all of you by now, and you are heroes. You are heroes for your love of books, for your skill at recommending the right books to the right people, and for your ability to say, "Do you need a bag?" three hundred times a day while still smiling. I promise I'll have another book for you to sell this time next year.

I am blessed with the most wonderful team of publishers too. Eternal thanks to my editor Harriet Bourton, at Viking, for her patience, wit and skill, and for being such an absolute pleasure to work with. The "sky pool" mentioned in the book is not only real, but is actually right next to the PRH offices in Battersea.

There are guards at the door of the American Embassy up ahead, and there's a group of young women going through the revolving doors of a publisher's building on her left.

In my mind's eye, that group is my wonderful Viking team of Harriet, Ella Horne, Olivia Mead, Ellie Hudson, Rosie Safaty and Lydia Fried, immortalized in print. Thank you for the incredible work you do: you're the best team in the business. See how close you got to Joyce and Elizabeth without realizing!

Thank you to the amazing Sam Fanaken, sales guru, for knowing how much I love to see a graph. And thank you to her brilliant team, Rachel Myers, Kyla Dean, Alison Pearce, Eleanor Rhodes Davies, Linda Viberg, Madeleine Bennett and Meredith Benson, and also to Samantha Waide and Grace Dellar.

I am indebted once again to the copyediting and production genius of Natalie Wall and Annie Underwood. Natalie is the first person ever to succinctly explain to me when I should be using "which" and when I should be using "that." It is a piece of knowledge that I will always remember.

And thank you too for the sterling copyediting work of Donna Poppy, who not only has an encyclopedic knowledge of Liverpool footballers, but also knows which Southern trains still have a trolley service. She also wins a prize for being the first person in the acknowledgements to be named after two separate characters from the Thursday Murder Club books.

The iconic front cover remains the work of the incredible Richard Bravery and Joel Holland. Often imitated, never bettered.

And thank you to Tom Weldon for the support, the wisdom and the Golden Penguins.

A career as an author is pretty much impossible without an amazing agent, and my agent Juliet Mushens is the best in the business. Endlessly supportive and imaginative, *and* a great gossip. Here's to many more Golden Penguins. Juliet is ably supported by Liza DeBlock, Kiya Evans and Rachel Neely. Every time a new book comes out, they have all moved one further rung up the ladder. Eventually we are going to need a bigger ladder. Also, Liza, I finally have that Bulgarian tax form for you.

I have so many lovely publishers around the world, and have been lucky enough to start meeting them in person this year. Thank you to them all, and I hope it didn't go unnoticed that I managed to continue my record of somehow mentioning Estonia in every book.

Special thanks, though, to my American publishers, Pamela Dorman Books/Viking, who are such an integral part of these books. To the incomparable Pamela Dorman, and Jeramie Orton, what an operation it was this time! Further thanks, from my side of the Atlantic to yours, to Brian Tart, Kate Stark, Marie Michels, Lindsay Prevette, Kristina Fazzalaro, Mary Stone and Alex Cruz-Jimenez. Thank you also to the wonderful Jenny Bent. Here's to a year of fewer Zoom calls, and to meeting lots of American readers and booksellers.

Thank you to Pauline Simmons for the name and to Debbie Darnell for the personality. Thank you to Angela Rafferty and to Jonathan Polnay for answering DNA queries with such speed and skill. You effectively convicted Andrew Everton, and, for that, we are all grateful. And special thanks to Katy Loftus. You'll always be part of the gang.

My family remains the heartbeat of my books. Thank you, as always, to my mum, Brenda, for the many things I will never be able to fully repay. To Mat and Anissa, to Jan Wright, and to my grandparents Fred and Jessie for their strength and their kindness.

Thank you to my children, Ruby and Sonny, who are now becoming increasingly monetizable, and who bring me joy and pride every day. I am so lucky to be your dad, even though one of you literally never lets me win at Mario Kart.

And, finally, all my love and thanks to Ingrid. That there was a time before I met you seems absurd. You fill my life with happiness and laughter, and to share the rest of my life with you is the greatest privilege I can imagine.

It should also be noted that Ingrid came up with the title *The Bullet That Missed*, and brought the wonderful Liesl Von Cat into my life.

And, speaking of Liesl Von Cat, I must go. I have shut the window in my study, and she is making it very clear that this is unacceptable.

Until next time . . .

A PENGUIN READERS GUIDE TO

THE BULLET THAT MISSED

Richard Osman

An Introduction to *The Bullet That Missed*

The Bullet That Missed, the third novel in Richard Osman's much-loved Thursday Murder Club series, sees the crime-fighting quartet of the Coopers Chase Retirement Village take on an ex-KGB colonel, several TV icons, a murderous money launderer, and more as they rush to catch the latest killer.

Joyce suggests that the gang investigate the death of Bethany Waites, a local TV presenter whose car was pushed off a cliff several years prior. Bethany had been investigating a tax fraud operation worth over £10 million and had told colleagues she was close to revealing the mastermind behind it all.

Now the Thursday Murder Club wants to know: Who killed Bethany? What happened to the £10 million? And why, since they started their investigation, have their two prime suspects in Bethany's disappearance turned up dead?

A Conversation with Richard Osman

The Thursday Murder Club returns for their third whodunit in The Bullet That Missed. *What was your inspiration for the novel?*

I really wanted to write a book set in the world of television, to draw on my former career a little bit. So much happens behind the scenes in television, and I have met so many extraordinary on-screen personalities who are definitely potential murderers. This book begins with our first meeting with local news legend Mike Waghorn. He was the perfect character for me. Nearly seventy years old, he is incredibly famous in his local area. He has a great mystery for the gang to solve, and I knew Joyce would immediately have a crush on him. Alongside that story line, as I always like to make Elizabeth's life as difficult as possible, I gave her a near-impossible task in this book, just to see how she coped with it.

What has surprised you most developing the Thursday Murder Club series? Has your writing process changed over three books as you continue to build the world of Elizabeth, Rob, Ibrahim, and Joyce?

I love how close readers have become to the characters. Everybody has a favorite, though my favorite changes day by day. They are all kind, but also all tough, and they each have their own ways of making us laugh and cry. I love the people who are drawn to them too, and how important they have become to the books. I'm always surprised how important Bogdan, Chris, and Donna, who are now honorary members of the gang, have become to the books. If I didn't put enough Bogdan in a book, for example, I know that my editors and my readers would be furious. Quite right too. There are a couple of new additions in *The Bullet That Missed* too, who I think will be sticking around for the next adventure. I just love throwing trouble at all of these completely different characters and seeing which one comes up with a solution this time.

Friendship and its importance are recurring themes in The Bullet That Missed *as our sleuths reflect on the relationships they have built later in life. As newcomer Viktor reflects: "People drift in and out of your life, and, when you are younger, you know you will see them again. But now every old friend is a miracle." Why was it important to explore this now?*

In *The Thursday Murder Club*, Joyce makes the observation that you always know when you're doing something for the first time, but you rarely know when you're doing something for the last time. Friendships are a very important example of that. There will always be people in our life who we are never going to see again. You don't choose your family, but you do choose your friends, and I love the strength of the friendships between Joyce, Elizabeth, Ron, and Ibrahim, and the lengths they will go to protect one another and to protect their friends. They know that one day they will lose one another, and they make the most of the days they have.

The cold case that the Thursday Murder Club is investigating in The Bullet That Missed *involves the disappearance of a local TV anchor. How did your experience as a television producer and host inform the mystery?*

There is a sequence in *The Bullet That Missed* where Joyce and Elizabeth visit the recording of a daily quiz show, and I adored writing it because I have been presenting daily quiz shows for many, many years. I loved writing it through their eyes. Though I should say that, without giving away spoilers, no audience member has ever brought a gun into one of my TV recordings before.

Every installment introduces readers to new "fan-favorite" characters. The gang's fixer, Bogdan, mob boss Connie, and this book's newcomers: ex-KGB officer Viktor and the mysterious Viking. How do you breathe so much life into each and every character?

When I introduce new characters, I try to imagine they're the lead characters in their own novel. Probably the only new major character in this book that I wouldn't want to write a whole novel about is Joyce's dog, Alan. Although, now that I say that, I'm kind of tempted to try. Dogs solving crimes, is that a profitable niche?

You just discovered that one of your ancestors formed an amateur crime-solving gang in nineteenth-century Brighton. Can you tell us a bit about these crime solvers? Will your discovery find its way into a Thursday Murder Club story in future?

Yes, I discovered on a British TV show that my great-great-great-great-great-grandfather, Gabriel Gillam, a fisherman and smuggler, uncovered the body in one of England's most notorious nineteenth-century murder cases. Even better, he was aided by his wife and mother, as they formed their very own band of plucky amateur detectives. I was able to visit the site of the murder, the old inn where the inquest took place, and the crown court where the murderer was convicted and sentenced to death. I would love to write a story one day about Gabriel, Mary, and Elizabeth (yes, the gang even had their very own Elizabeth) solving crimes in 1820s Brighton.

Questions and Topics for Discussion

1. How do you think the relationships among the members of the Thursday Murder Club have changed through the series? Have any dynamics remained the same? Discuss.

2. Who is your favorite of the new characters introduced in *The Bullet That Missed*, and why? Would you want to see them again in future books?

3. Elizabeth makes a rare mistake in keeping to the same routine, which leads to her capture by the Viking. What other flaws does Elizabeth have? What could she have done differently?

4. Joyce is shocked to discover that Elizabeth could be capable of killing someone. How far do you think Elizabeth would go to protect her friends? How far do you think Joyce would go?

5. During one of their therapy sessions, Ibrahim asks Connie if she has any secrets then refuses to answer the same question when it is turned back on him. Why do you think he avoids this question?

6. Joyce and Elizabeth are best friends—and yet even they don't tell each other everything. Do you think it's necessary in any relationship to keep a few secrets from each other? Why or why not?

7. Donna and Chris were each romantically uninvolved before they met the Thursday Murder Club and their network. How have they changed since then? And what do you think the future holds for Donna and Bogdan, Chris and Patrice?

8. What were your suspicions about the truth behind Bethany's disappearance? Were you surprised by the ending? Discuss.

ALSO AVAILABLE

The Man Who Died Twice

A Thursday Murder Club Mystery

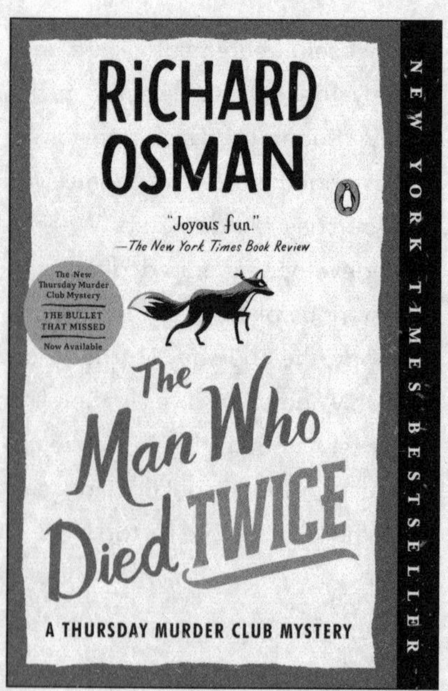

The Thursday Murder Club—Elizabeth, Joyce, Ron and Ibrahim—are looking forward to a bit of peace and quiet at their posh retirement village. But an unexpected visitor arrives, desperate for their help. He has been accused of stealing diamonds worth millions from the wrong men and he's on the lam. Then, as night follows day, the first body is found. But not the last. Can our four friends catch the killer before the killer catches them? And if they find the diamonds too? Well, wouldn't that be a bonus?

"It's taken a mere two books for Richard Osman to vault into the upper leagues of crime writers. . . . *The Man Who Died Twice* . . . dives right into joyous fun." —*The New York Times Book Review*